SEVEN-THIRTY THURSDAY

REED BUNZEL

A RICK DEVLIN NOVEL

SUSPENSE PUBLISHING

Seven-Thirty Thursday
Reed Bunzel

PAPERBACK EDITION
* * * * *

PUBLISHED BY:
Suspense Publishing

Cover Design: Shannon Raab
Cover Photographer: iStockphoto.com/ Brian Nolan

ISBN: 978-0-578-47562-2

OTHER BOOKS BY REED BUNZEL

PAY FOR PLAY

Jack Connor Mysteries
PALMETTO BLOOD
CAROLINA HEAT
HURRICANE BLUES (2020)
SKELETON KEY (2020)

Nonfiction
CLEAR VISION: THE STORY OF CLEAR CHANNEL COMMUNICATIONS
CALIFORNIA STYLE: THE JOE KORET STORY

DEDICATION

This one is for my brothers, Anthony and Jordan

PRAISE FOR REED BUNZEL

"Reed Bunzel's 'Seven-Thirty Thursday' is an emotional, tension-filled roller coaster that holds the reader's attention from the first page. Bunzel's voice is his own, but with a bit of Pat Conroy and James Lee Burke thrown in. This is a writer that every mystery fan should follow."

—Joseph Badal, Amazon #1 Best-Selling Author of the *Lassiter/Martinez Case Files* Series

"Bunzel peels away the layers of mystery like a master of the genre. The American south hasn't seemed this hot, menacing and filled with surprises in ages. Bravo to a fine writer and a splendid novel."

—T. Jefferson Parker, *New York Times* Bestselling Author on "Palmetto Blood"

"Lights up the Southern sky with taut, exciting action and a memorable cast of characters. Don't let this book pass you by."

—Michael McGarrity, Bestselling Author on "Carolina Heat"

SEVEN-THIRTY THURSDAY

A RICK DEVLIN NOVEL

REED BUNZEL

CHAPTER 1

A thin, orange line sliced the eastern horizon as the fading night released its grip on the coming day.

The sky was dark and thick and still sound asleep. Except for the brilliant seam along the edge of the sea, the lowcountry was a slumbering being not yet ready to shake off the cobwebs of sleep. Two points of light reflected in the headlamps reminded me that I shared the road with raccoons and possums and foxes, so I gently eased my foot off the gas. The dashboard clock told me it was just before five, which was why I had this stretch of roadway almost all to myself. As I accelerated up the long span of the bridge I caught sight of the massive shipping terminal along the sill of the marsh, massive cranes looming over illuminated steel containers that were stacked one atop the next like piles of Lego blocks.

The voice on the radio warned it was going to get well into the nineties today, and the heat quotient would make it feel well over a hundred. No such thing as a dry heat in Charleston, where humidity drives the summer days and the misery index rides shotgun. The forecaster went on to talk about pop-up thunderstorms later in the afternoon as a weather front moved through, with possible rip currents at the beaches and a chance of tornadoes inland. A real ray of sunshine, which I silenced in favor of whatever the next push-button on the radio would bring. It turned out to be an oldies station with James Taylor singing about how in his mind he was going to Carolina. What were the odds of that?

I was early. Or late, depending on how one looked at it. There was nothing I could do when the airline announced back in Dallas that Flight 801 to Charleston had been canceled. Severe thunderstorms, the gate agent had explained, although I could see now that any bad weather had blown through hours ago.

"I need to get to Charleston tonight," I'd pleaded with her. "My father is dying."

"I'm sure this is a difficult time for you, sir," she said, a genuine look of sympathy in her eyes. "I'll do my best to get you there."

Her best meant I had a choice: she could either put me on a flight into Charleston later today—still ten hours from now—or get me a seat on the final plane out last night to Columbia, which at the time had not been shut down. The lawyers had made it clear I had to be in town no later than noon today, so I'd taken my chance on Columbia. The jarring flight finally landed at the sleepy airport in the state capital a couple hours ago, and the rental agent had eagerly given me the keys to her last Kia. She'd looked tired and ready to go home, but she still tried to sell me the overpriced insurance.

Nothing around here looked familiar. Thirty years between then and now will do that to a person. This stretch of four-lane hadn't even existed the last time I was here, nor had the houses and apartment buildings, whose dim porch lights I could see through the trees. Mount Pleasant had been one of those small towns hidden along the Carolina coast, the meandering rivers and eddies and tidal marshes allowing for only a couple roads in or out. High school away games were thrill rides that began with a treacherous journey across the Grace Memorial Bridge and then snaked along ribbons of asphalt into the upstate hinterlands. Devlin family road trips—before *the night that changed things forever*—had been last-minute adventures that began at dawn's early light and had no fixed end point. No maps were involved; just get in the car and go. Traditional as he was, my father had an impulsive streak back when my sister and I were kids, the thrill of adventure always at the root of our childhood experiences. And our mother always went along with it like the good Girl Scout she was raised to be.

But we weren't kids anymore. Mom was one with the earth again, the passing tides having carried her ashes to the quiet glades and sand bars of Charleston harbor. My old man was a different story entirely.

According to the GPS app on my phone, he was about three miles up the road, under armed guard at an inpatient hospice facility until I got there. The nurses had been dead-set against harboring a convicted murderer in their midst, even for a few hours, but the choice was not theirs to make. The parole board had voted unanimously to release him, and in just a few hours he would be a free man.

I had grown up just a few miles from here—a place called Sullivan's Island—but now I felt as if I'd been dropped down in a foreign land. With no familiar reference points, I forced myself to trust the triangulation from the satellites orbiting thousands of miles overhead. I took the Mount Pleasant exit off I-526, then followed the simple directions to the address I'd fed into the GPS app back at the airport in Columbia.

My headlights cut a swath of light through the trees, exposing empty parking lots and office buildings that had replaced the dense forest that covered the land when I was a boy. Thirty years ago, this all would have been thick with pines and oaks and twisted tupelos, snarled with Carolina creeper and tangles of kudzu. The black man who had done odd jobs for my father used to tell me stories of how he had hunted around these parts when he was a kid, slogging through the muck of ancient creeks and runoff gullies. Rice plantations had thrived here before and after the Civil War, but long ago they had returned to dense overgrowth and wildlife. The land had been teeming with deer and possums and skunks, and once or twice old Ernie Collier had presented my mother with a venison steak or fresh-caught gator filets. The old Korean War veteran had offered them up with pride, but *The Joy of Cooking* had few suggestions on what to do with them.

Finally, I was there. I'd traveled twenty-four hundred miles since yesterday afternoon to get to this spot, and the sign verified I had arrived:

`East Cooper Hospice Center`

It was a simple guidepost, carved from red cypress and positioned between twin brick pillars. A single floodlight buried in a carpet of wild ferns illuminated the raised lettering, along with a street number that matched the address in my GPS. The building itself was unremarkable and ordinary: low-slung, fashioned from the same sort of bricks as the sign out front, plantation shutters angling out from hinges above the windows. No true architectural style other than the sort of clean and unobtrusive design one would expect of a medical facility where you go to die.

Three cars were parked out front: two small SUVs and a Dodge Charger with a strobe bar on its roof. Lettering on the side read "South Carolina State Police," and the vehicle's presence confirmed what I already knew. My father was inside, and so was an armed trooper assigned to make sure he didn't try to make a run for it. Considering what I'd heard about the old man's condition such an attempt seemed unlikely, but it appeared no one was taking any chances.

I parked my rental car in a space at the far edge of the lot, under the spreading branches of a sweet gum tree. I unfolded out of the car slowly, to give my large frame time to adjust after being squeezed into the cramped seat. Even at this hour the humidity outside collided with the crisp air conditioning of the car, and I felt as if I'd stepped from an ice box into a steam bath. My back and shoulders groaned as I flexed my bones; six hours on two airplanes and another two hours in a subcompact automobile reminded me why I drove an old Eldorado. Lousy on gas and bad for the environment, but it allowed me to stretch out my full six-two physique and feel as limber as when I'd trudged up onto the mound and toed the rubber. *Back in the day*, as they say.

The officer who belonged to the state vehicle was not dozing behind the wheel, so I figured he had to be inside the building. I rang a button at the front door, then waited for someone to buzz me in. It reminded me of the hotels I'd stayed at when I was playing minor league ball and riding on creaky old buses from one cow town to the next. When the lock clicked I slipped inside and explained to a tired aide who I was and why I was there.

"Down the hallway and to the left, Mr. Devlin," she told me after I offered her my driver's license. She did not seem pleased with my presence, nor that of my father.

I followed her directions past a vacant reception desk and down a long hallway bathed in a warm, subdued light. The floor was linoleum, the walls a muted cream, and framed photos of the marsh and the harbor and various lighthouses were arranged aesthetically along the corridor. Quiet and serene, peaceful and temporal.

I passed a half-dozen doors that led to rooms where I figured people were sleeping and, in all likelihood, dying. Maybe today would be their last day, maybe tomorrow. "Hospice" is one of those dreaded words because of its clear implications and unambiguous outcome, and simply being inside this place induced in me both a solemn reverence for life and an equal respect for death.

The state cop was seated on a rolling chair outside a door at the end of a short hallway. His head was tipped forward, and for a moment I thought he might be sleeping. Then one of my shoes squeaked on the polished floor and he glanced up, just as his hand went for the holster on his belt. I could see now that he'd been thumbing through a well-worn magazine which, when he finished it, would join the heap on the floor beside him.

"Who the hell are you?" he grumped in a gravelly voice. His hand remained on the leather holster, but he had not unsnapped his gun.

"Rick Devlin," I told him. "I'm early."

"You were supposed to be here hours ago," the cop said. He was pale, with a galaxy of freckles and bushy red hair that seemed molded to his skull. His ears protruded from the side of his head like wing flaps, and he had a fresh scar just beneath his left eye.

"Severe thunderstorms," I replied. I nodded toward the door the cop seemed to be protecting and added, "How's he doing in there?"

"Sleeping," the guard replied with a cool shrug. "And he's not going anywhere until his lawyer gets here. And the ambulance. That's—" he glanced at his watch "—another three hours from now."

"I'm in no hurry," I assured him.

It had been three decades since I'd seen my old man led away in cuffs, the jury foreman's pronouncement of "guilty" still ringing through the courthouse. The memory was always the same Frank Devlin looking back for one last glance at my sister and me as the guard led him through a door into the bowels of the courthouse. I had been stunned by the jury's decision, but I remember my father seeming resolute about the verdict, which many folks believed was moral and just. My sister and I both had tried to visit him in the first months after his imprisonment, but he had refused to see either of us and eventually we both stopped making the effort. Gone was the loving, caring father who had helped me build a treehouse in our backyard and had baked rock-hard muffins with Karen in her Suzy Homemaker oven. Whatever dignity the trial might have spared him, prison life had totally sucked from his body.

The cop nodded and took his hand off his holster. "I need to see some I.D.," he said. "Just to make sure you are who you say you are."

I dug out my driver's license again, then said, "Is there any place close by to get something to eat?"

"Don't know," he said with an impassive shrug. "This isn't my backyard. I live outside Orangeburg, needed the extra hours. Mind if I ask you a question?"

"Do you need to read me my rights?" I asked him.

The trooper hesitated, not sure whether I was serious or joking. A brass badge on his uniform identified him as Officer M. Egan. Finally he cracked a cautious grin and said, "Word is you haven't seen the old man since he got locked up. Why the change of heart?"

"Ask him," I quipped a little too easily as I nodded toward the door.

Fact is, I'd been asking myself the same thing ever since I'd received the first call five weeks ago. It was from the son of the high-priced attorney who'd defended my father at his trial. Not very well, obviously, but it turned out there hadn't been much to defend. That first lawyer's name was Myers Jenkins III, and he'd been roped into the job because he'd contributed to all three of my father's state senate campaigns. Never for a minute had he expected to take on the thankless task of defending the man who had been accused of brutally murdering his wife of twenty-two years. The trial had damned near killed Jenkins' legal practice, and after the lengthy—and fruitless—appeals process came to a close, he'd retired to a cabin on a creek down near Edisto.

The lawyer who called me was Myers Jenkins IV, a Clemson Law School grad about my age who had taken over the family business when his father drifted off into the setting sun. I wasn't sure what his legal interest in my father might be, since there was no money to be made from his parole and the Jenkins Law Firm now focused primarily on estate matters. The Roman numeral after his name was there as a reminder of how deep and red patriarchal blood runs here in the South, a reflection of the pride of southern lineage that predated the War of Northern Aggression.

When he told me the plan for my father's release, my response was a quick and resounding "no." Those were my second, third, and fourth responses, as well. The old man had shut me out of his world the second the prison door slammed behind him, and I'd managed to forge a life for myself despite his absence and enmity. No way in hell was I going to fly across the continent just to hold his hand now, as he lay dying. This was not a William Faulkner novel, and I was not Darl Bundren. Despite some lingering spores of affection I knew had to be hidden deep within me, he still was guilty of murdering our mother and destroying our picture-perfect, all-American family. He'd made it abundantly clear that he didn't want either my sister or me in his life, and I'd seen no need to change that decision just because the parole board had concluded otherwise.

Then came the fifth call, which took me off guard. Rather than hitting me with the same old speech about empathy and mercy and compassion, Jenkins IV passed the bludgeon of persuasion to a man of the cloth. The Reverend William McCann was an evangelical pillar of the South who was revered by an ever-increasing flock for his unapologetic fundamentalism, and equally reviled by political and theological progressives for the very same reason. He was the chief pastor of The Carolina Cross, a massive church based outside Spartanburg, and his televised crusades reached millions of followers every Sunday. Among his many distinguished claims to fame, McCann was known throughout the South Carolina correctional system as the "preacher to the prisoners," many of whom tuned to his weekly broadcasts for salvation and deliverance. For reasons I could scarcely comprehend—unless my father had found the love of the Lord during his thirty years behind bars—Jenkins IV had turned to him to induce me into changing my mind. Regrettably, my southern manners were too deeply etched into my upbringing to allow me to hang up on him.

The righteous Rev. McCann wasted no time, hurling his best stuff at me with an impassioned sermon about kindness and forgiveness, interwoven with threads of homespun piety and Bible Belt guilt. "As Matthew tells us, if you forgive other people when they sin against you, your heavenly Father will also forgive you," he implored as if he were speaking to a rapt congregation. "But if you do not forgive others their sins, your Father will not forgive your sins. And as Luke says, 'Do not judge, and you will not be judged. Do not condemn, and you will not be condemned. Forgive, and you will be forgiven.' "

"With all due respect to you and the Lord, sir, you're wasting your time," I told him when he had finished. "I'm not doing it."

But my protest did not stop Pastor McCann; in fact, it only seemed to encourage him. "All of time is wasted, and fleeting," he said. "As we know from Psalms, 'Lord, remind me how brief my time on earth will be. Remind me that my days are numbered and how fleeting my life is. You have made my life no longer than the width of my hand. My entire lifetime is just a moment to you; at best, each of us is but a breath.' "

"You're preaching to the wrong choir, sir," I replied as politely as I could when he was done. "As I said before, it's not working."

"Mr. Devlin, please—reach into your heart of hearts and see this moment for what it is," he replied. "'Get rid of all bitterness, rage and anger, brawling and slander, along with every form of malice. Be kind and compassionate to one another, forgiving each other, just as in Christ God forgave you.' Ephesians, chapter four."

I listened to his impassioned words with abiding patience, then said, "You can read me chapter and verse from now all the way to next Sunday, Reverend. My answer will remain the same. No."

By then he'd caught on that scripture wasn't doing the trick, so he switched to a more universal appeal. "C'mon, Mr. Devlin. *Rick*. Your father has suffered his sins long enough, and he deserves to pass his final days outside the walls of prison," he said. "Have mercy on him. It was God who told Moses, 'I will have mercy on whom I will have mercy, and I will have compassion on whom I will have compassion.' I'm telling you that compassion is the highest form of respect—of *honor*—we can pay to our Creator. That can be your God, or it can mean your father. Maybe both."

"He's made it quite clear he wants nothing to do with me or my sister," I told him. "Give me one reason why I should care now."

"If for no other reason than maybe to give you time to figure that out," the sanctimonious preacher responded.

It was an oblique answer, but Rev. McCann was relentless. I couldn't fault him for his energy or his effort, and his tactics eventually wore me down. Plus, there was just enough truth in what he'd said to make it sting. My father was dying, and no matter how the past had screwed with all our lives, very soon he would cease to exist in this world. Surely that mattered, didn't it?

That was why I now stood outside his room, against my better judgment. There were so many reasons for me to be someplace else, and so few reasons for me to be concerned with whether he died in a prison hospital or in his precious hometown of Charleston. A recent medical exam had found that his body was riddled with cancer, and the South Carolina parole board had granted him something called "conditional clemency for medical efficacy." This legal maneuver meant he would be allowed to die a free man, as long as an immediate family member accepted responsibility for his protection and well-being. In this case, "immediate family member" meant either a son or daughter, since he'd already killed his wife. My older sister Karen had been in and out of various treatment centers for years, a pattern the parole board had found troublesome. Therefore, the obligation fell on me, but only if I agreed.

I realized my mind had wandered and I still hadn't answered the state trooper's question. So I lifted my shoulder in a slight shrug and said to him, "Deoxyribonucleic acid."

"Deoxy-what?"

"The scientific name for DNA. It's what makes me part of him, and vice versa." In other words, *he's my father.* "Is the door locked?"

"No one's supposed to go in there. I have my orders."

"He's my old man," I pressed him. "I just want to have a couple words with him before the bureaucracy arrives. Like you said, it's been a real long time."

The cop hesitated, no doubt wondering if this somehow could reflect poorly on his next performance evaluation. I could see the cogs turning in his head, and not very quickly.

"Two minutes," he finally said.

"Much appreciated."

The cop didn't say another word, just motioned me inside with a jerk of his chin. Before he could change his mind, I turned the brushed nickel handle and slowly pushed the door inward on quiet hinges.

I slipped inside and closed the door behind me, leaving just a crack to cast a thin slash of light across the far wall. The room was dark and silent and smelled faintly of lemon. This was not a hospital, so there were no beeping machines with tubes and wires and sensors. No monitors announcing blood pressure and oxygen levels every second of the day. No video screen to show his pulse, no alarm that would scream if he began to code. No one was trying to keep this patient alive.

I waited for my eyes to adjust to the darkness, heard my father's ragged breathing coming from the bed. It was faint but steady and seemed a bit strained, as one might expect from a body that was shutting down. The cancer had only been found eight weeks ago, and was believed to have started in his prostate. By now it had spread just about everywhere: spine, brain, lungs, liver. The doctors who had submitted letters to the parole board had been unwilling to provide any kind of meaningful prognosis, other than the ominous words, "four to six weeks, at most."

That had been a month ago.

I stood in the dark, studying the shriveled, unmoving form tucked in under the bedspread. He was slightly curled on his side, not quite fetal, his back to the far wall. I wondered if that was a position he had adopted in prison, either as a precaution or a necessity. Thirty years is a long time, and he would have dealt with a lot of torment over the decades. State Senator Frank Devlin was a high-profile felon who would have attracted the roaches and piranhas of the system, and that would not have gone well for him.

A wave of anxiety flashed through me and I felt like a stranger in a foreign land. I had a life of my own, a daughter to look after, a book to write with a deadline to meet. Then I heard a voice that sounded like a twig scraping across an icy window pane.

"Hey, son. Did you win?"

The voice took me by surprise. I hadn't heard my father speak since that last day in the courtroom when the jury returned its verdict. The judge had asked him if he had anything to say, and he'd muttered six distinct words: "I'll see you all in hell." He sounded so much older now, exhausted and defeated. And definitely ill. Yet it was still the same voice I'd grown up with, the voice that belonged to the man who would wait up for my long bus rides home from night games in Greenville or Rock Hill or Spartanburg. He would always be waiting on the couch, where he'd fallen asleep watching The Late Show. And then, when I would come banging through the kitchen door with my equipment bag, he would say, "Hey, son. Did you win?"

Most times the answer was "yes," but that wasn't the point. Not then, and certainly not now. The fact was, he was always there.

And now he was *here.*

"You're awake," I heard myself saying.

"I tried to wait up for you," he replied. "But Carson had the night off, so I fell asleep."

Carson. *Johnny* Carson, who had retired in ninety-two. Damn; had it really been that long? I stood there lamely in the darkness, not sure whether the old man was messing with me or if his mind was more deficient than Jenkins IV had let on.

"It's been a long time," was all I could think of saying.

There was a slight pause, after which the dying man said, "Yes, son, it has. A real long while. And it's good to see you, considering the lights are off."

"You want me to turn them on?"

"As long as you don't scare easy," he said.

I flipped the switch and blinked as my eyes adjusted to the sudden change in brightness. Although I had been briefed on my father's condition, I was not prepared for the shriveled face that was staring at me from the tangle of sheets bundled up around his head. He looked like a creature from a Tolkien novel, and not one with a lot of goodness in its heart.

My reaction must have been obvious, because the mass of skin and bones in the bed said, "You'll have to forgive my appearance. My better days are behind me."

"You look good, considering," I told him, but I doubted I was fooling him.

His face was thin and his tissue paper skin was almost translucent, muddled by dark bruises where clusters of capillaries had burst. A large bandage covered one side of his head, and his scalp—which once had been covered with what I remembered as a blanket of hair—was pocked with scabs. His dark brown eyes seemed to be hiding inside deep caves, and large tufts of fur protruded from his ears and nostrils.

"You don't have to be kind," the old man said. "I know you don't want to be here."

I had no snappy comeback, nothing impertinent to say. Until now I had not given much thought to how he might feel about this arrangement, his estranged son coming home to Charleston to help count down the days until his life was gone. In fact, after his incarceration and his decision to shut me out of his life, I forced myself to stop thinking about what he might be doing. And feeling. I told myself not to care what friendships he might have nurtured, what humiliation and violence he had probably endured. I figured things had not gone well for him inside those walls, but I convinced myself not to lose any sleep over it.

Harsh, as my daughter would say, but truth is truth.

"If it makes any difference, they say I don't have much time," he said in a creak of a voice. "A week, maybe, no more than two. Then you're off the hook."

Jenkins IV had already explained this, and I'd suffered through Triple A road trips that lasted longer than that. I could put up with my dying father for a few days, especially since his life was already in the bottom of the ninth, with two outs.

"Why didn't you want to see me?" I asked him, out of the blue. I'd promised myself I wouldn't go there, wouldn't dredge up old animosities.

"What good would have come from it?" he replied. "What's done was done, and I saw no point in rubbing it in. But enough of the old days. You look good."

"Not a kid anymore," I pointed out.

"Youth is grossly overrated," he replied in a thin scratch that was painful to hear.

"So is being an adult."

My dying father said nothing after that, not for almost a full minute. I listened carefully to his ragged breathing, just to make sure his lungs were still functioning. One side of my brain was anticipating that final gasp, but in the depths of my heart I began to think of a few things I wanted to ask him before he died. Still, to hear him labor under the stress of a diminished life only served to remind me of what lay ahead in the days to come.

Eventually his lids flicked open and a faint spirit glimmered in those cavernous eyes. "I need to tell you something about that night," he said, his words soft and cracking.

"I don't want to talk about that," I told him. Truth was, I didn't want to relive one second of my mother's murder, or what had occurred afterwards. It had caused a severe downward spiral in my life, one that had taken me years to scratch my way out of. I didn't want to risk that journey down the rabbit hole again.

"Then just listen, and after I'm gone you'll never have to go through it ever again."

"Dad…please don't—"

"You wouldn't deny a dying man the privilege of uttering his last words, would you?"

Oh shit, I thought. I stared at the old mass of bones, hoping my silence would be contagious. It wasn't.

He closed his eyes again, and he kept them that way as he continued to speak. "I don't have much energy, so I'll try to be quick," he said. "I know what you must think of me. I know what you must think about that night. And I don't blame you. I'd be thinking the same things if I were you. I can't change one bit of what happened. Not what happened to your mother, or you, or your sister. And certainly not me. The past is malignant, and it has no cure."

"Dad, really—"

"Just do me the courtesy and hear me out," he said with a weak, tattered rasp. He fell silent as he collected his thoughts, then continued, "As you know, I don't remember much of what happened that night. You were off with the football team, warming the bench up in Darlington, I believe. Karen was away at college. Everything else is fuzzy, except that…well, when I finally came around…your mother was lying on the floor."

"Please don't do this," I said, almost begging him to let it go. "I've heard all this before."

"But you never listened," he said. "It's about time you did."

"I came to visit you in prison," I reminded him. "You could have told me then."

"Back then I hadn't had thirty years to think about things. But parts of that night have come back to me over time, in bits and pieces."

"Tell it to the jury." Harsh words, and they slipped out like a wild pitch that I couldn't take back.

"The jury wasn't allowed to hear it," the old man wheezed. "That goddamned judge ruled against us from the start. Whatever my lawyer tried to do was declared inadmissible."

I inhaled a deep breath, determined not to let the old bastard try to beat me down. "All right," I finally replied. "I'll play along. What sort of horse shit truth did the judge not allow?"

He cracked a wicked grin at that and gave just a slight shake of his head. Then he fixed me with his tired eyes, and said, "If you really must know, DNA."

"What?" I asked, just to make sure I'd heard him correctly. I'd said roughly the same thing to the cop whose ass was posted outside the door.

"DNA. They didn't test for it."

"I'm pretty sure DNA wasn't admissible back then," I said. "The trial was in 1990."

"I know when it was. The first court case where DNA was admitted as evidence was just a few years before that, in England. It wasn't a common thing here in the U.S. Not until the mid-nineties. I've had plenty of time over the years to do my research."

"Please, Dad—don't do this."

But the dying old man didn't seem to hear me. After thirty years we were both in the same room, alone, and he had a captive audience. "What I'm trying to say is I didn't kill your mother, son," he said in a weary, plaintive voice. "There were so many things going on back then, and none of it ever came to light. Lord knows we tried, but no one gave a damn."

"The jury took only two hours and fourteen minutes to convict you," I reminded him. "That's a half-hour shorter than *The Godfather*."

His eyes drifted shut again, and then he said, "Listen, Rick. I loved your mother more than words can say. Something affected my memory that night. It's like hours of my life were totally ripped out of my brain, and even after all these years I can only remember little fragments of what happened. I don't expect you to believe me; that's your right. And your choice. My memory is shot for good, but the science will exist long after I do."

"What are you trying to tell me?" I asked him.

"I'm not telling you anything. I just want you to think about it. Think about all that blood they showed on that screen in the courtroom. The blood on the knife, and your mother's clothes, and the floor. There has to be some of the killer's DNA in all of that. And I swear on your mother's grave, not one fucking speck of it is mine."

CHAPTER 2

Four hours later we were home.

In this case "home" meant a two-bedroom condo on the twelfth floor of Riverfront Towers, a high-rise building on the Charleston side of the Cooper River. Not my choice, but I had no input in the decision. I'd suggested a small house near the beach, or a private suite in one of the converted mansions south of Broad Street. Even a rustic cabin at the edge of a quiet marsh out of town was better than a concrete and glass tower with recirculated air and stuffy elevators.

Each room of the sterile condo had a panoramic view that swept from the Cooper River Bridge all the way out to the mouth of the harbor, and included the rooftops and church spires of the city itself. It was a million-dollar property that was owned by an investment firm whose financial roots I had been unable to trace. Jenkins IV had assured me that I had nothing to worry about; all I had to do was show up and take custody when my father was released.

"Who's paying for all this?" I had pressed him when he told me the plan on the phone.

"Put all of that out of your mind," the lawyer had said. "All the details have been taken care of."

The maxim of the devil being in those details floated through my mind, both then and now, but he'd refused to divulge anything further. He insisted everything was legal, but wouldn't say anything more. The official story—if anyone asked—was that Frank Devlin had squirreled away enough of his meager prison wages over the years to afford a few weeks in a water-view condo, and hospice was providing the home health aides. My suspicious nature and natural cynicism caused me to remain uneasy about the entire situation, but Jenkins IV swore there was no legal or financial catch in any of this.

"You don't have a dog in this hunt," was how he'd put it.

My old man had drifted off to sleep a few moments after his comment about DNA, and he'd only awakened marginally when the EMTs arrived at the Hospice Center with the ambulance. They'd transported him to the condo and then settled him into the room where he was expected to die. It was the master bedroom of the unit, with *en suite* bathroom and a balcony that offered a one-eighty view of the water. Hospice had provided an electric bed that could be raised up or down with a foot pedal, and a single upholstered chair was set to one side, next to an over-bed table.

"Where am I?" he'd asked wearily after the EMTs had departed, leaving only Jenkins IV and me in the room.

"Downtown Charleston," I informed him. "A block off East Bay Street near the river."

The old man gave me a blank look as if his brain cells were trying to recall just where that location might be. Then he said, "That's it out there?"

"That's right. You can see all the way from Fort Sumter up to the bridge."

"I heard they tore down that old death trap," he wheezed. "Always was a devil to drive across."

"Replaced it fifteen years ago."

My father uttered a grumble of either phlegm or approval, then closed his eyes again. Less than sixty seconds later he was snuffling lightly, a wet rattle coming from deep in his throat. Jenkins IV cocked his head toward the living room and I followed him out, gently pulling the door closed.

"So...what do you think?" he asked me as we both gazed out through the sliding glass doors at the million-dollar view.

"Is it too late to back out?" I replied.

Jenkins shot me a serious side-eye squint. "We're a little past that, Rick. Just take care of him and it'll be over before you know it."

I knew I was being insensitive, as if I were looking forward to the final out of the game. "That's easy for you to say," I told him.

"He's your father, for Chrissakes. You might just find you have a few things to talk about."

"He shut that down years ago," I said. "Look…I'm going to make the best of this, and we'll make it through. At least I will. But my father has never been the sort to do anything without making a ruckus. And at some point, word is going to get out that he's holed up here."

"The less attention, the better," the lawyer stated with a passive shrug. "For your privacy as well as his."

"Screw privacy. Sooner or later he's going to ask for a phone."

"He can't have one. No phone, no email, no internet. No communication at all. Just TV and movies, and music if he wants it. And under no circumstances is he to leave this condo."

I'd already heard all the rules, but no one else was going to be around when my father started yelling for things he couldn't have. "What if he goes over the balcony?" I asked.

"I'm going to pretend I didn't hear that," the lawyer said. "And now's your chance to let me know if there's anything you need before I go."

Jenkins IV's presence made me nervous, and I really just wanted him to leave. Then my brain went back to what my father had said just before he'd coasted off to sleep back at the Hospice Center. "There is one thing," I told him. "Earlier this morning he started going on about the trial. Insisted he wasn't guilty, that your father had evidence proving he didn't kill Mom. Said the judge wouldn't listen to him."

He let out a long sigh, then said, "No one in prison ever admits their guilt. They claim they were framed. They had an airtight alibi but a witness lied. Some snitch ratted them out. The judge wouldn't allow the evidence that proved they didn't do whatever they're in for. Listen to them and there are more innocent people inside the walls of a prison than there are at a convent."

"I've heard all that, and I get it," I replied. "But my father was talking about evidence and how no one tested for DNA back then."

"I'm sure he sounded pretty convincing," Jenkins said.

"No, just convinced. There's a difference."

"Listen Rick," he said in a fatherly voice, even though we were roughly the same age. "He's had thirty years to tell himself a bedtime story to help him sleep at night. But you were there, in the courtroom. You saw how quickly that jury came back with a verdict."

He was right: I'd been seated in the front row and I'd witnessed the whole thing. Like the jury, I'd eventually bought into my father's guilt, and I wasn't about to let him off the hook now just because of a few death bed murmurings. When I was fifteen I'd been caught with a half dozen airplane-sized nips of bourbon in my room, and my father had lectured me about how trust takes a long time to build and only an instant to lose. It was a learning moment I had not forgotten, although it didn't keep me from drinking during those formative years.

Now the tables were reversed. I'd erased any trust I'd had in my father long ago, and spending a week or two with him would not rebuild it. The old man had closed himself off during those three decades behind bars, surrounded by dirt bags, meth heads, gangbangers, skip rats, and junkies. No contact with Karen or me, or anyone else that I knew of. Why would he suddenly get all talkative and deny his guilt after all these years, now that he'd been released and was set to die? To clear his conscience? Con his way through the Pearly Gates? Convince me he wasn't the murderous bastard the jury had convicted, even though he'd been found with the bloody murder weapon?

"He said the judge ruled against him whenever he could," I pressed him.

"I wasn't there, but from what Dad told me it was all legal maneuvering," Jenkins IV replied. "The case was clear-cut from the start, no pun intended. I wouldn't make anything out of what he's saying now."

"Is it still around?" I asked him.

"What are you talking about?"

"The evidence that wasn't allowed?"

Jenkins shot me a guarded look, as if I was venturing off-script. "I'd have no way of knowing, and it was a long time ago. I really don't see any point in stirring up any of that shit again."

"To you it might be shit, but this is my father I'm talking about here. My mother, too."

He thought on this for a moment as he watched a water taxi chug up alongside the passenger dock down below. "I can't stop you from doing what you think you need to do," he finally said with a resigned sigh. "But I really don't see any point."

I wasn't sure I saw any point, either. It was all in the past, and whatever my father's motive, it wouldn't restore those thirty years to his life. Nor would it bring my mother back from the dead. I'd been a teenager back then, just starting my senior year of high school, and somehow I'd managed to carve out an entire life for myself without either of them. I'd earned a college degree, pitched three years of major league baseball, gotten married and divorced, and fathered a child of my own. I'd reinvented my career more times than I cared to remember, and suffered through the emptiness of drug addiction and alcohol dependence. My old man had been there for none of that, and I wasn't about to let him play any head games with me now.

Still, he'd planted a little speck of doubt that now nibbled at the back of my brain.

Jenkins IV spent the next few minutes showing me around the condo. Despite its age the place was modern, bright white with accent walls and polished tile floors. High ceilings, recessed lighting, bullnose corners. The kitchen had been updated with quartz countertops, contemporary cabinets, and stainless steel appliances. The living room was furnished with pieces that seemed to have been picked out of a catalog with a focus on decorator style, rather than comfort. "Sleek chic," Jenkins IV called it. The bathrooms matched the rest of the place, with raised sinks, oversized tile showers and a soaking tub in the master *en suite*.

I felt like a duck out of water, since my taste was embodied by the rustic cabin I rented on the fringes of L.A. My cramped kitchen was a Smithsonian curator's dream: ancient Coppertone stove, Harvest Gold fridge, *faux* mosaic linoleum that had worn through to the subfloor. The scuffed hardwood in the other two rooms was in desperate need of refinishing, and cobwebs had become a permanent fixture on the exposed beams. A glass slider consistently stuck in its runner, but it opened out onto a ground level patio where I could relax with a beer and watch the quail and rabbits scramble through the underbrush beneath the live oaks.

I missed it already.

After Jenkins departed I poked my head into the bedroom and again studied the tired old relic tucked under a layer of blankets. I'd always remembered my father as solid, big-boned, with a six-two frame and hard-packed muscles left over from his football days as a Citadel Bulldog. Crew cut, square jaw, deep-set eyes, slightly cleft chin. He'd been popular, gregarious, friendly, and loved to shake hands and kiss babies. He'd made a good living selling term life insurance before being elected to the state Senate, which in South Carolina was just a part-time vocation that paid more in power than salary. He was the epitome of the all-American alpha male, head of the flawless all-American family.

All of that was gone. Now he was little more than a ghostly apparition that reminded me of steam rising from a storm drain on a cold city street. His breathing was light, and the hospice nurse had warned me there might be times when I might not know if he was dead or alive. His chest was barely moving, just a slight rise and fall that told me he was still there.

The terms of his parole were clear: I was there as guardian only, not to play caretaker. Hospice was providing an aide who would visit once a day, and a home health nurse was available on-call. My father's taste buds had completely shut down and his appetite was gone, so he ate practically nothing. Just brief sips of water and apple juice, a little Jell-O. Nothing solid. That made his bodily functions much more manageable, which made everyone's life a whole lot easier. He'd been fitted with a GPS-connected ankle device to make sure he didn't make a run for it, although it was clear he wasn't likely to get out of his bed ever again.

Until now I hadn't given much thought to what I might do with my time. I had a book to write, an autobiography that would officially credit me on the cover as "with Rick Devlin." In the publishing world I'm known as a ghost, and my current gig was to sugarcoat the memoirs of a self-absorbed pseudo-celebrity whose star was fading rapidly. I also had an occasional fill-in role on a sports cable network, so I was able to scrape together enough money to cover the rent on my three-room A-frame in Topanga Canyon, and pay the child support for my fifteen-year-old daughter. The day my ex-wife remarried I'd actually wandered into a church down in the Valley and thanked the Lord for relieving me of the monthly alimony payments. Belinda's life had always been a hive of drama that buzzed with issues—some real and many imagined—and I had felt truly blessed to have shed her like a snakeskin.

On the other hand, my daughter was a pure gem and a delight to be around—even at the age of fifteen. I saw her on weekends and designated holidays, but that arrangement didn't seem reasonable or fair. Especially when her mother turned up in the E.R. or the drunk tank. I was paying a lawyer an obscene amount of money to rectify the injustice of the family court's decision, but thus far a decree was a decree.

Right now Adeline was out there in the SoCal smog, keeping pill bottles out of her mother's reach, while I was gazing out the glass sliders of a twelfth-story condo in downtown Charleston. Waiting for my father's chest to stop rising and falling, his eyes to close for the very last time. I felt like a stale sandwich, a slice of bologna caught between generations of old bread, dry and tasteless. Bad analogy, but that's what made me a hack writer.

My father's room was fitted with a monitoring device that connected to an app on my cell phone if he needed me. I'd given the app its own ring tone so I could tell if he was summoning me, like a duchess ringing her bedside bell. He'd been told there would be times he would be alone in the condo, which didn't seem to bother him one bit. In fact, he claimed to be thrilled to be surrounded by pure silence. He had a television with the basic cable channels and several dozen music streams. He had no desire to eat, no need to shit, and was permitted no visitors. Essentially, he was still in prison, but with a better view.

Once I was assured he was tucked snugly into bed and going nowhere, I made the impulsive decision to go to the beach.

Not exactly the beach; we have plenty of those in California, although the water there is almost always colder. In this case I elected to drive out to Sullivan's Island for a bit of ill-advised reminiscing. For some reason I had an unyielding desire to visit the place where my old house had stood before hurricane Hugo wiped it clean. The home where I had celebrated seventeen Christmases, pedaled my first bicycle, gotten laid for the first time, and where my mother had been killed in cold blood just days before the storm. The house itself was long gone; most of the island had been washed out by Hugo's monstrous winds and tidal surge. In the long run this had been a good thing: the looky-loos who had begun cruising past our house after the murder had stopped abruptly when the hurricane took out the swing bridge. Once the island was opened to the public again there were other things to gawk at, and the "murder house" was gone. A solitary chimney here, craggy ruins of brick steps over there, a big hole where an old oak draped with Spanish moss had toppled like David's goliath.

The destruction had been beneficial in another way. No one would have wanted to buy the old Devlin home, where a grisly murder had taken place. But a vacant lot was different. A new house meant a fresh start. No bloody memories from the past, no threatening ghosts whispering in the dusty halls. After all the detritus from the storm had been trucked away, Jenkins III had put the vacant lot on the market, then used the proceeds from the sale to pay my father's extensive legal fees.

The old property wasn't hard to find. The street on which I had grown up was now lined with garish McMansions that hugged the very edges of the lot lines. Like most of the island houses back then, ours had been a simple structure set up on reinforced cinder block pilings, theoretically high enough for almost any surge to sweep under it during a storm. Hugo defied all the theorists, however, and ragged chunks of the shingled structure were found several blocks away at the edge of the Intracoastal Waterway. Most of the furnishings had been washed out to sea by the powerful wall of water, or were scattered by the violent winds a mile out in the marsh. Months after the storm, a fisherman quietly poling his skiff through one of the lazy tidal eddies had found my Spaulding baseball glove, the thick layer of rosin I'd smeared on the heel now cracked from the salt and sun. My name was still legible on the leather thumb, and it eventually made its way back to me. I still have it.

The building that now sprouted from the land where my childhood had been framed could hardly be called a home. It was an architectural eyesore elevated on poured-concrete pillars twelve feet above the high-water line, painted bright white, with square lines and tight angles and sheets of glass that would have seemed more at home on Mulholland Drive in Los Angeles. A minuscule front yard was edged in brick, with polished river rock spread around clumps of sweet grass and knock-out roses. The house looked like a box that smaller houses might come in, extending far back into the grassy backyard where I had perfected the fastball that got me through the first years of my career. Also gone was the Pawley's Island hammock where I'd spent lazy summer afternoons reading Shelby Foote and Walker Percy and Pat Conroy, all of whom had served me well since then.

On the other side of the street was the public beach access that provided a quick stroll to the sand. I trudged up the well-worn path through the dunes until I crested the grassy mound where the Atlantic spread out before me like a vast pewter tray. The tide was well out, leaving an expanse of wet sand that on this July afternoon was cramped with parents lounging in beach chairs, children squealing and splashing in the surf. Far off in the distance I could make out the stone boundary of the shipping channel that always bared its ragged teeth at low tide.

There wasn't a breath of wind. The morning was already as steamy as a pot of boiling shrimp and, just as the voice on the radio had promised, the humidity was off the charts. These were the days I particularly enjoyed when I was growing up because no one moved fast, and there was nowhere to go in a hurry. Aside from my summer busboy job at an oyster joint on Shem Creek, I'd hung out most days right here on the sand, pitching balls into an overturned trash bin. I'd played both baseball and football for the Wando Warriors, but I was never really fast enough to accelerate off the line of scrimmage. Lack of leg speed was not a problem on the mound, however, and I'd hurled my pitches past enough confused batters to catch the eye of more than a few college scouts. My father had been pushing for The Citadel, where he had excelled as a wide receiver, but I was silently pulling for U.S.C.—the one in South Carolina, not California.

As I stood there on the fringe of the beach it occurred to me that my father never learned that I'd been kicked off the football team the same day that he killed my mother. It was just two weeks into the season, and I'd been caught with an open can of Rolling Rock on school grounds. I was on the football team only as a favor to my old man from the coach, who had been a Citadel running back, and I didn't have the foresight to realize that the athletic suspension might be noted in my academic transcripts. In any event, Coach Walters had laid into me hard that day and booted me from the squad, which meant I couldn't travel on the team bus up to Darlington that afternoon. After lengthy consideration he decided not to call my father, believing it would break his Bulldog heart. The only downside

I could figure in that moment was that my girlfriend Laurie was on the cheerleading squad, so I wouldn't be able to hang out with her, either.

Since I was supposed to be traveling with the team that Friday evening I couldn't go home, at least not until after the game ended and the bus rattled into the schoolyard. With a few hours to kill, I'd sneaked down to the beach with another six-pack I'd obtained in exchange for writing a book report for a teammate, and hunkered down as the moon and mosquitoes came out. Sometime around midnight I fell asleep amidst the sand and sweetgrass, and when I woke up my skin was peppered with crimson insect bites. The game had ended hours before and the six cans of beer had gotten me pretty wasted, so I staggered back over the dunes to where I'd stashed my car. I retrieved my unused football gear out of the trunk and carried it home, where I quietly dumped it in the screened porch that jutted off the kitchen. No lights were on inside so I took care to be silent as I scraped my key in the lock and let myself in through the back door.

It was in that moment that my self-absorbed adolescent universe turned upside-fucking-down.

CHAPTER 3

As I explained to the first officer on the scene twelve minutes later, I'd walked in to find my mother's bloody body lying on the floor in front of the dishwasher. My blacked-out father was sprawled on the linoleum beside her, the fingers of his right hand touching the butcher knife that forensic investigators later determined had been used to kill her. The autopsy report revealed she had been stabbed seven times, with at least two of those thrusts severing major arteries that caused her to lose more than half her blood.

The kitchen floor was gooey and slick when I'd tiptoed inside after my night on the beach. I'd let myself in quietly and kept the light off so I wouldn't wake my parents, whom I believed were upstairs in bed. I caught a whiff of a slight copper-like smell just before my foot slid out from under me and I dropped to the floor on my ass. My hands flew out sideways as I went down, both of them slapping the sticky linoleum at the same time. My half-functioning brain told me that the dishwasher must have overflowed, spilling sudsy water across the room. But when I picked myself up again and reflexively flicked on the light by the door I was greeted by the full horror of what had gone down.

My first thought was that both my parents were dead. There was so much blood everywhere that my mind couldn't comprehend that all of it could have come from just one person. I leaned against the door in shock, not blinking as I soaked it all in. Bad choice of words, but the imagery stuck with me for years. I'd never seen a dead person before, not even at the handful of funerals I'd been subjected to as a kid growing up in the American South. Even when the caskets were open I would shuffle past with my eyes closed, just to avoid the sight.

All that registered at that moment was the look of terror in my mother's eyes. Pure shock and consummate pain, as if a single frame of horror had been frozen on her face. By contrast, my father had a look of utter calm about him. His eyes were closed, his head lolled up against the refrigerator door as if he were using it as a pillow. He had a bruise on his cheek, and a trickle of blood seemed to have oozed from behind his left ear. Then I noticed a flicker of eye movement beneath his sodden lids, and I realized he was still alive.

I fought hard not to let my suddenly light head cause me to faint. I didn't want to collapse into all that blood, so I closed my eyes and tried to regain some sense of calm. Those first seconds gave me time to figure out what I had to do. First thing: I tried to revive my father. I yelled at him, slapped his cheek, even ran some cold water into my hand and tried to splash it on the old man's face. Bad move, the detectives told me later, since the water served to dilute the blood that had pooled on the floor.

"So fucking what?" I remember snapping at them. "There's plenty to go around."

Once I was breathing steadily I edged my way around the perimeter of the kitchen and took the phone out of its wall cradle. This was back when everything was still wired; no mobile or cordless devices. I dialed the number for the police that was listed on the faded sticker beneath the buttons, then waited for someone to pick up. The dispatcher apparently was not near the phone, but I let it ring and ring until she finally answered.

"This better not be a joke, young man," she scoffed when I told her my mother was lying in a pool of her own blood. "You are aware it's a crime to call in a false report—"

"She's dead!" I yelled into the phone. "Get a fucking ambulance here, now!"

"Don't swear at me, young man—"

"Yes, ma'am," I said, my southern manners kicking in as a matter of necessity. "Just get someone here fast."

The dispatcher coolly asked for my address, then said, "They're on their way. Stay put…it'll only be a few minutes. And this better not be a prank."

A "few minutes" take a lot longer when you're standing just a couple feet from your dead mother and comatose father. I had not yet connected the dots, and certainly had not figured my old man could have committed this vicious act himself. It occurred to me that whoever had done this might still be in the house, but I didn't want to go tracking blood from room to room to find out. Better leave that up to the cops.

Just then I felt the beer in my stomach start to churn. I didn't want to throw up in the middle of this grisly crime scene, so I pushed my way back outside. I barely made it out of the screened porch before I unloaded six cans of partially digested hops into the azaleas that choked the cinder block pilings. Suddenly I felt weak and lightheaded, and a cold shiver began to creep through my skin as the reality of what I'd just seen finally began to sink in. This was not a late-night rerun I was watching from the overstuffed couch in the living room; it was real. The knife, the blood, the empty eyes in my mom's ashen face. She was dead, no question about it, and as that clarity sank in I buckled under the weight of grief and collapsed to the ground.

I didn't lose consciousness, but I did lose the rest of the contents of my stomach. Eventually I managed to rise on wobbly legs again, one hand planted firmly on the side of the house to balance the dizziness. At that instant I heard the wail of a siren way off in the distance, and I knew I'd better sober up fast. I slowly stumbled around the corner of the house out to the street, where my father's black Dodge was parked at a crazy angle. I hadn't noticed it earlier when I'd slogged up from the beach, but one wheel was pulled up on the neatly trimmed lawn and the bumper was crushing a rose bush.

The police unit screamed up the road and lurched to a halt on the grass. A single uniformed cop climbed out of the driver's seat, his hand firmly gripping the butt of his service revolver. The gun was still in its holster, but I sensed an edge in the cop's swagger that suggested he couldn't wait to pull it out and exert whatever authority he thought he had.

"You the caller who reported a death?" he demanded, a coarse wariness in his voice.

I was still drunk enough to make some sort of wisecrack, but I also was smart enough not to. "In the kitchen," I told him. "Door's around back."

"Show me."

I led the way through the darkness, but held back as I gestured toward the screened porch. "In through there," I said.

The uniform nodded, seemed to grasp the concept that I didn't want to go back inside the house. "You stay here," he told me, as if it had been his idea.

He mounted the wooden steps, then pushed his way through the screen door. He turned and peered through the glass into the lighted kitchen, then froze where he was standing. "Holy fucking Christ," he cursed as the scene inside gripped his attention. "*Goddamn!*"

The next hour unfolded in a blur. The first cop did everything he could to hold down dinner from the night before, then radioed in for immediate assistance. More cop cars arrived within minutes, along with an ambulance and a pumper truck from the fire department. I wasn't sure what its purpose possibly could be, but I was not yet clearheaded enough to make intelligible conversation. Best to keep my mouth shut and let the experts do their thing.

They asked me a lot of questions and I answered them however I could. There was no point in lying about the football team, so I fessed up to hanging out on the beach with a six pack until it was safe to go home. The first cops on the scene were more interested in *what* and *when*, most likely because they had reports to file and thoroughness was next to Godliness. When the state investigator finally arrived, he burrowed deep into *where, who,* and *why*. Specifically, where was I last night? Who might be able to corroborate my alibi? Could I think of anyone who might have had a reason to want my mother dead? Did my parents argue a lot? Had I overheard any talk of divorce or separation, or relationships with other people?

At some point the questions began to zero in on my father. Nearly half of all murdered women are killed by their husbands or boyfriends, so he was quickly becoming suspect number one. I had no interest in promoting that theory, and I told this to the detective from the State Law Enforcement Division.

"I'm not going to talk about my father," I said.

"I'm only asking questions, son," the investigator assured me in a flat, creepy tone.

"Then ask better ones," I snapped at him. "Dad didn't do this."

"We're trying to determine that," he replied. "Just be calm and tell me what you remember."

I had not yet seen my father come out of the house, so he was either still passed out on the kitchen floor, or he had been revived from his drunken stupor and now was being questioned. Just as I was.

"I know he didn't do this," I assured the detective as firmly as I knew how. "Not in a million years."

"Did you see the crime scene?"

"Of course. I called it in."

"So you saw the knife?"

"I saw *a* knife," I replied. "On the floor."

"In your father's hand—"

"Close to his hand," I corrected him. "Not in it."

"But very close."

I nodded at that. No lies.

"Close enough for him to have dropped it?" the SLED guy asked. "His hands were covered with blood, and I'm sure we'll find his prints on it."

"It's a kitchen knife," I snapped again. "All our prints are on it."

The detective gave me a condescending nod, and I got the impression that each of my protests further congealed my father's guilt in his mind.

"You were the one who found them," he said. "The first person on the scene."

"Yes."

"And what was your initial thought? I mean, who do you think would do that to your mother?"

I remembered thinking the killer might still have been in the house, and I told him so.

"Right now it's looking like he was," the SLED detective said ominously.

Eventually my father emerged through the front door and was led down the steps to the oyster shell walkway. His hair was matted with dried blood, and a gauze bandage had been taped behind his ear. One of the cops had a hand on his shoulder and was guiding him toward a waiting police unit. When they reached it the cop opened the door, then gently shoved him inside with a hand that ostensibly was trying to protect him from hitting his head. With so many flashing strobes and glaring headlights it was not difficult to see the cuffs clamped around his wrists.

"They're arresting him?" I barked at the SLED guy.

"Taking him down to headquarters for questioning," he replied. "But I do feel obliged to tell you, your father is a person of interest. Now where were we—?"

Wherever we were, I was going no further. I was young and ignorant about how many things worked, but I wasn't dumb. I'd consumed way more beer than any seventeen-year-old should have, so my mind wasn't functioning as clearly as I would have liked. But I was sober enough to know that the police had already pinned my mother's murder on my old man, and whatever I said from this point forward would probably be used against him, in any way they could possibly misconstrue my words.

"I'm not saying another word unless a lawyer is present," I told him, and I didn't.

The trial was held the following spring, after the hurricane clean-up was finished and following a series of legal delays. I had been called to testify as a prosecution witness and was labeled as hostile. By that point I'd seen all the evidence and crime scene photos, and I'd suffered through enough testimony to seriously doubt my father's innocence. Still, I was in no hurry to convict the man who was instrumental in my very existence, let alone my upbringing, so I was as glib and aloof as I had every right to be. If they wanted to call it hostile, so be it.

Jenkins III did his best to get a hung jury. He'd come to realize that, with all the emotion surrounding the "trial of the decade," he couldn't win an outright acquittal. But a "no decision" in the form of a mistrial was almost as good, albeit only temporary. He tried to get the case thrown out because the crime scene no longer existed and therefore the jury couldn't view it for themselves, but the judge didn't buy it. He tried to introduce all sorts of hypothetical alternatives, but the prosecution batted everything away. He raised the possibility of other suspects and motives, but it all fell on deaf ears. He did his best to taint the state's evidence as circumstantial, but the jury evidently thought otherwise. In his closing arguments he maintained that the state had not provided a shred of proof that Frank Devlin was guilty beyond reasonable doubt. He accused the police of not conducting a proper investigation, and of railroading my father for the sake of expediency. He insisted that, with all this ambiguity clouding the trial, there was no way seven reasonable men and five reasonable women would conclude that Dad was guilty.

He was wrong.

Now my father was suggesting Jenkins III had attempted to introduce evidence that could have acquitted him, maybe even get the charges dropped. He also insisted that a DNA test might suggest someone else had wielded the knife that killed my mother. DNA identification was in its infancy back then, and there was no database that could have narrowed down a list of suspects. In any event, the judge had ruled against it all, which made me wonder whether the trial had been fair and just. I still had no reason to believe my father was anything but guilty, but now as I jammed myself behind the wheel of my rental, I wondered if the truth might have been eclipsed by the legal process.

Time to go. I didn't know what I'd hoped to accomplish, coming out here to the island for one last look. *The scene of the crime*, so to speak. Nothing of my childhood remained, unless I counted the memories. Which, I realized now, was exactly what I'd expected to find all along.

I still wasn't ready to go back to the condo. My father had managed to plant a nugget of doubt in my brain just a few hours ago, and I needed to think it through. Was the old bastard simply messing with my head, or did he actually believe he'd been incarcerated for a crime he did not commit? He was unable to recollect where he'd been or what he'd done that night, and he couldn't declare with any certainty that he had not slashed his wife with a knife taken from the block in the kitchen. His thumb and fingerprints were positioned on the handle in such a way that several expert witnesses said he'd gripped it while stabbing her. He'd also admitted to believing his wife had been shacking up with the father of a student in a Sunday school class she taught. A *black* father which, processed through his bigoted mind, was an incendiary and seditious accusation. No matter; to the prosecutor it all added up to means, motive, and opportunity.

As I drove over the swing bridge that spanned the Intracoastal Waterway I could think of only one place to go: Jake's Oyster House.

I had no idea if it still existed, but during the summer before all the shit went down I had spent the best three months of my life there. Jake's had been a casual joint known for its homestyle southern cooking and favored for its location right at the edge of Shem Creek. Eight hours a day, six days a week, I had bused tables, clearing away oyster shells and shrimp skins and leftover grits. Then, after the place closed down for the night, my girlfriend Laurie and I would drive off to a secluded spot we knew in a thicket of scrub near the beach where no one could see or hear us. There we would make out under the stars and all phases of the moon until just a few minutes before her midnight curfew.

Jake's had been owned by Laurie's parents and they had raised their little girl to be a proper southern woman. By definition that meant innocent and chaste and not given to the temptations of the flesh. Since I was the son of a local businessman and state Senator it was presumed that I was cut from the same bolt of cloth, so Mr. and Mrs. Cobb trusted me to be a gentleman and not take advantage of their daughter. My fondness for drinking hard and driving fast was not yet known to anyone but Laurie and me, and the swell of hormones—plus some convenient teenage logic—led me to determine that one could not take advantage of something that was offered freely.

Thirty summers ago, Jake's had consisted of a small, weather-beaten shack and a splintered deck, with picnic tables and umbrellas and a constant swell of hungry gulls milling about. No air conditioning or mist sprayers; just the blistering rays of the sun and the aroma of pluff mud and diesel exhaust from the boats that brought home the day's catch. Time had done its typical number, however, and as I pulled into the dusty parking lot I realized yet another memory from my youth was gone.

Sometime over the years Jake's Oyster House had been transformed into Jake's On The Creek, an upscale restaurant with an arched awning that shaded a set of polished wood doors. A fancy sign above the canopy read "Fine Dining and Dancing," while another explained that valet parking was available free of charge after four o'clock. The wood deck I remembered from years ago was now partially covered by a canvas enclosure, with clear plastic windows that could be rolled down during inclement weather. The rustic picnic tables were replaced with linen tablecloths and napkins, and twin AC units on the roof indicated cold air was pouring into the depths of the restaurant.

I'd already burned enough skin for one day, so I opted for a table inside at a window. Music from past decades was playing on speakers set into the high tin ceiling, and when a waitress walked up I asked her to bring me whatever her coldest beer on tap might be. She gave me the name of something I'd never heard of, explained it was a local craft IPA that was their best-seller.

Then she said, "You here just for the beer, or are you an eatin' man?"

"You still have your famous shrimp and cheese grits?" I asked her.

"Top sellin' item since this place opened thirty-nine years ago," she replied. She looked to be in her twenties, round face and over-starched figure, frizzy hair tied up with a black elastic band. A zircon stud was embedded in the side of one nostril, and an Asian symbol was tattooed on the inside of her left wrist.

"So bring me some of that, with a bottle of whatever hot sauce you have," I said.

"A man after my own heart," the waitress quipped. "Better not tell my husband."

She sashayed away and I gazed out the window at the creek. By now I had grown accustomed to things not being recognizable, and nowhere was that truer than here. There's no point to keep drawing visual contrasts between then and now, except to say that I felt as if I was at my thirtieth high school reunion and everyone but me had grown fatter and older. A lot of water had trickled down the proverbial creek since I'd left town, and now it seemed as if I'd just set foot in the middle of it again.

Then a voice behind me caused the time machine to shift into overdrive.

"Well, strike my match. Of all the shrimp joints in all the towns in all the world, Mr. Pitch Perfect just happens to walk into mine."

CHAPTER 4

I hadn't heard that nickname since I'd left South Carolina in my rearview mirror. It's been said that your past stays put even when you don't, although I'd made every effort to leave my well-worn baggage behind. Any whispers of a full ride baseball scholarship at either The Citadel or U.S.C. had disappeared within weeks of the murder, and my prospects of pitching for any halfway respectable school were almost nil. After I'd graduated from high school I headed west to California, where a sympathetic college scout had invited me to be a walk-on at Fresno State University. I'd successfully shed the murder stigma, and my father made it clear he wanted me out of his life. Despite my fondness for booze I had "fresh start" written all over me. For the record, my freshman year with the Bulldogs—Fresno, not The Citadel—I started six games and won five of them, with one no-decision.

That's why, when I heard the voice and the *Casablanca* reference to the perfect game I'd pitched my junior year of high school, I felt like a shrimp that had just been deveined. The paring knife sliced through my memory and brought that final summer crashing down on me hard, and for a second or two I didn't want to even turn around and remember those beautiful blue eyes.

But just for a second. Then I hardened my nerves and pivoted in my chair, staring at her for the first time in nearly three decades. "The last time we were together we said a great many things," I said, paraphrasing a line from the movie we had watched on her father's

VCR dozens of times. "We agreed that I'd do the thinking for both of us."

"You also said, 'where I'm going, you can't go with me,' " she replied, flashing me her most innocent and tempting Ingrid Bergman smile.

"Interesting, how life happens as time goes by," I replied in my best, totally awful Humphrey Bogart impression.

She giggled at that, then placed a firm hand on my shoulder and gave it a friendly squeeze.

I'd almost convinced myself that Laurie was the last person I hoped to see here when I'd sat down and ordered a beer, but that wasn't true. In fact, she was actually the only person I'd thought of when I'd pulled into the gravel parking lot, even if the restaurant bore little resemblance to the place where I'd cleared tables during that last summer of high school. Yet here she was: Laurie Cobb, my old heartthrob and midnight fantasy from my formative years.

I rose to my feet, gave her a proper hug and a chaste kiss on the cheek. "You are absolutely the only thing that hasn't changed in this whole town," I told her. "And the best part of it, for as long as I can remember."

It wasn't a lie. Sure, her face had filled out and her skin wasn't quite as silky smooth as it had been when she was seventeen. But her neck was still tight and her lips just as sensual. My ex-wife had been obsessed with tucking this and injecting that, and the periodic renovations had grown old very fast. But Laurie's eyes were just as blue as the sky on a summer morning, and her hair was still blonde—although she was showing some signs of darker roots. Still, I had no trouble mentally tussling with her in the warm sand, safely hidden within the cloak of shrubs and vines that formed our private thicket. Back when we were seventeen, of course.

She squeezed my shoulder again, then moved back a few inches and gave me that smile that won me over from the start. "I watched you pitch on TV," she said. "And I've read all your books."

"You're the one," I told her, my standard line whenever someone said that. "I thank you for the royalty check."

"Still the same old Rick Devlin," she said with a chuckle.

"I sure hope not." I couldn't help but force a furtive look at her ring finger, which was occupied by both a gold band and a very large diamond. *Damn.*

"What are you doing here?" she asked me then.

"I could ask you the same thing," I replied, not wanting to get into it. "Do your parents still own this place?"

"They both passed on a few years ago," she said, shaking her head. "Car accident. The short story is they willed the restaurant to me and my sister, and I bought her out."

"You own this place?"

"Me and my husband," she replied with a grin. "I caught you looking."

"Busted," I confessed. "I thought you said you'd never go into the family business."

"You're right, and I still can't look at a plate of cheese grits without feeling ill. So tell me…what brings you back to town after all these years?"

It was a natural and inevitable question, and I'd had enough time to concoct a cover story if it came up. But Laurie Cobb deserved more than a rehearsed line, not just because we had lost our innocence to each other way back when, but because I had never lied to her before. Not then, and I didn't want to veer off that path now.

"My father is sick," I told her. "I need to take care of some things before he dies."

"I'm sorry to hear that," she said, looking me square in the eyes. "Although in all honesty I'm not sorry at all, considering what he did. It's great to see you, though."

"You caught me looking at your ring," I admitted. "Does that mean family?"

"It does." She absently played with the gold band for a second, as if it was too heavy or constricting. Or maybe that was just me, searching for cyphers that weren't there. "A boy and two girls," she said. "Two in high school and one heading off to college in the fall."

"And what name do you go by these days?"

"Most times, 'Mom.' Or Mrs. Mitchell. But sometimes 'bitch' and 'shut the fuck up.' But that's a subject for another time."

I remembered now how Laurie always was able to use a minimum of words to create maximum impact. Clearly her style hadn't changed. An awkward pause set in, and I almost let too much time pass before lamely asking, "So when do you suppose that will be?"

"When will what be?"

"Another time."

She thought on that for a while, her fingers still playing with her ring. It seemed as if a light had gone out in her eyes as she gazed out at the creek, as if to find some vestige of truth out there. "Give me your number and I'll call you," she finally said.

My father was still asleep when I rolled in after finishing my lunch. I looked in on him and he seemed to be sleeping peacefully, so I gently eased the door closed and let him be.

A thousand things were churning in my head and, for the first time in weeks, not all of them had to do with him. At the top of that list was Laurie Cobb who, just for a moment, had seemed weighed down by the pressures of home, work, and family. Back when I had known her best, her biggest stress came from not perfecting a cheerleading routine, or getting a B+ on a paper when she felt she deserved an A. It didn't take a brain surgeon—or even a former major league pitcher—to see there were many things wrong with her picture. But I also knew enough to let her release some of that water over the spillway on her own time, and I would hear from her if she had a mind to call me.

Being twelve stories in the sky gives you a different perspective of the world than when you're at ground level. I stood on the balcony and watched the predicted thunderheads roll in toward Charleston from the west. Layer upon layer of gray clouds folded into each other, and tucked among those folds were bright flashes that went off like Union cannons firing on Confederate encampments. A distant rumble told me the downpour was still a few minutes off, but clearly the weather forecast was adding up to what the voice on the radio had promised.

I opened my laptop on the dining table in the alcove adjacent to the kitchen and turned it on. My intent was to spend an hour or so finishing a chapter of the biography I was working on. It was my seventh book and the process came a little easier now than it did in the beginning. All my southern literary heroes had bailed me out in college when I needed a major that could follow me on team road trips, and they still came to the rescue whenever I needed a literary hand. I had no delusions that my prose would ever be mentioned in the same reference as any of my idols, but they at least had taught me how to evoke emotion and compassion through the predominant themes of history, family, and social justice, and their role in preserving a legacy. I learned to write with a definitive voice—southern or otherwise—and to take chances in structure and dialogue. I even followed the advice of my champion, William Faulkner, who encouraged me to kill all my darlings.

But this afternoon my writing wouldn't coalesce. After fifteen minutes I found myself opening Google and typing in the name Frank Devlin. Before today I had not been concerned with how my father may have been referenced in the far reaches of the Internet, and now I weeded through pages of irrelevant links before I found one that mentioned him. It was a short squib from the mid-nineties announcing that a final appeal to overturn his murder conviction had been denied.

Appeals Court Upholds State Senator's Conviction

Lawyers representing former South Carolina State Senator Frank Devlin lost their third attempt to appeal his conviction in the 1989 murder of his wife, Kathleen Devlin.

In a 58-page unanimous opinion, the state's highest appeals court rejected Devlin's myriad claims of improper dismissal of evidence critical to the defense, witness tampering, and failure of the presiding judge to recuse himself from the trial. Through his primary attorney, Myers Jenkins III, Devlin also requested that DNA testing of blood evidence, a process that had not existed at the time of his original trial, be permitted. That motion was denied, as well.

Mr. Jenkins has continued to file appeals since his client's conviction in 1990, claiming that independent forensic tests would exonerate his client. During the initial trial Devlin did not testify on his own

> behalf, nor did he dispute the prosecutor's claim that he attacked his wife in a jealous rage after wrongly believing that she was involved in an intimate relationship with another man. In his appeals, Jenkins argued that investigators improperly focused on him as a suspect in his wife's death without looking at anyone else.
>
> Devlin, himself, has conceded that he remembers nothing of that night and has no recollection of how he came to be in the kitchen with the victim, who had been slashed multiple times with a knife. No medical tests were ever conducted to determine what caused the injury to his skull, nor how serious quantities of psychoactive drugs came to be in his blood.

I had not followed my father's legal maneuvers after the jury convicted him, although I'd heard via the family grapevine that he'd launched what appeared to be a vigorous appeal. I also remembered that, during the trial, Jenkins III had alluded that Judge Carter periodically attended a Friday night card game in which my father also was known to participate. The judge allowed that it was possible they'd met on at least one occasion, as had many folks in the lowcountry who donated to his legislative campaigns. But never, he insisted—emphasis on "never"—had they ever been in the same room under any sort of compromising circumstance. I can still hear his words coming out in their lazy, slightly softened southern style, friendly and firm.

But, witness tampering? What was that all about? Was it a legal ploy designed to hurl as many alleged violations of the legal code against a barn to see what might stick? Or did Jenkins III have information that the judge for some reason didn't allow, or that wasn't considered credible enough to be admitted? Again, my father had briefly mentioned to me just a few hours ago that Judge Carter wouldn't allow the introduction of certain evidence, which made me wonder if the fix had been in from the beginning.

Or maybe I was being sucked in by the desperate ramblings of a frightened old man clinging to the final threads of his life.

Since my father had been convicted long before the worldwide web was born, I was only able to find a few more references to him or the trial. I was about to give up when I stumbled across one more hit that mentioned him, which I clicked on. It was a summary of an arbitration case that was reprinted on an insurance industry forum, the subject being a property claim that had been denied by Gardiner Casualty and Life. I recognized the company as one of the underwriters my father had represented way back when, so I continued reading.

Apparently, a man named Avery Dunham had owned a multi-use warehouse in Hanahan, a mixed-use industrial community located just outside Charleston. In the aftermath of Hurricane Hugo the warehouse had caught fire and burned to the ground, and Dunham had filed a claim with the intent to collect on damage to the building, its destroyed contents, and loss of use. The only mention of my father was a sentence that read, "Dunham had purchased the policy six years prior from State Senator Frank Devlin, who at the time had owned and operated the Sumter Insurance Agency in downtown Charleston." The insurance adjusters refuted Dunham's contention that a wire had fallen on the structure during the hurricane and sparked the blaze. Instead, insurance investigators determined the fire began when ashes from a cigarette ignited an unknown quantity of nitrocellulose that had been stored on the premises.

Mr. Dunham had appealed the insurance company's denial, but adjusters pointed to a signed rider to the original policy that stated: "no incendiary material of any nature may be stored on the premises, either inside or outside the covered structure. Doing so shall render this policy null and void." Dunham claimed that he had not known that the nitrocellulose was highly combustible, but the panel of three arbitration judges ruled that ignorance did not negate a clause in a legal contract.

It was an interesting case summary but when I'd finished reading it, I realized it had nothing to do with my father. He had only been mentioned anecdotally, and there was no reference to the murder trial. Frank Devlin simply had sold the policy and was mentioned because of his former role as a South Carolina state legislator.

Just then a massive thunderclap rocked me out of my web search. I glanced up and saw that the afternoon had grown dark, and a jagged spear of light flashed out on the river. A few large globules of water splattered on the glass sliders, signaling that the main attraction was about to begin. An instant later a massive wall of rain cascaded down from the heavens as another bolt of lightning struck with a simultaneous crash that sounded like a roll of tin being unfurled with a vengeance.

A muted cry from the other room distracted me, and I realized the storm must have awakened my father. His faint screech was hardly a match for the earsplitting din, but his persistent wail managed to find its way between thunderclaps. I took one last glance at the wall of water, then went to see what he wanted.

Sure enough, he was wide awake, his hands gripping the blankets with tightened fists. His enlarged eyes told me he hadn't experienced a real southern thunderstorm in years, and the tempest unfolding outside the glass sliders seemed to both excite and terrify him. He had twisted his body so he could see the clouds and the rain and the lightning, and his mouth seemed stuck in the shape of a perfect 'O'. Then he noticed me watching him, and said, "There you are."

"I haven't been through one of these in years," I told him. "I'd forgotten all the power and fury of a summer storm."

"Nothing like the lightning and thunder we had inside the joint," he replied with a gloomy nod. "Sure did miss the real thing, though."

He said nothing for a long while after that. We both just watched the show, me from the doorway and him from his perch in his electric bed. It provided something for both of us to do without actually speaking, but after a while the repetitive flashes and booms grew tedious.

"A nurse came by earlier, while you were out," he finally said to me. "I didn't know where the hell you'd gone."

"I can't be here all the time, Dad," I reminded him, more than a little defensively. "It's part of the agreement."

"Don't get your jockstrap in a pinch, son," he said. "I wasn't meaning anything, just making an observation. This nurse, she asked if you were about, and I told her I didn't know."

"The nurse has a name," I reminded him. "It's Benita."

"That figures, given her mutilation of the English language," he rasped. "Next time she's here I'm going to ask to see her green card."

I'd conveniently forgotten two things about my old man: he was a sucker for lovely ladies, and he was a certified bigot. I'd been forced to tolerate his incendiary prejudice while I was still living under his roof, excusing his faults in favor of fatherly love. He'd always chosen his words carefully when he was in public, acutely aware that whatever he said could affect his insurance business or sway his poll numbers. But I knew for a fact that his lexicon of ethnic slurs was put to good use when he was drinking with his poker buddies, or trying to get a rise out of my sister and me.

"What did the nurse do?" I asked him, choosing to ignore his bait.

"The usual. Gave me water, wiped my ass, asked if I needed to take a piss."

"I see your discriminatory views haven't changed over the years," I pointed out.

He offered a puerile grin, apparently tickled that he could still get me riled up. "And all those years out west has kicked your southern heritage to the curb," he replied. 'Southern heritage' was his thinly veiled reference to the perceived superiority of white skin, and the social privilege freely accorded to it.

"The Confederate mindset never did sit well with me," I said.

"You come from a long line of proud men and women who fought and died to preserve a legacy of independence and liberty," he rasped.

"They died in order to protect a way of life that was built on the backs of slaves," I reminded him. "Black men and women who were officially counted as only three-fifths of one white person, if you remember your U.S. Constitution."

"Look, son," he wheezed. "You haven't been where I've been the last thirty years, so you don't know what you haven't seen."

"I know that Lady Justice is blind except when it comes to color," I replied. I knew I shouldn't engage him in his close-minded rhetoric, but for the first time he lacked the power to kick me out of his house for opposing him. "Black man steals a loaf of bread, he gets five years. White man embezzles a million dollars, he pays a wrist-slap fine."

"Typical snowflake bullshit, and you're missing the point." There was a heightened furor in his eyes, the same look that crossed his face years ago when he would embark on one of his white crusades. "Nigras are descended from African tribes, and they run their ghetto gangs like they run those jungle shitholes. Like John Wayne said, until they're educated and accountable, they shouldn't be allowed to teach our children or run a business. Or vote."

Yep, my father hadn't changed one bit over the years, and never would. As much as I'd loved him, I'd also done my best to avoid talking politics with him back then. I wasn't about to tread any further now, not with so little time left on his clock.

"Trip to the mound," I told him, as I had in the years B.C. It was a baseball phrase I'd come up with to allow us to both cool off and let tempers simmer down a bit.

The storm was still raging outside the glass, and I was sure every flash of lightning and cannon roar of thunder reminded him of Union blood being spilled at Shiloh. Frank Devlin had been born into a rabid Baptist family in the South in the late 1930s, and had been raised on motherhood, church, and apple pie. Jim Crow had long ago come home to roost, and institutional segregation was the law of the land. Miscegenation was considered a crime against humanity, racial fear flourished across the color spectrum, and any notion of civil rights was a cultural oxymoron. When I was a teenager he was still outraged that Hank Aaron had broken Babe Ruth's home run record the year I turned two, and he was still miffed that Rosa Parks had the audacity to take a seat in the front of the bus.

A long silence ensued as we watched nature's own fire and brimstone pounding the glass. His eyes slowly eased shut as sleep began to take hold, and I quietly edged toward the door. Just before I made my escape they flickered open, and he said, "I want you to ignore what I was babbling about earlier."

I stared at him blankly and tried to figure out what he was saying. "What do you mean, 'babbling'?" I asked.

"You know," his voice rasped. "What I told you about that night."

I said nothing to that, figuring whatever he was trying to tell me would come at his own pace. One more tremendous roar of thunder seemed to reinforce my thinking.

"Whatever I said about the trial was just the rambling of an old man who hadn't been out in the real world in over thirty years," he continued. Each word came out long and hard, like someone pumping a set of antique bellows to force them from this throat.

"Are you talking about the evidence you said the judge didn't allow?" I asked him.

He slowly adjusted his head in the slightest of nods, then said, "Whatever I said, it was because of all the pain meds they'd pumped into me before I got there. Don't give it another thought."

"It's hard to un-think something," I told him.

"You can if you're smart," he replied. "It's how I stayed alive the last thirty years."

Then his eyes closed for real, and within seconds he was asleep. His body had worn itself out from our five minutes of debate, as well as the unceasing appetite of the cancer that was devouring his body. I listened once again to make sure his lungs were still functioning, and had to bend down close to hear the coarse rasp in his windpipe. Another boom of thunder crashed outside the window, but he was already too far under to notice.

I gently pulled the blanket over his withered body, up to his chin. It reminded me of those early years of my own fatherhood, when I would tiptoe into Addie's room to tuck her in after she had fallen asleep. Just as my dying father had done with me when I was young. Cradle to grave, and back around again. I grasped his cold, withered hand that looked and felt like the outer skin of an onion, and moved it under the blanket.

That's when I felt the piece of paper tucked under his pajama-clad body. I gently tugged on it and eventually pulled out a small, cream-colored envelope that had been closed but not sealed.

My father was still asleep and presumably would be for hours, so I quietly backed out of the room and pulled the door closed behind me as the rain hammered the glass.

Not until I got to the kitchen did I open it. Inside was a white index card, the kind that was ruled on one side and blank on the other. Nothing odd about that, but the four words that were printed in block letters stood out plain as day. They read:

SHUT THE FUCK UP

CHAPTER 5

The words were handwritten in pencil, probably a standard Number 2, all upper case and carefully crafted to avoid any identifiable penmanship. Hard to trace or analyze, and as close to generic as possible without going through an inkjet printer. The envelope itself was blank, no name or address anywhere. Probably no prints, either.

The first thought to cross my mind was, *What the hell is this?* But that question didn't linger for long, since the note's purpose was plain and simple: a warning to my father to keep his mouth closed. Someone didn't want him yakking, and it didn't take much imagination to figure out who.

Jenkins IV. He was the only person I'd told about my father's mention of disallowed evidence and untested DNA, and it was a reasonable leap of logic to think he had a hand in writing the note. If there was a reason Jenkins or his father didn't want my dad talking about the trial, a veiled threat might cause him to think twice. I found it unlikely that either lawyer had delivered the message personally, but I was confident it had not been in my father's possession when he'd left the Hospice Center in the ambulance. If he hadn't smuggled it in himself, it had to have arrived at the condo after he did.

The easiest way to find the truth was to confront my father, ask him where he'd gotten it. I had every right to do that, since the terms of his release stipulated there would be no outside contact with anyone. He had always been a stubborn man, however, so I doubted I'd be able to change his mind. All I would get if I confronted him was a barrage of insults, and I didn't need that sort of shit.

I decided to pursue this from a different angle altogether. My father's pardon stipulated that he be housed in a secure building equipped with an alarm system that could be triggered by smoke or illegal entry. There was no mention of cameras in the papers I'd signed, and the only monitoring system I knew of was the one that triggered the app on my phone. And the device fastened to his ankle. However, I suspected the tastefully decorated foyer downstairs was equipped with twenty-four-hour video surveillance, and possibly even the six elevators that served the fifteen floors.

I went out into the hallway but saw no sign of cameras. Same thing with the elevator that arrived when I hit the button. I glanced up at the ceiling but didn't see the standard black plastic dome that typically covered a camera lens. Down in the foyer, however, I spotted at least three video devices that would capture the activity of anyone coming in or going out the front door.

Once I was back upstairs two quick phone calls gave me the name of the real estate company that managed the condo property. It was located in downtown Charleston on Meeting Street, and a quick call connected me to a cheery receptionist in the main office.

"Are you calling about a maintenance issue?" she asked in a soft, almost lyrical accent that suggested she probably was from the upstate area, or maybe western North Carolina.

"No, ma'am," I told her. "I'm at the Riverfront and it appears someone may have entered my unit. I don't think anything's been taken and no damage was done, but I was wondering if you have security cameras that might have caught the break-in."

"Oh, dear," she said. "That's horrible. Have you filed a police report?"

"No, ma'am," I said quickly. I didn't want her summoning the cops or making this any bigger than a simple question. "There's no proof of anything, but just in case...well, I wanted to know if you have video surveillance."

"We have a number of cameras on the premises, but individual unit security is the responsibility of the property owner." Typical cover-your-ass liability B.S., and completely understandable.

"Of course," I agreed. "I have an alarm system, but it was off. Do you think I might be able to take a look at your lobby video from this morning?"

She didn't say anything for a minute, then asked, "Are you a renter, or do you own your unit at Riverfront?"

I didn't see what difference it might make, but I said, "Neither. I'm housesitting for the current owner."

"I see. Which unit would that be?"

I gave her the condo number, then said, "I just arrived this morning."

There was another silence, presumably while she checked something in a file or on her computer. Then she said, "You would be Mr. Devlin?"

I didn't know if that was a good thing or a bad thing, so I said, "Yes, ma'am."

"Well, sir…you've sort of been flagged."

"Flagged? What does that mean?"

"I'm trying to figure that out…hold on." She said nothing for a good twenty seconds before continuing, "Okay, I see. There's a note here that says any request of any nature must be officially approved before it can be granted."

"Approved by whom?"

I could almost see her shrug over the phone. "It doesn't say, sir, except that everything pertaining to occupancy of that unit needs to be channeled through our head office."

"And where is that?" I asked.

"Spartanburg, sir. I can text them a message, if you want."

Dammit. Security seemed tighter than the airport. "No, that's all right, ma'am," I replied. "Like I told you, I'm not even positive anyone was in here."

"Right," she said. "But if you need any help, just let me know."

I told her I would, then ended the call. I wasn't surprised at the extra precautions that had been laid down to make sure my father's whereabouts remained private, and under normal circumstances I wouldn't be concerned. But someone had violated the no-contact rule just hours after his arrival, and if the note hadn't been delivered by Jenkins III or IV, someone else knew where he was. And how to get to him.

By now the deafening thunder had moved eastward, out to sea. The torrent of water that had erupted in an instant ended just as quickly. Dark mountains of gray continued to rumble across the harbor and marshland, while jagged wands of light stabbed the earth in the distance.

I didn't know what time it was, but I hoped it was close to a respectable drinking hour. Even though my body clock told me I was still on Pacific Time, my mental barometer was set to *now.* I grabbed a beer from the fridge, which had been thoroughly stocked at my request, then Googled Myers Jenkins III. I knew he'd moved an hour away to Edisto years ago, but I wanted whatever contact information might be available on the guy. I could have asked Jenkins IV, but I'd already committed the error of telling him about my conversation with my father. I wasn't going to make things any worse.

It took me a good twenty minutes to scour individual databases for an address and phone number, but eventually I had what I needed. Several more sites confirmed the address, and a few even told me how much the place was worth. Google maps gave me an eerily detailed aerial view as well as a map, which I roughly copied on a clean sheet of paper.

The satellite image told me the house was set back from the shore of a tidal estuary that emptied into the South Edisto River. There was one road in and out, no number or name, and it appeared to be either dirt or gravel. I could make out a dock with a boat nestled up to it, but I had no idea when the image had been shot. It could have been five days or five years ago. Either way, Jenkins III still seemed to be living there, so I committed as much of the terrain as possible to memory, then fed the address into the GPS app on my phone.

When I was a child my mother had been fond of saying, "there's no use poking through old vomit." Her message: what's done was done, and there's no point in revisiting the past since you can't do anything to change it. On the flip side, there's a philosopher named Santayana who taught us that if we don't pay attention to history, we're doomed to repeat it.

Because of the enormous spectacle my father's murder trial had evolved into, my sister and I had been assigned an armed bailiff who was with us at all times. He escorted us through a back door into the courthouse, guided us to a private room where we could kill time while the lawyers and judge were arguing, and ushered us to our front row seats behind the defense table when the trial resumed. I learned much later that this treatment was neither typical nor appreciated by the prosecution, but Jenkins III had been able to convince the judge. My sister had been in her second year at Clemson and I was a senior in high school, and he insisted that our courtroom experience should be as stress-free as possible. Good luck with that, since our accused father was seated at the defense table just a few feet in front of us.

Thirty years later, all I recalled about the bailiff was that he was black, bald, old, and went by the nickname "Stumpy." I remember him being particularly kind and compassionate, going the extra mile to make sure we had water or soda or coffee whenever we needed it. He personally delivered lunch to the small anteroom where we were sequestered from the spectators and reporters between trial segments. He told me stories about his family and seemed to know everything there was to know about my sister and me. I don't think Karen had the same appreciation for Stumpy as I did, which I blamed on the trial's poor timing. She was missing her final exams at Clemson, which meant she had received special dispensation to sit for them after the ordeal was over. Instead, she hunkered down in a corner looking glum and distraught, fuming about fairness and equality, while Stumpy and I discussed baseball, girls, and the rapidly approaching summer. Everything but the trial.

I spent my first bottle of beer and part of a second running all sorts of combinations of "Stumpy" and "Charleston County Court" through Google. The result was a lot of useless information that meant absolutely nothing to me. A town named Stumpy Point in North Carolina was the birthplace of a young pervert who had been convicted of a violent rape and abduction years ago in North Charleston. Also, a man charged with killing his wife and small son on James Island a few years back had been found floating face-down in Stumpy Pond, just outside Rock Hill.

Persistence and patience eventually paid off. When I took the "y" out of "Stumpy" and added "bailiff" I found my answer on the first page of results. Herman J. Stump had served as an officer of the court for twenty-seven years prior to his retirement eight years ago, which meant he would have been on the job during my father's trial. The newspaper squib actually included a color photograph of him with his wife of forty-one years during his retirement party, and I instantly recognized the large smile, the shaved black head, and the broad nose.

Now that I had his name, finding him was easy. I ran him through the same search matrix I'd conducted on Myers Jenkins III and found he had an address in the West Ashley section of Charleston, a few blocks from Old Savannah Highway. I also found the number for a phone that, I suspected, was still wired directly into the wall.

The former bailiff had to be close to eighty by now, very likely losing his eyesight and his hearing. Maybe even his memory. Still, I felt a strong urge to connect with him, since he had made such a difference in my life during that week at the courthouse. I never saw him again after that final evening when the jury announced its verdict, when he'd led Karen and me one last time out the rear exit of the courthouse. Uncle Andrew—our mother's brother—had been waiting for us in an alley, and Stumpy and I had shaken hands. His grip had been powerful, and I'd tried to match it, biting back the pain. Pain from the muscle strength, and from not knowing what my future might hold.

Uncle Andrew had been barred from the courtroom the day before the trial began. Judge Carter was tired of his repeated threats to attack "the sonofabitch named Frank Devlin who'd murdered his sister," and he implemented protective measures to keep him as far away from the jury as possible. Carter also made it clear that any member of the press who quoted even one word of what our uncle had to say would be held in contempt of court. Gag order in place, Carter then sequestered the jury, taking no chance that Jenkins III might get the mistrial he clearly was pushing for.

I punched in the phone number I'd found and a woman picked up after several rings. "Who's calling?" she answered in a naturally suspicious voice.

I introduced myself, then said, "Is Henry Stump home?"

"No, he ain't. You sellin' something?"

"No, ma'am," I told her. "This is nothing like that."

"They all say that. So what you want with Herman?"

"He and I go way back, ma'am. An old trial, and I'd like to talk to him about that."

"He retired eight years ago," she said. "On account of the heart attack."

I wasn't surprised by her words, since he always seemed to have a lit cigarette in his hand or mouth. "I'm sorry to hear that," I replied. "About his heart, I mean. Can you tell me when he might be home?"

"What did you say your name was again?" she asked me.

"Rick Devlin," I told her once more. "He and I met during my father's trial, a long time back."

She fell silent for a few seconds, then said, "Did you say Devlin?"

"Yes, ma'am. Rick Devlin. My father was Frank Devlin." *Was*, past tense, as if he already had ceased to exist.

"The murder trial," she said then, as it all seemed to click into place. "I remember that…it had to be what, twenty-five years ago?"

"More like thirty," I politely corrected her. "The trial was in the spring after Hugo."

"Lord Almighty," she said, her voice barely more than a wisp of air. "That long."

"Do you suppose your husband might have an inclination to speak with me? That is, if he's in any shape to do so."

"Heavens, boy," Mrs. Stump said. "Although I s'pose you ain't a boy no more. Sheesh, all he talked about during that trial was you and your sister. Are you in town?"

I told her I was, for a few days at least. "Do you think he might agree to see me?" I pressed her. "If his health is holding up?"

"His health? Lord Almighty, nothin's gonna stop that man. His heart quit pumping a few seconds and he done retired cuz of it. But he didn't stop working, not one bit. He still volunteers four days a week down at the federal courthouse, across the street from the old one. Tell you what. I'll let him know you called, lookin' for him, but if you just go up to the jury room tomorrow, after nine, that's where you'll find him. Still looks like ol' Stumpy, but older. *Lord Almighty*."

CHAPTER 6

I arrived at the courthouse early the next morning. Specifically, the J. Waties Waring Judicial Center, named for the pioneering civil rights judge. Since it was Thursday, most of the trials scheduled for the week had already concluded, so there was no line at the security checkpoint. Once I was past the metal detector I followed the signs to the jury selection room, where a handful of responsible citizens were waiting for their civic duty to begin.

It would have been difficult to miss Stumpy. He was standing outside the double doors where a simple sign read: "Jurors Only Beyond This Point." He looked much older than the last time I'd seen him, a little stooped from age, but he still stood apart from the other senior citizen volunteers. I had forgotten how tall he was, at least an inch more than me, and the midnight blackness of his skin. His head was just as bald and polished as I'd remembered, his dark eyes just as penetrating and alert. One mind-numbing morning during the trial, while the attorneys were arguing about something in the judge's chambers, he had taken the time to enlighten me on how his forebears had come to be in America. He'd explained that he was a direct descendant of the Gullahs, former slaves who had been brought to the Carolina rice fields from different regions along the western coast of Africa. His ancestors had mostly come from Senegambia and, following the Civil War, they had proudly maintained their distinct creole heritage—many of them living in isolated pockets along the coast and its remote sea islands.

I waited for him to finish passing out name badges to the handful of prospective jurors who were wandering in, inviting them to take their seats and thanking them for fulfilling their responsibility as U.S. citizens. I pictured him as he was thirty years ago: lean and solid, crisp bailiff's uniform, loaded gun strapped to his waist. Keeping an eye on every person in the courtroom, always looking for signs of potential trouble.

When he was done with the last of the jurors I casually wandered up to him and said, "Good morning, Mr. Stump."

He regarded me curiously, and I caught a flicker of worry that caused his brain to mentally reach for a gun that he no longer had. Then a glint of recognition flashed in his eyes, and he said, "Mr. Rick? Let me see…yes, you're definitely Rick Devlin."

I knew his memory couldn't be so good that he recognized me after all this time, so I replied, "Your wife must have told you I called."

"She mentioned it just as I was leaving the house this morning, said you'd phoned the house. My Lord, boy, you've gone and grown yourself into a man."

"There's no stopping the years," I replied.

"No, there ain't." He wrapped his big arms around me and gave me a hearty death squeeze, then pulled back and gripped me by both shoulders. "So tell me, what're you doing back in this town? Last thing I heard you say, you were never coming back to Charleston as long as you were alive."

"I was a bit of a dick in those days," I admitted. "Impetuous and hotheaded."

"I do recall you being a bit impulsive," he said with a grin.

"And one thing I learned since then is never say never. It's too long a time."

"That is a certainty. So what changed your mind? You here for a reason or just passing through?"

I didn't want to lie to my old friend, but I'd signed a stack of forms promising I would not tell anyone my true reason for being in Charleston. That restriction certainly included confiding in old Stumpy, but I knew I could trust him to keep our discussion confidential.

"Unfinished business," I explained to him.

"Thirty years is a long time to leave something undone," he

observed.

"Yes, it is. Especially when it involves my father."

"I figured it had to be that, else you wouldn't have called." He fell silent after that, letting me make the next move.

"Is there someplace we can talk?" I asked him. "In private?"

"This ain't like old times," he said. "They don't give me a ring of keys. But I know a place we can go, no one will hear us."

He led me to a secluded seating area tucked into an out-of-the-way alcove paneled with rich, dark wood and cramped with a sofa and several chairs. A large window looked out over a large plaza below, with iron grillwork and magnolia trees and a view of Broad Street. For everything that seemed to have changed from the Charleston of my memory, Broad remained exactly as I remembered it. Law firms, art galleries, banks, and churches extended all the way down to the Old Exchange at East Bay. Then and now the street embodied a sense of historic and economic prominence, a demarcation of an unspoken social hierarchy that defined the city's varied cultural spectrum.

"This is where lawyers huddle with their clients, so jurors won't see or hear them outside the courtroom," he explained. "Have a seat."

I did as he said, settling into in a comfortable high-backed chair that seemed to swallow me whole. Stumpy sat down in a similar chair positioned across a glass table from me. He checked his cell phone, then set it on the polished surface.

"Hope you don't mind, but I'm on call," he said.

"You do whatever you need to do, Mr. Stump," I replied. "I promise, I won't take more than two minutes of your time."

"You can have all the minutes you want, until the lawyers select their jury. And please—call me Herman. It's my name."

"Yes, sir." I found myself inhaling deeply, as if I had just wandered into a confessional and was about to bare my soul. "Like I said, I'm here on account of my father. Not *for* him, just *because* of him. I can't explain what I mean by that, but I don't expect my stay here to be more than a few days."

Herman Stump gave me a slow nod, a single dip of his head. "I'm listening. And whatever you need, just ask."

I thanked him, then gave him a thumbnail summary of the parole deal. "He's not expected to live much longer…a week, two at the most," I explained. "I'm here to watch over him until he's gone."

Stumpy nodded ponderously but said nothing until I was finished spinning my tale. "I don't guess that's on the list of tourist things to do in Charleston," he said. "And I don't know what it's got to do with me."

So I continued, explaining what my father had said about inadmissible evidence and DNA. I left out the part about him recanting what he had told me, as well as the note that told him to keep his mouth shut.

Herman Stump replied predictably, saying, "I've seen more prisoners than anyone in this building as they're led away after they been convicted. Almost all of 'em insist they're innocent, and they keep insisting it long after they get into the prison van."

"So I'm told," I replied. "But I'm not interested in any of them—just what my old man told me."

"Did he come right out and say he didn't do it?"

"He was very clear about it," I replied. "And he did plead 'not guilty' at his trial."

"You know how the law works. You don't get a jury unless you say you didn't do it."

"Still, he seemed pretty adamant yesterday about the evidence," I told him, reflecting on what my father had said to me yesterday morning. *I didn't kill your mother, son. I loved her more than words can say.* "He mentioned that his lawyer had evidence, but the judge ruled almost everything inadmissible."

"Judge Carter," Stumpy said, with a nod of recognition. "That man could be damned heavy-handed, if he was of a mind."

"And he should have recused himself on account of the poker games."

"I do recall hearing rumors of that," he said with a slow nod. "Lots of shouting went on in chambers during the trial."

I'd been leaning back in the cloudlike chair, but now I hunched forward and placed my hands on my knees. "Do you have any idea what that evidence might've been?" I asked him, looking directly into those big, dark eyes.

Herman Stump shook his head, almost pitifully. "I was privy to all sorts of things in that job," he explained. "Plea deals, compromises, sentence offers. Personal things I had no business knowing. But my main role during your father's trial was to keep an eye on you and your sister. Any legal wrangling that went on was far out of my range of hearing."

"Still, is there a chance any of it still exists?" I asked, suddenly feeling dejected. "The evidence that wasn't allowed, I mean."

His shoulders flexed in a spastic shrug and he shook his head again, side to side. Then he said, "If Carter didn't allow it, then it's not part of the trial record. But it could be your daddy's lawyer hung on to it across all these years."

"Who has the old trial records?"

"Well, it's a historic case, but it was long before the internet. Probably not available online, which means microfilm."

"Where do I start?"

"You're a persistent man," Stumpy said, flashing me a broad grin. "It's probably a thankless task, but if you insist on doing this, the Clerk of Courts is the place to go. And if you have any problems, give me a call."

The last time I'd been to Edisto was one of those Devlin family excursions when I was about twelve. One summer morning right after school had let out, our parents piled us into the Vista Cruiser and drove us down to a campground set right on the beach. It wasn't all that much different from the beach that was just a hundred yards from our front door, but that wasn't the point. We were on an adventure, and as usual we didn't know where we were going until we got there. My sister and I both tuned out our parents' bickering about the upcoming election—my father insisting Reagan was the second coming of Christ, while Mom had become a Gary Hart supporter after Ernest Hollings dropped out of the race.

We pitched a tent behind a sweeping dune topped with sea oats and feather grass, and swam in the surf and collected shells from the warm sand. We roasted hot dogs over a fire, burned marshmallows on sticks, and sang *Kumbaya*—which Stumpy told me five years later during the trial was a Gullah colloquialism that translated roughly to "come by here." Then we were eaten alive by clouds of no-see-ums that descended at dusk, and which quickly chased us into our tent.

I took the state highway down to the center of Edisto, arguably a tidewater island because of Watts Cut, a part of the Intracoastal Waterway that slices through the lowcountry from South Edisto to the Dawho River south of Charleston. Dozens of meandering rivulets and tidal tributaries course through the hummocks and marsh and mud, and this morning the egrets and herons were patiently scouting for breakfast along the banks.

The place I was looking for was located down a dirt road that took a sharp turn off the blacktop. The data package in my GPS app evidently didn't include the roads down here, because it stopped functioning when I left the state highway half a mile back. I was on my own, with nothing but scribbled directions and a crude map I'd sketched at the condo. I had to stomp hard on the brakes to get the Kia to stop in time, then pulled onto a narrow side road. Gravel crunched under the tires as I cruised past ancient oaks shrouded with Spanish moss and spindly pines that were corkscrewed with dead curls of creeper vines.

Jenkins III's private drive was not marked, but I knew where it was from the satellite view I'd uploaded to my phone last night. I slowed to a crawl, then edged up a two-rut lane a couple hundred yards until I came to a clearing at the edge of a river. The copse of trees from which I emerged provided a sublime backdrop to the tranquility of the south fork of the Edisto River, the water glimmering in the sun like crumpled tin foil. The light filtered through the leaves and the needles and moss, casting an illusion of an idyllic era long gone by.

The cabin itself was not really a cabin; it was a modern log home built on several levels, with a green tin roof, and a stone chimney at one end. The yard was neatly cropped, nothing fancy, just a small patch of knock-out roses turning their red petals to the sun. A silver Mercedes was parked in the open garage, which told me Jenkins was most likely home.

He was, and so was a black Labrador Retriever whose self-appointed job was to protect the kitchen door. He let out a throaty woof, and his tail thumped a few times as I got out of the car. As I came closer he sat up and stared at me intently, clearly thinking *friend or foe?* Or, more likely, *does he have a treat?*

Then the kitchen door opened and an old man appeared. My mental math told me Jenkins III had to be my dad's age, somewhere in his early eighties. He raised a hand to shade his eyes from the sun, and said, "If you're a Mormon or trying to sell me something, get your ass off my property."

"No, sir," I called back to him, raising my hands so he could see nothing was in them. "Not selling anything, Mr. Jenkins. Just thought I'd stop in and pay a cordial visit to an old family friend."

He squinted at me, and a spark of recognition ignited in his face. "That you, Ricky?" he asked. "Ricky Devlin? Damn, if that don't just beat all to hell."

He played the surprise perfectly. I knew he'd had a hand in arranging my father's deathbed deal, and his son would have updated him on my arrival in Charleston. But if he wanted to appear shocked at seeing me, why should I rain on his parade?

"Your son didn't mention we'd talked?" I asked him.

"At my age, if I don't write it down it slips right in one ear and out the other. My God, boy…you look like I last saw you just yesterday."

He labored down the kitchen steps, patting the dog on his head as he passed by. I closed the distance between us and we shook hands vigorously.

"Good looking dog," I said. "Got a solid bark in him."

"Much worse than his bite. Name's Diesel, and what he lacks in hunting instinct, he makes up for in the licking department."

I quickly learned what Jenkins meant. Now sensing I was "good people," the dog bounded down the steps and trotted toward me. I bent down to greet him, and he soon attacked my face with his tongue. I gave him a few seconds, then stood up and said, "I heard you'd retired down here a few years back. Nice spread."

And a good part of it made possible by defending my father.

"It's been a long time since I've written a legal brief or filed a motion, that's for sure," he said, almost longingly. "And it's getting a little warm out here…what do you say we go inside to visit?"

I followed him into the house, through the kitchen and into the rustic living room that offered a broad view of the river through a giant sheet of glass. A rolling field sloped down to the shore, where a dock stretched a good fifty feet over the water. Motor yachts and sailboats were cutting lazy arcs through the sapphire waterway, and a single cloud seemed to be pasted to the sky. I commended him on the view, which he told me was the reason he had picked this spot to build the house. "I moved in just a few years after your father's appeals came to a close. May I get you something? Water, coffee, sweet tea—?"

I hadn't had a glass of sweet tea since I'd left the south, and my L.A. dentist was certain it was why my mouth was full of silver today. Still, it sounded perfect for a warm July day, so I said, "If it's not too much trouble."

He left me in a chair looking out at the water and the boats, then returned a minute later with two tall glasses, complete with lemon wedges and straws. Once the requisite hospitality was out of the way he sat down, facing me as he gripped his glass in both hands.

"This isn't just a cordial visit, am I right?" he asked.

"Well, it's definitely a pleasure to see you, sir, but no. A good part of why I drove down here this morning is business."

"Look at that…there's a Cardinal," he exclaimed as he pointed at a red bird with a pointed top-knot perched on a bird feeder at the edge of his back deck. He watched it until it fluttered away, then said, "I presume this business has to do with your father."

"Do you speak with your son regularly?" I asked, not immediately addressing his observation.

"Now and then by phone, but he thinks it's too far to drive. Long hours in the office and at the courthouse, plus family things and fishing every weekend."

I nodded, a line from an old Harry Chapin song running through my head. *Cat's in the Cradle*. "You are aware my father was released yesterday," I said.

Jenkins III cracked a withered smile, and said, "I heard he's finally a free man."

"Not exactly free, and not for very long," I pointed out.

"I suppose that's true," the old lawyer said. I'd noticed when he came down the steps to greet me that he was slightly arthritic, and he'd winced once or twice as we were walking back inside. Now as he sat in his chair, he gently rubbed his right hip, his hand moving around toward his spine. "Goddamn disc," he cussed with a wince. "But you're not here to talk about me."

This was his not-so-subtle way of getting around to what I wanted, and he was right. I didn't wish to waste either of our mornings talking about his ailments.

"As you know, I hadn't seen my father since the trial," I said. "Not until yesterday. I knew he was in bad health, the cancer being just about everywhere that matters. As I told your son when he first called me, I didn't want to do this. I saw no need to put either of us through it, and couldn't figure out a single benefit."

"He relayed that sentiment to me," he replied. "And now?"

"The jury is still out on that," I said. "Certainly longer than the two hours and fourteen minutes it took to convict him the first time."

If Jenkins III took that as a subtle dig at his lawyering skills, fine by me. He studied me with eyes the color of dark oak, and said, "Have you tried looking at it through his eyes?"

"He brought this on himself," I replied, maybe a little too sharply. "But that gets me to why I'm bothering you on such a beautiful summer morning. Look: I know the line about how most convicts insist they're innocent long after the gavel drops. Someone else is always to blame, and all that. But yesterday morning Dad told me something that sounded kind of perplexing, and I can't shake it."

"Painted bunting," he suddenly blurted, pointing at a brightly colored bird perched on the feeder. He watched it nibble at a few seeds, then said, "Haven't seen one of those in ages. Go on."

"He mentioned the judge didn't allow some of your evidence to be introduced at trial," I continued. "Said you'd tried, but he excluded it."

Jenkins III closed his eyes, as if retreating into the past. When he opened them he said, "My memory isn't as sharp as it once was, my boy, but there were a few things I recall that might have cast a cloud of doubt. Maybe could've made it tougher for the prosecution to prove its case, and mine a little easier to win over the jury. Or at least hang them."

"Whatever you might remember could shed some useful light," I told him.

Jenkins didn't seem perturbed by my questions, nor alarmed that my father had raised the issue in the first place. If he'd been the one to pass the note on the index card, he was doing a damn fine job hiding it.

"Attorney-client privilege never expires," he replied tiredly.

"If you shared it with the judge then it wasn't privileged," I said, not caring whether I was correct in my thinking or hurling bullshit. "Whatever you wanted to admit into evidence wasn't going to remain private for very long."

He studied me with blank eyes for a minute, and then a smile cracked his lips. "I'm not going to get into a legal debate with you, son," he said. "You'd lose, hands down. But I'm old and weary, and there's no real reason not to let you in on my thinking back then."

"Much appreciated," I told him.

I waited for him to speak, and eventually he did. His words started slowly and carefully, framed with great caution. "You know all the circumstances of the crime scene. Your father was passed out, knife pretty much in his hand, his prints on it. Your mother's blood was on him, and he had a six-hour memory lapse. He had no explanation for anything, and couldn't rightly deny that he'd killed Kathleen. Couldn't remember a goddamned thing, in fact."

"Like you said, I know all this," I said, impatiently.

"Just setting the stage," he murmured. "There was no sign of forced entry, no defensive wounds on the victim. Your father had a contusion where the back of his head struck the kitchen counter. Blackwood insisted that injury had occurred when he came at your mother with the knife, and she pushed him away."

Daniel Blackwood was the Chief Prosecutor in the Charleston County Solicitor's Office who'd argued the case against my father. He was a vicious pit bull with widely assumed political aspirations, and he'd clearly been using his position as a stepping stone to advance his career. He'd been driven by power and ambition, and had been virtually untouchable until—as I learned years later—he was caught in a motel room with the family babysitter. His fall from grace reminded me of former Louisiana Governor Edwin Edwards, who once famously said, "The only way I can lose is if I'm caught in bed with either a dead girl or a live boy."

"Blackwood was a dick," I replied, feeling the need to say something crude.

"One of many appropriate adjectives. He also had what he thought was a slam dunk case, and Judge Carter didn't want the trial to grow into a spectacle. The SOB offered a plea, twenty years, with the possibility of parole in twelve. But your father figured twenty years was no different from thirty or forty, so he turned it down. We had to mount an impossible defense, and absent any evidence to the contrary, I only had reasonable doubt to go with. That meant suggesting that someone else could have killed your mother, which meant digging up dirt that might tie another party to the crime."

I knew all this; he had explained it all to me at the time. "Right, right," I said, hoping to get him to speed up.

"Bear with me," he said, sensing my impatience. "Context is just as important as content. As you may recall, the prosecution focused on a Mr. Brian Flynn as motive for your father to kill his wife."

"Flynn was the guy from church," I said. "The black guy, which got tongues wagging and racial tensions flaring."

"None of them more furious than your father."

The old lawyer was correct: the mere thought of my mother with a black man was enough to make my father apoplectic, and his courtroom outbursts proved that he'd fallen for Blackwood's race-baiting tactics.

"He made no effort to hide his anger," I said.

"Classic courtroom theater," Jenkins III said. "But the jury bought the notion that your father believed his wife had been rutting with a colored man. That gave him the motivation to kill her in what Blackwood described as a 'fit of jealous rage.' "

"Except you were able to prove there was no affair," I recalled.

"The best I could do was plant a few seeds of doubt," Jenkins III corrected me with a resolute sigh. He pointed out the window again, and said, "Red-bellied woodpecker. As for my evidence pointing to alternate theories...well, the judge wouldn't permit any of it."

"Those seeds of doubt—could they have turned the case around?" I asked him.

He studied the woodpecker until it flew off, then reluctantly turned his attention back to our discussion. "They were potentially poisonous," he replied warily. "But the nature of that poison is of no consequence now. Your mother is long gone, and your father will be soon. The waters of sin flowed under the bridge long ago."

Odd choice of words, I thought, but I didn't press him. "Please, sir. I have a right to know whatever you thought you had," I said instead.

He fell silent then, shaking his head slowly for a long time. By reputation he was an excellent storyteller and had won over many sympathetic juries because of his closing theatrics. Not the twelve men and women who decided my father's fate but, by his own admission, the scope of his case had been severely limited by the judge. Eventually he said, "In fact, son, you don't have that right.

Sometimes it's best to ignore the boogeyman you think is under the bed. Trust me: this is one of those times."

Try as I did, I couldn't get the old lawyer to budge. I pushed and prodded and cajoled, but he was having none of it. He was patient and polite, each time returning to the notion that revisiting the past would serve no good purpose, and might only harm my memories of both my parents. This made no sense, since my mother had been brutally murdered and my sonofabitch father had been locked up for it ever since. Eventually I gave up. Arguing with Jenkins III was a lost cause, and not even St. Jude could come to my rescue.

"Shakespeare was right about the lawyers," I snipped as I rose from my chair.

"No argument from me," he replied with a distinct indifference. He followed me to the door, where I hesitated long enough for him to say, "You probably can't see it, but you're not that much different from me."

"How's that?" I wanted to know.

"We both pitched a good game until we lost our stuff," he replied. "And as for your father, whatever he may have told you, I suggest you let him take his stuff to his grave."

CHAPTER 7

Fuck you very much, I thought, as I trudged down the kitchen steps, past the black lab named Diesel. By now I sincerely doubted that Jenkins III was behind the delivery of the handwritten note to my father, but whoever had sent it had accomplished what he—or she—had intended. In fact, my gut feeling was to take the old lawyer's advice and leave this alone.

On the drive back to Charleston I decided to do just that: let it go. I had brought seventy thousand words of transcribed interviews with me to edit into a coherent manuscript, and I was already behind on my deadline. I could either spend my time tilting at the windmills of the past, or make my editor happy. I'd already spent a good chunk of my advance, and I wouldn't see a penny more until I submitted a finished manuscript. I needed the money, and playing detective wasn't paying me one thin dime. Time to get back to work.

The phone call I received in the elevator on my way up to the twelfth floor changed all that. It was Herman Stump, and he told me he had done a little digging on a computer in a clerk's office and had found that the records for my father's trial did still exist. In fact, they were on microfilm at the County Clerk's office. This included the official transcripts, crime scene photos, and images of other evidence that had been allowed.

"Almost as good as the murder book itself," he told me.

I'd read enough Harry Bosch novels to know what a murder book was, but I'd never seen one in real life. That was a cop thing. I'm sure true crime writers encounter them during the course of research, but my books tend to be of the tabloid, sensationalist variety. The first two were profiles of baseball superstars who had been dragged down by steroids and opioids, and they wanted to erase the asterisks next to their names in the record books. After that came four more, sensational tell-all paperbacks promoted by Hollywood managers who clearly were trying to squeeze the last drops of notoriety out of their has-been clients. I was amazed that all of the books sold as well as they did, and the royalties have kept a roof over my head and allowed me to invest a few dollars in my daughter's college fund.

But now Herman Stump was telling me that he'd located the case files, and had actually reserved a time for me to review them, if I had a mind to.

"And they're expecting me when?" He'd already told me, but I wanted to make sure.

"Nine-thirty tomorrow," he said, then gave me an address. "Ask for L'Tecia. There's an apostrophe between the 'L' and the 'T'."

The bell for my floor rang and the door opened. "Thank you," I told him, not sure whether I was thankful or not. In about two minutes I had gone full circle, and my mind was engaged in a true tug-of-war. I felt like one of those old cartoon characters with an angel on one shoulder and the devil on the other.

When I opened the door, all the back-and-forth chatter instantly faded into reality, as I heard my father moaning in the other room. The monitoring app had buzzed while I was driving back from Jenkins III's house, but there was nothing I could do until I got home.

"Where the fuck have you been?" he called out. "Get your ass in here."

They were words uttered in a tone I had not heard in over thirty years. While our mother had been somewhat of a maternal pacifist, our father was reared in a family that believed in parenting by fear. Neither my sister nor I emerged unblemished; her mental potholes are the stuff of family legend, and our respective bouts with alcohol and prescription meds drove us both into rehab. But we had always been mindful and obedient children, and most of the trouble we did get into was of the inconsequential variety that rarely hit their radar screen. That's why hearing my old man raising his voice ignited an old fuse.

"Where the hell have you been?" he repeated as soon as I opened the door.

"I could ask you the same thing," I replied like the smart-ass I'd often reverted to when I was around him.

He glared at me and said, "Prick."

"Good day to you, too." I offered a slight shrug, then walked over to where the curtains were still drawn across the glass sliders. "You want a little light?"

He said nothing for a minute, a withered old man dying in a borrowed bed in which someone else most likely had died. Then he snarled, "I soiled myself."

This was why he wore an absorbent diaper, and why he had a home aide who came in to assist him once a day. "Has Benita been by?" I asked him.

"I told her to leave me alone," he grumped.

"She's here to help you, Dad," I reminded him.

"I don't want her touching me."

"She's not doing it because she fancies your six-pack abs," I replied. "It's her job."

"Far as I'm concerned she can find another one. Just help me out of this miserable thing."

I did, and the details aren't important. Except to say that life truly is a cradle to grave cycle, and you get to wipe asses on both ends. My father hadn't eaten in several days, but his digestive system was still doing its thing. The clean-up process was a mutual effort, and when we were finished, he said, "I believe I've lost something."

"Besides your dignity?" I asked him.

"Always the wise guy," he replied, his voice back to its usual rough-hewn timbre. "I had an envelope, with a note inside."

"Shut the fuck up."

He flashed me a bolt of anger. "Don't you dare speak to me like that—"

I raised my hand in a no-nonsense gesture. Not to hit him, just to let him know I didn't have the patience for his anger. "Give it a rest," I told him. "That's what the card said, right? 'Shut the fuck up.' "

That caused him to fall silent again, and he turned his head toward the wall.

"Who gave it to you?" I asked him.

My question caused him to slowly turn his head back and look at me. A malevolent darkness seemed to fill his eyes, but I couldn't tell if it was from anger or fear. "What the hell does it matter?" he finally replied.

"You know the terms of the deal," I reminded him. "No contact with the outside, other than the people who have been assigned to look after you. Someone wrote you that note, and that violates the rules."

"I spent the last thirty years of my life following the rules," he said with a snarl. "I'm done with that shit."

"Who was it from?"

He shook his head firmly; his lips tightened. "I don't know. It didn't say."

"Horseshit," I replied. "Who doesn't want you talking to me?"

Silence.

"You were out of that jail less than twenty-four hours and someone got to you," I pushed him. "Seems someone is worried about you talking."

Still nothing, except he twitched his shoulder in what I figured was an attempt at a shrug. I could have persisted, but it was obvious there was no use pressuring him. After thirty years behind bars, Frank Devlin no doubt had developed a skill for keeping the confidences of others, and nothing short of waterboarding would make him budge.

"Suit yourself," I eventually told him. "Anything else you need, as long as I'm in here?"

"I've got all a man could possibly want," he said.

"Good to hear," I turned to go, making it to the doorway before I looked back and said, "By the way, I visited an old friend of yours today."

He said nothing at first, but his interest clearly was piqued. "Who would that be?"

I stood there, letting the old fart puzzle out whether I was going to tell him or not. Then I said, "Myers Jenkins. Your old lawyer, not his son."

A spark of uncertainty flashed in his eyes. "Why the hell did you do that?"

"Because someone sent you a warning," I told him. "I aim to figure out who, and why."

On those words I left him there, tucked into his bed, a dying old man with everything he could possibly want, but no time left to enjoy it.

As I closed the door I tried to contemplate what was running through his mind. My father had always been a proud man, confident in his strengths and mindful of his weaknesses, and now he was confined to a bed where in just a few days he was going to die. I suspected he had no more desire for me to wipe his bottom than I did, but there was nothing he could do about it. His life was coming to an end, but I was certain it had not run out the way he had envisioned when he was my age. He'd been ambitious, outspoken, self-assured, and driven by success. Intolerance was his major fault, but most people were able to overlook it for all the rest of his charm. It had never been his plan to spend most of his adult life locked up with murderers and gangbangers; nor, I suspect, had he ever considered that he would spend his final days under the guarded eye of his scornful son. If he wasn't already dying, such a thought would have killed him.

Jenkins IV had provisioned the kitchen with a shopping cart full of frozen foods rich in carbs and sodium and saturated fats. Things I normally wouldn't have touched in California, but here in the land of barbecue and chicken waffles, everything was fair game. I zapped a couple of frozen burritos in the microwave and then took them out onto the balcony for a relatively taste-free lunch, washed down with a can of Cheerwine.

A regional beverage made with cherry-flavored soda, Cheerwine was a trademark of my childhood. I'd had my first sip when I was about ten, the day I'd been invited to the birthday party of a black kid in my school named Willie Thomas. When my mother dropped me off, I could tell she was stunned that I was the only white boy there, but she didn't way a word. My school was one of the last relics of discrimination in South Carolina, and many folks were bound and determined to keep it that way. Classrooms had been desegregated less than ten years before, so blacks and whites had been forced to comingle under the same roof in an attempt to erase any educational disparities. While that goal arguably had been achieved, the process also was fraught with distrust and suspicion, borne out of ignorance and fear. Many parents fought and screamed, but the law was the law.

When my mother picked me up after the party she'd made me pinky-swear that I would not tell my father about me being the only white kid in attendance. "We don't want him all riled up," she'd explained. Of course, there was no need for her to tell me any of this; kids pick up the subtle nuances of their surroundings long before their parents are aware that they know what they know.

That night, as I lay in my bed listening to the crackle of distant thunder in a land well outside my own, I puzzled over a world in which hatred could cause a heart to be so dark. Willie Thomas was just a kid like me: he liked baseball and monster movies and could name almost any model of car on the highway. He was a normal ten-year-old boy who lived in an unpainted shack down a dirt lane off a road known as Six Mile. He was one of my best friends, but I knew for a fact that he would never set foot inside my house. With enmity so firmly planted in the soil of the south, a decade earlier we never would have had the chance to even meet.

The sound of my phone ringing pulled me back to the present. I'd left it inside on the kitchen counter, and by the time I'd reached it, whoever was calling me had given up. I checked the call log, saw it was a local number. I knew a total of two people in the Charleston area, and both of those numbers were listed in my contacts, so this one was a puzzle. Then the phone chimed, telling me the caller had left a message. I clicked the voicemail icon, then waited while the system connected me to the server.

"Hi, Rick…it's Laurie. It was so great to see you yesterday, showing up out of the blue like that. I apologize for being rude…I was just surprised, is all. I was hoping I could make it up to you, maybe over coffee or a drink. Give me a call if that sounds okay with you."

She hadn't left a number, but as soon as I deleted the message I hit redial. I'd tried not to give too much thought to my old girlfriend after running into her at Jake's yesterday, but that had been impossible. The passing years had done nothing to rub out the memories of those times, when we were discovering all the secrets of this brittle world for the very first time. Every knee scraped, every ball game lost, every girl kissed, was a new lesson in our fragility, and we never forget that first time for everything.

"This is Rick," I said when she answered. "I ran to pick up the phone, but you'd already gone to voicemail."

"I probably shouldn't have called at all," she said, a little too quickly. "But like I said, I didn't mean to come across as short yesterday—"

"Yes," I told her.

"Yes, what?"

"Yes, let's grab a drink."

"Just like that?"

"Easy decision. It's your town, so just name a time and place."

She suddenly fell silent, and I hoped I hadn't sounded too impulsive or shameless. Then she said, "There's a little place on Sullivan's, off the tourist trail. They have a nice deck out back that's really private, great for catching up on old times."

Private, off the tourist trail. Which I took to mean that she didn't want to be seen, not by her friends or her husband. Which spoke volumes, in all sorts of ways.

"When and where?"

"Is tonight too soon? Maybe seven?"

"That's when *Wheel of Fortune* comes on," I said. There was a silence on the other end, so I quickly added, "I'm kidding. Poorly timed joke. Give me directions and I'll see you there."

Five seconds after I hung up, the phone rang again. I thought it might be Laurie, having second thoughts, but instead the screen read "Addie." It was my daughter calling from California, and my mind immediately went to the worst-case scenario. Which encompassed everything a father fears could happen to his fifteen-year-old daughter, and then some.

"Everything okay, sweetie?" were the first words out of my mouth.

"Yes, Dad. Just peachy. Nothing to worry about."

"Except—" I said, my parental instinct kicking into high alert.

"Except that Mom is acting weird again."

"Weird, as in not making sense and being moody, or weird like the last time?"

"They're all connected, Dad. You know that."

I did know that, and I also knew that Addie didn't want to trigger alarm bells before it was necessary. As the only child of an alcoholic mother and a rehabbed father, she had developed a strong codependent warning system. Something she didn't deserve.

"I hate that you have to see her like that, Sweetie. She's not the woman I married...I want you to remember that."

"I've done a lot of reading about this, Dad. And there's a bunch of videos on YouTube. It's not just the bipolar thing now. She has an addictive personality disorder and abuses herself because she doesn't think she's worthy of anything good."

"She had a rough childhood," I reminded her. "There's a lot of unresolved trauma."

When Addie's mother and I separated five years ago there had been a big argument that our daughter should not have overheard. A binge with a bottle of tequila had clouded Belinda's senses, and during a flurry of anger she let it slip that she had been abused as a young girl. The full package: physical, emotional, and sexual. I'd suspected this since the early days of our relationship, but we had always tiptoed around the edges of her trauma, for which she never sought help or guidance. Alcohol and recreational drugs had been enough to dampen it in the early years, and lately I'd been worried that opioids were pulling her into a dark hole so deep that not even light could escape. There was nothing subtle about the warning signs.

"All of which causes her to self-medicate," my budding psychologist replied. "Look, Dad. I'm going to be okay. I promise I won't get into a car with her when I think she's been using. She never does anything intentional to me, and she won't. Except to tell me I'm the only thing that keeps her going."

Emotional blackmail, which Addie and I had discussed on numerous occasions. "The first sign of any trouble I want you to let me know," I told her. "You'll be on the next plane here."

"I can't simply run out on my job," she said. "No one else wants to get up at five to grind coffee beans and bake muffins."

"That's my girl," I told her. "The conscientious and loyal daughter. But this is one of those times you need to put yourself first."

"Right, Dad."

"Promise me you'll call me first thing if Mom shows any signs of crashing again?"

"You're at the top of my speed-dial," she assured me. "Look—I gotta go. The lunch crowd is about to show up, and I'm the only tall blonde around here."

We both laughed at that, a reference to her first day on the job when a pudgy show biz wannabe in his thirties tried to hit on her. "I'll have a tall blonde, extra cream," he had said. "Or you, if you think you can get off."

He'd thrown her a dirty wink, but my spunky daughter played it cool. "It'll be a cold day in hell that I let a double iced Frappuccino like you get anywhere near me," she'd assured him.

Mic drop, as Addie described it to me later.

"I'll check in with you later," I told her now.

"Don't call me; I'll call you."

It was another inside reference that went to her mother, and not a particularly kind one. Belinda and I had met while she was shooting the third and final film of her short-lived movie career, a horror movie sequel in which she was killed off in the first scene. Stabbed in the shower, a blatant rip-off from *Psycho*. The director said it was *homage* but, as I learned much later, Belinda had a serious cocaine problem that transformed her into a bitch when she was high. She'd become intolerable on the set of the previous flick, and the producer ordered the writer to cut her out of the sequel as early in the script as possible. Her difficult reputation preceded her for the rest of her career, as casting agents curtly sent her on her way before she even had a chance for a screen test. The legendary words "don't call us, we'll call you" trailing out the door after her.

This had come out during the course of that nasty argument, too.

CHAPTER 8

The quiet hideaway off the tourist trail Laurie suggested was called Swampie's, named for the legendary Francis Marion—a.k.a., the historic and near-mythical Swamp Fox.

Anyone raised in the American South learns at an early age that Marion was a patriot who terrorized the Brits in the American Revolution. Even after King George's soldiers drove the Continental Army out of the lowcountry, he and his followers hung around, engaging in surprise attacks and sudden retreats that utterly stymied the Redcoats. He possessed an acute knowledge of the local terrain, which helped him and his men sneak in and out of British camps without detection. A determined nationalist who helped the colonies gain independence from the crown, Marion's unashamed cruelty toward his slaves—and his brutality against the native Cherokee tribes—eventually overshadowed his guerilla heroics, causing many contemporary historians to reassess his decency and legacy.

Still, he was the embodiment of southern ethos, evidenced by the sheer number of places in the Carolinas that reference his name. Swampie's being one of them.

I arrived first and found a small table in a corner of the back deck. A blistering July sun still simmered in the western sky, but the searing heat that had pushed the mercury near triple digits had begun to slip. It was still hot—there was no escaping the summer except to seek refuge in the constant thrum of air conditioning—but Laurie had suggested the deck, and I didn't want to contradict her. Someone had installed a cooling system that spritzed a light mist in an attempt to chill the air, but most of the moisture evaporated before its effect could be felt.

"Sorry I'm late," said a voice behind me. I started to rise but she placed a hand on my shoulder to keep me in my seat. She sat down across from me, hanging her purse from the back of her chair. "The problem with running a restaurant is there's always one thing after the other. Sometimes I wonder why I put myself through it, day after day. I should have bailed after my parents died, but I'm a glutton for punishment. Serves me right. But enough about work, at least for now."

She was chattering, something I remember she would do as a teenager when she was nervous. Back then it usually stemmed from doing something her parents might find out about, and that often involved me. Now I suspected it had to do with her husband, or maybe a friend who might see her having a drink with an unidentified male in an out-of-the-way Charleston bar. Which was pretty much the same thing, and ostensibly the reason she had chosen Swampie's in the first place.

I told her I'd only just arrived myself and hadn't had time to order a drink. As if on cue a waitress sidled up, dressed in a short maroon skirt and form-fitting white stretch top. Her face glistened with perspiration, and her hair was starting to come loose from a braided ponytail she had tied up hours ago. I really wanted a double vodka on the rocks but ordered a beer instead; Laurie went for a gin and tonic.

We broke the ice with small talk. I started by answering her questions about my life in the secluded reaches of Topanga Canyon, gradually easing into my attempt to reinvent myself as a ghostwriter after my baseball career tanked. I explained that I was divorced, which was a good thing, and the only ongoing positive force in my life was my daughter, whom I adored. My phone was sitting on the table, and I explained that if she happened to call me I would have to take it.

"Her mother is going through a really hard time," I said.

"No problem," she replied, seeming to understand. "Does she take after her dad and play ball?"

"She tried it, but found it too boring," I said, shaking my head. "Truth is, she's really into acting. Member of the Drama Club, just had a big role in the spring musical."

"Your wife was an actress, right?"

"Ex-wife, and it scares the crap out of me. But enough about me; now it's your turn."

She frowned, then took a dive into the pool that was her life. She remained near the shallow end, summarizing the parts of the story that posed little risk of drowning. Three children close to leaving the nest, a husband that still belonged to the ring on her finger, long hours at work that made her feel like a hamster on a wheel.

"Do you still find time to paint?" I asked her. She had been quite the artist in high school, watercolors of horses and dogs and shore birds. But she also could work wonders with the amber light seeping between storm clouds over a lonely marsh, and had sold a few of her works at local craft fairs.

"Haven't picked up a brush in years," she said, a flat distance in her voice. "Maybe when the kids are gone I'll find more time."

"I guess it's true what they say about life," I replied. "Other things getting in the way and distracting the dreams of our youth."

The waitress had delivered our drinks a few minutes before, and Laurie now reached her glass out and clinked the rim of mine. "To the dreams of youth," she said. "Looks like you got the chance to touch yours."

"Didn't take me long to get scorched, either."

"So what happened? Your fastball was unhittable. What caused you to quit?"

"It wasn't a choice," I told her. "One night I unloaded a particularly awkward slider and I felt a tendon in my elbow snap. I did the Tommy John thing and was expected to make a full recovery, but the next time I tried throwing it was pretty obvious my pitching days were over."

"Tommy John?" she said. "What's that?"

"In technical terms, it's something called ulnar collateral ligament reconstruction," I explained, one syllable at a time. "Named for the first pitcher to have it done. It involves a ligament graft, nerve repositioning, and a long period of recovery. Most pitchers do fine after the surgery heals, but not me. My career crapped out. The next year I was giving up home runs right and left, and when I was sent down to the bullpen as a five-pitch reliever I knew I was done."

And that's around the time the opioid dependency began, I conveniently left out.

"Sounds pretty dismal," she said.

"Didn't take me too long to hit rock bottom," I admitted. I nodded at her finger and said, "So tell me about the ring."

"There's nothing really to tell," she began. "Larry and I met my junior year at the College of Charleston. Art history class, of all places. It was my major and he had a requirement to fill. I know: Laurie and Larry. Cute. We went out, and he was a real charmer. We graduated together and got married a year later. Everything seemed ideal—perfect southern living. We renovated a house, went on some fun trips, bought a boat. Then the kids started arriving and he began to change. Subtly, no real clues, but I just sensed a difference. My friends couldn't see it, or didn't want to. And my folks thought I was poking a stick in a beehive. Eventually I found out about Rhonda… and then Lisa, and Tammy after that. Names have been changed to protect the guilty."

"That had to be rough," I said, a loss for any further words.

"Sure does a number on your self-esteem," she conceded. "Made me wonder what was wrong with me. Why didn't he love me anymore? What did those bitches have that I didn't? I tried losing weight. I tried being more seductive. I bought sexier clothes and wore skimpy bikinis at the beach. All the things women do when they convince themselves it's all their fault. But guess what? It wasn't my fault. He was the no-good lying, cheating, screwed-up sonofabitch, not me." She glanced around, checking to make sure no one had heard her blast of venom. "I filed support and maintenance on him four months ago."

"Support and what?"

"You can't get divorced here in South Carolina until you've been separated for a full year," she explained. "You have to file these legal documents—support and maintenance bullshit—and then make sure the rotten dirt bag doesn't spend another night under the same roof with you. Fat chance of that."

A hundred questions rolled through my brain just then, but I decided to leave them alone. At least for now. If they became relevant later on I could always come back and revisit them.

"So now you just throw yourself into the restaurant and your kids," I guessed.

"Both are more than full-time jobs," Laurie agreed. "I probably look like a total wreck."

"You'll always look like Ingrid Bergman to me."

She threw her head back in a laugh, as if she wasn't buying it. "It's your turn again," she said. "How did you go from major league pitcher to ghostwriter for the stars? Seems like quite a stretch to me."

"It's called survival," I told her. "My last major league contract was a one-year deal, and when it ran out I was left with almost nothing. I was in L.A. and had no real skill, and I'd burned through just about every dollar I ever made. I tried to land a coaching job, but got no offers. Then I opened a baseball camp, but only eight kids showed up. Not even enough for a team. I didn't want to sell shoes or used cars, or get my real estate license. I did some volunteer work with local kids, but that didn't pay the bills. Then one day a guy I knew at ESPN called and asked if I would come on his show to talk about the postseason. That led to semi-regular appearances. Not nearly enough money to live on, so I started doing background work."

"You mean, like investigative checks on cheating husbands? I hired someone to run one of those on Larry."

"No, nothing like that." I took a long sip of beer as my eyes followed a hawk soaring on a thermal far above. "I became an extra in TV shows and movies. You know—the people walking by in the background while the stars are getting paid the big bucks."

"For real? Anything I might have seen?"

I ran through a list of shows I'd been in and she seemed properly impressed. I assured her it was just low-paid work, not the glitz and glamour one tends to associate with Hollywood.

"So how did you meet your wife?" she finally asked. "Belinda."

I was pretty sure I hadn't mentioned her name when we chatted at Jake's On The Creek yesterday, which could only mean one thing.

"You Googled me," I said.

Laurie giggled and raised a single eyebrow, just as she used to do way back when. "You can never be too careful these days," she replied.

The worldwide web is a treacherous place. It can kiss you on the lips or stab you in the back. It can be your greatest friend or your most vile enemy. You have little choice about who sees what, there's no correcting the multitude of mistakes, and good luck trying to delete anything. It's the unfiltered landfill of the masses, a permanent reminder of one's mortality and vulnerability. In other words, deal with it.

"And after seeing what you found you're still sitting here?" I ventured, staring at her over the rim of my beer mug.

"Other than one story that called you 'the shameless pimp of empty-headed whores and skanks of the show biz set,' it was all pretty much positive," she replied.

I laughed at that and said, "Not far from the truth, really."

"So tell me about Belinda," she said again.

Damn. I thought maybe we'd moved beyond the question, but no such luck. "We met on the set of a movie," I told her. "Her last one, in fact. *Deathbed Two.* We were shooting on location, and I was an extra walking by on the sidewalk as she entered her house. We shot the scene a couple dozen times, from just about every angle. Over and over and over. Finally, after passing each other for about the thirtieth take, she stopped me while the camera was rolling and said, 'Imagine meeting you here.' The director was royally pissed at the ad lib, but afterwards we went out for a martini."

"Which I notice you're not drinking tonight," she said, nodding at my beer.

"Not good for my health or anyone near the batter's box. Anyway, her career was in a tailspin and I was doing bit parts and the occasional sports show gigs. Two total screw-ups and no future for either of us. We fed off the energy of each other's failures, and when things got just about as low as they could, we decided it was a good time to get married."

"I'm hearing drugs and booze in there," she observed.

"An astute guess, but it's all over the internet, so you don't get any points," I replied. "A year later our daughter arrived, and I knew one of us had to play grown-up. Around the same time a friend of mine—the same one who got me on ESPN—asked me if I might be interested in ghosting the autobiography of a pitcher who hurled a perfect game in the minors but never appeared in the majors."

"Why you?"

"You mean, why a drunk painkiller addict whose life was on the ropes, or why someone who had never written anything longer than a term paper in his entire life?"

"Both, I guess," she said.

I thought long and hard on this, even though I'd told the story many times. Interviewers tend not to be very inventive with their questions, even though they think they are. "I majored in English in college," I began. "It was an easy degree for someone who spent long days on team road trips. As a kid I could read for hours in a car, and it just made sense. After my elbow surgery I wrote a couple of articles that appeared in a few local papers, and I guess my ESPN friend thought they were good. Anyway, I wrote the book. It took six weeks to hammer it out, I got to hang around with baseball guys again, and it actually made some sort of bestseller list for a couple weeks. I got paid, it was fun, and afterwards the publisher asked for another one."

"And the rest is history."

"Along with my marriage," I conceded. No need to talk about rehab, or Belinda's overdoses, or the incidents that twice put her behind bars.

The waitress took that moment to wander up and ask if we wanted another round. I had no idea what Laurie's time frame looked like and was about to ask her when she reflexively said, "We've got a lot of years to catch up on, so keep 'em coming."

More small talk ensued after that, and then Laurie blurted out, "So how long are you going to keep me in the dark?"

"In the dark about what?"

"Why you're here. You mentioned the other day your father is ill, but the last I heard he was still in jail. Upstate somewhere."

Here it was again: a signed confidentiality agreement versus the truth, and keeping it from possibly the only person in this town that still mattered to me. "It's complicated," I told her.

"So is Sudoku, until you learn the tricks. C'mon, Rick—it's me you're talking to here, not some reporter interviewing you after a game."

"It's been so long I've forgotten what that's like."

Laurie studied me the same way she used to when she was trying to see if I was lying to her. Or stalling for time. Looking for eyes raised the wrong way, facial tics, twitching skin. Finally she said, "Out with it, buster."

I studied her then, my old hometown girlfriend who had evolved into a true beauty and successful businesswoman. Back then both of us were too focused on the day at hand to think about what either of us would be like thirty years in the future. Everything was about "now" back then but now, as I gazed at her deep blue eyes, all I could think about was "then."

"My father is dying," I finally said. "He only has a week or two left." I then explained about his cancer and his day-to-day lease on life, and the terms of the deal.

"You mean he's been released?"

I glanced around nervously to see if anyone had heard her, but no one was paying any attention to us. I lifted my brow slightly in a veiled gesture of affirmation, then replied, "It's important that no one finds out."

She nodded and clicked an imaginary lock on her lips. "I won't breathe a word," she said. "But I knew you didn't just happen to roll the dice and land on Charleston."

"I never could keep a secret from you," I assured her.

She stirred her new gin and tonic with the plastic cocktail straw, then said, "Mind if I ask you something else? It has to do with the trial."

By the time my old man's case made it to the courtroom, Laurie and I had broken up. The death of my mother and arrest of my father flipped my world upside down, charred on both sides like a scorched hamburger. For starters, I'd been forced to move in with my Uncle Andrew in Summerville, which meant switching schools during my senior year. I'd reacted predictably, mostly a stream of deliberate fury, fueled by bourbon and beer and anger at the entire world. I got myself ejected from four games that spring for hitting batters simply out of contempt. My insolence and disrespect ultimately caused me to miss out on the U.S.C. scholarship, which may have been the point all along.

"There's nothing about that trial I haven't relived a thousand times," I told her.

She still said nothing for a moment or two, then asked, "So, I've always wondered...who was the surprise witness who never showed?"

"The what?"

"You must remember," she pressed. "The last day of the trial, before it went to the jury. Your dad's lawyer was supposed to have a witness in his back pocket that would change the whole deal. It was all over the news."

"I didn't watch the news," I told her. "I was in the courtroom all day, and I didn't want to see it all replayed on TV later. Are you sure about this?"

Laurie leaned forward and looked me straight in the eyes. "I'm not making it up, Rick. And I didn't dream it. There was someone waiting in the wings."

It was my turn to fall silent as I thought this through. Had I possibly forgotten something, a secret witness who could have changed the course of Devlin family history? Was this what my father had talked about, evidence that wasn't allowed into play? Maybe the evidence was in the form of a person who was prevented from testifying. Or maybe it was pure gamesmanship, an attempt by Jenkins III to keep the competition on its toes. Planting a rumor that some mysterious person might be called to testify, but never showed. I honestly remembered none of this, and said so again to Laurie.

"Well, it probably doesn't matter," she finally said with a shrug. "Not after all this time."

I wished I'd known about this when I had spoken with Jenkins III that morning. If nothing else it would have been interesting to watch his reaction to the question. I could always ask my father, but he'd already clammed up—and I could think of no incentive that would make him change his mind.

Just then a loud blast split the evening in two. It sounded like a nuclear warning siren and, in that moment, it yanked me back to a distant, more innocent time when I was very young and my mother would get me ready for bed. Since my sister was older she got to stay up later, but Mom was strict about my bedtime and the need for a good, solid sleep. Every Thursday evening at exactly the same time—usually right after my nightly bath—the Sullivan's Island Fire Department would test its horn. It was loud and intrusive and annoying, yet I always felt oddly comforted by it. The abrupt explosion of sound would practically launch me out of my slippers, even though I usually knew it was coming. Then I would breathe a sigh of relief, reassured that the world was still there, and all was very much right in my little corner of it.

"Seven-thirty Thursday," I announced. "They still do that?"

"People still set their clocks by it," she assured me. "The only time they stopped doing it was after Hugo hit."

"I can't believe it's been so long," I sighed, shaking my head again at the span of time. "But who's keeping track?"

If I'd been keeping track I would have noticed the black pick-up truck parked in the dimming shadow of a live oak draped with drab green moss. Later I would learn it was a Ram 1500 quad cab, more old than new, but tonight it was simply backed into a narrow space at the far rear of the gravel lot next to Swampie's. The man slouched down behind the wheel would have been barely visible through the dark tinting, and the concealed gun would have been in either his hand or the pocket on the door.

Like I said, I didn't notice him at the time but, even if I had, nothing I might have seen would have clued me in to the storm that was building just beyond the horizon.

CHAPTER 9

The following morning, I arrived at the Charleston County Clerk's office on Broad Street when it opened at nine. My appointment wasn't for another half-hour, but this was a government facility and I knew inefficiency builds rapidly throughout the day. I managed to find a cup of coffee and an old copy of *Sports Illustrated* to keep me occupied while I passed the time. A few minutes before my appointed time a tall, attractive black woman poked her head through a doorway and said, "Rick Devlin?"

I tossed the magazine on the small table where I'd found it and stood up. "You must be L'Tecia," I replied.

"Sorry to keep you waiting," she apologized, glancing at her watch. We both knew I was early, so the wait was all on me.

"My bad," I confessed. "I get a little over-eager sometimes."

"Happens to the best of us," L'Tecia said. Her last name was Hayes, and she possibly was distantly related to the late great soul musician and songwriter Isaac Hayes, but she wasn't quite sure how. She told me this as she led me down a long corridor that smelled faintly of mold, finally stopping in front of a door that read "Public Records." She waved me inside and said, "Have you ever worked one of these things before?"

By "these things" she meant the microfilm machines that were positioned along a wall. I had encountered them during my college years, back in the dark ages of research when there was no such thing as the worldwide web. They were tedious and bulky devices that required you to scroll through a spool of film to find a document, which then could be read on a back-lit screen. There was no such thing as cutting-and-pasting right into a document; you either had to take copious notes or bring a bag full of quarters for the old-fashioned copier that was attached to it.

"It's been a while," I told her. "But I'm sure it'll come back to me."

She opened a white cardboard box and took out a six-inch spool of film, then refreshed my memory as she fed it through the spindles. "These are the records of the trial Mr. Stump said you wanted," she told me when she was done. "Transcripts, crime scene photos, images of any evidence that was introduced."

"What about evidence that was excluded from the trial?" I asked her.

"If it was excluded it wouldn't have been the property of the court, so it won't be in the file," she explained. "Use that foot pedal there to advance the film quickly, or you can go frame by frame using this dial here. Any questions?"

I assured her I would come looking for her if I needed assistance, then sat down at the controls and began to scroll through the film. L'Tecia had already cued it up to begin at a cover page describing what I would be looking at:

```
Official Records of Criminal Trial
Docket # 05141990
State of South Carolina v. Frank Devlin
May 14, 1990
```

I started slowly, advancing through the report page by page as I got a feel for the machine. After scrolling through endless pages of bureaucratic boilerplate language, I finally got to the transcript of the proceedings as memorialized by the court reporter. I remembered watching her, seated at a small table to the left of the witness stand, her nimble fingers rapidly taking down everything that was said.

The long, tedious hours sitting in that courtroom all came back to me now as I scanned the testimony. I began with the prosecutor's amiable but grim questioning of the dispatcher who had answered my call for help on the night of the murder. Her name was Mrs. Sandifer, and I remembered her as a mousy, waif-like woman with cat eye glasses and hair pulled back in an excruciatingly tight bun.

Maybe that's why her face always seemed to be pinched with pain.

"Do you recall anything about that phone call in particular?" he had asked her.

"The young man who called sounded very distraught," she replied. "I politely asked him to verify why he was calling, and when he told me the details of the scene I told him to stay on the line while police arrived."

"Did the caller do as you requested?" Blackwood had probed, according to the transcript.

"He did not. He was very impudent, which I guess was understandable because of what he had just witnessed."

"And what was that, Mrs. Sandifer?" the prosecutor asked.

"Well, I didn't know it at the time, but I later learned the caller was the son of the murderer, there—"

"Objection!" Jenkins III shouted from the defense table. I could see him now, jumping to his feet in a fit of well-rehearsed rage, although the theatrics were not revealed in the transcript. "Mr. Devlin is presumed innocent until proven otherwise. Move to strike."

"Sustained and stricken," Judge Carter had ordered, but the damage—as predetermined by Daniel Blackwood—was already done.

The prosecutor tried the same tactic with several other early witnesses—the first responder to the scene, the detective who had questioned me, and a neighbor who had claimed to have heard a struggle in the Devlin house earlier that night. Every time a witness implicated my father as "the killer" rather than "the defendant," Jenkins was on his feet, and the judge ruled in his favor. After the fourth such incident the judge called both attorneys to the bench for a sidebar, after which he stated for the record that all witnesses were to be advised not to pass judgment on the defendant's guilt or innocence during the trial. That was for the jury to do.

It was the last solid ruling in favor of the defense that Judge Carter handed down, and by now it didn't matter. Any member of the jury who was thinking of my father as a killer now had the words firmly planted in his or her head.

The transcript went on for hundreds of pages, and I skipped large chunks of it. I'd sat through all this testimony before, and I knew that none of it had gone well for my old man. Blackwood laid out his case in precise and unambiguous terms, building toward a murder conviction brick by brick. He focused on my father's inability to remember even a moment of what happened that evening, and played it for all it was worth. It was a Friday night and he had left his office at Sumter Insurance a few minutes after five o'clock, stopping off at a bar for a cocktail. He paid cash so there was no receipt, but detectives took a statement from the bartender, who claimed to have served him two martinis, straight up, with olives in both.

After that the barkeep assumed he had driven directly home, but the only witness who could verify that he'd actually walked through the kitchen door was my mother, and she was dead. No one remembered seeing his car parked in our driveway, aside from the neighbor who thought he maybe had heard a noise, which he described as a struggle.

"Objection!" Jenkins III had protested. "The witness has no evidence to draw that conclusion. How could he possibly know it was a struggle?"

"Overruled," Judge Carter stated. "The house was the scene of a homicide. There clearly was a struggle. The witness will answer the question."

"I heard someone yelling, and then a loud noise, and more screaming," the witness responded. His name was Arnold Gallagher, and he was a summer weekender who owned a furniture store in Raleigh. He had tried to sell my parents a six-piece living room suite, but my mother said it was made of cheap pine, not the rock maple she wanted. "Sounded to me like the Duran-Barkley fight," he'd added.

"Objection!"

"Overruled."

My testimony came the third day of the trial. Characterized by Blackwood as a hostile witness, I was treated with kid gloves, a well-conceived ploy hatched by the prosecutor. I had only been seventeen when the murder occurred, but I'd turned eighteen two months before the trial. I was not considered a minor, and there was no way Jenkins III could keep me from testifying. He had fought it in pre-trial motions, arguing that such a move could cause me undue stress. Blackwood had countered that justice for all outweighed the anxiety of one, and the judge agreed. By this point, three days into testimony—and after all the evidence had been presented—I'd begun to believe that my father actually could have done this horrific thing.

Still, a lingering sense of family loyalty caused me to come down on the side of insolence.

"Describe for the court what you saw when you came through the kitchen door on the night...excuse me, the morning in question," Blackwood had prompted me. I recalled that he was dressed in a lightweight suit, gray with white pinstripes, with a blue shirt and red-striped tie. Professionally styled hair, brown eyes, tortoise shell glasses that made him appear intelligent. I remember him standing near the lectern that was provided for opposing counsel to rest their notes on, dividing his glances equally between the jury and me.

"Nothing," I replied. If I was going to be considered hostile, then hostile—and precise—I would be.

This was not what Blackwood expected, and he seemed stunned by my answer. "Nothing?" he repeated.

"That's what I said."

"Objection!" Jenkins III exclaimed. "Asked and answered."

"Your honor," Blackwood interjected. "The witness, whom I have already described as hostile, clearly is showing contempt for this court."

"Young man," Judger Carter said, fixing me with a scowl. "You have sworn to tell the truth, the whole truth, and nothing but the truth. So please answer the court, and do so truthfully."

"I am being truthful," I replied. "When I came into the kitchen on the night in question" —I looked Blackwood directly in the eye when I said this— "I couldn't see a thing. The lights were off."

A slight chuckle rumbled through the courtroom at that, and I remember feeling pleased to have let a bit of air out of the windbag's trial balloon.

"When did you turn the lights on?" the prosecutor asked me patiently once the laughter had died down and the judge stopped pounding his gavel.

"A few seconds after I came in," I answered. "When I entered the room, my feet slipped out from under me and I hit the floor. I turned the light on when I got back up."

"I see," Blackwood said. "And at that point what did you see?"

I described the entire scene then, recounting the configuration of the kitchen and how my parents had been positioned on the floor. Crime scene photos had already been introduced to illustrate all of this, but eyewitness testimony from the defendant's son provided solid confirmation. Even though I was not looking at the jury, I remember twelve pair of eyes fixed on me as I spoke.

"At what point did you see the knife?" he asked me.

"There was a block of them on the counter," I replied. "And one was on the floor."

"The murder weapon?"

"I believe that's what you're trying to prove, isn't it?"

The drama wasn't reflected in the transcript I was reading, but at that point both lawyers jumped to their feet. "Objection!" they yelled in unison.

The judge ordered them both forward to the bench. They whispered their arguments over each other's, and eventually Carter told them enough was enough. What I understood from all this bickering was that Blackwood thought I was exhibiting impudence and contempt, while Jenkins argued that I was being asked to draw a conclusion I wasn't in any position to make.

My testimony concluded about a half-hour after that. Under cross-examination Jenkins did his best to discredit Blackwood's insinuation that I was protecting my father from the justice he deserved. One key point, which I now reviewed on the microfilm screen in front of me, was whether I might have accidentally moved the knife when I'd slipped and fallen in the dark. If my foot had touched the weapon it could have edged it closer to my father's hand when, in fact, he might never have touched it at all. At least not on the night in question.

Blackwood jumped all over this, of course. Crime scene photos showed no sign of a shoe print in the blood anywhere near the blade, which had been too far from the kitchen door for me to have possibly disturbed it. Still, if Jenkins had managed to introduce even a gram of doubt in the mind of just one juror, he had done his job.

I browsed through the rest of the testimony but found nothing surprising or new. I scrolled to the next section of the trial record and began looking at the evidence that had been part of the official case. It consisted mostly of photographs of various objects found at the scene, including the knife itself, and the clothes both of my parents had been wearing. There was a receipt from a gas station that showed my father had filled up his car the afternoon before the murder, and had bought a pack of cigars. Brand unspecified. Another receipt indicated my mother had spent sixteen dollars at the Piggly Wiggly, presumably on food she never had a chance to cook. Other receipts indicated that she had picked up some dry cleaning, and she had bought a new bra at a downtown clothing store.

The state Senate had already adjourned for the summer, so my father had not been traveling to Columbia two days a week as he did in the spring. He was in the early stages of his campaign for a fourth two-year term, but no receipts pertaining to the race had been introduced. Likewise, he had kept his business and household expenses separate, so nothing from the operation of Sumter Insurance was introduced, either.

Blood alcohol was a different matter altogether. Frank Devlin had been in no condition to breathe into a tube when he was brought into the police station, but he supposedly had consented to having a blood sample drawn. It tested at .20, well over the legal limit to drive in any state. He also had a substantial amount of benzodiazepines in his system, which he was unable to explain.

At that point I scrolled through the microfilm to find my mother's toxicology report. I hadn't paid close attention to the scientific findings during the trial, but now I saw that her alcohol registered at a somewhat respectable .04, about what her two regular glasses of Chardonnay would have shown at the time of her death. She also had trace levels of diazepam in her blood. I knew she had a prescription for valium, so this did not surprise me.

Next, I read the summary of the post-mortem exam. I remember thinking it hideous that my mother's body had been violated with a circular saw and other cold steel implements, when cause of death was so obvious. Fortunately, no photos of the procedure were introduced as evidence; the crime scene pictures had brought back more than enough grim memories. Of the seven stab wounds she had received, two were potentially fatal while five were described as superficial. The medical examiner had stated that he thought the first blow, to her left carotid artery, most likely had killed her, which would have explained why she had no defensive wounds. No torn fingernails or skin particles under them, no slash marks on her hands where she might have tried to fend off her attacker. Jenkins III had objected when Dr. Butler—whom I remembered as amiable and elderly, with a gray buzz cut and wire-rim spectacles—had suggested she likely had known and trusted her killer. It was one of the few protests he'd lodged that Carter for some reason had sustained but, again, the damage was already done.

The knife itself had undergone extensive forensic analysis, as had the blood on it. Dr. Butler stated that my mother's blood had been A-positive, which was the type that had been found on the handle and the blade. He testified about alleles and antigens and other technicalities of blood, and then took great pains—under close direct questioning by Blackwood—to explain that type-A blood contains about twenty different subgroups, with A1 making up close to eighty percent of all type-A people. This was important, he maintained, because all the blood samples lifted from the knife came back from the lab as A1.

"And what type of blood does the defendant have?" Blackwood had asked.

"Objection!" Jenkins III had shouted. "As the witness just stated, millions of people have type A1 blood. Including the victim and, I would guess, a few members of the jury."

"The expert testimony of this witness will prove much more beneficial than your guesswork, Counselor," the prosecutor countered.

"Your honor—"

"Both lawyers will approach the bench…now," Judge Carter ordered.

After yet another counseling session, he reprimanded both sides for conduct unbecoming of the court, and then Dr. Butler was told to answer the question. As expected, my father's blood also turned out to be A1, which meant it could have been part of the sample that had been tested. "At this time we don't have the ability to examine the properties of blood down to the specific individual," the pathologist had said. "Scientists at this very moment are working on something called DNA sampling, so someday we might have that capability. But not at present."

Someday was now, which was why my father had mentioned DNA testing to me the day before yesterday. And then he fell silent about it, at the urging of an unknown but clearly interested party.

A few minutes later I came across the witness lists that had been submitted by both parties. I scanned both documents and found that Blackwood had called every person on his list, while Jenkins III had skipped two of his. One of these was Alice Marion, whom I remembered was my father's secretary at Sumter Insurance. She was tall and wiry, coke bottle glasses that rested on a nose that came to a point. Whether she was related to the legendary Swamp Fox she did not know, nor did she seem to care. She always seemed to be hunched over the green screen of her IBM PC, one of the very early office machines equipped with dual floppy drives and a primitive financial software package.

The second uncalled witness on the list was a man named Rudy Aiken. His given occupation was listed as "various," which suggested he had no steady, full-time employment. Jenkins III had provided neither an address nor the reason Aiken was on the list; if Blackwood wanted to know what my father's lawyer was planning to ask him, he'd have to figure it out on his own. There was no indication of whether Blackwood had tracked Aiken down, and now I wondered if he had been the surprise witness Laurie Cobb had mentioned.

I fast-forwarded through the rest of the case file but found nothing I didn't already know, or that provided any fresh insight. Yes, Judge Carter had been tough on Jenkins III and his efforts to sway the jury any way he could, but the evidence introduced by the prosecution was damning. It was perfectly understandable that the jury had returned a "guilty" verdict, and I'd neither heard nor seen—then or now—anything to reverse that decision. My sister had been so distressed by the whole process that she left town immediately after the verdict was delivered. She turned up four weeks later in a campground outside Mobile, Alabama, having hitchhiked there with a man she'd met while walking the Appalachian Trail in northern Georgia. And thus began a long, slow slide into alcohol, pills, dysfunction, and depression.

When I'd finished with the film roll I rewound it, then slipped it back into its box. I had difficulty getting it to fit properly, and when I checked to see what was blocking it I found a slip of paper inside. It was an official sign-out sheet designed to list the names of those who had checked it out, like an old library card. L'Tecia Hayes had signed it out on my behest that morning, and I now wrote "11:15" in the box marked "time returned." That's when I noticed that the last time this particular reel had been looked at was almost fifteen years ago, before the county had shifted from microfilm to online archives.

The person who had last viewed it was Lily Elliott, and the name rang a bell. She had been a reporter for the Charleston *News and Courier* and the co-owned *Evening Post*, and had covered all aspects of my father's trial. Since then the two newspapers had merged into the *Post & Courier,* presumably eliminating a number of journalistic redundancies in the process. The reel of film I'd just reviewed included the records of Charleston County court cases for the entire month of May 1990, many of which Ms. Elliott might have covered as a journalist. No coincidence there. But the Frank Devlin case had been billed as the "trial of the decade," so I'd assumed it was the most important legal case on that spool of film. Was it possible she could have been reviewing the same case fifteen years after the fact—and if so, why?

The answer to that question wasn't nearly as important as the way it jiggered my mind. I had forgotten about Ms. Elliott who, despite Stumpy's best efforts, more than once had cornered me in the courthouse hallway to ask a probing question or to provoke a response to that morning's testimony. I didn't really blame her; that was her job and she was doing it the only way she knew how. I remembered her as an unremarkable woman with straight hair of nondescript color, freckles, and tight lips that reminded me of my strict Aunt Betty. Eyes so close together she could have looked through a keyhole with both of them at the same time. Every day she wore the same thing: skirt and blouse, mix and match colors, with a scarf tied around her neck. I recall thinking that if that scarf were to be loosened, her head might roll off.

To my best recollection Lily Elliott had been in her early thirties back then, which put her in her early sixties now. Journalism was a revolving door occupation, so I doubted she still worked at the newspaper, especially after the merger. She might not even still be in the Charleston area—or alive, for that matter. Nonetheless, she had written thousands of column inches on the trial, and therefore had known every nuance, every rumor, every whisper of gossip surrounding anything that touched on it.

If there had, in fact, been a mystery witness, Ms. Elliott would have known about it.

CHAPTER 10

When I arrived back at the condo my father was awake and making noise again. As I let myself in through the front door I could hear him in the bedroom, trying to stretch his tired vocal chords further than they would permit. Every word sounded like a gust of wind in a winter storm, icy and raw. His home health aide wasn't due for at least another hour, and I'd left him alone all morning. He'd been asleep when I sneaked out after downing a cup of coffee on the balcony, and I'd hoped he'd be in the same state when I returned.

"Good morning, Dad," I said cheerily, after checking my watch to make sure it was, indeed, still morning. "You're up."

"You left me alone again," he wheezed, each syllable coming out with great effort.

"I can't be here all the time," I reminded him.

His head seemed to dip in a slight nod, then he said, "Where's the remote?"

"On the table next to your bed." I walked over and picked it up, then placed it in his withered hand. "Do you want to watch something?"

He seemed hesitant, something distant in his eyes. Then he let the device slide from his fingers, and he said, "For almost thirty years all I thought about was getting out. Parole or pardon, it didn't matter. Always thankful that sniveling judge didn't sit me down in ol' sparky. Or pop me with a needle like they do now. Thirty years, and it turned out I was sitting on Death Row all along."

There was nothing I could say to ease the sting of irony. Yes, he was dying, and he was running out of good days. Death is an imprecise variable, and my father was proof in the flesh.

"Are you hungry?" I asked him. The hospice aide had already told me that eating is what a body does to stay alive, and not eating is what happens when it's shutting down. I had not seen him take a bite since I'd arrived, and he shook his head now.

"The thought of food makes me want to throw up," he replied.

I subtly checked my watch, then said, "I can turn on the cable news for you."

"Same thing as food," he rasped.

"You used to be a total news junkie," I reminded him.

"That was then, when the world still held meaning. Now I don't give a shit if some priest diddles an altar boy or some crazy-ass psycho pops his whole family. I don't have to worry about any of that, 'cause I'm checking out. Not my problem."

"Are you afraid?" I asked him. The doctors had told him there was a strong likelihood he would pass away in his sleep, and probably wouldn't even be aware of his death. Still, it's natural to think about one's own mortality, and I had an almost perverse desire to know what was going through his mind.

He inhaled deeply, and for a while I thought he was going to leave me right at that very moment. Then he said, "Don't expect me to come up with any great revelations you can sell to your publisher after I'm dead. I hate to disappoint, but you're not getting any final words of any philosophical value from me."

"Thanks for clearing that up," I replied with a shrug.

He flashed me a look of contempt but said nothing. Maybe he didn't have the energy for any more verbal sparring. Still, he seemed to be contemplating something, and eventually he said, "You know what I truly hope?"

"What's that?" I asked dutifully.

"I hope Heaven's filled with dogs and deer," he said.

"Given your history, you might be headed to an alternate destination," I told him.

It took him a moment to figure out what I was suggesting, and when he finally did, he said, "I guess I'll know soon enough. And just so you know, no—I'm not scared. It'll be a relief, in fact. Like I said, no great revelations and no mountaintop wisdom."

"The human race will be greatly disappointed," I assured him.

"Anything else you want to say before I go to sleep?"

"As long as you're asking, sure. Tell me what happened that night."

He released a tired sigh. "I already told you—I had nothing to do with what happened that night."

"So talk to me about it, instead of shutting me out."

But he just shook his head at my suggestion and coughed. He closed his eyes and kept them that way a long while, as if he were trying to force himself to die right then. Pass away inside his own transience and just go gentle into this good night. But Dylan Thomas was not there to turn the final page on my father's life, and eventually his eyes slid open, just enough to let me know he was still there.

"I pled 'not guilty,' honest and true," he finally said. "Like I told you the other day, I loved your mother more than anything."

"And now you've clammed up like an oyster."

His body quivered, as if he was trying to suppress a lingering urge to finally bare his soul. "You're mixing your mollusks," he finally said. "And what fucking difference does it make?"

"Unarmed truth is stronger than evil triumphant," I said. "To paraphrase Dr. King."

For obvious reasons the Reverend Martin Luther King Jr. had never been one of my father's favorite Americans, and the mention of his name brought a bitter darkness to his eyes. "The best part of that man ran down his momma's leg," he said.

"Are you deliberately trying to squeeze out every last ounce of hate in your soul before you kick the bucket?"

"Hate?" he wheezed. "That actually was meant as a compliment."

I shook my head and turned to go. I had no further words for him, and I had no desire to debate him. When I was younger I'd revered this man because he was my father, but as I'd grown older I'd learned to balance that unyielding love with contempt for his consummate bigotry. I'd been able to deal with it as a boy because children naturally view their parents with unconditional love, no questions asked. But as we grow older our perception matures and we see the warts and blemishes as the imperfections they are. Love endures, but it also changes as our sight improves and our peripheral vision expands.

I looked back once, just as I got to the bedroom door. He was staring at me, his lips moving as if he wanted to say something but didn't know how. Finally, he squeezed out seven short words: "Everything I did, I did for you—"

I didn't doubt him, but I still was far from forgiving him for all he'd caused. I could fulfill my promise to watch over him until he died, but any compassion or empathy Reverend McCall had convinced me I might find was still hiding in the shadows.

"Do what the note said," I snapped at him as I left. "Just shut the fuck up."

After that I felt miserable, just as I always had after a fight with Belinda. There are words and deeds you can never take back, and you know the words that have come out of your mouth have done lasting damage. When I was seventeen I had blamed my father for flipping my life upside down, not just for killing our mother but for slamming the door in our faces afterwards. My anger simmered deep inside over the passing decades, and only after enduring some serious addictions and spending a lot of time on the couch did I learn that anger is a wasted emotion that accomplishes nothing. I'd thought I'd put all the fire and fury behind me; such are the little lies we tell ourselves as we try to make sense of who we are.

I hoped my animosity would dissipate over time, but that was one thing my father did not have. His body was failing rapidly, and he only had a few lucid days remaining. Maybe only hours. I stood outside his bedroom, trying to separate my ego from the greater picture. It was like separating the yolk from the whites of an egg, an imprecise endeavor that never yields the exact results you want.

I opened the door again gently and looked in on him. I wasn't sure what I might tell him, but I felt I needed to say something. Not an apology, but maybe an acknowledgement of the wall that had come between us. Given the few days he had left I wanted to see him for who he really was, not how I remembered him to be. But he was asleep, or at least pretending to be. His head was turned toward me just slightly and I could see that his eyes were closed deep inside those dark, cavernous sockets. I waited a few minutes to make sure he hadn't died on me, then slowly closed the door again.

It was lunchtime but I had no appetite. I walked out on to the balcony and watched the power boats cut through the steel blue water of the harbor, but after a few minutes I came back inside. I felt nervous and fidgety, like when I consumed more than my daily limit of caffeine. Or a few years back when I was popping pain meds and I'd run out of my prescriptions too early.

One of the perks of condo living was the large indoor swimming pool. A few laps in cool water always helped distract me whenever the old monkey mind started swinging from branch to branch. That's what I needed just then, and five minutes later I was downstairs, carving a lane through the water. Arm over arm, drowning the ghosts of the past. I don't know how many laps I swam, but when I finally hoisted myself out of the water I felt cleansed in many different ways.

I'd left most of my enmity at the deep end, but a malignant antagonism still remained as I dried off and wrapped myself in the terrycloth robe I'd found in the closet upstairs. I tried to push everything from my mind as I tossed my towel in the laundry bin and made my way through the glass door to the central corridor. The pool was on the second floor so I hit the "up" button and waited for the elevator to arrive. When it did I thought it was empty so I started to get on, but then a small dog crept up to me and started licking my bare ankles.

It was a white Maltese with a shaggy coat and brown eyes that seemed to be begging for help. His tongue was rough as he went after the chlorine and salt on my skin. I bent down and checked the metal tag crimped to the blue collar around his neck. It told me his name was "Sparky," and he belonged to a Beatrice Adams on the fourteenth floor. How he had ridden all the way down to the second on his own was a mystery, but I was certain Mrs. Adams had not given her consent. The tag had a phone number on it, but I had not brought my cell with me to the pool.

I punched the button for "14" and rode it all the way up. A quick visual check confirmed Sparky was a male, and I gave his chin a gentle scratch as we rode up together. He appeared to think we were old acquaintances, and rolled onto his back and permitted me to rub his tummy. Then the bell dinged and the door opened, and he bolted out and raced down the hallway.

Sparky seemed to know where he lived, because he came to a halt outside the condo that was directly above mine. I was staying on the twelfth floor and this dog lived on the fourteenth, but I'd noticed in the elevator that there was no "13." Humans truly are a superstitious lot. The doorway was flanked by twin jade foo dogs, light green with pale accents that made them look like alabaster. One of the carved figurines—actually imperial guardian lions—was a male, resting his paw upon a globe-like sphere, while the other depicted a female restraining her boisterous cub. They were quite common in L.A., especially in Chinatown and other Asian neighborhoods.

I hit the doorbell and waited, then hit it again. A shadow obscured the peephole, and then a voice called out, "Who is it?"

The voice belonged to a woman who sounded a little on the elderly side.

"My name is Rick Devlin," I replied. "I live right below you."

"Is my TV too loud?" she said through the door.

"No, ma'am. I come bearing dogs."

"You found Sparky?"

"Would he be a white ball of fur?"

I heard movement on the other side as locks were being turned and a chain was unfastened. Then the door opened and a woman who looked to be in her seventies poked her head out. "Where is that little rascal?" she said.

That little rascal was sniffing one of the foo dogs, and when she saw him she bent down and bundled him in her arms. Then she stood up and looked at me with eyes that beamed of appreciation.

"I've been worried sick about my little boy," she gushed as she rubbed his ears. "Thank you so much for returning him."

"Not at all, ma'am," I said. "Does he get out often?"

"More than I'd like. I try to keep him inside, but sometimes my husband leaves the door open and he goes exploring. Sparky, not my husband."

"Well, if I ever see him again I'll know where to bring him," I told her.

She thought for a moment, then said, "If that happens—and I'm sure it will—we may be out. If no one answers the door, I keep a key under that lion, there." She used her chin to indicate the male statuette that Sparky had been sniffing.

"I'll keep that in mind," I told her. All of a sudden I felt underdressed, standing there in a white terrycloth robe and bare feet.

"I think I'd better get back to my place and get some clothes on."

She nodded. "Well, thanks again for bringing home my little scoundrel," she said. With that she closed the door and left me standing there in the hallway, dripping on the carpet.

When I got back to my floor I felt refreshed and back on track. My father was still asleep, so I set my laptop on the table and made my way to Google. Over a snack of grapes and Ritz crackers I typed "Lily Elliott" and hit enter. Less than a second later the search algorithms returned over a million hits, and I saw that I'd hit pay dirt.

There were several Lily Elliott's out there, but the one I was looking for dominated the entire first page of results. It turned out that more than a decade ago she had traded in her reporter's notebook for a publishing contract. Since then she had written nine romance novels, all of them set in coastal Carolina and all of them hitting various bestseller lists. They weren't my kind of books, but they'd received modestly good reviews and one had even been described as "the must-read beach book of the summer."

The bio on her official web page said she lived full-time in Beaufort with her seven cats, three dogs, and two horses. There was no mention of a Mr. Elliott, which I suspected might be related to all the animals. An email link said I could contact her through her agent, but that didn't suit my purposes or my time frame. I began to dig around through the usual public info sites, and eventually learned that she owned a house on Oyster Catcher Road, across Harbor River from Beaufort proper. I fed that address into a pay website I occasionally use and came up with a phone number. The 843 area code told me it was local, not her agent or editor up in New York.

My call went right through, and a woman picked it up after several rings.

"Ms. Elliott?" I said in my most pleasant and engaging voice. "Please don't hang up. I'm not selling time shares or running a scam, but I am a flash out of the past. You probably don't remember me—"

Click.

A few seconds later I called her back, but the phone just kept ringing. Not a good sign. I tried one more time, but now a message on the screen read:

`Number Blocked`

Damn.

There was no point in dialing again, since any call I placed with my cell would result in the same message. I knew my father didn't have a phone, nor was there a wired line in the condo. That was part of the arrangement.

For about five seconds I considered driving down to Beaufort right then on the chance that she might be home, maybe working on her next book. Just as I should be doing instead of chasing old ghosts. But my father's presence in the next room, laboring under every breath while cancer cells consumed his body, created a distraction I couldn't get around. I had not come home to Charleston to poke through the mire of the distant past, and so far that pursuit had done nothing but spin my wheels. The specter of inevitable death lurked only a few feet away, and I had a deadline to meet.

Just then there was a knock on the door, and the knob turned. I had not locked it when I returned from handing over Ms. Adams' dog, just as I rarely did with my own A-frame out in Topanga Canyon. Then a voice called out "Hello?" and I felt my muscles relax. It was a woman's voice, young with a soft accent that sounded like warm tequila. She practically jumped when she saw me and almost dropped the large bag that was slung over her shoulder.

"Come in," I told her as I rose from my chair. "I don't think we've met, but I'm Rick Devlin."

"Benita Juarez," she replied, lightly shaking my hand. "You were out when I came by yesterday. I'm your father's home health aide. Activities of daily living, fundamental care, bathing. That sort of thing."

"I understand he sent you away," I said. "I apologize."

"It's a difficult time for him, Mr. Rick. He's scared."

"You're a courageous woman," I told her.

"Sir?"

"Never mind. It's just that…well, not many people would want to do what you do."

"That's why I make the big bucks," she said with a laugh. "How's he doing today?"

"A bit ornery, I'm afraid," I told her. "We've been snapping at each other."

"He's in a very bad way," Benita reminded me. "I'm sure he

doesn't like this any more than you do."

She was right. He was the one doing the dying, trapped in a room not much larger than the cell he had lived in for the last thirty years of his life. He had a better view now, but it was tainted by the certainty of his demise. When he died I would lose a father I had not seen in years, but he would lose everything he'd ever known. While I still was having difficulty feeling sympathy for him, I sensed a genuine sorrow for both of us.

"He spends a lot more time asleep than awake," I replied.

"That's to be expected," she said. She had lovely, smooth skin the color of honey, and her hair was cropped just below her ears. She wore baggy, light blue scrub trousers and a floral top, with a plastic name badge pinned to it. "It's in our nature to want to keep people going, make sure they eat, sip a little water. Get better and heal. But at this stage in life there is no getting better. And no healing."

She clearly saw a lot more of this sort of thing than I did, so I deferred to her sensitivities. "Anything I can do?" I asked.

"Just be here for him." I must have blanched at that thought, because she quickly added, "I don't mean hang around this place twenty-four-seven. Just that he might need to hold a hand or share a thought. Or a tear."

Benita Juarez obviously didn't know my father's back story, and I wasn't about to fill her in. She was possessed of genuine compassion and empathy in her heart, and I envied her.

"I'll keep that in mind when we start to butt heads," I said.

"Good idea, sir. Now, if you don't mind, I'm going to give him a sponge bath."

I shuddered at the idea as she started toward my father's bedroom. Then I said, "Do you have a phone I could borrow? The battery in mine died. It's a local call."

She handed me an iPhone from her bag. It was an older model with a pink glitter case, not one of the newer, pricier upgrades. "I have unlimited minutes, so talk all you want."

After she had disappeared into the other room I went out to the balcony and dialed the number I'd found on Google. It rang three, then four times before someone answered.

"Hello?" It was the same voice as before, and just as suspicious.

I got right into it. "You covered the Frank Devlin trial many years ago. I'm his son, Rick. Please don't hang up."

She didn't, but I knew she had the option to do so at any time. There was a lengthy pause, and then she said, "Why are you calling me?"

"I'm in town, and I have a few questions."

"What town, and what questions?" I wasn't sure, but it sounded as if her hard shell might have just cracked.

"Charleston," I replied. "I'm here on family business."

Another silence followed. Then: "How's your father?"

"That's the family business," I explained.

"The sonofabitch finally passed away?"

Ouch. It was clear where Lily Elliott's sentiments lay. "Any day now. Please forgive me for calling you out of the blue, but I have a few things I'd like to ask you while I'm here."

"That was you on the other phone," she said.

"Guilty as charged," I told her. "Please don't hold it against me."

"You have no idea how many calls I get from strangers, scammers, marketers, and fans."

She still hadn't hung up on me, which I took as a good sign. "I don't blame you for your suspicion," I said. "And I thank you for your time. Is there any way we might be able to meet, maybe for a cup of coffee? I can drive down there if you like."

"Down where?" she asked, and I instantly knew I was busted.

"Beaufort," I said. "I admit it…I had to do some research to find you."

"Which is how you got my very well-protected cell phone number?"

"Not as protected as you might think, but yes," I conceded.

She fell silent again for a couple of seconds, then said, "How large a cup of coffee? I'm in the middle of a draft and my time is precious."

"I understand. I'm a writer myself. Twenty minutes' worth?"

"That's not much coffee. I can do thirty."

"Deal," I told her. "Does tomorrow work?"

"When tomorrow stops working, we have a big problem," she said. "We'll meet here at my house, since you already know where I live. You bring the coffee. I take mine black. Ten o'clock is good."

"Yes, ma'am," I replied. "I really appreciate this."

"You might, if you bring the right questions."

CHAPTER 11

Benita spent close to an hour with my father. It was way more than I could have done and I was grateful for her help. I'd had to clean him up yesterday, but I couldn't imagine dabbing his body with a sponge, toweling him off, and putting on another diaper. All the while tolerating his bigoted jabs. I heard them talking in there, her asking polite questions and him replying with his sandpaper voice. I couldn't hear what they were discussing, but I was glad he had someone with whom he could share his thoughts.

Eventually she opened the door and slipped out of his bedroom. From the way she was tiptoeing I could tell he was asleep again, and hopefully would be for hours.

"How's he doing?" I asked, for lack of anything more brilliant to say.

"Tired but hanging in," she replied. "He's all set until tomorrow, but that will be someone else. Probably Alicia. I have weekends off."

I watched her as she stuffed a few items back into her large cloth bag, then said to her, "Do you mind if I ask you something?"

She lifted a shoulder in a shrug. "Go for it."

I wasn't sure how to get into what was on my mind, so I went right to it. "You were here Wednesday, the day we moved him in?"

Without thinking, she nodded and said, "That's right—Wednesday, Thursday, today. Why do you ask?"

"Well," I said, buying time while I framed the question properly. "Did you by any chance give my father something?"

I saw a slight hitch that confirmed my suspicion, and she said, "You know, Mr. Rick…I think I did."

"I need you to tell me what it was," I told her in a serious voice.

Benita pretended to think about it for a second, and then replied, "A small envelope. Is there a problem?"

"Any outside communication to my father is supposed to go through me," I told her. "It's part of our agreement."

She made a good show of not knowing what I was talking about, then said, "Oh, Mr. Rick. I am so sorry. I was not aware of any agreement."

I realized that I'd slipped up, but didn't want to belabor the point. So I asked, "This envelope…where did you get it?"

This time Benita took a second or two to reply. Truth or lie, fact or fiction? Finally she said, "A man handed it to me down in the parking lot as I was walking from my car. He asked me if I was visiting the person in unit twelve-oh-eight. I told him I was, and he asked me to give it to him."

Who could possibly have known where she was going, unless he had her license plate number? "Did he give you anything else?" I asked her. "Like…maybe money?"

Benita bristled at the accusation, then shook her head rapidly. "No…no money. He just asked me to bring it up to your father, and I didn't think anything of it. Look…is there going to be a problem? I can always ask to be transferred."

I didn't want to create a scene, and I needed her help, so I quickly said, "No, no. I think my father actually likes you, so please don't even think about that. But maybe you can tell me what this man looked like."

She said nothing while she thought this through. She didn't want a dissatisfied customer filing a complaint, especially when she didn't do something she felt was wrong. Finally she replied, "He was white, but dirty, like he worked in a warehouse or garage. Forties or early fifties. No beard or mustache, black hair. Black truck. His breath smelled of cigarettes and booze. Whisky, not beer. He didn't tell me his name, but he made it sound like him and your father were old buddies."

"Did you see what was in the envelope?" I asked.

Benita shook her head. "No. Mr. Frank just took it from me and slipped it under the covers."

Whatever was going on here had nothing to do with her, and I felt sorry for grilling her. I thanked her as I handed her phone back, then said, "Please don't worry about any of this. It's just a family thing, so let's keep it between us."

"Yes, Mr. Rick," she said. "You have a good weekend, now."

"You, too, Benita. And please let me know if that man approaches you again. Any time, for any reason."

"Yes, sir," she replied. And then she was gone.

My father slept until a little after eight, when the approaching night cast a granular duskiness upon his room. That's when the app on my phone buzzed, telling me that he wanted to see me. After the way our last encounter ended I wasn't looking forward to this one, but I looked in on him anyway to see what he needed.

"You've developed quite a mouth," he rasped, when I poked my head through the door.

"Learned from the pro," I replied.

He seemed to contemplate that, then made a weak motion with his head that I took as an invitation to come in. I sat down in the chair next to the bed, and said, "Can I get you something? Maybe some water?"

He nodded, so I gave him a sip from the cup on his nightstand. "This isn't what I chose," he said when he was finished. "None of this."

I didn't know if he meant this room, or the cancer that was devouring his strength, or the way his life had turned out. Probably all of the above. "Nobody ever did, or ever will, escape the consequence of his own actions," I said lamely.

"The philosopher son," he wheezed, cracking the faintest of grins. "Maybe you can enlighten me on the meaning of life while you're at it."

"I'm all out," I replied, with an apologetic shrug.

Neither of us said anything then, the friction between us still palpable. Lights were winking on all over the lowcountry, and I could see a line of red taillights streaming up and over the Cooper River Bridge. When it became clear neither of us had anything further to say I stood to go, then said, "Do you mind if I ask you a question?"

"Is this like all the others?"

I knew he'd been warned not to talk, but in a few days he would be dead and my questions would still be alive. Now was my chance.

"Who was the mystery witness who was supposed to testify at your trial but never showed?" I asked him.

He didn't feign ignorance, didn't express a look of surprise or shock. He just lay there stone-faced, eyes seemingly focused on a spot well behind my head. I knew he'd heard me, but he said nothing.

Seconds pass very slowly when you're in the middle of an awkward silence, and at least thirty of them ticked by before I said, "What are you afraid of? You're going to die anyway."

"It's not me," he finally said.

"What does that mean?"

He drew his head tiredly from side to side, then rasped, "It's so much more than me. Always has been."

"What are you talking about?"

"Leave it be, Rick. All of this dies when I do."

"All of *what*?" I asked.

But he didn't answer. His eyes simply settled into a deep state of sleep, and within a few seconds he was snuffling rhythmically, although with great labor. I watched him for a good minute, just to make sure he wasn't faking it to get rid of me. Eventually I convinced myself he was asleep for real, and I quietly let myself out of the room.

The following morning, I was up and out of the condo a few minutes past eight. Before leaving I made sure Dad was alive and awake. I opened the drapes so he could see the harbor sparkling like a sheet of glass. I refreshed his water cup, absorbed his rebuke when he said he wasn't hungry, *goddammit*, and assured him I'd be back in time to do it all again at the lunch hour. I turned the TV to a classical music channel, and showed him how to turn it off with the remote. He didn't ask me where I was going or why, and actually seemed pleased to be rid of me for a few hours.

It was Saturday, so I knew I'd miss the drive time rush, but I wanted to get down to Beaufort with a few minutes to spare. I knew where Lily Elliott lived but still had to pick up coffee on the way, so at the edge of town I stopped at a cozy breakfast joint that looked locally owned. Weathered clapboard siding, blue shutters, small patch of red flowers out front. I'd passed several of the mega-chain coffee shops on the way, including the one my daughter worked for in L.A., but I figured Miss Lily was someone who preferred to patronize locally owned businesses. I ordered two large coffees to go, plus a couple of blackberry scones.

Her house was large and tidy and smacked of the antebellum South. It was a white frame structure with a wrap-around veranda, twin rocking chairs and a long joggling board suspended from twin braces. A porch swing moved lightly in the morning breeze, and straw baskets dripping with fuchsia and impatiens and lobelia hung from the *haint* blue ceiling. A tin roof angled past second-floor dormers, and a brick chimney with a tarnished rooster weathervane protruded above its peak. Weeping willows and magnolias and large live oaks bordered the lush lawn, which carried the aroma of freshly cut grass. A neat meadow rolled down to the edge of the river, where a pair of horses grazed in a fenced field.

Ms. Lily met me at the door with a broad smile that belied any doubts she might have had yesterday. She took the cardboard tray with the coffee and scones and welcomed me inside. I noticed two Siamese cats sleeping on a pet bed in the foyer, and another feline of undetermined variety rubbed against my leg as I followed the romance writer through her house.

"Ten o'clock on the dot," she said as she led me into a solarium that had a broad view of the water. "I like a man who respects another person's time."

"Time waits for no man," I told her. "Or woman."

She had lost a lot of the mousiness I remembered from the trial. She also had added a couple of pounds, which had been sorely needed, and had employed the skills of a good hair stylist. She also appeared to have made full use of the make-up counter at Belks. She had transformed herself into an elegant-looking woman in her sixties, gracious and confident and comfortable in her skin. Quite a contrast from the nervous waif that had seemed so stressed as she chased people down the halls of the courthouse.

She waved me into a wicker chair that swiveled and rocked, covered in leafy fabric upholstery that carried the outdoors inside. She produced napkins to go with the scones, about which she said, "I'm not sure I can eat those."

"They're vegan," I advised her. "But not gluten-free."

"I stand corrected," she replied, and chose the smaller one.

I knew I was on the clock here—thirty minutes was what she had said—but I didn't want to dive right into my questions. I was curious what she considered "the right ones," but I suspected we would get to that.

"I want to apologize for my demeanor on the phone yesterday," she said. "Like I told you, I get all sorts of crank calls. There's no sense of privacy anymore. People just get your number and feel they can bother you any old time."

"I think I should be the one apologizing," I replied. "I intruded on your life, and that was rude."

"Nonsense. I just didn't know who you were. Now I do."

She took a nibble of her scone, which she quickly washed down with a sip of coffee. "After we hung up I did a Google search of my own. I must say, you turned out okay, considering."

"Every life has its ups and downs," I replied, not wanting to venture too far into any of mine. "You've done very well yourself."

"Thanks to Ellie Carrington," Lily said. I guess I must have looked confused, because she added, "She's the heroine in my books."

I realized I should have brushed up on her background and literary success, but her path on to the bestseller lists now allowed us to break the ice. Eventually we came to a natural pause and she said, "So you have some questions about the trial."

"Yes, ma'am—"

"You can stop that polite southern shit," she said, grinning again. "It's pure pretense, considering how duplicitous folks down around these parts can be. Just call me Lily."

"It's how I was raised, but I'll try," I told her. I paused a second or two, then dived right in. "I was going through an old microfilm transcript of the trial yesterday and saw that you'd also looked at it, about fifteen years ago."

"Why were you putting yourself through all that, after all these years?" she asked, deflecting my question.

"Same thing I was wondering about you."

Lily considered this a moment, took another sip of coffee. "There would have been quite a few trial records on that reel," she said. "What makes you think I was looking at that specific one?"

"I wasn't sure until just now," I replied.

Lily Elliott smiled and gazed out the window at the river, which was part of the Intracoastal Waterway that snaked all the way from New Jersey down to southern Florida. I sensed she was weighing how much to reveal to me, which only served to make me more curious. Eventually she leaned forward, as if she were going to share some long-held secret.

"I'd been thinking about writing a book," she finally said. "I'd connected with an agent in New York who was intrigued when I told her about your father's trial, and she thought it might make for a good true crime story. This was before the Ellie Carrington books, and I didn't know where my career might take me."

"Writing a book about a case you covered makes sense. Did you do it?"

"I drafted a proposal, and my agent sent it around. There was some interest, but not enough to lead to a contract. Meanwhile I finished the manuscript for *Pelican Creek*, and it got sold. The true crime idea got shelved."

"So why did you review the trial records?" I asked her. "I'm sure you kept your notes and clippings."

"I did," she admitted. "Held on to everything, until we got the hundred-year rains a few years ago. The attic roof leaked like a sieve and everything got destroyed. But you're right…I wanted to review the trial again, and going through the transcript seemed the best way to do it."

"A refresher course?"

"Of sorts." She was gazing out the window again, as if focusing on a lingering memory from the past. "You know…there was something about that trial I never could put my finger on."

"How do you mean?" I asked. "What sort of thing?"

She shook her head and sat back in her chair. "That's just it…I could never figure it out. And it wasn't just one thing. I'd covered a lot of trials before then, even a few murder cases. That one seemed pretty straightforward, nothing out of the ordinary. Defendant, witnesses, evidence, jury. Guilty verdict. But there just always seemed to be a…a vibe that made me feel uneasy. Edgy. Maybe even duped. Like knowing your husband is having an affair but having absolutely no way to prove it."

My thoughts drifted to Laurie Cobb and how she must have

felt when she learned of her husband's serial infidelities. "Were you looking for something specific in the microfilm file?" I asked her.

"Nothing in particular, just something I might have missed at the time. Or that might jump-start my memory."

"Did you find it?"

She shook her head. "If I had, I probably would have written the book anyway, even without a contract. In all honesty I was thinking I might come to a different conclusion than the jury."

I stared at her, probably longer than I should have. "You think my father is innocent."

"I hoped I would come to that assumption, because the book would have been a bestseller if I could prove it. Big bucks, movie deal, all that."

"Let me rephrase—"

"Now you sound like that doofus lawyer your father had," she said with a snicker.

"Objection!" I quipped, and we both had a quick chuckle. Then I made an effort to look serious again, and said, "So you're not convinced that my father was guilty beyond a reasonable doubt."

"Well, that's not really phrased in the form of a question," she replied, a glint in her eye. "And I did tell you to bring the right questions. But yes, the thought crossed my mind—more than once—that your father spent thirty years of his life in prison for something he did not do."

CHAPTER 12

Her words did not surprise me, but they still came as a shock. Thirty years ago I had accepted the decision of the jury foreman as legal gospel, despite the fact that the accused was my own flesh and blood. It was hard not to, considering the way the prosecutor had laid it all out, from arrest to conviction. But now I wondered if I'd allowed myself to be played, along with those seven men and five women.

"Do you remember anything about there being a surprise witness who never appeared?" I found myself asking her.

At that point she rose to her feet, and I thought she was being strict about my thirty-minute time limit. Was it time to go already? She wandered over to the glass and studied the pair of horses nuzzling the grass in the far-off field. It was as if she were a trial lawyer herself, taking command of the courtroom with her sincerity and candor. Then, without turning to look at me, she said, "There were more rumors floating around that courthouse than bats flying out of a cave at sundown."

"So, was that a right question or a wrong one?"

She turned and I could see a look of distant resignation in her eyes. "I'd put it in the 'close enough' category," she replied. "The whole thing moved so quickly, as if the judge was following a well-crafted script. Your father's lawyer—I forget his name—was in so much quicksand he didn't know how to save him."

"Myers Jenkins the Third," I said, refreshing her memory. "What do you think was going on, looking back at it now?"

"Like I said, I could never put my finger on it. Gut feeling, intuition, blind hunch…who knows? But something was off. And you're right about the rumors of a witness."

"The funny thing is, I don't remember a thing about him," I told her. "I just happened to come across it by accident."

She came back over to her chair and sat down. She arranged herself comfortably, tucking her floral skirt under her thighs. Then she folded her hands in her lap and spoke, "First of all, it wasn't a him, it was a her. Or at least that's the impression I got."

I thought back, trying to recall any woman who might have been lurking in the wings to help save my father's hide. The witness list mentioned his former secretary, Alice Marion, by name, so I doubted it would have been her. No mystery there. Was there someone else intertwined with my parents' lives I didn't know about?

"This witness…I assume her name never came up?"

She shook off my question. Her coffee was getting cold, but she didn't reach to pick it up. "That's what was so curious. There was some speculation that it may have been the wife of the man your mother was thought to have had been involved with, but she was kind of obvious. So was your father's Chief of Staff up in Columbia, and his secretary was already on the list. It was someone else altogether, and whoever it was, her identity was protected with a Kevlar vest."

"What do you remember about the judge?" I asked her then, shifting the subject.

"Ernest Carter." Lily Elliott rolled her eyes, and I could tell this was another of the "right" questions. "That man was a snake," she said with a noticeable shudder. "Should have recused himself from the case from the beginning."

"Because of the poker games?"

She wrinkled her nose as if one of her cats had just passed gas. "That was just the tip of it," she said, shaking her head. "What I remember is people saying 'the judge has got a grudge.' Rumor was it had to do with a real estate deal, or an old debt, or a political conflict. Or it could have been something more personal dating back to their days at The Citadel."

"They went to college together?" I asked.

"I'm pretty sure their years overlapped," she replied. "They may have known each other, maybe even dated the same girl. Whatever the circumstances, there was some bad blood between them."

"Enough to rig a case against an innocent man?" I asked her.

"I don't for sure that your father was innocent," Lily Elliott said, raising her palms as a way to create distance between herself and the verdict. "Or that the trial could have been compromised. Just that there were some irregularities."

"But you were going to write a book," I pointed out. "And you said you thought there may have been another explanation for my mother's murder."

"A book I ended up not writing. Look, Rick. I don't know what happened in that courtroom thirty years ago. A lot of the people who were part of it are old and probably senile, and more than one has died. Like the judge. You ask me, karma is one vengeful bitch."

"You think there's a connection?" I asked.

She raised her eyebrow in a noncommittal gesture, then said, "That's not for me to say. But I have come to believe that all things in this universe are intertwined in one way or another. I can understand your interest in your father's trial, but remember, this is South Carolina. If you start turning over rocks, you never know what might crawl out."

When I'd agreed to take custody of my father I'd also agreed to keep his parole confidential, with one exception. I insisted that I have the right to reveal his release to my uncle, who had taken me in during my last year of high school. At that time my father was in jail, my mother was dead, our house on the island had been wiped out by the hurricane, and my entire high school baseball career in Mount Pleasant had been flushed down the toilet. My closest blood relative was Uncle Andrew, who gladly fixed up a space in his garage and enrolled me in Summerville High. It was an old rival school that I'd shut out twice in my sophomore and junior years, and I found it painful to pitch for them against my old Wando teammates. Although I did hold them to three hits and one unearned run.

Judge Carter had prohibited Uncle Andrew from setting foot inside the courtroom, and at one point he had clamped a gag order on him to keep him from ranting to reporters about my father's guilt. He was a decent man with a warm heart who had dearly loved his deceased sister, and he continuously asked the good Lord why he had taken her so young. I don't think the man was a true believer—there was too much booze and gambling and carousing in his life to call him devout—but he'd been suffering an honest and very deep grief over his loss, angry at anyone who might have had a hand in taking her from him. And leaving my sister and me without a mother.

Even though I owed a good part of my reinvented life after high school to my uncle, I never felt particularly close to him. He had an imprecise relationship with the bottle, as did I at the time, and he enjoyed picking a fight just to experience the ensuing battle. He had an obsessive fondness for creating friction whenever more than two people were in the same room, and he derived a perverse pleasure from watching an evening devolve from civility into chaos. He craved conflict and turmoil, and seemed energized whenever calamity rolled through his front door.

That's why I'd waited three full days to give him a call.

"Oh, my fuggin' Christ," he said now, when I told him who was calling. "I thought you'd done near walked in front of a truck and died. How long's it been, Rick?"

The last time we'd spoken on the phone was Christmas a couple years back, early in the day before the holiday drinking kicked in on the east coast. "Way too long," I said, a dry alarm in the back of my head telling me he'd already cracked the seal on a bottle of vodka. "Good to hear your voice."

"My Lord, boy...what brings you to suddenly call me out of the deep blue?" he asked.

"I'm here in Charleston," I told him. "Taking care of family business."

"Please tell me the old bastard finally died," he replied, deep sincerity in his voice. "I need to hear some good news for a change."

"Not yet, but soon," I informed him. "How are Bradley and Randy?"

Bradley was his oldest son, a cold-hearted bastard who had worked in a paint store when I moved into the garage all those years ago. I knew for a fact that he was dealing drugs, and he'd threatened to turn me into a girl the one time I questioned him about it. Randy was closer to my age and had been responsible for the disappearance of numerous small animals throughout the neighborhood. I wondered if he had progressed to larger prey over the years.

"No good comes from talking 'bout those two assholes," he replied. "Neither of 'em amounted to more than a mound of horseshit. Got two wives, three ex-wives, and seven kids between 'em, and debt higher than the steeple at St. Michael's. Pieces of shit, both of them. But they're my boys, so I guess I got to love 'em."

This was Andrew Wheeler, my mother's brother and a genetic contradiction in the flesh. Crass, opinionated, stubborn, critical. How Mom possibly came out of the same womb I could not comprehend, and she never explained. She was yin to his yang, day to his night. Light to his dark. North to his South. Maybe that's why she got along so well with my father.

"How much do you remember of the trial?" I asked him, doing my best to catch him off-guard.

"The trial? Shit, boy...that was last century."

"That's why I'm asking," I pressed him, gently. He'd taught me enough about fishing for me to know you gently set the hook, wait for the fish to bite, then reel him in slowly. "How's your memory?"

"No one in the Wheeler family's ever fallen into the well of dementia, far as I know," he boasted. "Why you asking?"

"I just have a few questions," I told him. "Things I'm trying to work out before Dad passes away."

"What sort of things?" I couldn't determine whether he sounded edgy or tense, or a combination of the two.

"Mostly random," I said. "Probably best to discuss it all in person. And in private."

"Oooooh," he said, going for ghostly and mysterious. "Sounds mysterious."

"You still live in Summerville?"

"Nah...moved to Goose Creek the winter before last. Tell you what. Remember that place we used to go bowling? I still hang out there sometimes, just to chill. What do you say you meet me there tomorrow, maybe three o'clock?"

It was a local joint called Ten Pin Alley, and I remembered it from high school. He'd brought me there once or twice, him to drink and me to roll a few frames to strengthen my pitching arm. That was the excuse, but I knew it was because he liked to sip his vodka and sneak a peek at the bartender's breasts in the mirror.

"On a Sunday?" I asked, mindful of how southerners are about ecumenical things.

"And on the seventh day the Lord hoisted himself onto a stool, ordered a cold one, and raised it to his lips," he said. "You in?"

"I look forward to it," I told him, instantly reconsidering the idea just as soon as I ended the call. *Too late.*

Even though it was Saturday, I called Herman Stump. Since he'd phoned me when he set up my date with the County Clerk's microfilm machine I had his number in my phone. I found it and hit redial, then waited for it to connect.

"I apologize for bothering you on the weekend, and I'll only take a second," I said hurriedly when he answered.

"No rush. I'm just sitting here in my boat listenin' to John Lee Hooker and waitin' for a fish to happen by. Nothin' could be finer. What's up, my brother?"

I pictured him, lazing on a still, green pond somewhere with nothing but the sky above him, the gentle rocking of a flat-bottomed skiff countering the rhythm of the old blues icon.

"Just a quick question," I told him. "I was thinking about the trial, wondering if you remember there being a mystery witness who wasn't called to testify. May have been a woman."

There was a long—and I mean very long—pause, and for a moment I thought maybe the call was dropped. But the screen indicated the signal was still connected, so I waited.

"That ain't a quick question," he finally said.

"Well, I hate to impose on your time on such a fine Saturday," I told him. "Maybe I can catch you at the courthouse on Monday."

There was another pause, much shorter than the first, and then he said, "No use going to all that trouble. Just tell me somethin', will you?"

"Sure thing."

"Where'd you get that sort of notion? About this witness."

"It's come up a couple times, different folks. My mother used to say that rumors have a longer shelf life than canned peaches, and this seems to be one of those times."

"If I were you, I'd pay this one no mind," he advised me. "Ain't nothin' that doesn't go bad over time."

"So, there's nothing to the rumor, then?"

"Just a nothin' sandwich," he assured me.

"About ten seconds ago you made it sound different," I reminded him. "In fact, you said it wasn't a quick question."

"Does it sound quick to you?"

It was my turn to hesitate. I was heading north on Highway 17, coming back from Beaufort, and the car ahead of me had just braked for a man who had darted across all four lanes of traffic. "Please, sir," I said. "It's important, at least to me. And maybe to other folks, as well."

"Son," he said, making the word sound more serious than it was meant to be. "Some things truly are best left alone, you know what I mean?"

"That's what everyone keeps telling me," I replied.

"Maybe everyone is right. You ever think of that?"

"Mr. Stump, sir," I said. "Two days ago you went out of your way to help me take a look at the old trial records. Now you're telling me to leave it all be. Please excuse me, sir, if I can't figure you out."

"Damn," he said, slow and measured. "You sure do know how to ruin what looked to be a fine day of fishin'."

I let his own words hang there, like a hook he had dropped into his own conscience. "All I need is a name," I pushed him. "I can take it from there."

"The name you're looking for, I don't have," he said with a reluctant sigh. "And like I said, nothing good can come of any of this."

"If you can't tell me who, can you at least tell me what?" I asked.

"What do you mean, 'what'?"

"What was this woman going to testify about? What did she know, and in what way did it pertain to my father's case?"

"Christ on a cracker." There was another of those long pauses, and finally the old bailiff breathed, "Jimmy Holland."

"That's the witness' name?" I asked.

"Lord Almighty, boy. Can't you look past your own nose?"

"I'm not sure I follow—"

"Do I have to spell it out for you?" Herman Stump said, exasperation in his voice. "Jimmy Holland wasn't the witness. He was a boy, just sixteen-years-old when he died. And that's it; no more. I've already done told you too much as it is."

My father was awake when I got back to the condo, but just barely. He was thirsty, so I helped him with a drink from his sippy cup. When he finished I walked over to the glass sliders and peered out at the harbor, which was shimmering like a sheet of tin foil.

"Looks like it's raining out past the shipping channel," I observed, for lack of anything better to tell him.

He didn't respond, instead inquiring, "What day is it?"

"Saturday. A little after noon."

"I used to like Saturdays," he said, his words coming out hard and labored. "Way back… before. Remember then? You and me, we'd head down to the breach if the tide was right, set our poles in the sand and see what was biting."

"Good times," I agreed. The beach had always been one of our favorite fishing spots because of the strong tidal current that flowed through the narrow gap between Sullivan's Island and Isle of Palms.

"This is my last one," he said then.

"Your last what?"

"My last Saturday."

What could I say to that? Lie? Tell him he had plenty more where this one came from? Or comfort him by encouraging him to enjoy every minute of the day?

"We never know how many tomorrows we have," I told him, my words sounding lame and unconvincing.

"If you ever stop writing books you could get a job at Hallmark." He coughed, and when he wiped his mouth with his sleeve I saw a small spot of blood.

"I appreciate the encouragement," I said.

"Where've you been all morning? I called for you a couple times, but you didn't seem to be anywhere around."

"I had a few errands to do," I told him, providing no details.

"You're up to something."

I remember my father as always being astute, even if he didn't know all of my teenage secrets. I knew it would be best if I just changed the subject, put the trial behind us and forget about this "mystery witness." But I never was able to leave an itch alone, and this one was bothering me big time.

"Does the name Jimmy Holland mean anything to you?"

My father's eyes, as deep-set into those cavernous sockets as they were, practically bugged out as the name collided with his memory. He stared at me, then looked away in resignation. Or was it fear? Finally he said, "My God, Rick What the hell have you done?"

"All I did was ask around, came up with a name."

"You sure as shit did." His voice came out more ragged than before, and the words segued into a minor coughing fit. When he finished, he said, "Who you been talking to?"

"Doesn't matter," I told him. "I'll find out the truth sooner or later. Why don't we start with you?"

If looks could kill he would have shredded me with those razor-sharp eyes. "You don't understand," he said. "None of this."

"So enlighten me," I challenged him. "Tell me what I don't understand. Remember: you brought it up in the first place."

He knew I was right and he turned his head away again. I had been standing in the glare of the glass slider, but now I edged over and lowered myself into the chair beside his bed. "What do you gain by keeping silent?" I pressed him. "Like you said, this might be your last Saturday."

"It's not *my* Saturdays I'm thinking of," he growled through a wad of bedcovers. "Never has been. When I saw you the other day, after all those years…well, I should have just kept my goddamned mouth shut."

"Too late for that, Dad. Just tell me what you've been hiding all these years. Before—"

"Before I go down for the count?"

"I can think of some Hallmark words that might be more comforting, but yes. Before you run out of Saturdays."

He studied me with those dark eyes that had made my mother swoon and voters eagerly mark his name on the ballot. "I heard you pounding away on a computer out there," he said, tipping his head in the direction of the living room. "Do we have internet in this place?"

"High speed Wi-Fi."

"So put it to use. If you're so fucking interested in Jimmy Holland, he shouldn't be too hard to find."

"Then what?" I asked him.

"You'll have to figure that one out without me," my father said with a deep, throaty rattle. "Just keep your eyes open, and remember:

the past is never as far behind you as it seems."

CHAPTER 13

He was right—Jimmy Holland wasn't difficult to find.

It helped that there weren't any athletes or other erstwhile celebrities that shared the name. In fact, the Jimmy Holland I was looking for was the top hit on Google, despite the fact that it referenced an incident that happened more than thirty years ago. *Thirty years,* which seemed to be an increasingly common thread here. It linked to an article from *The State*, a daily Columbia newspaper that's been around since the 1890s and whose co-founder—in true South Carolina style—was gunned down by the then-Lieutenant Governor.

The story I was looking at was published almost one hundred years after that, in the summer of 1989. July 17th, to be precise.

Wolfton Teenager Was Likely Dragged To Death

State Law Enforcement Division officials confirmed that a young man, whose remains were found alongside State Road S 38-60 Saturday, likely had been dragged behind a vehicle before he died.

Jimmy Holland, 16, was pronounced dead after a resident in the area discovered his partial body lying in a patch of brambles clogging a run-off trench. Authorities said the remains found at the scene included the victim's torso and both legs; additional parts of the young man's body were subsequently

> discovered in a ditch at the side of the road. Investigators and the Orangeburg County Medical Examiner reported there was significant evidence to suggest that a rope had been used to tie Holland to a vehicle, which then dragged him along the paved road for at least a mile. Officials say they have identified no suspects or witnesses at this time, and are asking anyone who has any information about the incident to step forward. An anonymous telephone tip line has been established so informants may call without having their identity revealed.
>
> Because Jimmy Holland is African American, authorities believe his murder may have been a racially motivated hate crime.

Damn. This was not at all what I expected, although I suppose I didn't have a clue what I might actually find when I started flipping rocks. Certainly not a story about a black kid who'd been murdered in such a heinous and cruel way, tied to a bumper and then dragged to his death by a bunch of shit-kicking rednecks joyriding along a Carolina highway. I presumed more than one was involved because, in my experience, cowards always traveled in packs.

The story went on to provide some background on Jimmy Holland, who was going to be a senior at North High School in Orangeburg. He was the second youngest of four children; his father was a plumber and his mother worked in a day care center after school. Jimmy was known as the local fix-it kid who was always tinkering with small engines and building electronic gadgets. Sometimes he would help his father unclog pipes on weekends, and he was known to the women at the day care center as a bright, fun, easy-going kid who eagerly helped out whenever he was asked. Following high school he was planning to attend South Carolina State University, a four-year historically black college, where he could pursue his interest in mechanical engineering. A relative quoted in the story said the kid actually had his eye on Clemson, but family finances made that dream unattainable.

On the morning of July 15th, Holland and his cousin, Darnell

Davis, had planned on going fishing at a place called John Smith's Pond. Darnell told police that Jimmy never showed up, which he thought was strange because Jimmy had visited the Davis' mobile home on numerous occasions and had never gotten lost. No, he didn't call the police because his parents didn't have a phone.

Subsequent articles pieced together additional parts of the monstrous crime. By Tuesday a story was floating around town that Jimmy had been seen walking with a white girl, maybe even holding hands, and the rumor was that he'd been punished accordingly. Wolfton was in the heart of the South Carolina midlands, where races did not mix, and this was doubly true for black males and white girls. In fact, Orangeburg had a long and rather dark history of racism that dated long before the Civil War, and state laws had institutionalized the intolerance and bigotry over the years. When local black residents demanded full integration of the city's schools in the 1960s, the white power elite took matters into their own hands by firing them and booting them out of their rented homes. In 1968, a group of blacks protested the segregation of a local bowling alley, whereupon local police descended on the scene and opened fire—killing three of the protesters and wounding twenty-seven others. All nine officers involved in the fatal shooting were acquitted, claiming the demonstrators—none of whom was found to be armed—shot at them first. In a system where white justice prevailed, no one was surprised.

Eventually an anonymous witness to the death of Jimmy Holland came forward and tried to set the record straight. He had been driving along the same state road where Jimmy had been found, and claimed to have seen the young man strolling along, talking to the white girl who seemed to be about his age. The witness had not seen them holding hands, just talking, but he had only observed them for a second or two because just then a red pick-up of undetermined make and model raced past. The anonymous witness watched in his rearview mirror as the truck skidded to a stop, and several people piled out. By now he was at too great a distance to see them very well, but he believed they were white. He had considered stopping, and had slowed down before realizing it was none of his business, and he wanted to keep it that way.

The identity of the white girl was never learned, and she never came forward with any details. It was speculated that she may have left the state or had gone into hiding, or may have even been tracked down and killed by Holland's attackers. SLED investigators scoured the county for red pick-up trucks, which were a dime a dozen on the dusty back roads of South Carolina. No suspects were ever named, and Jimmy Holland was buried in the Orangeburg Cemetery following his funeral at the Williams Chapel A.M.E. church.

A loud blast out on the water suddenly jolted me from my laptop. A large container ship was edging up to the dock at the port just a hundred yards upriver, and I sat back in my chair and watched it maneuver alongside the quay. I checked my watch and found I'd been lost in the internet for close to an hour. I'd learned just about all there was to know about Jimmy Holland as well as the Orangeburg Massacre of '68, which I'd heard of but was never taught in school. It had occurred before I'd been born, and in the land of Dixie that was as good a reason as any to leave it out of the history books. Any scurrilous truths of the past were thoroughly scrubbed of treachery and sin, then whitewashed with ignorance and deceit.

When I'd asked Herman Stump about the mystery witness at my father's trial he had pointed me in the direction of Jimmy Holland. He did not say why, and now I could only guess. The truth had to fall somewhere within the young man's fate and the events that had transpired on that horrific summer day in 1989. He'd been in the wrong place at the wrong time, and had run up against a pack of rabid, racist shitkickers consumed with hatred and self-loathing. I tried not to imagine the torment the poor kid had suffered during the ghastly torture that had ended his life, and I felt my blood steam as I thought that whoever had been in that truck had spent the next three decades gloating about how they'd gotten away with murder.

Despite the thick summer heat, I walked out onto the balcony and tried to erase the images from my mind. I studied the ship piled high with steel containers, goods from all over the world. Some of them were bound for stores and factories across the South, while others would continue on, maybe through the Panama Canal and into the Pacific. Global commerce in action.

The distraction worked for only so long. My mind kept drifting back to my father, who was lying in bed just a few feet from me. What did he know about Jimmy Holland, and how was that incident connected to his trial? How could the racially motivated death of a black kid one hundred miles upstate have any bearing on whether my old man was convicted or found not guilty? Henry Stump had drawn a straight line from the rumored mystery witness to Holland's agonizing death, so there had to be a link.

I went back inside and pushed the bedroom door open, just a few inches. I watched my father from a distance, his withered body totally without complexion, like a recently shed snakeskin. His weary face was discolored by bruises that were the color of dried prunes, and his mouth hung open like a carnivorous plant waiting for its prey. I felt like shaking him awake, demanding that he emerge from the shell of silence in which he'd hidden for thirty years. Tell the truth, or at least whatever version of it he might recall.

But that was not going to happen. If the humiliation of prison hadn't been enough to break his spirit, why would he crack now? As much as it pained me to think, he most likely was going to take his bleak secrets to his grave.

As I gently closed his door I remembered what Benita had told me yesterday. She'd been passed the handwritten note by a white guy who smoked and drank and drove a black truck. Who the hell was this dirt bag, and how had he come to know the whereabouts of my father? The number of people in South Carolina who even knew Frank Devlin had been paroled could be counted on one hand. Not even his caregivers—Benita included—had been told the true identity of their patient. For all they knew he was just an old man who had moved into his son's high-rise condo until he transitioned from one plane to the next.

For some reason my brain drifted to Judge Carter. I knew he'd passed away a couple years after my father was convicted, but other than that he remained an enigma. Until today I'd never had a reason to even think about the man, but now he seemed to take on a new stature—at least in my mind.

His background was a little more difficult to trace than Jimmy Holland's. For starters, I couldn't remember his first name, although Lily Elliott had mentioned it to me. I quickly learned there had been more than two dozen judges named Carter in South Carolina just in the past one hundred years. Not to mention a former U.S. president from Georgia, who dominated most of the first ten search pages.

Eventually I found him. Circuit Court Judge Ernest Carter had presided over South Carolina v. Frank Devlin in 1990, and had served a total of twelve years on the bench before he was struck and killed by a vehicle while crossing Rutledge Avenue in Charleston. The accident had happened just three days before Christmas in 1992, and the driver who struck him was never found. Nor was the vehicle, although tire racks and paint chips on the judge's body suggested it was a blue, late-model Chevy Silverado pick-up. At least one headlight had been broken upon impact, and a piece of chrome trim was found a hundred yards further up the street. Investigators said that skid marks indicated the truck had been travelling at around forty miles an hour, and apparently had braked before suddenly speeding off.

Because the victim was a sitting judge, extra effort was taken in trying to track down the truck and its driver. Body shops all over the state, as well as in coastal Georgia and North Carolina, were contacted repeatedly, but no one reported any repair work that matched the damaged Silverado. No abandoned pick-ups were found in swamps or rivers, and the few calls that were received about vehicles in barns or old garages turned out to be errant leads. Whoever had run down Judge Carter was never found, and the investigation eventually turned ice cold.

Many of the references speculated whether the judge's death was accidental or intentional. He had presided over a number of criminal cases—my father's included—and it was not much of a stretch to suspect that someone had killed him out of retribution or revenge. Carter may even have had a trial in the works and the killer wanted to silence him before it ever got underway.

I was in the middle of reading a rather uninteresting ruling Judge Carter had issued when my phone rang. The screen told me it was my daughter, so I stopped what I was doing and answered it on the first ring.

"Hi Addie, what's up?" I asked her.

"Dad…I…I'm sorry for calling you, but…well, Mom died!"

"What? Mom died? Slow down. What are you talking about?"

"Well, not *died*, died. I mean…I guess she did, but the guys in the ambulance revived her. They used something called Naloxone, I think. Still, her heart stopped and everything, and now she's on her way to the hospital."

Naloxone. That meant opioid overdose, and with Belinda that meant heroin. This was the last thing my daughter needed. Me, too, but I could deal with it. Adeline, I wasn't so sure. Not after last time.

"Sweetie, please…calm down and tell me what happened."

"You know what happened," Addie said, her voice shaky and clogged with tears of panic. "She said she was clean, except for the gin, which she was never going to stop. But then…well, I was just heading out for the lunch shift and found her in the kitchen. *The needle was still in her arm!*"

If I wasn't on the opposite coast away and if Belinda wasn't already on the brink of death I would have strangled her on the spot.

"You called 9-1-1?"

"She was *blue*, Dad. *Blue!*"

I could tell Addie was on an emotional ledge, ready to fall, and I couldn't let that happen. Not with me here and her there. I had a thousand questions, but almost all of them were going to have to wait. Still, I needed information, so I said, "Do you know where they're taking her?"

"Yes," she replied, and she gave me the name of a hospital two freeway exits away from where she lived.

"Where's Carl?" Carl was Belinda's husband, the one who had saved me from the alimony work farm. He and Addie tolerated each other, but he was a second unit TV director and a narcissist, and had little time for a blended family.

"He's up in Seattle on a shoot," she said.

Damn. "Okay. Here's what we're going to do," I said. "I'm going to call Pam Thayer, remember her? She's just a couple minutes from you, and she's going to go right to your house. I want you to stay there until she arrives, okay?"

"I need to be with Mom," Addie said. "And what if Pam doesn't answer? What if she's moved?" There was a pause, and then she added, "What if Mom doesn't make it?"

"One thing at a time, sweetie. Let me call Pam, and then I'll call you right back."

She didn't want to hang up, so I told her to stay on the line while I put her on hold. Pam was a woman I had dated for a while a couple years ago, but the flame that had burned between us had gone out after fire season ended. At least, that's how she put it when she broke the news to me. In any event, we'd remained friends—the kind without benefits—and now I needed her more than ever before.

Pam was outside pruning a lemon tree and agreed to drop everything and head right over. I managed to connect her into a three-way call with Addie, and I could sense my daughter was breathing easier already.

"Addie, you need to listen to me," I said. "Your mother is very sick, and the hospital is not going to release her right away. Not tonight. Not for a few days, in fact. She needs help, the kind of help you can't give her."

"But—"

"No buts, sweetie. Now, this is what we're going to do, and there's no debating it."

Ten minutes later I'd booked her a seat on the next flight out of LAX, a red-eye that left at ten-ten that evening and arrived in Charleston tomorrow morning at nine-thirty. I had hoped there might be something that got in late that same night, but the three-hour time difference meant I was shit out of luck. I hated to put my daughter on an overnight flight that would only drag out her worry and fear, but I had no choice.

Addie did her best to protest, but I also sensed relief in her voice. She made noises about not being able to leave her job, the house needed tending to, and she had no way to get to the airport. But Pam took care of all the details, and assured me Addie would be on that plane. There was one stop, in Charlotte, but my daughter had flown by herself before so I knew she could handle the layover.

When I hung up I realized I was shaking. Not because my ex-wife had almost died—for all I knew, she still might not make it—but because I'd been absent during the worst crisis of my daughter's young life. I kept picturing Belinda's sorry, blood-shot eyes and her track marks and thinking *bitch*, over and over again. I closed my eyes and drew in a few deep breaths. My heart rate eased, and I felt my muscles relax. I would get through this. *We* would get through this.

I took one more deep breath, and that's when the doorbell rang. I'd watched enough B-grade thrillers—including my ex-wife's horror trilogy—not to put my eye to the peephole, so as I approached the door I called out, "Who is it?"

"Home health agency," came the reply. "My name is Alicia Hernandez."

Great…another Latina for my father to harass, I thought. Still, my tension level dropped appreciably, and I quickly unlatched the deadbolt.

"Please forgive my caution," I told her as I waved her inside. "The sign out front says 'No Solicitors,' but they keep showing up."

"No one reads anymore," the young woman said with a thin smile. She was short, smooth complexion the color of a mocha latte, very pretty in a J-Lo sort of way, but younger. "It's mostly Jehovah's Witnesses and roofing scams where I live."

We shook hands and then she asked about my father. She apparently had been fed the standard line about him being from upstate, near Rock Hill, and that I'd brought him down to my home in Charleston for his final days.

"How's his appetite?" she asked me.

"He stopped eating several days ago," I explained. "His body has begun shutting down."

She nodded at that, as if it made total sense. "Do you mind if I go in to see him?"

"I'm told that's why they pay you the big bucks."

That brought another grin, and then she said, "Show me the way."

I led her to the door that opened off the living room, and gently pushed it open. My father still seemed to be out like a light, so I whispered, "He seems to sleep pretty deep, so it may take a bit to wake him up."

"I'll be gentle," she assured me.

Without another word she went inside, and I quietly closed the door behind her. Then I took out my phone and thumbed a text to my daughter:

`It's all going to be fine. You'll like this place. And you'll finally get to meet your grandfather.`

Half a minute later I received a return text, which eased my mind a bit.

`Just heard from the docs. Mom's hanging in there. Can't wait to see you. Do they drink coffee there, or is it all mint juleps?`

To which I replied:

`Coffee and sweet tea and shrimp with cheesy grits. Plus pulled pork and ribs and chicken waffles.`

Addie had become a vegetarian last fall, just before Thanksgiving, so I knew what her response was going to be.

`Yuck. No cooked animal flesh for me.`

We texted back and forth a few more times. I echoed her sense of relief that Belinda wasn't going to die, then talked up all the fine things about Charleston that I barely remembered. I told her I was looking forward to going to restaurants and the beach and maybe paddle boarding, and she slowly seemed to actually turn this trip into a mini-vacation rather than an escape from the home where her mother had almost died. She sent me one last text that read "`TTYL`," followed by a bunch of brightly colored emoji hearts.

Crisis averted.

I couldn't sink myself back into the internet, not just then. And I didn't even have a chance, because two minutes later Alicia Hernandez came back out of my father's room. I had wandered into the kitchen to grab a beer, so I only half-heard her say, "Mr. Devlin, sir. Can you come here, please?"

I casually wandered back out into the living room, my brain already going through the deposition in which I would make it clear that Belinda was no longer fit to have custody of our daughter. Cold-hearted, considering the timing, but my daughter deserved better. I wasn't looking at Alicia's face, but when I finally glanced up I could read it in her eyes. They were open wide, dark pupils staring at me, and she seemed to be trembling. I knew what she was about to tell me, but still I had to ask.

"What is it?"

"Mr. Rick, sir…I was going to give Mr. Devlin a sponge bath," she began, a shiver in her voice. "I'm pretty good at them even if the patient is asleep, but, well…. Sir, I hate to tell you this, but I think he's with the angels."

I stared at her dumbly, and the first words to come out of my mind through my mouth were, "Angels? What are you talking about?"

"Mr. Devlin, sir. I've been doing this a long time, so what I mean is, your father is dead."

CHAPTER 14

Jenkins IV had given me a private number to call when my father died. The man who answered was extremely professional, reverential even, and when I explained why I was calling said he would take care of everything. He expressed his deepest sympathy for my loss, informed me that his thoughts and prayers would be with my family in this time of need, and then hung up.

"You want me to wait around?" Alicia asked when I ended the call. She sounded shaken and contrite, even though my father's death clearly was not her fault. "At least until they get here?"

I wasn't sure who *they* might be. Certainly not EMTs; it was clear that my father was beyond resuscitation. In fact, I didn't really know who might be coming, or what they would do when they arrived.

"No, I can take care of things from here," I assured her. "I know what to do."

She balked for a second, then gave me a look of genuine relief. She didn't want to be here any more than I did, but at least she had a choice. "Thank you, sir. I am so sorry for your loss—"

"I appreciate that, and I want you to know it wasn't your fault," I assured her. "We all knew his condition was terminal; we just didn't know when his last day would be."

She gave me a quick hug and a smile, then turned and was out the front door before I could change my mind.

My next call went to Jenkins IV, who simply said, "Well, that didn't take long. At least he didn't suffer."

"After thirty years of hell he finally found some peace," I agreed. *Not without some verbal ballistics at the end,* I added in my mind.

We talked about funeral arrangements, the fact that my father had insisted on being cremated and then having his ashes scattered in Charleston Harbor. This wasn't exactly legal and was frowned upon by environmentalists and government agencies, but red tape can always be cut for the right price.

Then Jenkins reminded me, "No public service. That was a strict part of the agreement."

"Who do you think would show up?" I replied, my thoughts suddenly going to Adeline. Less than a half-hour ago I'd made her flight arrangements, telling her she would be able to meet her grandfather when she arrived. I'd always described him as a hard-assed bastard and sonofabitch, but she still sounded grateful that she'd get a chance to meet him before he died.

"I just want to make sure we're clear on this," Jenkins IV insisted.

"I have to tell my sister," I replied. "If she decides to drive down here I'm not going to stop her."

"Family is fine, but keep it low-key."

"Don't worry, Myers," I assured him. "No party, no media. Which reminds me: how long do I have to get my father's affairs in order?"

"That's no concern of yours at the moment," he said stiffly.

"What I mean is, when do I have to move out of this place?" I pushed him. "My ticket was open-ended because I didn't know exactly when I might be going home."

"The condo was rented month-to-month, so you can take your time. In fact, there's some paperwork and legal issues we'll need to finalize. Stick around a few days, see what's happened to Charleston over the years."

"What kind of legal issues?" I asked, not liking the sound of that.

"Standard stuff, nothing to worry about right now."

I thought about asking him what he knew about Jimmy Holland, but didn't feel like getting into a sparring match with him. He'd either deny ever knowing the name or, more likely, tell me to leave it alone. Especially now that my father was gone. Sleeping dogs, and all that.

My next call went to Uncle Andrew. He was elated at the news, proclaiming, "Ding-dong, the sonofabitch is dead. Good to finally be rid of the old bastard."

It seemed a little early to be dancing on his grave, especially now that I had a somewhat good reason to think he may not have been guilty of the crime for which he'd been convicted. At least not in the manner everyone had previously thought.

"We should probably postpone getting together tomorrow," I suggested.

"Why the fuck should we do that? Now we got something to hoist a glass to."

I didn't mention that I'd have Addie with me, the niece he'd never seen. He'd only come out west once, when Belinda and I had tied the knot, but I'd sent him pictures of my daughter almost every Christmas. All of a sudden I realized that, without my father around and no memorial service to plan, my days were totally freed up.

"See you at Ten Pin Alley, then? Three o'clock."

"Wouldn't miss it for the world, son."

For the next call I knew I needed medicinal fortification. I went into the kitchen and grabbed a beer, which I carried out onto the balcony. The afternoon was still a scorcher, but I needed the ripples of subtropical steam and the ice-cold buttress of alcohol to ease the apprehension I felt building inside. I wished there was something a little more potent in the condo, but no good would have come of it. Especially with my daughter arriving in the morning.

Even though I rarely called my sister, I had her number in my contacts. I scrolled through the list and punched it before I could have second thoughts. She had known I was coming to Charleston to supervise our father's dying, and had made it clear at the time that she wanted absolutely nothing to do with the deal. She'd wished me well in my endeavor, and had asked me to let her know when the death vigil was over.

"Ricky," she said when she finally answered, letting out a breath of silence before continuing. "Since I never hear from you, I assume this is the call I've been expecting?"

"It is," I told her. "Dad passed away in his sleep about an hour ago. He doesn't appear to have suffered."

She said nothing for a long time after that, finally muttering, "I don't know what I'm supposed to feel."

"Join the club."

I thought I'd be hit with a wave of relief when he died, a sense of welcome liberation from the persistent truth of the last thirty years. Our lives had been irreparably shattered by the events that transpired that horrific night, like a vase that's been dropped on a tile floor. The pieces could never be collected and glued back together, but at least the last shards of the mess now could be swept away. I could relate to what my sister meant about not knowing what to feel, but I couldn't help sense that so much of the bitterness and resentment I'd harbored for so long had all been a waste.

"You think I should come there?" my sister asked. She lived outside Atlanta, or at least she did the last time I'd mailed her something. She moved around a lot, never being able to hold down a job and always seeming to be one step ahead of the demons that seemed to guide her wildly fluctuating moods.

"There's plenty of room here in the condo," I told her, instantly realizing the trap I was setting for myself and Addie.

"I'll let you know tomorrow," my sister said. "I have to see what my star chart says."

"I'll be around," I told her.

She didn't reply, not at first, and I could hear her breathing on the other end. Then she said, "He's really gone?"

"As gone as it gets," I assured her.

"Maybe finally this'll all go away for good."

I didn't know what she meant by that, but I didn't press her. We all process things in different ways, and Karen had taken the hard route, through the dark tunnels of a troubled mind. I'd suffered my own addictions but had emerged in relatively one piece, give or take a momentary lapse or two. I could not say the same for my sister.

"Let me know what you decide," I told her. "It would be good to see you."

The representative from the pre-paid crematorium arrived not long after that. He was a pale, lanky man, dressed in black trousers and a black polo shirt. He looked like a priest without the collar, and moved with quiet reverence as he went about his business. He showed me papers that said he was authorized to proclaim a body dead, which he did in a very perfunctory and routine manner. No postmortem was necessary; that had been stipulated by the parole board. He had a sheaf of forms for me to sign, and then he and a colleague—also dressed in black—lifted my father onto a wheeled gurney. Since there wasn't going to be a church funeral or formal viewing I realized this would be my last chance to see him.

"Wait a second," I told the man who was running the show.

I approached the gurney solemnly and stared down at my father. I tried to find some serenity in his face, a hint of everlasting peace now that his life had ended and his personal torment was over. Whether he deserved it or not, thirty years in a concrete tomb filled with violent hard-timers was not the way he'd envisioned spending the last years of his life, especially if it turned out to be for something he didn't do. The jury had proclaimed its judgment, but reality sometimes has a way of burying its difficult truths forever. This very well could be one of those times.

I bent over and slipped my hands under his tired body and hugged him to me. He'd taught me so many things as a child, things I would never forget and would hold close for the rest of my life. It was all borne out of an absolute love that bind parents with their children, something I came to know only when my own daughter was born. There's an inevitable growth in consciousness from infancy to adulthood that changes how we relate to our parents, but until four days ago I'd never had the chance to speak one word with him since the trial, when I was eighteen. I'd missed the opportunity to relate to him as an adult, and now I felt an emptiness that I knew could never be filled. Still, this man had given me my life, and as I held him I realized that when I let him go it would be for the last time.

Once the men in black had rolled my father out of the condo I found myself overcome with a vast sense of calm. In an odd way it reminded me of whenever I turned in a final draft of a book, or handed the ball to my pitching coach in the late innings of a game. I had done all I could and he was now out of my hands, hopefully in a far better place. Ashes to ashes, dust to dust. I suspected a wave of grief would wash up around me at some point, but at the moment I just felt as if the tide was out.

I sat on the balcony without moving for a few minutes, my mind a collage of memories both past and present. Bouncing and giggling on my father's knee when I was three years old. Sitting on the living room floor Christmas morning, assembling a wooden train set in a figure-eight pattern. Playing catch with him on a Saturday afternoon, hurling my fastball into his weathered and heavily padded glove. Gripping the wheel of the old Vista Cruiser for the first time while he sat beside me in the passenger seat, talking me through every cringe worthy turn.

Then: walking into the kitchen that night and finding him passed out in a pool of my mother's blood. And eight months later, hearing the jury foreman state, firmly and unequivocally, "We find the defendant guilty of murder in the first degree."

There seemed to be so much to take care of, but actually there was very little. We come into this life with nothing, and essentially we leave it the same way. My father's life had been downsized tremendously, and every item he owned could be stuffed into a bag from the grocery store. I know, because that's what I did. It struck me that I could ignore Jenkins IV and be on the first flight home if I wanted to, and for a second I thought about calling Addie and telling her to stay put. She could spend the night at Pam's, and I'd be home tomorrow to get her. Then I realized she needed a break from her routine, some time to chill and process her mother's condition. Besides, my father had left behind some truths that had outlasted him, and I still felt an unyielding urge to learn what they might be.

There was unfinished business to settle.

I spent the rest of the afternoon getting the condo ready for my daughter. The hospice folks were amazingly efficient, arriving less than an hour after my father left. They seemed to understand how important it was to clear away the detritus of death, and were in and out of the place in under thirty minutes. Once they were done I re-assembled the original bed and moved my things in, then tidied up the spare bedroom. I found a set of clean sheets and made up Addie's bed, cleaned the bathroom, and opened the glass slider to trade the stale air for the freshness of Charleston.

A few minutes before five I switched from beer to wine, a glass of which I carried out to the balcony. The humid mantle of summer had settled in, and the air was thick and moist. Fortunately, a trace of a breeze was coming in off the water from the east, making the approaching evening just bearable. I settled into a chair and propped my feet up on the rail, watching the tourist boats chugging in from

Fort Sumter. Closer in, the cranes along the busy waterfront had already begun to offload the massive containers that held everything from pre-wired dashboard assemblies for the BMW plant upstate to bulging bales of dog food.

No sooner had I lifted my glass to my lips than my phone rang. It was Laurie, whose number I had entered into my contacts after our evening at Swampie's.

"I've got to get out of this madhouse," she said, her voice sounding as if she were at her wits' end. "Let's grab dinner somewhere."

"Rough day at work?" I asked her as I watched an airplane bank over the harbor on its way into the airport.

"Never, ever get into the food-and-bev business," she said. "It's the most thankless endeavor invented by man. But enough about me...how has your day been?"

Other than my father dying, my ex-wife overdosing on heroin, and my daughter boarding a plane in a couple hours, pretty much a typical Saturday. I didn't say that, of course; talk about killing the mood. Instead I said, "Let's back up a bit," ignoring her question. "Were you serious about dinner?"

"Dinner, margaritas, plunging an oyster knife between my ribs—anything."

"Drama queen. What do you have in mind?"

"I can take it here for about another hour," she replied. "Tell you what...are you home?"

"Sitting out on the balcony as we speak," I told her.

"Do you think your father would mind if I came to your place and cooked dinner?"

"I don't think he'll say a word," I assured her. No need for details; not yet.

"You're in that big high rise off East Bay, right?"

"Near the aquarium." I gave her the unit number, then said, "I have plenty of wine, both red and white. Anything else you want me to pick up?"

"Just me, after the day I've had," Laurie replied. "I hate Saturdays. See you in a bit."

It was well past seven by the time she arrived. I didn't mind; in fact, I needed time to decompress and rid myself of three decades of emotional debris. I had flown east to Charleston less than a week ago with a deep-rooted antipathy in my heart. I suppose if I were more of a merciful man I would have forgiven him years ago, but that voice of absolution had yet to speak to my soul. Now he was gone, and the darkness I had always associated with him seemed to have evaporated like a shimmer of water on a steamy summer's day. On top of that, there was every reason to think that he'd been responsible for none of this.

I felt it was my obligation to learn the truth, one way or the other, once and for all.

Laurie came armed with all the fixings for shrimp linguine with parmesan cream sauce and a salad, straight from the menu at Jake's On The Creek. She'd even brought tiramisu, even though I was sure I wouldn't have enough room once we'd finished the main course. She hauled it all through the front door in two sturdy reusable grocery bags, which she deposited on the granite counter in the kitchen.

Then she said, "Do you think your father would mind if I tell him a quick 'hello'? Despite all that happened back then, he was always very nice to me."

"That's going to be a little problematic," I told her. She was dressed in embroidered jeans and a white button-down shirt that was tied in a knot a few inches above her navel.

"If he's taking a nap I can wait," she said. "I wouldn't want to wake him."

"No chance of that," I said, almost too glib, and then explained what had happened.

"You mean…he's dead?" she gasped.

"Passed away this afternoon."

Her eyes had turned into big, wide orbs, and she said, "He's not still here—?"

"No, they picked him up a few hours ago."

"You should have told me, Rick. Your father just died, and here I was, inviting myself over to cook dinner for you."

"I didn't have plans," I told her. "And you're a far sight better than whatever the alternative might have been."

"Is that meant to be a compliment?"

"I'm all out of witty repartee," I said with a tired sigh. "And I guess the truth hasn't really set in yet."

"You're sure you're up for this?"

"The fact is, I can't think of anyone I'd rather spend the evening with," I assured her.

She shot me a glance, not sure if I was talking about dinner or whatever might follow. She fell silent for a minute, then said, "Me, too. Just tell me if there's anything else I should know before I start making a mess of your kitchen."

"Well, my daughter's arriving on the red-eye in the morning."

Laurie stopped unloading her grocery bags and braced her hands on the counter. "To pay her respects to your father? Damn, you work fast—"

"Actually, I booked the ticket before I knew he was dead. Her mother OD'd this morning, so she's coming to spend some time with me while I wrap things up here."

"OD'd, as in dead?"

"Not quite, but it's serious. Addie—she's my daughter—she found her."

"Jesus," Laurie said, letting out a short breath. "And I thought *I* had a bad day. Is that it? Any more surprises?"

"That's it for now, but don't look in the coat closet."

"What?"

"Humor," I told her as I placed two bottles of wine on the counter. "Red or white?"

"Right now I need two of each." She glanced at the two bottles, then said, "But I'll start with the Chardonnay."

Back when we were kids there always seemed to be an urgency whenever Laurie and I got together. It was as if there was a reverse bucket list that caused us to rush into things, both of us anxious to get a lot of firsts out of the way. First time we held hands, first time we kissed, first time we fooled around. Nothing ever seemed slow and measured. We were two young people cursed by glands and hormones and carnal urges, and we fumbled our way through our days and nights as if the world was new and had never been experienced by anyone else in human history. We were impetuous and impulsive, which more than once took me to the very precipice of her parents' wrath. Twice I'd had to slip out her second-floor window, shimmy down the metal roof, and then gingerly let myself down to the front porch railing. Both times the risk of a broken arm far outweighed the consequences of her father blowing my head off with the shotgun I knew he kept behind the water heater.

Not so tonight. Laurie took her time making the linguini sauce and boiling the water for the pasta, while I tore the romaine lettuce into bite-sized pieces. There was no physical touching but plenty of conversation, probably the first time we had actually discussed anything other than my pitching, her cheerleading, Mr. Givens' biology class, and who had slashed the tires on the principal's Volvo. Until tonight I had never known that Laurie had an older brother who died from a fall when she was three, or that her mother had been married once before, in a quickie Las Vegas wedding. A lot of water had spilled over the dam since then, and we covered that, too. Peace marches in Washington, a progression of boyfriends in college, and falling in love with the man of her dreams who now had become her worst nightmare.

When my turn came I told her about how my love affair with booze had continued to grip me through college and into my professional life. Half the time I was on the mound I was high on something, self-destructing just sixty feet and six inches from home plate. I'd conveniently blamed it all on my family dynamics, with my mother dead and my father in jail. Not one of my teammates had the cojones to call me out; maybe they understood something I didn't, or maybe my plight wasn't that far from their own personal paths.

I told her about my downward spiral with booze and drugs, which was almost a cliché in the majors. The elbow surgery had tugged me into hardcore drugs, OxyContin and oxycodone and other opiates. I'd drawn the line at needles, but everything else was fair game and a welcome relief to my daily drudgery. Then I met Belinda, and things only got worse.

"What cheerful conversation for a first date," Laurie observed as she stirred the cream sauce. Slowly, like everything else tonight.

"We're way past our first date," I reminded her. "Just making up for lost time."

"Tell you what," she said. "Let's turn this around. You say one positive thing—anything that comes to mind—and I'll do the same. Deal?"

I nodded, then considered her challenge. At this point in my life it was easy to focus on a string of negatives, but without thinking I said, "Addie. My daughter."

"Okay, that works," she said, encouraging me. "Tell me something positive about her."

So I did, beginning with the day she was born in the back seat of my first Eldorado in a traffic jam on the San Diego Freeway. I described her smile and the absolute confidence she had in herself and a crowded city that others found dismal and bleak. "'Smile, breathe, and go slowly,' is one of her favorite sayings," I said, as Laurie poured more wine into both of our glasses. "Right along with 'I will never stop dreaming, I cannot predict the future, and all I have to learn already resides within me.' "

That got us to talking about her own children, a conversation we carried to the table. By now the summer sun was kissing the western horizon, casting soft hues of pink and purple and orange against the soft underbellies of a few passing clouds. We sat at the corners of the table so we both could experience the approaching evening, lights blinking on all over Charleston and in the boats scattered on the dark water.

As we ate I felt an unspoken temptation lurking in the room, a tacit sense that we both were enjoying this meal more than we'd expected to and eventually a decision might have to be made. Not now, not until dinner was over and the tiramisu had been served, and maybe one more glass of wine was consumed. But that decision was coming, and it seemed both of us were putting it off as long as we could.

"Did you think about what I said the other night?" Laurie asked me at one point, adeptly changing the subject to something more neutral. "About the no-show witness, I mean."

I was both disappointed and relieved at the shift in discussion. "I've done a little digging," I told her. "I'm not sure where it might lead."

"Any idea who it was?"

I shook my head and scooped the last bite of dessert onto my fork. "It may be connected to something that wasn't even part of the case," I told her. The less she knew the better.

"And now that your father's gone...what happens next?"

"You mean, when am I going home?"

"Yeah, that." Letting it hang there.

"I've never liked loose ends," I told her. "I get the feeling there's a bit more dirt where I've been digging. And besides, like I said, Addie arrives tomorrow. I'd like to show her a few things about my hometown before we turn around and go west again."

"I'd like to meet her," Laurie said. "I think I'd like her."

"I have no doubt you will," I replied.

What happened after that involved no fumbling, no rushed moves. No slipping out of second-floor dormer windows in the dark of night, no sand on beach blankets in the dark. No mad dash to the finish line, no groping. Well, some of that for sure, but instead of being frantic and rushed we fell into a rhythmic cadence, maybe even musical.

There's a reason we slow down as we grow older, and never was that truer than the next hour. Two, was more like it. Our anxious searching of youth had evolved into a fine dance of aged confidence, both of us more self-assured and relaxed in our desire to give, as well as to receive. Details are neither necessary nor appropriate, other than to say we both made up for lost time.

And then some.

CHAPTER 15

Laurie left a little after midnight. It was a decision she suggested and I agreed with, not just because I was picking up my daughter from a long overnight flight in just a few hours, but because she still had teenagers at home. Saturday had faded into Sunday, and the Bible Belt was tightly cinched around the weighty concepts of church, sin, and family values. It would not look good for her to roll in at dawn's early light after a night of carousing, especially since she was going through a divorce that no doubt would get messy.

I left for the airport almost an hour before Addie was due to land. It was a bit of overkill, since it was only a twenty-minute drive, but I wanted to make sure I was standing there when she came through the security gate. She was a veteran traveler but I knew she was distraught about leaving her mom in the hospital, even though she needed to disconnect from all the drama. She had called me around midnight, right after Laurie left, heaping a ton of guilt on herself for phoning me so late. She was totally convinced she was doing the wrong thing by leaving at a moment of crisis and coming east to see me. I spent the next half-hour assuring her that her mother was getting the help she badly needed, and it wasn't Addie's job to take care of her. I eventually talked her out of her panic. She calmed down, and after we hung up she texted me a full row of heart emojis. She was too young for this sort of shit, and I wasn't ready to forgive Belinda for the melodrama. My advice: never marry an actress.

As focused as I was on my daughter, I still noticed the black truck in my rearview mirror as soon as I pulled out of the condo's first-floor garage. It was parked in the shade of a magnolia tree, and as soon as I edged out onto the empty street, it moved away from the curb and fell in behind me. I probably wouldn't have noticed it except that traffic is quiet on Sunday mornings, at least until church lets out and everyone heads for the beach, their boats, or a bar.

The truck hung back about a hundred yards, but it was still easy to spot. We don't have as many pick-ups per capita in California as in South Carolina, but I'd grown up around them. I know the difference between an F-150 extended bed and a GMC 3500 dually, and I knew this one was a Ram 1500 quad. South Carolina law doesn't require a front license plate so I couldn't get the tag numbers, but I wasn't concerned. Whoever was behind the wheel was going to make it easy for me sooner or later.

He followed me up East Bay Street and onto the I-26 interchange. When I hit the exit that transferred me to the 526 loop he followed right behind, and we both took the off-ramp for International Boulevard. When I turned right, toward the airport, he waited a few seconds and then made the same turn. He trailed back—still hovering at the same distance—as we passed the massive Boeing plant, where the 787 Dreamliners are assembled. As I neared the airport I passed the cell phone lot, where a dozen cars were parked, their occupants passing the time until whoever they were picking up called to say they had arrived.

I pulled into the enclosed parking deck and took the corkscrew ramp up to the second level. Laurie had told me this was the best place to park for an arriving flight, and had suggested I find a space as close as possible to the far end, which was nearest to baggage claim. Sure enough, the black pick-up followed me into the parking enclosure, hanging back in the shadows while I hunted for a place to park.

The more he lurked, the more pissed I got. Whatever game this goober thought he was playing had nothing to do with Addie or me, and I was getting angrier by the second. Following me on the highway was one thing, but stalking me in a parking garage when I was about to pick up my daughter took this stunt to another level.

I hung a quick left, as if I had spotted an empty space, then gunned it to the end of the lane of parked cars and turned left again. The driver of the truck momentarily lost me as I swerved down another lane and gently eased to a stop. I could see the roof of the cab slowly moving, the driver peering through the glass to see where I might have gone. My Kia was lower than his truck, so he couldn't see me as easily as I saw him.

Eventually the black Ram 1500 turned down my lane, then braked to a stop. It sat there with its engine running, the driver evidently trying to figure out his next move. There wasn't enough room for him to pull around me, so he would have to shift into reverse and back his way out. Since there seemed to be only one way out of the garage—and I was closer to the exit—I could block him in.

In the end he laid on his horn, as if trying to get me to move. I waited a couple seconds, then threw the shifter into reverse and tapped the gas. The rental car flew backwards, shimmying on the polished concrete as I came close to ramming his front bumper. Then I stomped on the brakes, threw the transmission into park, and jumped out of the car.

"Move it, asshole," the driver yelled from the open window of the truck cab.

I ignored him as I walked the length of the truck and snapped a photo of the rear license plate with my cell phone. He screamed a string of obscenities but did not get out of the cab. Not yet, at least.

I marched back past his door and took several more pictures, one of the VIN tag affixed to where the dashboard met the windshield, and one of him, his face lit up with rage. He had stringy black hair, a heavy brow that shaded his eyes, and a day-old growth of stubble.

"What the fuck you think you're doing, asshole?" he screamed. "Move your goddamned turdmobile!"

I stepped back, anticipating what was to come next. "Who the hell are you?" I snapped back at him, clicking off another photo with my phone. "Why are you following me?"

"Give me that," he yelled as the door flew open and he charged out.

It was not my intent to start a fight, but as he jumped out of the cab I caught sight of a gun in his right hand. That jacked this up to another level, and my brain shifted from sound reason to gut instinct. He was burly but a good four inches shorter than I, which was a good thing on any day. But what this asshole didn't know was that during my days at Fresno State I had developed a wicked sidewinder designed to catch batters off guard. When I unloaded that waist-high pitch, which was a hybrid of a curve and a fastball, the ball did screwy things after it left my hand. I'd rarely used it, and when I got to the big leagues my pitching coach told me to never, *ever* throw it again. Too little control and too much showboating.

Right now, I didn't give a damn about either of those things. What mattered was the arm motion itself, which was designed to confuse the batter before the ball ever left my hand. And that's what I was counting on now as I let loose with a resounding sidearm blow that I know he didn't expect, and never saw coming.

My fist collided with his jaw, hard. A spasm of pain shot through my hand, and my wrist jammed the instant my knuckles connected with his head. But I wasn't thinking about any of that as I saw the gun fly out of his hand and clatter under a parked SUV. The force of the blow knocked him against the front fender of his truck, and he collapsed on his ass on the concrete floor of the garage. My hand was covered with blood, but most of it seemed to be from his mouth, which appeared to be missing a tooth. The entire left side of his face looked like raw steak, and he looked dazed and confused.

"You fucker—"

"Shut your face and listen to me," I snarled at him. "I don't know who sent you or what the hell you think you're doing, but it ends now. My father's dead, so whatever score you think you're trying to settle, it's done. Got it?"

"Up your ass," he growled through blood and bone. "You don't know shit what this is all about."

"I sure as hell do," I told him. "And I've got your plate, your face, and your VIN."

"You think you're so smart, lay it on me."

"Jimmy Holland," I told him, then snapped one last photo of him. It was the best one so far, his jaw hanging open wide enough to show his bloody gums and the gap in his teeth. Still, the look in his eyes left no doubt what he was thinking:

This ain't over, not by a long shot.

After that I parked my car in the outside long-term lot, one silver vehicle in a sea of thousands. I doubted he'd come looking for me, but I didn't want to take any chances. I'd thrown the first punch in a fight I didn't want, just like so many other stupid things I'd done during my darker days. On the plus side, I now had his gun, which I'd fished out from under the parked car before I drove off. As a boy growing up in the American South it was a rite of passage to shoot a gun, and Uncle Andrew had initiated me into this club when I was about twelve. He took me to his deer stand in a thick second-growth forest in the middle of nowhere, where we waited for six bone-chilling hours until a hungry buck wandered by, nibbling at a trail of deer corn. It was like shooting shrimp in a barrel, and I totally failed to understand the thrill of the hunt.

In any event, the driver of the truck clearly knew where I lived, which meant he might be back. I doubted he'd show up alone, but if he got his nerve up—reinforced by a bottle of rot gut and a few of his fellow numb-nut bubbas—it could become tricky. I hated to involve my daughter in this—*whatever this was*—but he'd forced my hand. At least that's what I kept telling myself as I ran my knuckles under cold water in the airport men's room, hoping Addie wouldn't notice the bruising. After a few minutes the swelling had subsided and my hand was feeling a lot better. I could wiggle my fingers, which told me nothing was broken. Still, I was angry at myself for landing the first blow and, in doing so, pissing in a hornet's nest.

Addie's flight arrived five minutes early, but she was seated in the back of the plane so it took her a while to disembark. She dragged herself through the exit gate, hunched over from the weight of the pack on her back, and I threw my arms around her. I didn't care if she was fifteen, or who might be watching. She was my daughter and I was damned glad to see her.

"My, how you've grown," I joked as she squeezed back. It was a line I used every time I saw her, which was just about every weekend.

"And you've lost a few more hairs," she said, her standard comeback. "You didn't tell me it would be like a sauna here."

"It's called humidity. That's how we do summer here in the South."

She had checked a bag, which took forever to come down the luggage chute. We passed the time with her telling me about the flight—"I slept most of the way"—and giving me an update on her mother—"she's resting peacefully." The doctors were very guarded about Belinda's prognosis; this wasn't her first rodeo and certainly not the first time she'd been thrown off the bull and rushed to the hospital. Even though we'd been divorced for five years and she'd remarried, I still cared about her. Misguided as she was, she was still the mother of my child. But any empathy I might have had for her had evolved into criticism, which Addie picked up on.

"Don't be too hard on her, Dad," she said. "She's pretty fucked up."

"*Language*," I warned her. She was too old for me to clean up the vocabulary she'd learned from her mother and kids at school, but I still felt it was my duty to try.

"I'm just saying you should go easy on her. She knows that shit—that *stuff*—is going to kill her if she doesn't stop. She just needs help."

"Yes, she does, and lots of it," I agreed. Last night after Addie called I spoke briefly with Carl, Belinda's husband, who was rushing home from Seattle. He was directing a second unit shoot of a new cable drama, and wasn't pleased to have to delay the production schedule. "Carl will deal with all that," I told her. "Right now, we need to think about you."

"I'm fine," she protested in an uncertain voice that told me she was trying to convince herself.

"I know you are, Addie," I assured her. "And we're going to keep it that way."

There was no one left at the baggage carousel by the time her suitcase finally tumbled down the chute, and Addie protested when I made the effort to wheel it away. "I can do this," she said. "I'm not a little girl anymore."

No, she wasn't. She had maxed out at what was probably going to be her final height, about five seven, just like her mother. Her naturally blonde hair had been feather cut to fall around her face, almost touching her shoulders, and she was dressed in a combination of Dodger-blue yoga leggings and a baggy shirt embroidered with dragonflies and lotus flowers. Her sixteenth birthday was still six weeks away but she had blossomed into a young woman that I knew drew hungry stares. Again, just like her mother.

Most of the drive back to the condo was spent talking about drug addiction and rehab centers. Addie was divided by conflicting emotions: she had a deep, abiding love for her mother, but she was exhausted by the constant upheaval involved in living with such a high maintenance woman. Yesterday's escapade was just the latest test of empathy and patience, for both of us.

"We'll call the hospital a little later to see if we can speak with her," I assured her. "It's still early out on the west coast."

Addie nodded, but I could tell she was still deeply troubled by the events of the last twenty-four hours.

Just wait until we get to the condo, I thought.

We didn't discuss my father until we were riding up in the elevator. I'd avoided the subject on the drive from the airport, and we already had enough heavy material to occupy our time. Then, just as the steel doors slid shut and we started moving upward, Addie said, "I've never met a murderer. At least, not that I know of."

"It's probably best that you don't remember your grandfather that way," I told her.

"Remember him? I've never even met him. And all you've ever said about him—when you've said anything at all—is that he was a racist sonofabitch and a cold-blooded killer."

She was right, and now I realized that she learned some of her off-color vocabulary from me. I should not have clouded my daughter's opinion of my father, nor should I have spoken that way in front of her. I'd been so hell-bent on trying to distance myself from him—after he'd distanced himself from me—that I hadn't given much thought to the impact of my words.

"Well, you still shouldn't think of him that way," I insisted. The bell rang and the doors slid open. Twelfth floor. I waited for Addie to step out, then added, "And before we go inside there's a couple things you need to know."

Addie said nothing, just turned and studied me. I knew that look, deep and intent, waiting for a shoe to drop.

"First, I have some reason to believe that your grandfather may have been wrongly convicted," I said in even, measured words.

"You mean he's *innocent*? After thirty years in jail? That's harsh!"

Harsh wasn't the word for it.

"I don't know, not for sure," I explained quickly. "I'm hoping to learn more before I can draw any real conclusion. But the other thing is…well, I didn't want to hit you with this before now—after what you went through yesterday—but…well, your grandfather passed away yesterday."

"He did what? I flew clear across the country and then we drove all the way from the airport and you didn't tell me until now?"

"We had other things to discuss. Things that involved living, breathing people whose lives are a little shaken up right now. Life or death things. But your grandfather…well, his was a death thing, and we all knew it was coming."

I led her down the hallway to the door and inserted a key in the lock. "Don't worry," I told her. "Everything is going to be fine."

"He's not still in there, is he?"

"No. The medical people came and took him away." I anticipated her next question, so I added, "And I'll be sleeping in his room. I didn't want to put you through that."

"Jeez, Dad. Thanks."

I opened the door and let it swing open so she could enter first. She did, and immediately raced over to the wall of glass. "Holy shit, this is some view."

"Addie—"

"Holy *crap*. Same meaning, different words."

George Carlin's famous routine on the seven dirty words came back to me, and I let it go. Pick your battles, pick your time. "It seems a little sterile to me from this high up," I said instead. "I prefer being a little closer to the ground."

"Like your little cabin in the trees?"

"Exactly. Give me some dirt and flowers and bees and I'll be happy as a pig in slop. Are you hungry?"

"I had a banana in Charlotte," she replied, not really an answer.

"I can make you some oatmeal," I offered. Addie had been hovering between vegetarian and vegan for the past six months and I wasn't sure which way the dietary winds might be blowing.

"I read about grits on the plane," she said. "Can we go out for breakfast?"

Sundays in Charleston are ritualized by the merger of breakfast and lunch into brunch. That way people can eat and drink more without feeling guilt, which most of them have just processed out of their systems by sitting in church. With this in mind I took my daughter to a place Laurie told me was known for its southern cooking and homespun hospitality, and by the time we got there we'd missed most of the post-congregant crowd. Addie seemed ready to throw up when my biscuits and sausage gravy arrived, but she loved her cheesy grits, which told me two things: she'd fit right in here in Charleston, and she was on the vegetarian side of the dairy fence these days.

Toward the end of brunch, she studied me across the table. She looked as if she were contemplating something serious, which she finally blurted out. "What makes you think Grandpa was innocent?" she asked. "After all these years?"

"I'm not sure he is innocent," I told her. "The jury thought he was guilty, so there's still a good chance he was."

"That's the lamest thing I've ever heard. People are wrongly convicted every day in this country. Usually black people who were in the wrong place at the wrong time."

"And that's a great injustice that needs to be corrected," I said. "But Grandpa was neither of those. Have you ever heard of Occam's Razor?"

She shook her head, looking puzzled. "You mean, like something you shave your legs with?"

"No. It's sort of a scientific rule that says that if there are two possible explanations for something that happened, the simpler one is probably more likely to be correct."

"Yeah, I've heard of that. I just don't get the razor part."

"I think it's because it forces you to shave off layers of unlikely explanations. In this case it implies that the most likely scenario is that your grandpa was guilty, even though there may be some reason to believe otherwise."

"Like what?" she had to ask.

I didn't want to go into any of the details right then, mainly because there weren't very many. Also because of the sleazeball in the black truck; no telling what sort of knee-jerk reaction he might have to getting his ass kicked. Obviously I wanted to deflect the fallout as far from Addie as I could.

"I'm still working on that," I replied. "And I might could use a little help."

"*Might could*?" she repeated.

"It's how we talk down here," I explained.

Before we left for the restaurant, Laurie called me, mostly to assure me that she wasn't the love 'em and leave 'em type. "Chew and screw," as she so crudely put it. When she was finished with her contrition, I let her know that Addie had arrived safely and we were on our way out to get a bite to eat. I avoided the details of my altercation in the garage, but I did remember something she had told me when we'd had drinks a few evenings before.

"You mentioned that night at Swampie's that you had someone run a background check on your husband," I said.

"Should've done it years before," she said. "Would have saved a lot of time and a shit-ton of grief."

"This person who did it…was he local?"

"It was a she, and yes, she's here in Charleston. Her name is Kat Rattigan, and she's a licensed P.I. Very solid, and she does most of her work online. You can just input stuff right into her website, and you get your results back the next day. Sooner, if it's a simple search. Does this have to do with your father?"

"Good guess," I said. "How do I find her?"

"I'll text you the URL," she said. A few seconds later my phone dinged, and there it was.

All I'd had to go on was a license plate number and the black truck's VIN, but I figured I could backfill any information those data points might eventually produce. Kat Rattigan's website listed a number of services for people looking for specific categories of information, and I found one designed for motor vehicle searches. The DMV report would set me back nineteen-ninety-five, tax included, but I wanted to know who the redneck SOB was. I gladly ponied up the money and typed in the info, then hit the submit button.

I mention all this because the internet doesn't take Sundays off. It works twenty-four seven, which meant that just as the waitress brought the check my phone pinged. Because I was only looking for a name and related contact info the search was fast, and the results were now waiting in my inbox.

"Is that from the woman you were talking to before?" Addie said.

"What woman?"

"C'mon, Dad. It's no big deal. Whoever it was who called you."

"Actually, it's from a detective I contacted about Grandpa," I told her, stretching the truth a bit.

"Cool," she replied.

Still, I smiled at my daughter's perceptive words; she was very astute and possessed a strong intuitive sense. Intuition like that might spare her a shit-ton of grief, as Laurie would say, and might just save her life someday.

I had no idea at the time just how soon that day would arrive.

CHAPTER 16

The owner of the truck was listed in the South Carolina DMV database as George Kovacs. He lived on Limehouse Lane in Ladson and owned the truck outright. It was a 2013 Ram 1500, with a bank note that had been paid off just a few months back. Although I hadn't requested it, the report also included Kovacs' driver's license number and other data that listed him as five-ten, one hundred ninety pounds. The grainy color photo, as viewed on my phone's tiny screen, confirmed he was the man whose jaw I had busted. The file also gave me his phone number, which I had no intention of calling. At least not yet.

After brunch I gave Addie a casual driving tour of Charleston. It was as much of an adventure for me as it was for her, since the city had changed in many radical ways since I was her age. I took her past the mansions on Murray Street and the Civil War canons in White Point Gardens at The Battery. She was impressed—as much as any fifteen-year-old can be—by the pastel houses on Rainbow Row and the intricate wrought-iron gates and ornate *clairvoyees*. Equally notable were the quaint cobblestone streets and in the old French Quarter, the flickering gas lamps, and the ancient pre-war cemeteries on Church Street.

"That's pre-*Civil* War," I explained to her.

"I know, Dad," she replied, rolling her eyes. "They have these things called schools now."

Addie was not so impressed by the Custom House, where

thousands of slaves were bought and sold in the city's early years. More of them entered the colonies through Charleston than any other city in North America, and over the years the steps in front of the Custom House saw a thriving and profitable business in human trafficking. When the trade of foreign slaves was abolished in 1808, a lot of businesses suffered, although the buying and selling of those born in the U.S. continued until the end of the Civil War. In 1856 the city passed a law prohibiting the sale of humans within view of the public, so merchants simply moved their concerns to enclosed yards and indoor markets.

"Pigs," she said simply. "And disgusting."

"Without a doubt," I agreed. "But it's part of your heritage."

Her mouth dropped open. "We were slave owners?"

"Not to my knowledge," I quickly told her. "Slaves were expensive, and Devlins were pretty simple folk. But that's the way it was back then, just like in *Gone with the Wind*."

"That's on my summer reading list," she replied.

"You might want to start it while you're here."

"It's over a thousand pages, Dad. How long are you planning on staying, now that Grandpa's dead?"

"Not long, sweetie," I said. "Just a few days."

By mid-afternoon I'd worn her out. She was still on west coast time, and she'd only had a few hours' sleep on the plane. She was in dire need of a nap, but as a teenager she was never going to admit it. Plus, we had one more place to go.

"How do you feel about bowling?" I asked her.

"You mean like with balls and pins?"

"You got it," I said. "Before I knew you were coming I made plans to meet with Uncle Andrew at a place up in Summerville. He'd be your great-uncle."

"You get Christmas cards from him, right?"

"Yup. Just so you know, after my father went to jail I moved in with him until I finished high school. He was very good to me and my sister back then."

"My sister and me," she corrected me with a grin.

"Yes, Miss Adeline," I said, thick sarcasm in my voice. "Anyway, we agreed to meet at a place called Ten Pin Alley, about half an hour from now. I hope you don't mind."

She yawned and said, "Sounds like a blast."

Ten Pin Alley was an iconic bowling joint right out of old-time Americana. It was a low, flat building with a large animated neon sign out front that, at night, depicted bowling pins being knocked over by a ball. During the day it just looked stark and lifeless, with a few cars scattered through the patchwork lot out front. Glimmers of heat rose from the gray asphalt, and the tires of my rental car popped on loose gravel. The dashboard thermometer said it was ninety-six, which I knew also mirrored the humidity.

The inside was pretty much the same as outside, except the AC was ice cold. It was like stepping off a plane in the Arctic, except we were looking at twenty lanes of polished hardwood rather than icy tundra. The clatter of bowling pins reverberated off the walls, accompanied by someone occasionally yelling "strike!" Off to one side was a snack bar where hot dogs and burgers were served, and beyond that was a dimly lit cocktail lounge with pink and green neon letters that spelled "The Gutter." I didn't see Uncle Andrew, so I figured I had time to get my daughter settled on a lane of her own.

I paid the young kid behind the rental counter for two games, assuring Addie that after my uncle and I discussed a few things we'd join her. She seemed okay with that, but balked when the desk kid asked her for her shoe size.

"What for?" she wanted to know.

"To get you shoes that fit," he told her, as if she had two heads.

"I'm not wearing anything that had other people's feet in them," she protested. "That's just wrong."

"We spray them with antiseptic after every use," he told her. "They're clean."

But she wasn't having it. Whenever Belinda and I had taken her bowling as a kid she never had a problem with the shoes, but now she did. And I didn't really blame her. Finally the desk kid told her she could go barefoot for all he cared, as long as she took the shoes with her.

We selected a lane not far from The Gutter, and I assured Addie that I'd be right there, keeping an eye on her.

"Don't worry, Dad," she admonished me. As if nothing could

happen to her in a run-down joint that reeked of stale sweat and urine. "I'll be fine."

Uncle Andrew arrived as close to on-time as a man in his eighties can be. In my mind he had remained the ornery ex-Marine with a buzz-cut who had sat in the bleachers behind home plate watching every pitch I threw. That distant Spring of my displaced senior year, before the trial and afterwards, he never missed a game whether I was playing or not. I realized back then that he bore a strong resemblance to my mother: same angled chin, high cheekbones, strong nose, chestnut eyes. Now, as I watched him shuffle across the carpeted lobby, I wondered what she might have looked like today, if she were still alive. Would she have the same white hair, the same hunched shoulders and knobby knees? Would she have the same beaming smile of recognition as he did, once his tired eyes found me in the dark, sitting there at the bar?

I slid off my stool and walked over to greet him. I extended my hand for a polite "hello," but he was having none of that. He wrapped his arms around me in a ferocious hug that defied his age. Then he pulled back and gazed into my eyes, as if he were expecting to find a clue to the meaning of life in there. I hated to disappoint him.

"Damn, it's been a long time," he said.

"Close to twenty years," I told him.

The only time I'd seen him since the trial was the day of my wedding. He was terrified of flying, but he insisted he wouldn't miss The Big Day for anything in the world. Neither of my parents could be there, and he wanted family blood to be present and accounted for. He'd managed to survive the flight west with lots of booze and sleeping pills, but had taken the train home.

He joined me at the bar and ordered what I figured was his usual. The bartender, a busty young woman with green hair named Teena, brought over a bottle of Absolut and poured him a double. She left the bottle on the Formica counter; it was mid-afternoon on a Sunday and evidently she wasn't expecting a run on vodka. Since I had the wellbeing of my daughter to think about I ordered a glass of sweet tea.

"May the sonofabitch rot in hell," my uncle said, raising his glass.

"I believe he already did that," I reminded my uncle. "Whatever the truth of yesterday, may he find himself in a better place today."

"Works for me, as long as the flames are a million degrees. Centigrade."

"Whatever happened to the idea of 'love the sinner, hate the sin'?" I asked him.

"Whatever happened to the young man who didn't have a drop of spit for his father the day he was led out of the courtroom?" my uncle countered.

"First take the log out of your own eye, and then you will see to take the speck out of your brother's eye." The words of Matthew were my mother's favorites, and she had repeated them frequently when I was a child. For a second I wondered what she would have thought of Reverend William McCann and his firebrand form of fundamentalism.

He shot me a curious glance that didn't distract from taking a healthy sip of vodka. "You sound just like Kathleen," he sighed. "Forgiveness always was her strength. And maybe, in the end, her weakness."

"Like I told you yesterday, I've been thinking a lot about the trial," I explained.

"Well, don't. It's not smart to pick through old vomit."

"Mom used to say that, too," I told him.

"Your mother was one very smart woman," he replied over the tumbler in his hand. "Except for when it came to your old man."

"I know how you feel about him," I said. "For reasons that are obvious. But I want you to push that all aside for a minute. There's just a couple things that have been bothering me."

I sensed another retort—probably another verbal assault on my father—trying to get past his lips, but he managed to hold it back. "Can't help you with what I don't know, so go ahead—tell me what's on your mind."

I took a long sip of my sweet tea and said, "What do you remember about a witness who was never called during the trial? Someone Jenkins had waiting in the wings."

Unlike my father, Uncle Andrew had always been a disaster at cards. The one time he'd been coaxed into a Friday night poker game he'd quickly lost everything he had. The reason for this, my father later explained, was that my uncle had an obvious "tell"—a wayward nerve in the skin beneath his left eye that quivered whenever he got excited or told a fib.

That's how I knew Uncle Andrew was lying when he said, "Never heard anything about that."

I knew enough not to press him, not just then. He wasn't telling the truth, which meant he felt he had a reason not to. Whatever it was, he wasn't going to share it with me, so I simply went on to my next question.

"What did you think about the judge?" I asked him. "He did everything in his power to screw my dad."

"As I recall in these sunset years of my life, Judge Carter was a wise and impartial man," Uncle Andrew replied.

I was surprised he'd remembered the man's name after all these years, but didn't say so. "So why did he go out of his way to deny evidence and testimony that might have helped the case?" I asked instead. "Or have you forgotten?"

"My mind is old and my memories are thin, Rick. You'll have to illuminate me."

"Let's just say that I read through the old trial transcripts and Carter came down on them—Dad and Jenkins—with a hammer."

"You did what?"

"I went through the old records. You might find it a fascinating read, since you weren't allowed inside the courthouse. And despite what you may remember, the judge had a real hard-on for my father."

The bartender made a half-turn at my choice of words, then went about her business. Uncle Andrew downed his drink, then splashed himself another from the bottle at hand. Finally he said, "Your father was guilty as the hordes of hell, Rick. The jury was clear about that. The judge didn't want a circus in his courtroom, so he did his best to keep the monkeys in the cage."

"Is that why he didn't allow you inside?"

"I wasn't allowed inside, as you put it, because I had no tolerance for your father or his lawyer's horseshit."

It was obvious he remained one hundred percent convinced my father was guilty as sin, and nothing was going to change his footing. Or the line he was toeing.

"What about Jimmy Holland?" I asked him. "Does that name ring a bell?"

It sure as hell did, and the deep scowl on his face told me more than I expected. He leaned forward, his nose no more than a foot from mine, and said, "God locked that door tight many years ago."

"Well, guess what? He just opened a window."

My uncle stared at me as if I'd just lost all my senses. "You can't even be thinking about that name, son," he said.

"That name had a face," I reminded him. "And a head, and arms and legs, until they were ripped away from the rest of him."

"I know the story," Uncle Andrew said with a heavy sigh. "It's part of our very uncivil and murderous history in this state. And pretty recent, at that."

"History is a vain reminder of the inglorious sins in our blemished past."

"Let me guess: Oliver Wendell Holmes."

"Rick Allen Devlin."

He said nothing for a moment, just stared at me with uneven eyes. Then he asked: "Who told you that name?"

How I got it was unimportant, and I told him so. "Tell me how it ties in with my mother's death," I challenged him.

My uncle contemplated what I'd asked, then pounded back the rest of the clear liquid in his glass. "Your father was a very duplicitous man," he said. "Well-heeled in the course of business and politicking, but two-faced when he was among his closest friends."

"He was a racist and a bigot," I agreed. "Tell me something I don't know."

"'Though his hatred be covered with deception, his wickedness will be exposed in the assembly'," my uncle recited from memory. "That was another one of your mother's favorite quotes—from Proverbs, I think."

"What does any of that have to do with Jimmy Holland?"

Uncle Andrew dug into his pocket and threw a few bills on the counter, then stood up as quickly as his frail legs would let him. "The sonofabitch judge prohibited me from entering that damned courtroom, but that didn't keep me from hearing things. Things about secret meetings and treachery and evil men with blackness in their hearts. You want to know the truth about that trial, you have to be prepared to accept your father for all that he really was."

I wondered how much vodka my uncle had already consumed before he'd come here, and how many cylinders in his brain were still firing after all these years. "Exactly what are you trying to tell me?" I asked him.

"The men and women on that jury reached a reasonable conclusion, and your father's wickedness was exposed. That's all that matters, and all that ever did."

"Just tell me how the Holland kid fits in."

"I don't know the answer to that, and I don't care to," he insisted, and the lack of any nervous twitch indicated he meant it. Still, there was a drowsy look of caution in his eyes as he added, "Just do what's best for you and the ones you love, and leave the past alone."

I sat there watching as he limped back across the grimy carpet and pushed his way through the double front doors that were covered with reflective film that had begun to peel. A blast of light enveloped the lobby for a minute, then faded again as the doors slowly swung shut. The bartender glanced over at me, and I gave her a noncommittal shrug.

"Must have been something I said," I said.

She told me it was fine if I brought my sweet tea down to the lanes, so I picked up my glass and went down to join my daughter. Addie was halfway through her second game and appeared tired and frazzled, and when I looked at the digital read-out of her score I could understand why.

"A little rusty?" I asked her.

"I just remembered what I don't like about this frigging game," she said. "Unless you're really good at it, you totally suck."

"Addie—"

"*What?* They use that word on TV all the time."

She had me there, so I let it drop. "Your Uncle Andrew had to leave suddenly," I told her.

"Yeah, I saw. He looked pretty upset."

"He's an old man and set in his ways," I said. A poor excuse, but I really didn't want to get into the whole Jimmy Holland story with her. My uncle's parting words still rang in my ears: *Do what's best for you and the ones you love.* "I'm sorry you didn't get to meet him."

"His loss," she said, offering up a cynical grin. I think she got that from me.

When we got back to the condo Addie flopped on her bed and slept for two full hours. She probably could have gone for a lot longer, but evening was coming on and I didn't know what she might want for dinner. When she finally wandered out from the bedroom she was rubbing the sleep from her eyes. "I assume there's going to be a funeral, right?"

"Your grandfather didn't exactly have a lot of friends," I replied. "It would just be you and me, maybe my sister."

"Aunt Karen? She's the gonzo mental one, right?"

"Borderline personality disorder," I corrected her. "With issues of self-medication and addictive behavior."

"I just remember her talking really fast, like one of Carl's old records turned up to high speed." Addie's stepfather collected antique jukeboxes and vintage turntables, and she was fascinated by old vinyl. "And she drank a lot."

I glanced at my own glass of wine, wondering if there was a hidden message in my daughter's words. "Aunt Karen has been known to overdo things every once in a while," I conceded. "She's unpredictable."

"Still, there should be some sort of thing. Especially if Grandpa turns out to be innocent."

"Well, I already called her," I said. "She didn't know if she could make it here or not."

"Where does she live?"

"Atlanta," I told her, then explained that Karen didn't have the patience or focus to spend five hours on the road. "We'll just have to see how it goes."

"Well, you and I should at least do something for him," she insisted. I could tell when Addie was serious about something, and this was one of those times. "Maybe at the beach. Toss rose pedals in the waves. Something."

"Okay. You've sold me. Let's just see whether my sister makes it or not."

By now it was after six and Addie decided she wanted sushi for dinner. I reminded her that sushi is raw fish, but she explained that avocado rolls were fine. No fish or crab, just things that grew out of the ground or on trees, with a little seaweed wrapped around it. A little of that and some miso soup and she'd be fine.

She wanted to change her clothes, so she disappeared into her bedroom. While I was waiting for her to freshen up I turned on the local news. I wasn't paying much attention to the talking heads until I heard the name "Lily Elliott."

I snapped my eyes to the screen and stared at the live shot of flashing blue lights and emergency vehicles. In the background I could make out the roofline of a familiar house, familiar because I had been there just yesterday. I couldn't see what was going on because of all the commotion, and then the reporter on the scene began to explain.

"Authorities were called to the house after a gardener discovered the front door was open," she said in a cordial on-air voice. "When he saw the victim's body he immediately called 9-1-1 and waited for police. We are told that when emergency medical personnel arrived, they took immediate resuscitative measures, but Ms. Elliott was pronounced dead at the scene. Cause of death will be determined pending an autopsy, but one official who asked not to be identified said it appeared she had been shot in the head."

My entire body felt as if it had been bitten by a deep frost. *Lily Elliott, dead?* That couldn't be right. Who would have wanted to kill the poor woman who only wished to be left alone to write her romance novels and care for her animals?

The answer hit me like a line drive up the middle of the infield: George Kovacs. If the bastard had followed me to the airport that very morning, it was highly possible he had trailed me down to Beaufort yesterday. I wouldn't have noticed him a hundred yards behind me because traffic was thicker than it was this morning, and I'd been focused on what I was going to ask Ms. Elliott. The fact was, I probably led him right to her, and when I mentioned the name Jimmy Holland to him, he must have figured she'd been the one who'd spilled it.

Do what's best for you and the ones you love.

CHAPTER 17

How do you tell your daughter that your own action—innocuous and innocent as it might have seemed at the time—possibly led to the death of an innocent person? How can you explain that idle conversation over coffee and scones earned a woman a gunshot to the head? How can you keep from worrying about the safety of your own family and everyone you came into contact with since you started asking questions that ripped open a mound of fire ants?

The answer is: you don't. You can't. You go on as if nothing happened, biting down on the guilt and trying not to focus on the harm you've caused. You accept the blame and responsibility for your actions while trying not to let your daughter peer into the anguished reaches of your heart, no matter how much it might be pounding.

The bottom line was, Lily Elliott was a fine woman with a large spirit who did not deserve to die. She did not deserve to have someone walk up to her front door, fire a bullet into her skull, and then leave her on the cold flagstones of her foyer. Yet that's what happened, and there was not a shred of doubt in my mind about the bastard who had done it.

Nor did I question that he would do it again. George Kovacs was the sort of man who would do what he had to do until he was convinced he'd cleared up all the remains of the day. A day that I had every reason to believe was July 15th, 1989.

The info on Kovacs' license told me he was in his early fifties, which would have put him in his early twenties when Jimmy Holland was brutally murdered. Since no one was ever arrested for the crime, there was no way of knowing the age of the killers when they tied the poor kid to the bumper. I naturally assumed more than one was involved, since it would have taken several of them to overpower Holland and bind his hands and feet. And now I wondered what role Kovacs might have played in Holland's death that day, in some reprehensible way. And why he had wanted to keep my father quiet.

Google didn't have much to say about him. I already knew he was a totally unremarkable man who lived an unspectacular life, and most likely would die an unheralded death. I also knew he lived on Limehouse Lane in Ladson, but a short newspaper squib told me he worked at a service garage that repaired large diesel semis and had an ex-wife who was a waitress at a local steakhouse. Beyond that he seemed not to stray very far outside the lines, and he avoided social media at all costs. Still, I believed a professional search would turn up a few details that would paint a clearer picture of who I was dealing with.

I dropped twenty-five dollars on another background check, this time one that would provide Kovacs' full employment history, personal data, and rap sheet. I knew there would be no smoking gun that placed him directly on State Road S 38-60 outside Wolfton thirty years ago but, as Lily Elliott had told me just yesterday, "if you start turning over rocks, you never know what might crawl out." If Kovacs was one of those crawling things, I owed it to her to stomp him out.

I rolled into bed just past midnight and stayed there until my phone rang a little after seven the next morning. It was Laurie, who apologized for calling so early, but she had an idea that she admitted up front was probably stupid and I could tell her to mind her own business if she was overstepping our rekindled friendship. Once she got the disclaimer out of the way she explained that her daughter Kelli—spelled with an "i"—was going to the beach with some friends and she was wondering if Addie might be interested in joining them.

"I don't mean to intrude, but I thought she might like to be around some kids her own age."

"I don't know if she's up yet, but let me find out," I told her. "I'll call you back."

In fact, Addie was awake and talking on the phone. I checked my watch, just to reconfirm the time and do the mental math. My daughter knew no one here in South Carolina, so she had to be talking to someone on the west coast. As far as I knew she didn't have a boyfriend, but she was part of a group of kids that seemed to have interchangeable parts. Life shifts so quickly at that age it's hard to keep track. She was sitting in a lotus position on her bed and invited me in when I knocked. Then she mouthed the word *hospital* and I understood. She talked for another thirty seconds, and when she hung up she said, "I was worried about Mom."

"Me, too," I told her, impressed that she'd taken the initiative to call on her own. "How's she doing?"

"Serious but stable. The nurse said she has an infection, probably from the needle, and there could be complications. But she's resting and out of immediate danger."

We talked about her mother a bit more, and then I broached the subject of the beach. She was hesitant—almost guilty—when I explained the beach offer. How could she go have fun at the beach when her mother was in the hospital? I explained that one was totally unrelated to the other, and she was not responsible for what had happened to Belinda. Then I assured her there was no pressure to go to the beach, that it was totally her choice and if she'd rather do something else there was plenty in Charleston to keep us busy. Or I could take her to the beach myself, if she preferred.

That's when she looked me in the eye and said, "If I go, what will you do?"

"I have a lot of paperwork to take care of," I told her. "There's a lot of red tape involved when someone dies."

Addie mulled this over, then said, "How do you know these kids? You haven't even been here a week."

"One of them is the daughter of an old friend," I explained, without explaining too much.

"The woman you talked to on the phone?"

Addie had always been sharp as a tack, and there was no use denying it. "That would be correct," I conceded.

"You do move fast," she said, her lips creased in a broad grin.

"I ran into her at lunch the other day. We knew each other in high school."

Addie had an impulsive side and clearly wasn't the best at filtering her questions. "Knew…like in boyfriend-girlfriend?" she asked.

"It's been known to happen," I admitted with a smile. "We were both older than you, and that hasn't changed."

She spent a few seconds digesting this new batch of info, then seemed to accept it. "Okay, the beach sounds good," she agreed. "Is it warm enough to go swimming?"

"This isn't California," I told her. "You're going to love this beach."

I dropped Addie off at Laurie's house, which was located in the Old Village section of Mount Pleasant a couple of blocks from the water. Unlike her parents' two-story home from which I had made my hasty escape several times, it was a one-story lowcountry design with a broad porch and square pillars supporting a tin roof. Matching black shutters, gardenias planted along the brick foundation, crepe myrtles and magnolias in a yard defined by a black picket fence. Flower baskets hung from a porch ceiling that was painted *haint blue* to ward off evil spirits.

A half-dozen kids around my daughter's age were loading things into the back of a gray SUV, and I caught a lingering look of apprehension in my daughter's eyes. Or was it fear? She hesitated only briefly, then opened the door and slid out of the car, slipping her overstuffed pack over her shoulder. She brazenly walked over to the group of kids, and within seconds she was squeezing her things into the growing mound in the back of the vehicle.

I waited until Laurie came out of the house and approached my car. She leaned over and rested her hands on the windowsill. "Looks like she's already part of the gang," she observed.

"They all look so young," I replied. "I sure as hell wouldn't want to be that age again."

"We did all right," she reminded me. "I wish I didn't have to work all day."

"Maybe you'll need a break at some point." It was a suggestion, not a question.

"Keep your phone on you," she said, raising her eyebrows suggestively. "It's Monday and slow spells come and go without much notice."

"Just like high school."

"I don't like to think about that," she replied. "Like you said, they all look so young."

After I left Laurie's house I drove directly to the airport, where I turned in my rented Kia and picked up a Chevy Impala. I made sure I wasn't followed, and actually circled through the airport twice just to make sure. Now if George Kovacs or one of his posse was gunning for me, they'd be looking for the wrong car. I didn't exactly feel emboldened, especially after what they did to Lily Elliott, but it was a move in the right direction.

Over the weekend I'd made a few calls and left almost as many voicemail messages. On my way back from the airport one of those calls got back to me, a woman who instantly gushed with effervescence when she heard my voice. Her name was Alice Marion, and she had been my father's loyal and devoted secretary when he'd owned Sumter Insurance on King Street. She also was one of the witnesses that Jenkins III had not called during the trial, and I wanted to ask her about that.

Like all the other folks who knew my father back then, Alice was nearing eighty. She was suffering from spinal stenosis and a few other ailments that had forced her to move into an assisted living facility, where she was confined to a wheelchair and spent her days watching game shows and HGTV reruns. I got the sense she was lonely and bored, and when I told her I'd like to meet with her she enthusiastically invited me to drop by. Yes, later that morning would work very well, thank you.

An hour later I pulled into a visitor's space in front of Plantation Run, a gated "premiere independent living community" that looked more like an upscale country club than an old folk's home. Several of the residents sitting in a pocket of shade greeted me with a nod as I approached the front door, which opened automatically as I got close. A state police vehicle slowly cruised through the covered *porte cochere*, presumably making a security run through the grounds. As I walked inside I felt as if I were stepping into a walk-in freezer, and I was sure I saw several older folks shivering under their summer sweaters.

Alice had suggested we meet in the downstairs library, and as I walked in she looked up from something she was working on in her lap.

"Mr. Rick," she said, understandably making no effort to get up.

"Mrs. Marion," I greeted her, lightly shaking her tired hand when she raised it. "It's wonderful to see you after all these years."

"I'm knitting Christmas stockings for my grandchildren," she explained to me, her fingers struggling with the long needles. "I know it's summer, but my hands don't work as quickly as they once did. My physical therapist says it's good for maintaining manual dexterity and mental acuity."

I hoped her therapist was correct, since I was counting on her memory to clarify a few things. "I can't believe how long it's been," I told her. "You're looking marvelous."

"Just as charming as your father," she said with an endearing smile.

She waved me into a chair and then we went through the usual stuff about how much I'd grown, what was I doing these days, how my sister was doing. She didn't want to talk about herself except to say that Edward, her husband of fifty-four years, had passed away two winters ago, which was why she felt inclined to come to this place to live. The eyes that once required coke-bottle glasses had declined further, one of them defeated by glaucoma and the other looking glossy and nebulous. She wore a plain cotton dress with little pink and green flowers on it, lace collar, and a string of faux pearls around her neck.

"I see my children every month or so, but they have lives of their own," she observed. "And frankly, I do better without all the chaos."

Eventually we got around to the point of my visit, which she correctly assumed was not just to offer my regards. "This has to do with your father," she ventured, narrowing her eyes on mine. "Do you ever talk to him?"

"He was diagnosed with cancer a couple months back," I explained. "Non-treatable. He passed away on Saturday."

"I am truly sorry to hear that," she said. "He was such a nice man, and I never could believe he could do such a horrible thing."

"That's why I wanted to speak with you," I replied. "You knew more about him back in those days than anyone who's still around."

She considered this a moment, then nodded. "Probably true, but I don't know what I can tell you that could change anything now."

"Do you mind if I ask a few questions anyway?"

"Go ahead," she said, setting her knitting aside. "My fingers can use a break."

I led off with why she had been on my father's witness list but was never called to testify. "What caused the change of heart?" I asked her.

"That trial was a farce," she said with a sniff of disdain. "Lynch mob mentality."

"What makes you say that?" I asked. I had my own suspicions, but I wanted her personal take on it.

"The judge, for one thing. He had no business sitting up there, presiding over that case."

Alice Marion wasn't the only person who had told me that, but so far no one could put a solid finger on why. "I remember hearing rumors, but what makes you say that?" I pushed her.

"It's pretty simple, really. Judge Carter donated a lot of money to your father's campaign. The first one. There were real contribution limits back then, and Carter spent the max. Then one day about six months into your father's first term he got a call from him, looking for a favor."

"Do you remember what kind of favor?"

"Like it was yesterday. Carter wanted help passing a bill that would legalize pari-mutuel betting on horse racing. He had some friends who stood to make a lot of money, and he'd invested a large sum in getting your father elected to the state senate. Money is power, and power corrupts."

"And absolute power corrupts absolutely."

"Something your father learned pretty quickly. A lot of people leaned on him, but Frank held firm. He wouldn't do it. And that outraged the judge."

"So, when Dad went on trial for murder, Carter wanted to see him fry," I said.

"You know what they say about revenge being served cold," she said, dipping her head in a nod. "He couldn't exactly recuse himself, because that might expose his corruption."

"Why didn't my dad's lawyer raise the issue?"

"You'd have to ask him," she said with a shrug.

I already suspected how that would go, and chose not to go into it. "Interesting coincidence that Carter was killed in a hit-and-run just a few years later," I pointed out.

She smiled and touched a finger to her lips. "Careful," she said, her voice no more than a breath. "That kind of talk can get you killed."

"Other than the judge, do you remember anyone who might have had it in for my father back then?" I asked her. "Or my mother?"

She gave my question considerable thought, staring up at the ceiling while the aging cogs in her brain got to work. Eventually she shook her head and said, "That was the hardest part about the trial. No one could come up with a reason why anyone would want to kill your mother, especially so violently."

The prosecutor had hammered that point home time and again during the trial, particularly during his closing arguments. Countless witnesses had stated—over Jenkins III's objections—that no one else but the victim's husband could have possibly stabbed her so viciously. As Blackwood repeatedly alluded, it was a crime of passion that only could have been committed by her husband. When the jurors started nodding I knew he had them clenched in his tight little fist.

"Of course, that was long before the Avery Dunham case," she added.

The name sounded familiar, but I couldn't remember where I'd heard it. Or seen it. "Who was Avery Dunham?" I asked her.

"Mr. Dunham bought an insurance policy sometime in the late eighties, about a year before...well, before your mother died. This must be hard for you to revisit after all this time."

"It is, but that's why I came to see you," I reminded her. "Please go on."

"The policy covered several buildings that he used for his transportation business. He had a fleet of trucks that moved dry goods from Jacksonville to Norfolk and back. When Hugo struck, one of the buildings burned to the ground, and Mr. Dunham tried to collect on the insurance."

Her words rang a distinct bell. A few days ago, when I first Googled my father's trial, I'd come across a link to Avery Dunham on an online insurance industry forum. "I think I read about this," I told her. "He stored explosives in that warehouse."

"Which negated the policy. None of his losses were covered, and he blamed your father."

"Did Avery Dunham ever say what he was doing with all the

explosives?" I asked her.

"He claimed a client was moving a shipment of scrap material from point A to point B, and he—Avery—didn't know what it was," she explained. "Turns out the material was nitrocellulose. The arbitration judges unanimously ruled that ignorance of law is not an excuse, and they found in favor of the insurance company. Same thing with all the appeals. By that time your father was in prison, but I remember it well. Mr. Dunham was furious."

"But this was after my mother was killed," I pointed out.

"That's right—it had nothing to do with her death. But Avery has the blood of a lot of other people on his hands."

"Is there some connection between him and Dad?" I asked.

She flashed a look that said *be patient*, then said, "You're too young to remember this, but right around that time—a couple years on both sides of Hugo—there was a rash of church bombings around the state. Parts of Georgia, too. Black churches; ten or twelve in all. More than a dozen people were killed, and a lot more were injured. No one had a clue who did it, and probably never would have except for a set of fingerprints the FBI found on the underside of one of the charred pews, near where the explosives were planted."

"Avery Dunham?"

"Actually, his stepson. The FBI tried to get him to turn on his old man, but he didn't. The feds raided Dunham's business and found trace amounts of the same type of explosive that was used in the church blast, but they never could make a case."

"How do you remember this?" I asked her.

"Maybe it's the knitting," she said, glancing at the yarn and needles in her lap. "Plus, I do a lot of memory games and brain teasers."

"Do you know where I might be able to find him?" I asked her. "Avery Dunham, I mean."

"Last I heard he was in federal prison in West Virginia," she replied. "He was convicted of blowing up a doctor's car outside a family planning clinic in Charlottesville."

"Nice guy."

"At least it got him out of the gene pool," she said with a shrug. "Just like the stepson."

"Meaning what?" I asked her.

"Meaning his body was pulled out of the Congaree Swamp a

couple years after the church thing, sometime in the mid-nineties. The coroner was able to match prints or DNA, I can't remember which. Anyway, as I recall he had a large hole in the center of his forehead."

The Congaree Swamp is a massive expanse of wetlands in the middle of the state where two large rivers flow through a forest of old-growth hardwoods. During heavy rains the swelling streams and oxbow lakes overflow their banks and flood the bald cypress and water tupelos and pines. Throughout history the sloughs and creeks provided refuge to everyone from Francis Marion's marauders to escaped slaves on the run, and it had been the destination of yet another Devlin family adventure when I was about ten. I remember slowly paddling a canoe through the waterlogged bottomlands as cottonmouths sunned themselves on dry streambeds and water moccasins dangled from branches overhead.

"Someone shot him?"

"That's what the coroner said. The animals got to him pretty good, but there must have been enough left to write a conclusive report."

"This stepson...was his name Dunham, too?"

She stared at a blank spot near the ceiling for a second, then gently shook her head. "I believe his first name was Gerald, and he was from the mother's side of the clan. Last name was Aiken, just like the town. Funny thing is, his cousin Rudy was supposed to testify in your father's trial, but the week before it started, he just up and disappeared."

CHAPTER 18

I called Jenkins IV as soon as I was back on the road. His cell phone went straight to voicemail, so I left a brief message and hung up. I knew he wanted me out of his hair—out of South Carolina—so I figured he'd call me back sooner rather than later.

As I merged into thick lunchtime traffic I couldn't help but wonder if Alice Marion's memory really could have been as good as it seemed. Even if she did work on puzzles and brain teasers, could an octogenarian brain really recall so many details of a story, all these years after the fact? She would have been an excellent witness on the stand, which made me wonder even more why Jenkins III decided not to give her the chance.

My phone rang and I answered it without looking at the screen. I assumed it was Jenkins calling me back, but instead I was greeted by a woman who said, "Is this Rick Devlin?"

"Who's calling?" I asked warily. I was in no mood for time-share pitches or IRS scams.

"My name is Kat Rattigan," the voice said. Pleasant, upbeat, neither young nor old. Professional and polite. "You submitted a request to my website for a background check on an individual named George Kovacs?"

"I did," I confirmed. "Got the name of your company from a friend. I ran a DMV check on him yesterday and then submitted a more thorough background this morning. I wasn't expecting to talk to a real live person."

"It's not usual protocol, not with most reports," she said. "The computer network is very efficient and hardly ever requires a human touch."

"I take it this time is different?"

"Sometimes the software red-flags a report that could be problematic for the customer," Kat Rattigan explained. "That's when I step in."

"You're telling me George Kovacs is bad news."

"Of the highest order," she confirmed. "A lot of my clients are either checking out a new partner, or backgrounding a prospective employee. If you fit into either category—totally off the record—you might want to consider dumping this dirt bag now."

"Too late," I told her. "I already had a run-in with him, and I suspect he was involved with a murder down in Beaufort just yesterday."

"The writer? Jesus…I saw that on the news. I love her books."

"I don't have any proof. He followed me to the airport and we had a bit of a scuffle. It looks like he may have paid a visit to Lily Elliott after that, and I'm pretty certain he'll come back to settle his score with me."

"If the report I'm looking at is any indication, you're in for some serious fireworks," she said. "I'll email it to you now."

"I'm in my car," I told her. "Do you have time to read the pertinent parts to me?"

"Given the circumstances, sure." I heard a rustle of pages, then she continued: "Let's see…three charges of assault with intent to kill. Two were dismissed, and the third one the victim—his girlfriend—never showed. And by never showed I mean she disappeared, and is presumed dead. Then we have six individual cases of aggravated assault, the last time against an elderly black woman at a Walmart in Orangeburg. The case went to trial but the woman dropped the charges. Same thing with all the previous cases, apparently. The witnesses clammed up or disappeared. Mr. Kovacs is suspected in three murders, all of the victims black, but was never charged for lack of evidence. He was convicted on several weapons charges and served a year at Broad River, where he was believed to have shanked a fellow prisoner. No proof, charges dropped. He was arrested twice for domestic abuse, charges dropped. Lots of petty crime stuff, several armed robberies—charges all dropped. There's a juvenile record as well, but it's sealed."

"Sounds like a total rat turd," I said when she was finished.

"And you picked a fight with him?"

"I know—buy the ticket, take the ride. Anything else you can tell me?"

"Just that he's known to associate with white supremacists," she replied. "He likes to go to marches and bust heads."

I soaked this all in, checked my rearview mirror out of paranoia. No black trucks, nothing out of the ordinary. At least not that I could see. "Does the report say where he was born?"

"Yeah…a place called Livingston, in Orangeburg County. Where his juvie record is still secure under lock and key."

Orangeburg. Just a fair piece down the road from Wolfton.

"What do you think I should do about the Beaufort murder?" I asked her.

"Let me handle it," she said. "I know a few of the guys at SLED, and I'll forward Kovacs' sheet to them. It might carry more weight that way and keep you out of it."

"Much appreciated," I told her. "I want to thank you for this. Looks like Kovacs is one nasty shitkicker."

"A genuine bad-ass sumbitch," she concurred.

"Listen…I'm planning on running another report as soon as I get home. If I give you the name now can you feed it into the computer for me, and when I log in I can pay up?"

"Your payment info is on file," she reminded me. "Just give me the name and any other data you have and I'll get it rolling."

"Rudy Aiken," I told her, spelling the last name. "Just like the town. He may have had a brother named Gerald, and a stepfather named Avery Dunham. Sorry, but that's all I've got."

"It's enough to start," she replied. "I'll get back to you when the report's done."

I ended the call and thought on what I'd done. George Kovacs was a mean sonofabitch and I'd stepped right in the middle of his shit. He'd pretty much laid it on my doorstep and lit it on fire, like a Halloween prank, and maybe I'd overreacted. I'd only intended to photograph his license number and VIN, not hurl a fist into his jaw. But when he'd opened his door and I saw the gun I knew I needed to land the first punch. That made me the aggressor, but if I hadn't knocked him flat there's no telling what he might have done.

The problem was, he knew where I lived. Not just what building, but the exact unit number. I had no idea how he'd come by that info, since it had been closely guarded by only a handful of state officials, and both Jenkins lawyers. He'd used it to get to Benita Juarez, who had passed along the warning note to my father. And he'd been lying in wait for me yesterday morning.

All of which meant he had someone on the inside. Inside of what, I didn't have a clue.

Jenkins IV called me back a few minutes after that, just as I was heading up the arching span of the Ravenel Bridge. It was one of those architectural wonders with soaring towers and white cables designed to resemble the sails of old merchant vessels that carried sugar and spices from distant ports around the world. And slaves, from Africa.

"I've been meaning to call you," he said when I answered. "We need to meet."

"Does the name George Kovacs mean anything to you?" I asked, ignoring him.

"Not right offhand," he said. "Should it?"

I filled him in on the events of yesterday, how I was followed to the airport and then what I suspected might have happened to Lily Elliott.

"Did he say what he wanted?" Jenkins asked me when I was finished.

"He came at me with a gun," I said. "We didn't do much talking."

"And what's the connection to that woman's murder down in Beaufort?"

"If he followed me to the airport he probably tailed me to Beaufort, too," I replied.

"What were you doing down there?"

All of a sudden I felt that Jenkins IV had slipped into courtroom mode and was cross-examining me. "It had to do with what my father mentioned the other day," I told him.

"So what's the connection to the woman who was killed?"

I told him that Lily Elliott was a newspaper reporter who had covered the trial, and had moved to Beaufort to write romance novels.

"I had a few questions and she agreed to answer them," I said.

"And what makes you think he followed you there?"

"Kovacs looked like a fox caught in the hen house when I cornered him," I explained, losing my patience. "If he also followed me to Lily Elliott's house on Saturday he could have figured we talked about things he wanted dead and buried."

"If P does not necessarily equal Q," the lawyer pointed out.

"Dammit, Jenkins," I snapped at him. "That woman is dead, and I'm pretty sure I know who killed her."

Jenkins IV fell silent for a moment, then said, "I can see why you're worked up, Rick. But it still doesn't prove anything."

"Then you won't mind if I slip him your name, tell him you're the one who told me about Jimmy Holland." Yes, it was a threat, and I might have even meant it.

"Shit on a stick...what does that colored boy have to do with all this?" Jenkins IV said. I pictured him cradling his face in his hands, wondering how things could have gone this far.

"Why didn't your father let Rudy Aiken testify at my dad's trial?" I asked him, ignoring his question. "He was on the list."

"You'll have to ask him."

"C'mon, Jenkins. Everything he knows, you know. And piece by piece, I'm finding it all out." I took a moment to settle down, then said, "So what was it you wanted to talk about?"

"You called me," he said in a voice that was cracking from anger. Or was it worry?

"True, but you also said you'd been meaning to call me, that we needed to meet. What about?"

He inhaled deeply, then let out a long breath. "Your father's trust," he said.

"I don't think he trusted anyone, and vice versa, right up to the very end."

"I'm talking about his *legal* trust," Jenkins IV clarified, suddenly sounding tired and exasperated. "Whatever you might have thought about him, he made a few good investments back in the day."

It was my turn for silence, and I must have held it a while, because I heard him say, "Rick...you still there?"

"Yeah, I'm here. You're talking about a trust, like a will?"

"Well, there are a lot of differences, but yes," he replied. "And we need to start the legal balls rolling."

This was all news to me, and it sounded as if it would delay Addie's and my return to California. "Tell me what works for you and I'll be there."

He gave me a time and an address, then said, "Look, I'm sorry I can't help you about that other stuff, but it's attorney-client privilege material."

"The client is dead," I reminded him. "I don't think he's in any position to sue."

It had not been my intent to unload on Jenkins IV, but lawyers are a particularly tight-assed breed. When they shift into legal mode they lose any sense of empathy and compassion, and in return they deserve no more respect than a genital disease. I'd never had a good experience dealing with one, and I expected that streak would stay alive as I now called Jenkins III from my speed dial.

"Mr. Jenkins," I said brightly when he answered. "Rick Devlin here. I was just talking to your son and he suggested I give you a call."

"He mentioned he was going to talk to you about the trust," the retired barrister replied. I pictured him sitting in his log home overlooking the marsh, watching the egrets and wood storks poking through the pluff mud for lunch.

"We're going to meet tomorrow, but that's not why I called. He said I should ask you about Rudy Aiken, what he was going to say at Dad's trial."

I'm certain I heard him curse under his breath, and he said nothing for a good five seconds. Then he replied, "My son knows nothing about any of that."

"Which is why he said I should ask you about it. So I'm asking: What did a shit bag named Rudy Aiken, whose stepfather is now serving time in federal prison, have to do with my father's case?"

"Absolutely nothing," Jenkins III said. "Which is why I never put him on the stand."

"But you were going to," I pressed him. "He was on the witness list you submitted during pre-trial discovery." I wasn't sure I had my legal jargon correct, but it didn't really matter.

"Aiken was a false flag," Jenkins III explained. "I only put him on the list to throw Blackwood off."

"That's bullshit and you know it," I countered. "You didn't just pick out a name at random and put it on a witness list. He was on that list because of something he knew."

"Believe what you will." The lawyer was silent a moment, then added, "I warned you about poking through old shit."

"Like I told you the other day, Dad dropped a hint that something wasn't right with the way the trial went down. That was before a Nazi named George Kovacs got to him, told him to shut up."

"Jesus Christ, son," Jenkins III sighed. "What do you think you're doing?"

"Obviously something that's been left undone for a long time," I snapped at him. "Just tell me about Rudy Aiken…and don't give me any of that attorney-client privilege bullshit."

He bought a little time collecting his thoughts, or maybe fabricating a lie. Eventually he said, "It's not at all what you think, Rick. And in the long run it wouldn't have saved your father."

I got the feeling that Jenkins III was delaying the inevitable, calculating how much he might be able to tell me while actually revealing very little. "So go ahead—tell me what I'm thinking," I said.

As far as lawyers go Jenkins III was quite an actor. I knew he'd taken drama classes as an undergrad at Duke and had learned enough to perform a one-man show in the courtroom. He knew the value of a well-timed pause, the significance of an orchestrated sigh, the importance of a bombshell being dropped precisely at the right moment. He knew how to articulate his words in such a way as to evoke passion or tears or sympathy, and he recognized the influence of sincere eye contact. He also had learned the high cost of a mistake, which was why he almost never made them.

"Putting Rudy Aiken on the stand would have been a huge error," he finally explained to me. "He was a scrawny, pale-faced redneck who refused to shave or use deodorant. No one—and I do mean no one—would have related to him in any positive way. Whatever I stood to gain would have been lost in the first five seconds."

"So why put him on the list in the first place?" I asked.

Another pause, either for effect or to further mold the story. "Because he said he knew where your father was the night your mother was killed."

CHAPTER 19

This was not what I expected, and I almost rear-ended a plumbing van that had braked for a bicycle in front of me. I should not be having this conversation while driving, so I pulled off the highway and came to stop in the corner of a Kangaroo filling station.

"Where he was? What the hell are you talking about?"

"You've gone through the records," he said. "You know your father was shit-faced that night. Drunk as a skunk. And tox tests showed he had other substances in his blood system. Mostly benzodiazepine."

"I saw that," I replied. "Isn't that a depressant?"

"That's right. When you found your father on the floor he was still blacked out, and the benzos were to blame."

"So where was he? Where did he get these benzos?" I asked.

"That's where Rudy came in," Jenkins III said. "He swore that Frank—your father—had been at a gathering out near Cottageville, and he probably was given them there."

"Dad popped enough pills to make him pass out?" I asked.

"Aiken didn't know how they got in his system. Someone probably spiked his drink. And anyway, Blackwood would have shredded him up there on the stand."

His story had a thin ring of truth, and I had no real reason not to believe him. "What kind of gathering?" I asked.

"That's not pertinent to what you're asking," he said.

"My father wouldn't have been in Cottageville unless he had a reason," I said. "It's out in the middle of bum-fuck nowhere.

C'mon…I'm going to find out anyway."

Jenkins III let out an audible sigh, which I suspected was part of the overall drama. Then he said, "It was a meeting of an organization called White River. A nicer group of southern gentlemen you'd never want to meet."

I noted the sarcasm in his voice. "I assume you're not talking about the river that flows through the Ozarks."

"You assume correctly. You know your history of this state, Rick. Not exactly a bastion of tolerance and understanding. Behind every polite smile and 'yes, sir' and 'thank you, ma'am' is a thin dusting of suspicion and distrust. Suspicion of the unknown or the indefinite—which around these parts is considerable—and a distrust of anything that's unfamiliar or threatening. It's a history founded on prejudice and hypocrisy."

"This White River—are you talking about the Klan?" I asked him.

"Not in the strictest sense," Jenkins III replied. "But a close blood relative."

I'd always known my father was a bigot, but I never figured him for a white hood. "So what was my old man doing there that night?"

"That's what Rudy was going to explain," he said. "But then he disappeared, and we didn't have time to track him down. I tried to get an extension, but the judge said 'no'."

"But you knew," I pushed him. "You're too good of a lawyer not to know everything there was to know about that night."

"I appreciate your confidence," he replied. "And yes, you're right—up to a point. I vetted Aiken before I ever put him on the list. But like I told you, whatever I stood to gain would have been lost in the first five seconds. Just leave it be, Rick. Let it go."

I was about to lodge another protest but heard the signal click off. The old lawyer had hung up on me, and I knew that calling him back would yield the same results.

I phoned Laurie mid-afternoon and learned that the kids had grown tired of the beach and had moved on to go-carts and miniature golf. I asked her if she thought Addie was enjoying herself, to which Laurie reported that she'd only seen them for a couple of minutes but that my daughter seemed to be fitting right in. In fact, she seemed to be particularly besotted by a certain boy in the group named Sam.

"Besotted?" I repeated.

"Smitten, enamored, whatever. Your little girl is fine. A better question might be whether I'm enjoying myself."

There was a sensual quiver in her voice that told me there definitely was a correct way to respond. "That could be a very loaded question," I told her. "What might the answer be?"

"That the lunch rush is over, and things are a little slow here right now."

"Slow is good," I replied. "Care for some company?"

"What do you have in mind?" Laurie asked.

"Maybe an early start to happy hour."

"We don't have a happy hour at Jake's."

"I wasn't talking about Jake's," I told her. "I was thinking of a different gin joint in this corner of town, and it goes by the name Rick's."

She laughed at the *Casablanca* reference. "Now that's an offer I can't refuse."

"You're mixing movie dialogue, but I'll overlook it. So happy hour at my place, then?"

"I'll be there as soon as I can get out of here," she agreed. "But just for the record, I never said anything about just an hour."

I'm quite sure everyone had an enjoyable time for the duration of the afternoon. The group of teens had tried to arrange an extension of the day, this time a get-together for burgers at a local joint, but the other parents put the kibosh on that. Plus, Addie didn't eat burgers and was reluctant to sermonize on healthy diets, saving the environment, loving all animals, and all the other things that made people roll their eyes at her plant-based advocacy. Especially those who've been raised on Carolina barbecue and fried chicken. She was new to this group and didn't want to be voted off the island the same day she arrived.

When I picked Addie up she exchanged the vital "4-1-1" with Sam, and they both promised to text and FaceTime later. I knew well enough not to grill her on how her day was, nor did she volunteer any details. On our way back to the condo we stopped to pick up fixings for tacos, something Addie could eat because hers were a mixture of black beans and veggies. I had not gone the "full Monty," as she called it, but when we made meals together on her weekends at my canyon A-frame I honored her vegetarian choices. Tonight we did it full restaurant style, with Mexican rice and chips and guacamole, which we ate out on the balcony as lightning crackled in the west.

Halfway through the meal she asked the question that I knew would come up, sooner or later. She hadn't said anything when I'd picked her up, or while we were driving home, or even unloading the groceries out of the trunk.

"Why the new wheels, Dad?"

I hated to lie to her, since we had a solid relationship built on mutual trust. But sometimes the truth is hard to explain, and this was one of those times. "I rented the Kia up in Columbia in the middle of the night when I landed, and drove it down here," I said. "It was getting expensive, and getting a local car was cheaper."

She mulled that one over a few seconds and seemed to accept it. At that age you don't know exactly how things work, and there was an ounce of truth to what I'd told her.

"Have you given any thought to a service for Grandpa?" she asked me then.

"As a matter of fact, I have," I told her. "His body was cremated today, and they should have the cremains ready tomorrow. We can do it right after that."

"Cremains?" she asked with a noticeable shudder.

"That's the word they used. I didn't come up with it."

"Still, it's kinda creepy."

We then segued into what her day had been like. She'd liked most of the kids, except for one of the girls who kept trying to put her down. "Kardashian wannabe" and "left-coast nuthatch" was how the girl had defined her. Addie had chosen to ignore the insults, which had irritated the girl even more.

"I thought middle school ended years ago," I observed, not knowing what else to say.

"It did, but some people never got the text. No big deal."

Next morning Addie went with me to Jenkins IV's office. It was located on the third floor of an old building constructed of weathered brick and granite corner blocks and decorated with wrought iron grillwork. Thick bolts at the corners suggested it had been seismically retrofitted years ago, and real gas lamps flickered on either side of a massive oak door that opened in from the veranda. Baskets of begonias and lobelias and sweet alyssum hung from the outside ceiling, and pools of water beneath them suggested they had recently been watered.

Stepping inside took us a hundred years into the past. A grand staircase climbed from a large foyer of wide polished boards, while framed portraits of long-deceased patriarchs and dignitaries hung on plaster walls that were painted light yellow. A massive crystal chandelier hung from the coffered ceiling, and the window over the front door appeared to be genuine Tiffany glass. I had a vague recollection of being here once or twice many years ago, but at the time I would have been too preoccupied to have noticed the architectural details.

Jenkins advised us that Addie might be better off finding a comfortable seat in the waiting room, since our meeting involved complex financial and legal matters that would probably bore her. I expected her to protest, but she just picked up her phone and said, "I promised Sam we'd Snapchat." The waiting room looked as if it came right out of Tara, complete with a chest-high fireplace and green velvet curtains hanging from the windows. Addie found a mahogany chair finished in deep burgundy upholstery, tucked her feet up under her, and took out her phone.

Once she was comfortable, Jenkins IV showed me into a conference room with a long, rough-hewn wood table and a dozen chairs pushed in around it. A wall of windows overlooked a traditional garden out back: magnolias and oaks oozing tufts of Spanish moss, whitewashed gazebo, a placid pond with a gurgling waterfall and golden koi.

I took a seat at the near end of the table, and Jenkins chose the chair opposite me. He set a large accordion file down on the table and placed both hands on it, as if it might try to escape. He settled his eyes on mine for a minute, then said, "I understood from the start that this was going to be an unusual and difficult situation for you, coming back here to Charleston to care for your father in his final days. Given the family history and circumstances of his incarceration, and all. Not many sons—or daughters—would have done that."

I wondered how long he had rehearsed that line, practiced with the solemn gaze of a doctor providing his patient the grim diagnosis of metastatic cancer. But I also knew that I'd given him a hard time from the start, as well as yesterday, and I didn't want to get off on the wrong foot today with a snide remark. So I said, "Much appreciated, Myers. And I want to apologize for any crap I've thrown your way. The last few days have been a little stressful."

"No apologies necessary. You'd be surprised the way most people treat lawyers, and most of the time we deserve it. Anyway, let's get down to business."

He thumped a hand on the file and then removed a thin manila folder. From it he pulled out a few pages held together with a black alligator clip. From where I was seated I could see the Jenkins & Jenkins logo and lettering at the top of the first page. He held the sheaf of pages in two hands and said, "I was hoping your sister might be able to make it, but she told me her travel plans were indefinite. Then she told me to go to hell. So we'll proceed without her."

"When did you speak with her?" I asked.

"Yesterday afternoon. She said you had called her about your father and invited her to come, but she was not of a mind to accept. Those are my words; hers were a bit more colorful."

That sounded like Karen, and I had no reason to doubt him. "So what's that?" I asked, nodding at the pages in his hand.

His hands were still guarding the clipped stack, but now he set them down on the table. "You may not have known it, but several years before your mother's death your parents put their joint assets into an irrevocable trust," he explained. "They'd had a standard will, but my father convinced yours that a trust was a better way to proceed legally and financially. They offer a number of legal protections, as well as tax advantages."

I gave him an idle shrug; I'd talked to my own attorney about doing the same thing, but at this point my financial security was on life support. If I had to pay a lawyer, I was more concerned about rewriting the language of a custody agreement. A trust could wait.

"My father was always interested in saving taxes," I told him.

"He also was into new technology," Jenkins IV replied. "He didn't have a lot to invest, but what money he and your mother did have they put into a couple of small stocks. Over the years they performed quite nicely."

"Over the years?" I asked him. "My father was in jail for the last three decades. I'm sure the state took whatever assets he might have had."

"People have a lot of misconceptions about how the law works," Jenkins IV replied, shaking his head. "Neither the state nor the feds have the right to seize the assets of an inmate. They can take what they believe might have been used in the commission of a crime, or the profits therefrom. But not the contents of a trust."

"I see," I told him. "Go on."

He did. He went on to explain that from the time my father began toying with the stock market he dabbled with several companies, most of which had lost more money than they made. But as he got savvier, he focused on long-term growth, and what was happening in new tech and commerce. "In the mid-eighties he bought his first office computer, an IBM PC. He liked how it saved his secretary time in the office."

"Alice Marion," I told him.

"Good memory. I don't know where she is now, but she was very loyal to your father."

I was one step ahead of him; I'd spoken with her just yesterday. "She was on your father's witness list," I said.

"Could be," he said, swatting aside my comment as if it were a fly. "Anyway, at the time IBM was a big multinational company that manufactured typewriters, copiers, and computers of all sizes. Your father liked what he saw, and decided to invest."

"He bought IBM stock?"

"No, no. They manufactured the machines, but he believed the true value lay in what ran them. IBM was already too established, too entrenched in a highly competitive business with little upside, and he didn't like the risk. But he was intrigued by two start-up companies that created the operating systems that made the computers function. I remember him telling Dad that the sky was the limit when it came to what these programs could do."

I felt the hairs on my neck stand at attention. "What two start-ups are we talking about?" I asked him.

"Microsoft and Apple. He didn't invest much—ten thousand in each, give or take. And that was it. Your mother died not long after that, and he went to jail. But it turns out he made two very wise choices."

"And it's just been sitting there all this time?"

"Reinvesting dividends and compounding in value year over year. As you know, the sale of your parents' house paid your father's legal bills, but the trust itself was never touched. Aside from a modest sum set aside for legal fees resulting from probate, your parents made it so you and your sister are two fairly wealthy individuals."

"You're joking—"

"I'm dead serious," he said. "And since you were named the sole successor trustee, you have a few things to take care of."

"What does that mean…successor trustee?" I wanted to know.

"It means it's up to you to disburse the assets of the trust according to your parents' wishes. Starting now."

I walked out of there twenty minutes later thinking two things: life for Addie and me had just changed in a big way, and I needed to revise my own will.

I also was questioning whether I should leave well enough alone. Forget George Kovacs, Rudy Aiken, Jimmy Holland, and whatever had really gone down the night of my mother's murder. Nothing I did or learned would change the course of Devlin family history: my parents would still be dead, my ex-wife would still be in the hospital, and my daughter would still be in the passenger seat next to me, texting furiously with a boy she had met only yesterday. Jenkins IV had assured me I could handle all the legal paperwork from my home in California, so there was no need to remain in Charleston any longer than I wanted to. The condo apparently was paid up for three more weeks, but there was no practical need to hang around. As soon as we scattered my father's cremains in the harbor we could pack up and get the next flight out.

It was still early and even earlier in L.A., but Addie and I placed a call to the hospital to check on her mother's status. Because she had been intubated following her overdose she had contracted aspiration pneumonia, and the infection was proving to be stubborn. They'd put Belinda on antibiotics, which hadn't had time to go to work yet. Bottom line: she was in guarded condition, not critical but certainly not out of the woods, either. The nurse we spoke with did her best to tiptoe around any prognosis, trying to sound upbeat about eventual recovery. Addie asked some good questions, listened to the answers, and when we ended the call, sat silent for a long while.

Eventually she said, "I should be there, but I don't think there's anything I can do."

"She needs time to heal," I assured her. "The hospital is open twenty-four-seven, and we can call anytime you want."

She accepted this, but I could tell from her prolonged silence that she was struggling with guilt, responsibility, and concern. And the unexpected presence of a boy named Sam in her life, which tangled her anxiety even more.

The crematorium director had said that my father's ashes wouldn't be ready until mid-afternoon. He'd also told me that federal regulations prohibited the scattering of ashes less than three miles from land, while the EPA had its own set of restrictions. But then he told me he knew a guy with a boat who would take us out on the water for two hundred bucks, no questions asked. The boat would be available at three o'clock and the government could piss up its red-tape, he proclaimed.

"Sam wants to know if I can go see a movie," Addie said suddenly, looking up from her screen.

"When?"

"Just now," she said, showing me her phone.

I stole a quick glance at her; besotted didn't seem to be the proper word for the look in her eyes. "I mean, when is the movie?"

"Whenever," she said. "He works at Chick-fil-A, and he's through at five."

"What movie?" I asked her.

"I don't know," she told me. "Just a *movie*."

"We're doing that thing with my father this afternoon," I reminded her.

"I know. So can I tell him 'yes'?"

It was obvious that she really wanted to do this, and the kid named Sam was keeping Addie's mind off her mother's issues. While I had a hundred things I wanted to do with my daughter while we were here, most of all I wanted her to be happy. So I said, "Under one condition."

She shot me a suspicious look. "What?"

"I get to meet him first."

"Jeez, Dad. You're going to drive us. He doesn't have his license yet."

Two minutes after we got back to the condo my phone rang. It was an 843 number I didn't recognize, but I'd grown accustomed to that over the last few days. "Hello," I answered with a slightly distrustful tone.

"Who is this?" a brusque voice growled on the other end.

"You called me," I said. "Who were you expecting?"

There was a brief pause. "This is Detective Amos Brady with SLED. Is this your phone?"

SLED was the State Law Enforcement Division, South Carolina's version of the FBI. My first and only encounter with them was the night my mother was killed, and I wondered why this guy was calling me now.

"Yes, sir," I said, resorting to my inbred southern manners. "I'm Rick Devlin, and this is my cell. What can I do for you?"

"Did you place a call to a Miss Lily Elliott last Friday?"

In an instant I could see what this was about, and my brain started to work fast. "Yes, I did," I replied. "I had some questions for her and I asked her if we could meet."

"She blocked your call," Detective Brady said. "After about six seconds."

"Yes, she did. She didn't recognize the California area code and thought I was a marketer, maybe a realtor trying to tell her how much her house is worth."

"Ten seconds later you tried calling her back," Brady pressed.

"Because I didn't know she'd blocked me. When I figured it out, I borrowed a phone from someone and called her again. If you have her records there you can see another call a few minutes later. We talked for a minute or two."

"Eighty-six seconds," Detective Brady said.

"Sounds about right," I said. "I assume this is about her murder?"

"She was ambushed at her front door," he confirmed. "Shot in cold blood. We're talking to anyone who might be a person of interest."

I glanced over my shoulder at Addie, who was sitting on her knees in a chair in the living room. She'd barely looked away from her phone since I'd collected her from Jenkins' waiting room, but I knew from years of experience that she was a good multi-tasker. Her fingers were texting a mile a minute with Sam, but I had no doubt that her ears were tuned in to my side of the phone call.

"I'm not your guy," I told him. "I was busy all day Sunday."

"Can you prove it?"

"I picked up my daughter at the airport and she was with me all afternoon. She was right here when the story came on the news."

He said nothing for a few seconds, then continued, "We're going to want to talk to her."

"Not a problem," I replied. "But can it wait until tomorrow? My father died Saturday and we're holding a small service for him later today."

"We're on a tight timeline to crack this, Mr. Devlin."

"I understand, sir. I just don't know how I can help you."

"You can start by telling me why you called the victim. You said you wanted to ask her a few questions."

"That's correct, but I'm sure it had nothing to do with her death. I just had some questions about an old trial she covered back when she was a reporter." I didn't want to go into what sort of trial, or the fact that my father had been convicted of murder thirty years ago. He hadn't connected those dots yet, and I wasn't about to spur him along. I didn't want him thinking *like father, like son.*

"Did she agree? To answer your questions, I mean? I have no record of any further calls from you."

"She invited me down to her house for coffee Saturday morning," I explained. "We spoke for about a half-hour, and then I left."

He was silent for a moment, then said, "How would you describe her frame of mind at the time?"

"On the phone she told me she was on a deadline, but when I got there she was very hospitable. She didn't seem to be preoccupied with anything, at least not that I could tell."

There was another silence, and then he said, "Have you ever heard of a person named George Kovacs?"

Wham!—there it was. Kat Rattigan must have fed the name to her contacts at SLED, and now this Detective Brady was asking me about him. I hesitated a few seconds, then said, "Not right offhand. Who is he?"

"Just a name," Brady replied with a grunt. "We got a tip, and I'm just following up on all leads. And I'm still going to want to talk to your daughter."

CHAPTER 20

Addie and I met up with Maxx Mason right at three at the Patriot's Point Marina, just a stone's throw from where the *U.S.S. Yorktown* was moored. "Maxx, with two x's," he'd explained, as if I might have a reason to spell it later. He'd brought the brass urn that held my father's ashes, a thoughtful gesture so we didn't have to drive out to the crematorium to pick it up. I signed a few forms, accepted the urn with both hands, and stepped over the gunwale onto his Sea Ray inboard. Addie followed right behind, admiring the swim platform protruding from the transom.

"Sweet," she said.

Mason took us into the outer reaches of the harbor, past Fort Sumter on our right. "Starboard side," he reminded me. I figured him to be about my age, shorter and huskier, skin about as dark as the black paint on the side of his boat, which was cleverly named *Miss Conduct.* His hair was showing little coils of silver, and when he moved he had a noticeable limp that caused him to wince.

He provided a full summary of Civil War history as we raced through the water, the hull slamming against the crests and plunging into the troughs. The old tales had been ingrained in me in elementary and high school, and armor-plated by southern lore. He pointed out where Citadel cadets had opened fire on the merchant ship *Star of the West* as it was entering the harbor, and where Brigadier General Pierre Beauregard ordered the bombardment of Fort Sumter, with cannon fire raining down on Union troops. Later during the war, a massive fire started at East Bay Street, over there, and destroyed most of Charleston. And the battle of Secessionville pushed back the Union forces right over there, he informed us, saving the city from a land invasion of dreaded Yankees.

Eventually he slowed the engine and shifted the throttle into neutral. A heavy chop was coming from the southeast, and a steady wind pushed a thick billow of clouds across the sun. We were a good half-mile from the southern tip of Sullivan's Island, where a handful of fishing boats bobbed in the running tide. In the distance, the beacon of what I always considered the world's ugliest lighthouse flashed its rhythmic wink.

Mason gave me a nod and said, "This is the best place for what you have in mind, unless you want to go way out."

"This'll do fine," I told him.

Over the years I've attended my share of funeral services, which usually were defined by bountiful tears and solemn prayers and black veils, with clergy reciting words meant to remember the recently departed with great exultation and evoke even more tears. Lots of references to God and Jesus and "our daily bread" and the "Valley of Death," words about not being led into temptation and delivering us from evil. Growing up in the heart of southern piety I fully understood the unctuous pleas made to a Supreme Being in an attempt to have one's own sins forgiven. This was the land of some of man's most egregious transgressions against other men, and forgiveness was in high demand.

But I mentioned none of that now. In fact, I said nothing as Addie reached for the brass urn that contained my father's ashes. Together we unscrewed the lid, and then moved to the back of the boat.

"Do you mind if we use the platform?" she asked Mr. Mason.

"That's why it's there," he replied from the captain's seat behind the wheel.

Taking my cue from my daughter, I followed her over the transom and moved to the port side of the swim deck. She stared up at the heavens a moment as if collecting her thoughts, and at that moment the large cloud that had darkened the day lifted its veil and the sky lit up like a thousand suns. This brought a smile to her beautiful face, and in that instant I saw my father's eyes, only younger and brighter and still full of wonder.

Then she said, "Because of tangled fates we may never comprehend, I never got to know you, not as a fellow human being or my grandfather. But on this beautiful afternoon we have come together on the waters of this historic and embattled harbor to share your passing, and to honor your life. In the words of the great Shawnee warrior, 'When your time comes to die, be not like those whose hearts are filled with fear of death, so that when their time comes they weep and pray for a little more time to live their lives over again in a different way. Sing your death song, and die like a hero going home.' "

I stared at her with what I presume was a gaping mouth, because she then flipped me a slight shrug and said, "Tecumseh."

I was up next. As a major league pitcher in the American League I never once was called on to step into the batter's box and take a swing. Pitchers simply can't hit, and fans cringe in despair after three quick strikes send them back to the dugout. That was how I felt at that moment, because it was my turn to speak and I was totally unprepared. After all these years of uncertainty and disappointment I was left with no eloquence in my heart or soul. Too many questions, too many memories, too much doubt cramped my mind to conjure the sort of compassion or unconditional love my daughter had just spoken of.

So I simply said, "Dad...you were my father, my hero, my coach, my mentor, and for far too long the shadow in my being. With your passing I hope you have found peace and serenity. I pray that truth will come to show itself, and that your life—and death—will someday be viewed with honor and distinction. Our brief existence in this world comes from the stuff of stars, and we now return you to the earth and the sea. Ashes to ashes, dust to dust. Rest in peace, old man."

Addie and I then both raised the urn to the edge of the swim platform and sifted my father's cremains into the churning water of Charleston Harbor. We spoke not another word, but my brain was a steady stream of memories as his ashes tumbled from the brass jar. My life with my father seemed to pass before my very eyes as his charred flesh and bones joined my mother's in the very waters where her own star stuff had been scattered thirty years before.

The brass urn was a loaner so we had to give it back. That was all right with me, since I had never been one to hang on to mementos of the past. I still had the baseball that had gotten me the final strikeout in my perfect game in high school, and the glove that had been fished out of the marsh after the hurricane. But that was it. An empty urn on a mantle would only serve as a reminder of hollow promises and untapped possibilities that had been truncated by tragedy.

Once we returned to the condo, Addie started to fret about what to wear. When she left L.A. she'd hurriedly tossed a jumble of clothes into her suitcase, and now was convinced she couldn't be seen at the movie theater wearing any of them. Over the last few years I'd come to understand the hysterics of adolescence which, in L.A., carried more pent-up stress than the San Andreas Fault. Fashion nuances were dictated by unwritten trends that seemed to change on a whim, so that a pair of shorts or skirt that was "*V lit*" one day was "*total sus*" the next. (I had the internet to thank for helping my vocabulary stay "*woke.*")

She eventually settled on cut-offs and a pink T-shirt with a bejeweled image of the Hindu God Ganesh on it. She could explain what it was to anyone who asked, and those who didn't probably would think it was just an elephant. She matched it with a pink Angels cap, which I had given her for her last birthday, as I had done every birthday of her entire life.

Sam lived in a townhome on stilts in a gated community built on mud dredged from the Intracoastal Waterway. As soon as we pulled into the driveway the front door opened and Sam appeared, dressed in cargo shorts and a U.S.C. T-shirt. He wore a baseball cap backwards on his head, and had blue sneakers the size of small cars on his feet.

Sam's father was a dentist and his mother did all the bookkeeping for the family practice. They seemed like pleasant folks, and didn't flinch when they learned that their son was going to the movies with a girl from the left coast. Even more important, they didn't seem to have any knowledge of the Devlin name or that Addie's late grandfather had been a convicted killer. I promised them I'd have their son home no later than eleven, even though both young moviegoers groaned in unison.

When I got back to the condo the SLED investigator was waiting for me. Detective Amos Brady said he wanted to verify a few things we had discussed on the phone earlier, and just decided to drop by. A sharp spasm briefly seized my stomach, then subsided just as quickly as I invited him inside. My plan had been to come home, grab a beer, and see what Kat Rattigan might have turned up on Rudy Aiken. But that was going to have to wait.

Detective Brady declined my offer of beer or water, insisting he wasn't going to stay that long. That was fine with me, but I still was a bit spooked by why he had shown up unannounced, rather than call me as he had before. He cleared that up quickly and directly.

"You weren't exactly up front with me," he said, his voice accusatory and bordering on threatening. "But you already knew that."

"I'm not sure I'm following you," I replied. "What are you talking about?"

"I'm talking about lying to an officer of the law. Specifically, about a man named George Kovacs you said you didn't know."

"I'm still not sure what you're driving at," I told him, quickly deciding to stick with my previous story. "I don't know anyone with that name."

"Not according to him," Brady pressed. "In fact, he said the two of you got into an altercation at the airport Sunday morning."

"There was a bit of an understanding with a guy in a truck, but I had no idea what his name was. You're telling me that was George Kovacs?"

He studied me, almost challenging me to keep my story straight. "According to him, you tried to keep him from pulling into a parking space," he said. "Of course, he had a little difficulty telling me this, because of the bandage wrapped around his swollen jaw. A jaw he indicated got banged up because of your temper."

"And he just happened to know my name?"

"What he said was he got your plate number, tracked you down because he intends to sue your ass off for pain and suffering."

I doubted that Kovacs had any intention of going anywhere near a lawyer, but I could see where Brady was going with his questioning. "Like I told you, I didn't know his name," I said. "And you're the one who linked him to Lily Elliott's murder. Is there something about him you're not telling me?"

"I told you, we got a tip," Brady clarified. He waited for me to say something more, but when I didn't, he continued, "Tell me about this altercation at the airport."

I had two ways to play this: lie or tell the truth. But I already could see where lying to this man might take me, while there was no reason not to go the straight and narrow. It was a phrase I remember my mother telling me, something that went: "Straight is the gate, and narrow is the way, which leadeth unto life."

So I said, "He was parked out on the curb when I left here to pick up my daughter, and he followed me all the way to the parking garage. I snapped a photo of him with my phone, and he went berserk. He came charging out of his truck at me, and I defended myself." I almost mentioned the gun in his hand, but then I remembered I'd stashed it on my closet shelf after I'd fished it out from under the SUV in the parking garage.

"Why do you suppose he'd do that?"

"I don't know, and I didn't ask him. But if there's a connection to Lily Elliott's death, it's possible he followed me down to Beaufort on Saturday, as well."

"What I don't understand is why you believe Mr. Kovacs was following you," Brady said.

I began to tell him again how I had noticed his car Sunday morning, but he raised a hand to stop me. "Save your breath," he snipped. "What I'm asking is why he'd be tailing you in the first place."

Aside from landing a wicked punch into Kovacs' jaw I'd done nothing wrong—not yet—and having the state cops on my side could only help me in the long run. My father was already dead and his ashes scattered, so whatever covenant I had signed no longer existed.

"I believe Kovacs was following me because of my father," I explained, then launched into my mother's murder and my father's conviction, and his diagnosis six weeks ago with terminal cancer. "The parole board released him last week because of his health, and I agreed to take custody from the state," I said.

"Which still doesn't explain one damned thing about Mr. Kovacs," Brady replied.

I didn't feel like going into my father's thin attempt to revisit his innocence, or the note warning him to keep his mouth shut. "No it doesn't," I agreed. "But he's stuck his nose in my family business, for some reason. Maybe you should take a harder look at him."

Brady leveled me with a dark, almost accusatory look, then went on. "Kovacs has a file a foot thick. He's done some despicable things in his short time on this planet. Maybe he had something to do with the Elliott woman's death, maybe not. Too early to tell. And I don't care personally if you landed those bruised knuckles on your right hand on his jaw or not. He probably deserved what he had coming. But if you are responsible for laying him up, you'd do well to stay way clear of him."

"Your concerns are noted," I assured him. "I have no intention of going anywhere near that dirt bag again."

"Wise choice," Brady said. "Just keep in mind that, in the long run, it may not be yours to make."

I hadn't checked my email since before we'd scattered my dad's ashes, and after Detective Brady left I found a bunch of them. Most were spam from marketers or Nigerian princes, but one was from my publisher. It was just a gentle nudge, reminding me that my deadline was approaching rapidly and hoping that all was on schedule. I assured her I was on top of things and she had no need to worry. The book would be delivered on time.

One other message snared my full attention, and I saved it for last. I knew that once I opened it I would be pulled back down the wormhole, and I needed to clear my mind of all other issues. The email was from Kat Rattigan, and the subject line simply read: "Rudy Aiken." Kat had not called me back the way she had when I'd submitted my George Kovacs search, and I didn't know if that meant anything. I was about to find out:

Mr. Devlin: Attached to this email is the full background check for the Rudolph Aiken you requested. My computer search found records for two persons with that name, but since one of them was born only twelve years ago, I assume he is not the subject you are profiling. As you will see from the report, very little data is available, and none of it from any year after 2003. The final document is a newspaper notice that indicates he passed away at some point before that.

Thank you, KR

The background report told me that Rudolph Clarence Aiken had been born March 9th, 1969 in Newberry, South Carolina. Sixteen years later a driver's license had been issued to a person with the same name, and it had never been renewed. At some point the family must have moved because Aiken had graduated from Orangeburg-Wilkinson High School in 1987, just a few miles from where Jimmy Holland had been killed in July 1989. Coincidence or not, the implication was not lost on me.

Not long after turning eighteen, Aiken had two scrapes with the law. The first was an arrest for petty larceny in 1988, details not provided and charges dropped. Six months later he was apprehended again, this time for possessing and pointing a firearm. Again, charges were dropped. During that period Aiken had paid minimal state and federal income taxes, after which he became a ghost. There was absolutely no mention of him after that, except for a brief newspaper story that said his remains had been positively identified through dental records in August 2003. There was no location or cause of death given, except for a notation that said his remains had been found in Berkeley County.

Berkeley County bordered Charleston County to the northwest and included almost all of the soggy woodlands known as the Francis Marion Forest. The mention of dental records told me Rudy Aiken had either met a very gruesome death, or his body had not fared well after his demise. Maybe both. His last known address had been in Orangeburg—a town that was now highlighted in my mind—and the last time he paid state and federal taxes was 1989. The same year my mother had died. The same year Jimmy Holland had died, and one year before he failed to show at my father's trial and dropped out of the system.

I typed "Rudy Aiken + Berkeley County" into Google and got absolutely no results of any meaning. I considered this for a moment, then changed the entry to read "Rudolph Aiken + Berkeley" and this time got a solid hit. It was a link to a story in the Charleston *Post & Courier*, noting that a body had been pulled out of an old rice bog near Dog Swamp Road A in the national forest. The remains had been identified as those belonging to Mr. Aiken, last known address in Orangeburg, South Carolina. Cause of death was unknown pending autopsy, but the county medical examiner offered little hope that anyone would ever know how, or even when, the man had died.

CHAPTER 21

The next morning Addie went with me to the Berkeley County Clerk of Courts office in Monck's Corner. The South Carolina Department of Health and Environmental Control—acronymically known as DHEC—issues birth and death records for all such events following 2005, but Rudy Aiken's body had been found before that, so the county was the place to go. My daughter wanted to know why I was looking for a death certificate for a man I'd never met, then astutely said, "This has to do with Grandpa, doesn't it?"

There was no point keeping the truth from her—except, perhaps, about George Kovacs—so I conceded that I was following a lead that might somehow determine whether her grandfather was innocent or guilty. She considered this while we waited for the county computers to cough up the data for which I had just paid twelve dollars, then said, "Seems like a lot of effort to go through for something that might be nothing."

Seizing on a teaching moment, I told her, "In my best baseball days I usually threw ninety, maybe a hundred pitches during a game. Not all of them were strikes, and only a few ever won or lost a game. But every single one of them contributed to the outcome, one way or another."

She seemed to accept the message, and said, "You're going for the win."

"Never settled for less," I replied.

Eventually the document was ready and my name was called.

Addie had never seen a death certificate and was curious to know what it looked like. When I handed it to her she studied the elaborate engraving, similar to the artwork found on a dollar bill.

"Cool," she finally said.

"It's called *guilloché*," I said, trying to impress her. It was a word I remembered from art class during my junior year in high school, when Mrs. Bowen tried her best to deflect our collective—and lusting—attention from her very ample bosom. "It's a graphic ornamentation that you find on everything from dollar bills to stock certificates."

"That's really interesting, Dad, but what I mean is it says here that death was likely caused by a gunshot wound. See?"

She handed the certificate back and I let my eyes go to where she was pointing. My daughter was correct: the coroner had certified that Rudy Aiken had suffered a single gunshot wound, which likely killed him instantly. There was a brief note that explained that C.O.D. was not precise because of the dearth of actual remains, but it probably was connected to small fragments of a bullet that were found lodged in the C-4 vertebra, severing the spinal cord. I knew from my chiropractor that the C-4 was in the midsection of the cervical spine, near the base of the neck, and any injury in that area was bound to cause catastrophic damage to the central nervous system. Judging from where Aiken's body had been found in the Francis Marion Forest, if he hadn't died instantly, he'd suffered a slow demise. Although not necessarily painful, since he probably wouldn't have felt anything from the neck down.

"Who was this guy?" Addie asked me as we were walking back to where I'd parked the car. The sun was well above the tree line and steam from a band of thundershowers that had moved through the lowcountry last night was rising from the warming asphalt. I glanced around the lot at the cars and trucks, checking to see if anyone was slumped down behind the wheel of any of them. I was reasonably sure we had not been followed here from Charleston, but I was taking no chances. I also figured that a state police vehicle I saw at the edge of the lot would serve as a deterrence if any trouble did arise.

"Rudy Aiken was supposed to testify at your grandfather's trial," I told her. No reason to hold back the truth; she was entitled to know her family's history, warts and all. "Just days before he was supposed to go on the stand it seems he disappeared, only to turn up thirteen years later in the middle of an old rice swamp."

"Gross," she said with a shudder. "You think he was killed because of what he knew?"

"Could be any number of things," I replied. "Or it could just be coincidence."

It also could have been coincidence that Addie wanted to grab lunch at the Chick-fil-A in Mount Pleasant, the same restaurant where Sam had a summer job taking window orders and directing traffic through the crowded noontime lot. I reminded her that it was fast food chicken and she was a vegetarian, to which she replied, "I hear they have great salads."

She insisted we eat inside, where for the next twenty minutes she did her best to waggle a finger whenever she caught a glimpse of him. He stopped by our table to say "hello" twice, and Addie appeared to blush both times. He seemed to be a decent kid with a good work ethic, and college plans that would lead to heaps of success. I couldn't find anything to fault him for, except that he was interested in my daughter, and I remembered all too well what was going through my mind when I was not much older. Laurie's mind, too, come to think of it.

Addie attended an academic magnet school in California that assigned a modest reading list for the summer. She had plugged away at it but still had three books to finish before classes began in just over a month, and on the drive back to the condo she informed me she was going to follow my suggestion and dig into *Gone with the Wind.* She had put off the trials and tribulations of Scarlet and Rhett since early June, but her sudden and fervent interest in Sam and all things southern had shifted her perspective. She'd grown up about as far from the land of Dixie as she could get, yet she was plunging herself into the ethos of the Civil War. I'd done the same when I was just about her age, and the book had instilled in me a deep, abiding appreciation for my Carolina lineage and all the inconsistent pathology that went with it.

That was the plan for the afternoon, but as Addie had learned from her Robert Burns reading at the start of summer, "The best laid schemes of mice and men often go awry." When we stepped off the elevator on the twelfth floor I saw that the door to the condo was ajar.

Not open; someone had pushed it closed but not far enough for the bolt to latch. My first thought naturally went to George Kovacs and what had happened to Lily Elliott, and I motioned for Addie to stand to the far side of the door while I gently eased it open. There was no sign of damage to the wooden jamb or the lock mechanism itself, which told me entry had not been gained violently. Still, someone was inside, and I didn't see that as spelling anything but trouble.

Having grown up in South Carolina I was raised to appreciate the Second Amendment, even though no one I'd known was a member of a well-regulated militia. In my youth, pistols were used to pop beer cans at the dump, and that was where I'd drawn the line. I'd never been interested in stopping a beating heart, human or otherwise, but as long as Kovacs had me in his sights I was glad I'd hung on to his gun. I had no idea if the sonofabitch had come to own it legally or what he might have used it for in the past, and none of that would matter if I ever had to use it.

Problem was, the gun was on a shelf in the bedroom closet and I was out here in the hallway.

"Stay put," I told my daughter, reaching out my arm in a gesture to nudge her further away from the door.

"What is it, Dad?" she asked me.

"Let me go in first, make sure it's safe."

"Why wouldn't it be safe?" she pressed. "Does this have to do with why you switched cars the other day?"

I didn't answer; I just put my finger to my lips and slipped inside.

At first I saw nothing out of the ordinary, but an odd aroma hit my nose almost instantly. My mind flashed on my early days with Belinda, before we were married and she lived in a studio apartment not much larger than a garden shed. The floor was always covered with empty food containers and dirty laundry, and the place often reeked of an incense stick that was burning on the cluttered coffee table. She insisted the smell eliminated toxic fumes from the air and tantalized your sensory nodes as you sank into meditative bliss, but to me it was just noxious.

That's what the condo smelled like now, except not the same scent. Belinda's apartment always had the odor of a cat that had jumped on a hot burner, but this scent was softer, less invasive or toxic. A mixture of pine and lemon, with a sweet fragrance of walnuts.

What the hell?

My question was answered three seconds later when a woman poked her head out of the kitchen and saw me pressed up against the wall in the foyer, my hand balled up in a fist that was ready to let fly.

"Ricky...there you are," my sister said in a voice that always reminded me of nails on a blackboard. "I was starting to get worried."

"Karen...what the hell...how did you get in here?"

She cracked a large grin. "Practice, just like Carnegie Hall." Then she lunged at me, wrapping her arms around me like the extended sleeves of a straightjacket. She hung on tight and far longer than was comfortable, then pushed away and said, "My God, it's good to see you."

I edged back a step, just in case she decided to go for a second squeeze. I hadn't seen her in ten years, and was not expecting the streaks of green mixed into her dishwater hair. Tight lines emanated from the corners of her steely gray eyes, and faint signs of aging accented her typically pale skin. "I had no idea you were coming," I said.

"Well, surprise!"

At that point I heard Addie say, "Dad—?"

"Who's that?" my sister said, peeking around me at the open door. "Holy Mother of God...Adeline? Is that really you?"

Karen had come out to California once about ten years ago, just after Addie had turned five. She had stayed with Belinda and me for forty-eight excruciating hours, and had been sober or straight for about three of them, although not all in a row. This was after my twenty-eight-day stint at Rehab Ranch and I'd had no tolerance for the tequila, weed, uppers, coke, and painkillers that kept my sister company all hours of the day and night. After a non-stop two-day party, I'd finally screwed up the courage to boot her out. We hadn't spoken for months after that, but I was not about to expose my young daughter to that kind of shit. Her mother already had that sort of education well in hand, and Addie didn't need to be double-teamed.

My sister didn't appear to remember any of that right now, although I was sure it would come back to her at some point. Despite all the ways she had tried to mess up her mind, she never seemed to destroy a single memory cell. Instead she opened her arms wide, like a massive trap, and Addie fell right into it.

"Is that incense?" she asked, as soon as she extricated herself from the jaws of life.

"It is," Karen said, pushing a strand of hair behind her ear. She took Addie's hand and led her into the kitchen. "Frankincense, in fact. It's used to promote calm and peace and reduce stress and anxiety. But it's also good for easing ongoing conflicts and bringing peace and harmony between longtime adversaries."

She let the last few words dangle, indicating they were meant for me. And signaling that her cynicism was just as sharp as ever.

Judging by her rapid cadence, Karen clearly was in one of her "up" moods, which I knew eventually would suffer the inevitable plunge. While she chattered at Addie in the kitchen I quickly glanced around, saw no sign of luggage or an overnight bag. I took a quick look into Addie's room: nothing. Same with mine.

As I closed the front door Karen poked her head back out of the kitchen, and said, "I know what you're thinking, so don't worry. I'm only here for one night, and I'm staying with a friend. Well, not exactly a friend, just someone I met at that place in Georgia last year, the one who'd been in that horrible crash that killed two people in the other car. Her name is Tonya. She had to go into pretrial substance abuse intervention or something like that. The judge approved it instead of a prison sentence, but she has to pay restitution, which she can't afford because her husband left her, but she has a cousin who lives on James Island, on the other side of Charleston, and she said I could crash there. When's the service?"

"The what?" I repeated. I knew the answer to her question, but I needed to buy time to sort through all the info she had just downloaded.

"The funeral," she explained. "For Dad. Or have you forgotten that he died?"

"Not easy to forget," I said. "I was here."

"Don't guilt me," she snapped, then quickly creased her lips in a tight smile. "I don't need that sort of thing right now."

I hesitated a second, trying to release the sudden tension from my nerves. The frankincense obviously wasn't doing its peaceful, non-adversarial thing. "There isn't going to be a funeral," I informed her. "No one knew he was here, and no one knows he died."

"But—" She stared at me, her eyes dark with contempt and

disbelief. "Where is he? Where's his body?"

"You said you weren't sure if you could make it here," I reminded her. "I couldn't just tell the folks at the crematorium to keep him on ice until you made up your mind."

"Crematorium?" she snapped, her voice almost a scream. "You can't just...burn him up!"

"Too late." Those two words came from Addie, who was standing behind my sister in the kitchen.

"What do you mean? Too late for what?"

"We had a small service and scattered his ashes yesterday."

"You...did *fucking what*?"

"Karen...keep it down," I told her. The line from a Johnny Cash song jumped into my mind, the one about hearing the train a-rolling 'round the bend. A mood change was fast approaching, and there was nothing I could do to delay its arrival. "Please...take a breath and settle down."

But that was not my sister's style. There were no breaths and definitely no settling down in her repertoire. With one massive swing of her arm she swept the incense burner to the floor, glowing stick and all. She almost caught my daughter with her hand, but Addie moved back with the same speed as a batter being brushed back by one of my targeted fastballs.

"You went ahead and burned up his body and then scattered him...*where*...at the beach? From a bridge? A boat? And where was I during all this? Didn't you even think to include me? He was my father, too, for Chrissakes. I should have had some input in this, but you just went ahead and did your thing, just like you always did. Just like during the trial, oblivious to what was going on around you, joking around with that black friend of yours. You didn't even know what that was about, did you? Protecting us from reporters, my ass! What a joke. You never gave a shit about me, or what I was going through. Everything was about you. Then and now. Always was, always will be."

Each word of her raging diatribe was delivered at the decibel level of a jet fighter doing a low fly-by. I'd witnessed the spectacle before, on more than one occasion, so I was accustomed to the rage. But Addie had never experienced such a display, not even from her mother, who typically became quiet and morose when she slipped into what she called the crypt of darkness.

"I called you right after Dad died," I said in an even tone that I knew would only inflame my sister's rage. Inevitably, anything I said—no matter my tone or choice of words—would escalate into a fire fight. "You said you didn't know how to feel. And you wouldn't say if you wanted to come here or not."

"I told you, don't go throwing blame on me for this!" she screamed. I was afraid she might put her fist through a wall, which made me wonder if Jenkins IV had paid a damage deposit when he rented the place. "You call me out of the blue and tell me Dad just died and you expect me to drop everything, come running to see him? I have a life, you know? *A life!* It's not like I could just pull up everything and come nurse him in this fancy condo, wait for him to die. I didn't do this! *It. Is. Not. My. Fault!*"

My sister was blocking the doorway, one hand firmly planted on either side. Addie was trapped in the kitchen, and there was no way she could get around her. I knew from experience that when Karen got going there was no easy way to stop her. Not until she burned herself out. That could take minutes or hours, depending on the depth of her rage and what sort of chemicals were raging in her blood. Her doctors had prescribed a virtual pharmacy of medications over the years, but I had no idea what kind of pills she was popping these days.

"Let's go, Addie," I said, looking past her to my daughter. "We're late."

"Late?" my sister yelped. "What the fuck are you late for?"

I didn't answer, a voice in my brain screaming *disengage!* Addie picked up on my cue right away, ducked down and slid under Karen's outstretched arms.

"I said, what are you fucking late for?"

I didn't utter another word as I waved Addie past me toward the front door. I made eye contact with my sister just once, for less than a second, then slipped out into the hallway and pulled the door closed behind us.

"Don't you fucking walk out on me!" she screamed, the volume of her voice muffled only slightly as the latch clicked.

"Stairs," Addie suggested, cocking her head at the steel fire door that opened into the exit stairwell.

We hurried down a flight of steps and emerged onto the eleventh floor. I cautiously pushed the door open and peered out into the corridor. Empty, no yelling. "We can take the elevator from here," I said.

She nodded, then said, "What was that?"

"I'm sorry I didn't get the chance to properly introduce you," I said, feeling miserable. "As you know, your Aunt Karen has some anger issues."

"You think?"

"She experiences major mood swings and personality shifts," I explained.

"What do you think she'll do up there?"

I shook my head and said, "Scream and yell, throw a few things. Probably break stuff. Eventually someone will call the cops, and then she'll simmer down. Until next time."

"You don't seem to care—"

Addie was right; I didn't care. Not a good lesson to teach your daughter, but I'd grown weary with my sister's over-the-top rants. She was not well—hadn't been since before the trial—and she'd never made it possible to reach out to her. Get-togethers of any length eventually devolved into chaos and uproar, which then led to a visit from the police. I had not wanted to expose Addie to that, which was why I admittedly had not gone out of my way to include Karen in the memorial plans for our father.

"I care very much about Aunt Karen," I assured her. "But when she gets into one of these phases the only thing that works is for her to push through it on her own."

"How long will that take?" Addie asked. "The pushing-through part?"

I hated to sound indifferent, especially when my sister obviously was in so much pain. But I was all out of teachable moments, so I said, "A couple hours, usually. Then we can go back and see what kind of storm damage there is."

My phone rang just as we reached the ground floor and the doors slid open. I glanced at the screen, saw the call was from a Los Angeles area code. It was not a number I recognized, and definitely not in my Contacts. I shot a quick glance at my daughter, then said, "Rick Devlin—"

"Mr. Devlin," a voice on the other end said. Male, sincere,

concerned. Indian. “I’m Dr. Verghese, at Valleyheart Hospital. It’s about your wife, Belinda.”

“Ex-wife,” I corrected him. After my sister’s flare-up I was in a lousy mood, and probably came across as blunt. Probably even terse.

“Such as it is,” he said. I had no idea what that meant, but decided to let him do the talking. “She is the mother of your daughter?”

“Yes.”

“Well, then I am calling you to let you know there are some complications.”

CHAPTER 22

The complications weren't necessarily life-threatening, but the bottom line was that Belinda was in bad shape. The doctors had prescribed a series of antibiotics that still had yet to do their thing, and had placed her in quarantine to guard against any outside bacteria that could morph into acute respiratory distress syndrome. Plus, there was the risk of severe sepsis, which in her condition could prove fatal.

I glanced at Addie, who fortunately had just received a text from Sam. He must have been on a break, and couldn't have found a more opportune time to reach out to her. I took a few steps away and said to Dr. Verghese, "This sounds pretty dire."

"Yes, Mr. Devlin. She's been downgraded to critical condition, and we need to move her to a more suitable place."

"You mean, like another room?"

"No, sir," he replied, polite and professional and measured. "I am talking about another facility that is more appropriate for her immediate requirements."

I glanced back at Addie to make sure she was still texting; she was. "What sort of place do you have in mind?" I asked him, my voice just above a whisper.

"Cedars-Sinai. She would receive much better care there, although there are some risks involved in the transport. That's why I'm calling you, sir."

"Why me?"

"Because she isn't mentally competent to make a decision and you're listed as her durable power of health care attorney."

This was nuts. Belinda and I were divorced five years ago, and she'd gotten remarried since then.

"She's not my wife," I told him. "You should be talking to Carl, her current husband."

"We haven't been able to contact him, sir. She hasn't changed the form, and we need a signature in order to move her."

Jesus Christ, could the day get any more screwed? "I'm in South Carolina right now," I explained in the calmest voice possible. Wondering what my sister might be breaking upstairs in the condo at that very instant.

"So I am told, sir," he replied, cheery as could be. "I do believe they have fax machines there, is that correct?"

I told him to send whatever forms I needed to sign to Jenkins IV's office. I didn't have the fax number but gave him the office line and told him I could be there in fifteen minutes to sign them and send them back. He thanked me politely, then said, "I watched you pitch once."

"You did what?"

"I went to an Angels game when I was doing my residency at UCLA. A colleague wanted to prove to me that baseball is better than cricket, so we drove down to Anaheim."

"So what did you think?" I asked him.

"He was wrong."

I considered lying to Addie about my conversation with Dr. Verghese, but that was not how we rolled. Instead, I calmly explained that her mother had developed some complications—nothing really serious—and she needed to be transferred to a hospital where she would get better care. Cedars-Sinai, one of the best in all of L.A. Addie seemed to understand, but I could tell from her silence as we drove to the lawyer's office that she was worried.

After signing the necessary forms and faxing them back, we drove north on Highway 41 to the Frances Marion Forest. In between periodic texts Addie asked me where we were going, and I explained that I wanted to check something out in the middle of the trees and tangled vines that had grown up where rice plantations once had been.

"Looks more like a swamp than a forest," she observed once we got there, peering out the window at the dense woods.

"Lots of mud and muck, that's for sure. Many years ago there was a booming rice business around these parts. The climate and terrain were perfect for growing it, and it's part of what made Charleston the hub of the south."

"So were slaves," she observed. "Just what are we looking for?"

"The place where that body was found."

"Really?" She cast me a curious glance, as if I might be toying with her. "The one on the death certificate?"

"That's right. I want to get a sense of where the man died. Or at least where he was found."

Dog Swamp Road A was a sharp right turn off—*what else?*—Dog Swamp Road, which in turn was about five miles up Steed Creek Road from the state highway. It was an unpaved stretch of pure isolation cut through dense stands of loblolly and longleaf pines, wrapped tightly with creeper and kudzu and wild jessamine. From the satellite photo the road seemed no more than a mile long, just a few gentle curves that conformed to the topography of the area. Maybe there was an old creek running through here, or a run-off ditch that had been carved through the land decades before.

"This is where he died?" Addie asked, staring up through the tinted windshield at the towering trees.

"Hard to say," I replied. "His remains were found at the edge of the road, but it seems no one knows for sure where he was killed."

"He was shot in the back, right?"

"The neck, actually. Just below the base of the skull."

She looked around at the dense trees and snarled creeper that seemed to form an impenetrable curtain at the edge of the dirt lane. "I think he was killed here on the road," she said. "He couldn't have gone in there."

The same scenario had occurred to me. If Rudy Aiken's body had not been dumped in the ditch at the edge of the road, he had been brought here and kicked out of the car. Or truck. The coroner's report had said he'd been hit in the C-4 vertebra, and the placement of bullet fragments suggested he'd been shot from behind. Unless he had been hogtied and forced to the ground face-down, he had been fired upon right here on the road, possibly while he was running from his assailant.

I pulled over to the side of the road and shifted into park.

"You're getting out?"

"Why not? It's a beautiful morning."

"Then I'm coming with you."

"Fine by me."

Whenever I was on a baseball road trip—college, minor league, or the majors—I always liked to arrive at the ballpark early. Way early, when the place was empty and I could walk out to the mound and get a feel for the place. I would anticipate the excitement that was going to come in a few hours as thousands of fans rooted against us. I'd inhale the aroma of freshly mown grass, fresh lime in the base paths, infield dirt that had just been raked. There was a distinct mysticism down there on that empty field, a filament of connectivity between the quiet present and the electricity that was yet to come.

I'd had a pitching coach at Fresno State who approached the game with a Zen-like spirituality, and he had instructed me to use all six senses when preparing for a game: sight, sound, taste, touch, smell, and the vibrancy that connects us with the cosmos. He would say things like, "You don't find greatness; it finds you" and "Your destiny is written in the stars, so find yourself a good internal telescope." His favorite was, "Fate has a way of putting in front of us, that which we most try to leave behind." At that point I'd attempted to leave behind so much in the few short years since my mother's murder, and Coach Thayer had brought it all back around with those simple words.

Addie and I got out of the car and stood there on that dusty road. There wasn't another vehicle in sight. I drew a deep breath into my lungs, just as I'd done when I walked onto the mound in an empty ball park and sensed what I could not hear and felt what I could not see. The woods were teeming with life just beyond the fringe of trees—snakes and raccoons and lizards and deer and whatever else called this patch of forest "home." That connection caused me to slip back to an earlier time to see how Rudy Aiken's murder had played out.

I closed my eyes and imagined a vehicle coming up the road in a veil of dust, transporting what felt like a cloud of human fear. It was not real, not now, but I sensed the car pull to the very edge of the road and lurch to a stop. Then the doors opened and several men dragged out a young man who I could only imagine was consumed with terror. This was all conjecture on my part, but I sensed him wriggling free and then running up the road in a frenzied fashion, gaining speed until a loud rifle blast dropped him to the dirt.

I stared at the point where I imagined he'd fallen, then glanced away.

"You look like you just saw a ghost," Addie said from where she was standing on the other side of the car.

"Could've been, sweetie. It just could've been."

It wasn't my intent to freak her out, but for the next few minutes as we drove out of the forest she was silent. Except to say, "There's no signal out here."

"You'll have to tell Verizon," I told her.

She shot me a look that suggested I wasn't being funny, but eventually she cracked a smile. A few seconds later she added, "You really did look like you saw something back there."

I shook my head. "Just trying to play out in my mind how it might have gone down. The way a director blocks out a shot in a movie before the camera starts rolling. Like your stepdad Carl."

She pondered that for a bit, then said, "Okay, I get it."

As soon as we got back to the state highway we picked up a cell signal. My phone pinged, and when I sneaked a peek at the screen I saw it was from my sister:

`Sorry about this afternoon, and the plates. Hope you get your deposit back. Headache is gone. Going home tomorrow. Maybe breakfast? I barely got to see Adeline.`

Plates? Deposit? Shit...what the hell had she done? The headache part I could understand, but breakfast? I wasn't so sure about that. Not unless there were witnesses present. My first inclination was to just ignore her and move on, but something my sister had said during her rant had stayed with me, and I wanted to get to the bottom of it.

When we arrived back at the condo building three Charleston Police units were parked near the front entrance. A cop was standing in the foyer, talking to a man and woman who had just come out of the elevator. I pressed the "up" button just as the officer finished his conversation, and then he turned his attention to us.

He flashed his badge and said, "Sergeant Marsters, Charleston P.D. Do you live in the building?"

"Short-term rental for a couple weeks," I told him, as truthfully as I could. "Is there some sort of a problem?"

"We received several reports of a disturbance," the officer said. His dark blue uniform appeared too big for his shoulders, and his broad ears seemed to be holding up his hat. His skin was a pasty white, like freshly sifted flour, and pocked with acne scars. "Where were you for the last two hours?"

"My daughter and I were hiking in the Francis Marion Forest," I replied. "What kind of disturbance?"

"We're trying to figure that out. It appears someone threw some crockery from one of the balconies, broke a few windshields."

Jesus Horatio Christ. "Do you know which condo it came from?" I asked him.

"Not yet, but high up. Has anyone been in your unit today?"

I glanced at Addie, who gave a very convincing noncommittal shrug. "No, sir. It's just me and my daughter, and like I said, we went hiking. In the forest."

"Whereabouts?" he pressed.

Addie took the reins on this one and said, "A place called Swamp Dog Road. I'm working on a summer project for school, and I wanted to check it out. Kinda creepy."

Sgt. Marsters studied her for a second, then said, "You're not from around here."

"No, Officer," she replied. "L.A. born and raised. You can probably tell from the way I talk. But my dad, here, is made of oysters and fried okra."

Marsters nodded at that, then turned back to me. "Do you mind giving me your name and phone number?"

I told him slowly, so he could write it down in a small notebook. "You're welcome to come up and have a look, if you want," I invited him.

"No need," he replied. "I'll call you if I have any further questions. Have a great day."

As far as I could tell my sister had destroyed only the dinner plates in her rampage. The cupboard still contained six bowls and salad plates, but all the large dishware was gone. The condo itself was neat as a pin, and even the scent of frankincense was gone. I glanced around, then pulled open the glass slider and went out onto the balcony. I looked down and saw that the damage was confined to a handful of vehicles twelve floors below, where the cops that belonged to the other police cars I'd seen were speaking to their owners and taking photos of cracked windshields and dented roofs.

"Looks like Aunt Karen tidied up," Addie said.

"The calm after the storm," I said. "I probably should have reported her."

Addie shrugged, as if it were no big deal. "It's nothing Mom hasn't done before, which reminds me. I probably should give her a call."

I checked my watch, remembering that hospitals operate at the speed of a glacier. That meant Belinda probably was still waiting for an ambulance or, more likely, somewhere in the tangle of Southern California freeways on her way to Cedars-Sinai. "Let's give her a bit more time, so she can get comfortable in her new room," I suggested.

Fifteen minutes later Addie was in her room, either reading about Tara and antebellum plantation life or texting with her own teenage Rhett Butler. She poked her head out once to let me know that some of the kids she had met on Sunday were planning another group event, but she didn't yet know the what, when, or where. Then she slipped back inside and closed the door.

I seized the quiet and settled down in front of my computer, again with all the best laid plans to get some ghost work done. I got about two paragraphs into it when I realized I was turning the words "white river" over and over in my head. Jenkins IV had mentioned that my father had attended a meeting of a group by that name the same night my mother was killed, and I had put it out of my mind until now. Despite my deadline and flagging discipline, I found myself typing the two words into Google.

The results were numerous and varied, producing everything from a lumber company to a state park to the title of an old movie. And, of course, a number of rivers around the U.S. I modified my search by adding "racism" and "South Carolina" and came up with entirely different results. Jenkins IV had described an organization founded in fear and knee-jerk hatred, fueled by bigotry and hypocrisy, and the first "hit" told me I'd found what I was looking for.

I clicked through story after story, mostly old newspaper accounts of mayhem that had been inflicted by a group of grass-roots extremists committed to terrorizing blacks and civil rights sympathizers throughout Georgia and the Carolinas. The organization was a loosely knit cadre of small local units that spent much of their time congregating in rural barns, drinking beer and whiskey and ranting about how kikes and blacks and beaners were destroying the fabric of America. They fumed, they raged, they pontificated, and occasionally they would get so worked up that a small band of them would set fire to an African American church or shoot up the home of a Jewish doctor. The intent was multi-fold: to release a pent-up orgasm of racial hatred and thereby destroy a symbol that threatened their already low self-esteem, and generally to spread terror through a segment of the population they feared might upset a cultural norm that had existed for hundreds of years.

Most of the articles I found referred to White River in indefinite terms, as in, "a local splinter faction of the nationalist group White River was believed to have been involved," or "the attack is alleged to be the work of members of White River." No one ever took credit for the death and destruction, and no one was ever arrested for any crime. It truly was a stream of hateful consciousness that raged from the mountains to sea, the undercurrent of fierce self-loathing and anger obscured beneath the cloak of anonymity.

All that changed about seven years ago when another group of racist thugs going by the name White Makes Might absorbed the White River movement. Their Grand Poobah, a smug-looking cracker with stringy blonde hair, a weak lower jaw, and a pointed nose, was named Ed Landry. A self-proclaimed "white spiritualist," he widely and soundly proclaimed the absolute truth of white superiority above all other races. Inflaming the sensitivities of his fellow haters, he called for a rapid and full return of the U.S. to the white "ethnostate" it had been before social apologists began calling for a mixing of the races. A few years back he'd cobbled together a thesis that proclaimed the biological superiority of "Americans of European Descent," a treatise that drew criticism and scorn from most major social historians. Undaunted by the derision, Landry published his creed under the title "A Call For A White America," a paperback tract that Google told me had sold over half a million copies on the internet.

Google also told me that Landry had been arrested four times for inciting violence. Charges were dropped three times, but on one occasion he'd been convicted and given probation. Undeterred,

Landry apparently stepped up his rhetoric and violence. The number of church burnings escalated, while the number of black homes that had been torched more than doubled. Landry was always quick to deny his involvement with any violent acts, but his group always seemed to be hovering on the periphery whenever a newsworthy fire or hate crime went down.

This had all happened after my father's conviction, and from what I could see had absolutely nothing to do with why he would have been at the meeting of White River the evening my mother was stabbed. Jenkins III had told me that Rudy Aiken could place him there that night, which may have been the reason he'd been shot in the neck and left in a ditch in the Francis Marion Forest. For a moment I'd simply been swept up in the undertow of Landry's radical extremism, but now I realized it would tell me nothing about what happened in the kitchen of the Devlin home thirty years ago.

That was my thinking…until the name Avery Dunham popped out at me.

I almost missed it. There's something about how your eyes sometimes detect a word on a written page that makes you go back and check whether you actually saw what you thought you saw. In this case I was just closing out of a news story about a protest rally outside a women's health clinic in Charlottesville. It seemed that just moments after Landry had been hauled away in cuffs, a doctor was killed when he came out the back door of the clinic and got into his car. A bomb exploded when he turned the key, killing him instantly. After a thorough investigation, state police arrested Dunham and tried to get him to roll over on anyone else who might have been involved, but he kept his mouth shut. This was probably the incident Alice Marion had mentioned during my visit with her. He was still doing time in federal prison while Ed Landry was ramping up his violent, racist rhetoric.

It took me a few minutes to locate the website where I'd previously seen Dunham's name. I'd forgotten the search terms I'd originally entered, but eventually I found the site I'd scanned several nights ago. The online story began with a summary of the insurance claim, and why it had been declined by Gardiner Casualty and Life. A link at the bottom of the page took me to various abstracts and motions submitted by attorneys for both sides of the appeals.

Then I found It. "*It*," with a capital "I."

Under a subheading titled "Losses" were two paragraphs that catalogued everything Avery had lost in the fire. It began with the building itself, described in the policy as "a fifty by forty-foot structure that provided two thousand square feet of space under secure cover from the elements." Part of that space had been converted to small offices and a restroom, while the rest was used to store assorted materials and equipment. These included, in no specific order, six sealed bales of ammonium nitrate fertilizer, four drums of oil, several gas generators, unassembled sections of steel scaffolding, the nitrocellulose that had ignited the flames, a Caterpillar front loader, one Massey Ferguson tractor, a hydraulic scissor-lift, a large assortment of old tires and dozens of wood pallets. Plus, one 1978 Ford F-150, red, registered to a Gerald Aiken of Orangeburg.

Rudy Aiken's brother.

CHAPTER 23

The next morning Addie and I met my sister for breakfast at a Waffle House in West Ashley, across the river from Charleston.

Gone was the wild, frenetic look in her eyes, and the mad nerve in her brow that quivered at any hint of stress was motionless. Whatever fury had gripped her yesterday had been cleansed from her system, and now she looked like a different person. Maybe it was her hair, which had been washed and dried and done up in a painfully tight French braid. A thin coat of rouge brightened her cheeks, and she smiled brightly as I led my daughter to the corner table where she was slowly stirring a spoon in a cup of black coffee.

Addie scooted into the booth first and I sat beside her. The plans her newfound friends had been hatching last night had evaporated, which was just as well because she had a thousand-page novel to fall into. She'd stayed in her room reading and texting until after midnight, and had fallen asleep on her bed without even crawling under the covers. The social scheme now called for a picnic at the beach, which gave us plenty of time for waffles and coffee before I had to drop her off at the home of one of her friends, a little before noon.

A stack of laminated menus with color photos of breakfast food lay at the edge of the table, but none of us reached to pick one up. "Okay, I want to get this out of the way first thing," Karen said as we settled in. "Yesterday never happened. Take that card out of the deck and throw it away. Today is a do-over. Deal?"

I knew from experience that everything with Karen was a do-over, but now was not the time to go into it. Nor would be any time in the future. Being around her was like tiptoeing around a floor covered with eggshells.

"No worries," I assured her. "Today is another day."

She seemed to tense and said, "Why should I be worried?"

"Precisely," I agreed as blithely as I could. "No one at this table has any reason to worry about a thing."

At which point Addie said, "Are you really going back to Atlanta this morning? You just got here."

Karen brightened at that, and replied, "I'm afraid so, Adeline. I have a lot going on, so I need to get going."

"I'd love to visit Atlanta someday," Addie replied, tentatively feeling her way. After yesterday and a quick review on the drive over this morning she, too, was cautious of the eggshells. "I'm reading *Gone with the Wind*. It seems like an awesome place. A part of American history."

"You can ride back with me today," my sister offered. "I'd love the company."

Addie looked at me with a flash of panic in her eyes. Then Karen said, "Don't worry...I'm just kidding. Besides, as Clark Gable—Rhett Butler—said, Charleston is the true city of grace and civility."

"I haven't come to that part yet," Addie said, looking relieved. "It's a long book."

Breakfast seemed long, too, although it only took forty-two minutes. Karen seemed to have forgotten about the plates and the memorial service and our father's ashes. None of that came up, although I was afraid that every breath might swing her back to the inner wrath. I don't know if she'd popped some Prozac or lithium or had consumed some other substance this morning, but she seemed as normal and cheerful as I'd ever seen her. We chatted about everything from coffee beans to movies to General Sherman's march, and never once did I see a hint of a spark.

Which was why I was reluctant to steer things back around to the trial. I knew it was a sore subject with Karen, one that always seemed to darken her already quixotic mood. Still, she'd mentioned something yesterday that I wanted to clarify, and now seemed the time. Especially since she had picked up the tab and already laid down the cash.

"I know we agreed that yesterday has been removed from the

deck of cards," I ventured, waiting for the nerve in her brow to start quivering. It didn't, so I continued, "But you mentioned something I didn't quite understand."

She stared at me, no tic in her brow, no fire in her eyes. No storm clouds building on the horizon. No train coming around the bend.

"You'll have to enlighten me," she said.

So far I was on solid footing. We were in a public place, with about twenty other diners peacefully eating their waffles and omelets and home fries. I could feel Addie tense a bit in the booth beside me, but I was all in on this. "You said something about the trial, and the bailiff who was there to keep an eye on us."

Karen picked up a salt shaker and dumped a few crystals into her hand, then wistfully blew them to the floor. If it was a meaningful gesture, it was lost on me. "His name was Stumpy," she replied.

I nodded. "We were told he was there to keep us away from all the reporters, and I believed him. But what you said yesterday made me think maybe I was a bit naïve."

"What was it I said?" she asked as she shook more salt into her hand.

"Something like, 'protecting us from all the reporters, my ass.' "

My sister set the salt shaker back on the table and leaned forward. Not a great distance—just a few inches—but the intent was clear. Our mother used to do that when we were children, and it always meant *listen up, because I'm only going to tell this to you once.*

"There was a lot more going on during that trial than you knew," she said, her voice almost a whisper, like a light breeze at the beach. As if someone at one of the neighboring tables might overhear.

"Care to enlighten me?" I asked her.

"It was a long time ago," she said. The nerve in her brow twitched once, twice. Then it stopped. "That deck of cards has long since been played out."

"Dad is dead," I reminded her. "There's nothing that can hurt him anymore."

"Dad was never the issue," she said. Then she did something she'd never in her life done: she reached out and took my hands in hers. "Please try to let it go, Rick. The past is never where you think you left it."

The line was from Katherine Anne Porter, whom I remembered

was one of Karen's favorite writers. Mostly because of her dark themes of betrayal, death and the flashpoints of human evil. Even back then my sister was dipping her toes into black waters.

"Then give me an idea of where to find it," I suggested, squeezing her hands in return.

My sister surprised me and actually gave this some prolonged thought. Eventually she let go of my hands and slid out of the booth. "If you really must visit the outhouse of our lives, talk to Stumpy," she said. "If he's still around maybe you'll find what you're looking for. And tell him I say 'hi.' "

Then she blew a kiss to Addie, and was gone.

Addie had brought her book and was content to read it in the same furnished alcove where Stumpy and I had talked a week ago. Since this was late July a number of judges and lawyers were on vacation, and the trial docket was light. Still, a few cases were being heard, and that meant jurors were needed.

I found Stumpy right where I thought he would be, outside the jury selection room. I waited until he had a moment, then approached him in the hallway.

"Mr. Rick," he said, visibly surprised—and maybe a little perturbed—to see me show up out of the blue. "I heard about your father. I pray that he's gone to a far better place, where maybe he can make some peace with his world."

I wondered to whom he had been talking about my father, but decided to let it go. "I'm hoping we all can," I replied. "There's something I need to talk to you about."

He fixed me with a glum look, one that carried a hint of warning in its depth. "You're staring way too much at the past rather than looking at what lies up the road," he observed.

"I just need to know one more thing," I told him. We were alone in the hallway, and I was certain no one could see or hear us. "It has to do with something my sister brought up less than an hour ago."

"Your sister? Lord Almighty…how is she?"

"The same, but older. And she made a point of mentioning your name."

"In regards to—?"

"I think you know, sir," I told him.

It was obvious that Herman Stump was unsettled, maybe even a bit scared. "Look, Mr. Rick. I already put the key right in your hand. It's up to you to find the lock."

"Just point me toward the right door," I urged him. "I promise it's the last thing I'll ask of you."

The old black man sized me up, as if he were peering into my soul through his old wire rim glasses with a chip in the lens. He said not a word for the longest time; then he leaned forward and cupped his hand to my ear.

"Ernie Collier," he whispered. I started to repeat the name out of simple reflex, but he put a finger to my lips. "And you didn't hear that from me."

Ernie Collier was the handyman who years ago had done odd jobs for my father. He repaired screens that got torn in summer storms, painted trim and hung rain gutters, and replaced the lattice work around the foundation of our house. On occasion he would show up with fresh venison steaks or wild pig ribs from his latest excursion into the woods, and a cousin generously provided us with fresh shrimp when it was the season. Ernie had a source that could provide ground oyster shells for the driveway, and he'd recommended the man who had carved the beautiful red cypress mantle over our fireplace.

I had never once been to his home but I knew he lived in a historically black neighborhood in Mount Pleasant called Snowden. The word "snow" rhyming with "plow." The families that resided there were descendants of former slaves and sharecroppers who began purchasing plots of land following the Civil War, and over the years those properties were passed down to their sons and daughters, grandsons and granddaughters. They had been farmers and hunters and laborers, drawing their living from the same land that their ancestors had plowed and worked under the steaming southern sun and the stinging whips of their beastly masters.

When I was a child Ernie had told me tales of years long gone, stories passed down through word of mouth and parable. He spoke of days stalking deer and foxes through dense woods that now were expensive housing tracts and golf courses. He reminisced about poling second-hand canoes through the rich drainage culverts that were left over from the rice plantations, and watching bald eagles and red-shoulder falcons plummet from the sky in their quest for squirrels and rabbits. He captivated me with stories from his time in Korea as a sharpshooter in one of the first integrated Army units, how he could pop the enemy between the eyes from a couple hundred yards out. On those lazy summer afternoons, I would hang on every word he said, picturing a world of simpler things and easier times. Times that, despite the ingrained injustices of my young conscience, seemed more chastened and humble.

Even though I didn't have his address, it wasn't hard to find him. Despite the built-in suspicion aroused by a white man driving a rental car and asking the whereabouts of an old black man in an African American community, the folks who lived here harbored little animosity from the past. Thirty years ago seemed just like yesterday, and the Devlin name still brought a glint of recognition even in the most guarded eyes. Almost everyone in this quiet community was related by birth or marriage, which therefore meant that everyone knew where old Ernie Collier could be found. It also meant that he knew I was coming long before I pulled into his driveway and cut the engine.

The last time I'd seen him was a week before the trial. I don't recall the reason, but I remember him looking withered and tired. Then again, to a teenager almost everyone past fifty seemed older than dirt. I figured he'd probably been in his early sixties back then, which placed him in his nineties now. A lot of years had fallen under his feet, a lot of rusty screens patched and window frames slathered with paint.

I got out of the car and pulled the door closed on quiet hinges. It would be a shame to disturb the afternoon that was so noiseless I could almost hear the rustle of feathers of a hawk circling on a thermal high overhead.

"Mister Rick, is that you?" the old man said from the wooden rocker on his small veranda. He slowly rose to his feet, his back stiff and bent from the passing seasons. His legs seemed more bowed than I remembered, and he grimaced from some hidden pain in his pelvis. "I heard you was drivin' around these parts, getting' more lost by the minute."

"Mr. Collier," I replied as I approached the wooden steps that led up to his porch. "You don't look like you've changed one bit."

"Now, that is a damn lie," he replied with chuckle, flashing a set of teeth that seemed too perfect to be real. "Come on up and let me get a look at you, boy."

He'd always spoken with such authority that I never hesitated to obey his commands, and I found myself doing that now. When I got to the top of the freshly painted steps he sized me up, then gave me a hug. He was too frail and tired to give me anything more than a gentle squeeze, then said, "Care for some sweet tea?"

That sounded ideal on this hot July day but I didn't want to put him through the effort. So I said, "No thank you, sir. I won't be bothering you all that long."

"No bother, Mister Rick. You're welcome to stay as long as you want. Set yourself down in that chair, and I'll be back in the blink of an eye."

He pushed his way through the front door, while I took a seat in a wood rocker and glanced around. His house was small and neat, gray clapboard with white shutters and a porch that stretched along the front. The lawn looked a bit shaggy, but the magnolia trees looked freshly pruned. Twin window boxes were clumped with weeds, which made me wonder about Mrs. Collier. In my mind she had baked the best peach pie that ever touched my lips; I could almost taste it now.

A couple minutes later he came back out, carrying two tall glasses of sweet tea. "You have a nice place here, sir," I told him as I took one from him.

"I was born in this house, don't you know," Ernie Collier replied as he settled into the chair next to mine. "Nineteen and twenty-nine, it was. No bathroom or running water back then, but my daddy built it strong and true. She's gotten herself a bit of a facelift across the years, and a new roof from time to time. She may be plain and small but, unlike some folks I know, her beauty goes all the way through to the heart. And she's paid for."

"I hear you," I said as I took a sip of sugary tea. Then, sensing I already knew the answer, I asked, "How's Mrs. Collier these days?"

"My sweet Geraldine is with the Lord," he replied in a sad but resolute voice. "She transitioned a good ten years ago. It's just me now, but our kids and grandkids all live around here. Except Booker, who went off in pursuit of a song as soon as he was able."

"He'd be your son?"

Ernie drew his head from right to left. "Grandson. Picked up a trumpet in the Wando marching band, hustled himself off to Memphis soon as he got that diploma tucked in his hand."

"I didn't know there was music in the Collier blood," I said. Truth was, I knew very little about Ernie, except for the food he brought my mother and the lazy tales of summer he'd spun while he was painting or fixing something at our house.

"Is that a fact." It was a statement; no more, no less. "You come with me."

He rose on wobbly legs and motioned for me to follow him inside. I worried that he might topple over any second, but his shuffling gait was steady yet slow. He held the screen door open for me, and as I entered the living room I realized the inside of the house was just as hot as the outside.

"AC's broke, and my nephew Freddie ain't found time to get around to fixin' it," he apologized. "Come…follow me."

He led me into the dining room, really just a small nook that separated the living room from the kitchen. A hand-hewn oak table that looked about a hundred years old was pushed against one wall, with four chairs tucked neatly under it.

"Back when Geraldine was still on this earth this was where we ate breakfast and dinner," he explained as he stood in the doorway. "Fifty-nine years. Most times now I just eat out there on the veranda with the birds and squirrels. This here's where I play my sax."

He shuffled over to a corner of the room and gently lifted a battered old saxophone from its stand. It was tarnished and scarred from years of use, just like its owner. He gazed at it fondly, then touched the mouthpiece to his lips and began to blow. He held the first note for a long beat, then let loose with the opening bars of a melancholy melody I instantly recognized as *Rainy Night in Georgia.* For an old man with severe arthritis and porcelain teeth, he knocked it out of the park, and when he finally stopped after a good thirty seconds he cracked a big smile.

"Brook Benton," I said, stunned by what I'd just heard.

"Tony Joe White laid down the music," Ernie replied. "Benton took and ran with it, turned it into eternity."

"I've never heard it played so sweet," I told him.

"Well, you can thank your daddy for that," he said as he gently tucked the instrument back in its stand.

"My father?" What could Ernie Collier possibly say about him that I didn't already know? "What's he got to do with it?"

"Come back outside, let me tell you a few things about that daddy of yours," he said. "Might cause you to change your mind about him for all of time."

CHAPTER 24

This is what he told me: Sometime, a good forty years ago, not long after Ernie had first come to our house to patch some cracks in our old brick chimney, he and a few friends were jamming at a juke joint on Four Mile Road in the middle of a pine forest. It was blacks-only by decree of folks of all colors, and rare was the night when anyone as pale as the moon set foot on the property. That particular evening, a steamy night in August when a breeze was seeping through the trees and fireflies were winking at the edge of the woods, Ernie and a couple of his friends were wailing on an old John Lee Hooker song on the wide front porch. Rhythm guitar and bass, trombone and drums, and Ernie on his sax. The air was thick and sticky, and the beer and bourbon were flowing without care as the jam band segued from *Big Legs, Tight Skirt* into *Blues Before Sunrise.*

That's when a pick-up truck swerved off the road and braked to a sudden stop in the tall grass. It could have been black, maybe dark blue or brown. No one much remembered later. What they did remember was that a couple of white crackers climbed out of the cab and began taunting the folks who were sitting at picnic tables, eating shrimp and sweet potato fries, minding no one's business and listening to some of the finest music around.

The two white guys—clearly drunk and expressing their limited intelligence with four-letter words—began what was widely known as "nigger knocking." One of them flicked an index finger hard against the skull of a black man sitting on the surface of one of the wooden tables, feet on the seat, and said to him, "Didn't your momma learn you that tables was for the food, monkey man?"

"Whatchoo care where I park my ass?" the man sitting on the table said. "You'd best get back in that truck of yours and leave."

"Or what?" the white man said, flicking him again with his finger.

The other cracker—the driver of the truck—thought this was funny and flicked his own finger on the skull of another of the black men. "Yeah…or what?" he snapped.

The first guy then helped himself to one of the boiled shrimp sitting on a piece of paper in a red plastic basket. "Niggers do know how to boil their shrimp," he announced to the crowd. Then he grabbed the basket and headed toward the porch, where the music had suddenly gone quiet.

"What…all of a sudden you boys forgot how to play?" the shitkicker said. "Or maybe we're not good enough? Get that music going. Something good, like Johnny Cash. Not this black and blues shit."

But no one in the band responded, and no one played. They'd seen this sort of thing before, each of them in their own time and place, and nothing good ever came of it. Race-driven confrontations were like a storm front moving across the land; they had to run their full course before passing on. It was the nature of things, and you couldn't change nature.

"C'mon…eat one," the white man with the shrimp ordered Ernie, who was sitting in a wooden chair with his saxophone standing in his lap. The man tried to press the shrimp into his face, but Ernie casually brushed his hand away.

"What the fuck!" the redneck snapped, and then tossed the basket of shrimp in Ernie's face. "I said fucking *eat*!"

But Ernie wasn't going to eat, and he wasn't going to put up with any of this cracker's horseshit. He rose from his chair and set the saxophone down on the floorboards of the wooden deck. Then he balled his hand into a fist.

The blow landed square in the drunk shitkicker's stomach, hard. This was at a time when blacks were still the equivalent of a stray dog, and stray dogs were treated with disgust and revulsion. The redneck doubled over in agony, coughing ragged gasps as he tried to catch the wind that had been knocked all the way to Charleston.

Not a noise filled the night. Even the crickets knew enough to remain silent. The drunk man slowly straightened and flexed his shoulders, trying to minimize the pain in his gut. He glared at Ernie, and drew his eyes over the throng of black men who were waiting for any sign of an invitation to whip his ass. But Ernie raised a silent hand, signaling them all to stand down and let it ride.

"Dr. King came to Charleston once, more than fifty years ago," he told me now. "It was summer, and my brother begged and begged me to go with him to hear him speak. I didn't want to do that; I was an angry man who had suffered the scars of indignity and racial inferiority. I didn't want to hear some pacifist preacher tell me that I had to drive out my anger if I was going to find peace in the world. But I went anyway and I stood there in the blistering sun, and I listened to what he had to say. And my brother was right: I needed to hear those words, on that day, and put away all that anger that was pounding in my heart."

"So, what happened that night?" I asked him. "After that redneck tossed the shrimp in your face."

Ernie closed his eyes and drifted back to that time once more, then opened them and let out a long sigh. "I allowed my fist to speak first," he admitted. "It was driven by years of anger and resentment and futility. But then something Dr. King said came to my mind, and I heard myself repeating the words to everyone who could hear me. 'Darkness cannot drive out darkness; only light can do that,' I said. 'Hate cannot drive out hate; only love can do that.' "

I was still wondering how my father figured into this story, but I allowed the old man to tell the story his way, in his own time. Still, I said, "I don't suppose that went over well with the crackers from the pick-up."

"It did not," Ernie replied with a throaty chuckle. "There was almost a full moon that night, but its light was not enough to drive out the darkness. What followed was almost over before it began, but not before a couple of beer-drenched skulls and one truck windshield got busted."

I watched a ruby-throated hummingbird dart toward the mouth of a honeysuckle bloom and dip his beak in for a taste of nectar. "And your saxophone?" I asked, sensing where this was going.

"That's right, Mister Rick. After that fence-fucker threw the shrimp at me, he done drop-kicked my ol' sax so hard it pretty near wrapped around the trunk of a magnolia. That was my own daddy's instrument, got it when he was but a boy, and he taught me to play it when I was still sittin' on his knee. But after that night it never played another note. Neither did I, till your father came by the house a couple days later—right up on this porch, where you're sittin' now—and handed me a brand new one."

Ernie Collier was right: I'd never heard this story. My father, who was a contradiction on so many levels, had never said one word about it, and neither had my mother. "That one in there?" I asked him, cocking my head toward the room where the old sax was perched on its stand.

"Your father was a good and kind man," he told me, a sad smile further creasing his wrinkled face. "He was conflicted by so many things, in so many ways, but I can tell you for a fact he didn't do none of what they said he done."

"You're saying he didn't kill my mother?" I asked him.

"Frank Devlin? Not a chance. That man was many things to many people, but he was not a murderer."

"The jury said otherwise," I reminded him.

"That jury was high on emotion and low on information, Mister Rick. Look—you didn't come here today just to shoot the breeze with an old black man who's got maybe a year to live. The docs say cancer's going after my kidneys, and then I'll be in the arms of my sweet Geraldine again."

"I am so sorry to hear that," I said, and I was.

Ernie took a long sip of his tea, gently rocked in his chair as he watched a butterfly light upon one of his roses. Then he said, "You never once paid a visit to my home when you was a boy, and I don't fault you. There was no need to. But here you are, thirty years later, which tells me you got your own doubts on this matter. And you're thinkin' maybe I can shed a little light on 'em."

"You're a good judge of human character," I acknowledged.

He tipped back in his chair so far that his head touched the windowsill, then slowly eased forward until his eyes met mine. "Had to be, to get to be a ninety-one-year-old black man in the south, where it's so easy to loop a strand of rope into an instrument of death."

"Things some of us don't see from the other side of the lens," I replied. "What can you tell me about that night, why you're so sure my father is innocent?"

Ernie Collier said nothing for a long while after that. He massaged his temples with a bony hand, then rocked to and fro a few times as he considered my question. Then he said, "You ever hear of a black kid name of Jimmy Holland?"

Wham! I felt as if a clean-up slugger had just lined my own fastball back at me, right into my chest. I swear my heart skipped a beat as the name reverberated in my head. I sensed Ernie Collier watching my reaction, but he said nothing.

"How does he fit in?" I asked, after I visibly recovered from the shock.

He didn't answer my question, not directly. Instead he asked another of his own. "What do you know about him?"

"I know he was seen holding hands with a girl and got dragged to death because of it."

"That's something you just happen to know, is it?"

"His name came up and I did a little digging," I acknowledged, not wanting this to get back to Herman Stump unless fate took it there. "My father sure seemed to know the name, but refused to tell me how."

Ernie wiped a bead of sweat from his brow and rubbed his hand on his jeans. "Jimmy was a good kid, had a real gift for mechanical things," he said slowly. "Helped install my water heater off the kitchen, still workin' like it was new after all these years."

"You knew him?" I said. "Jimmy Holland?"

"Knew him? Lordy, Mister Rick. That boy was my wife's cousin's son. That made him her second cousin, or something like that. Fact is, you met him. I brought him to your house one day while I was fixin' somethin', don't remember what. You boys played catch."

My heart missed a beat again as I went back to a time when I was maybe fourteen, and Ernie showed up with a boy just about my age. I don't remember what Ernie had come to the house to do, but I'd given the kid my old glove and then set him on the grass at the edge of the backyard. The glove was a Rawlings my father had given me when I started Little League, and my hand had outgrown it. Jimmy Holland didn't seem to mind that it was a little tight, and I'd thrown fast balls into that glove until my arm got tired. As I recall, he'd caught every one of them.

"That was him?" I asked.

"Three summers before he was killed," Ernie said. "He still had that glove when they buried him."

Damn. I'd forgotten until now that I'd let him keep the Rawlings, since I had no use for it anymore. "Shame, what happened to him."

"He encountered a load of hate that day, that boy did. No light in the world could have saved him from the darkness."

I was still having difficulty making sense of what Ernie was telling me, and why it had taken thirty years to come to light. "So tell me, Mr. Collier. What does Jimmy Holland being dragged to his death have to do with my father, and why that jury convicted him?"

"Let me tell you something else about your father," the old man said. The rocking chair creaked under his weight as he softly moved back and forth. "Frank Devlin was a man tore up by humanity and at great odds with his soul. He was brought up with the same anger and fear as most young men in the south, white and black, and he fastened onto the same sort of hate that's passed down one generation to the next. He was taught to be a racist and a bigot and a misogynist in a world swaddled in Bible Belt sanctimony. Lured by the fire of the Devil all week long and then swept into the arms of Heavenly repentance on Sunday. He did his best to overcome it all, but the gates of Hell open wide when sin invades the soul."

It had been years since I'd heard so much fire and brimstone talk, and never from the lips of Ernie Collier. His words about my father served to explain how he could have so much love in his heart for my sister and me, yet succumb to the vile cloak of bigotry toward others.

"Jimmy Holland died that same summer when my mother was killed," I said, trying to steer him back on track. "Did one thing lead to the other?"

"I can't rightly speak to any of that," he said. His eyes closed softly and I heard him inhale a ragged breath. "You're gonna have to talk to your sister."

"My sister? How does she figure into it?"

Ernie closed his eyes and said nothing for a while. I couldn't tell if he was sleeping, or just taking a break from the steamy afternoon. Then he opened them just a crack, and said, "She was with him when he got himself dragged that day."

CHAPTER 25

Questions bounced off the inside of my skull as I waited for him to say more, but he didn't. What he'd just told me didn't make sense, and then all of a sudden it made all the sense in the world. Henry Stump clearly had known about Jimmy Holland, and so had my father. Jenkins III, too, most likely. What did they all know that they tried to keep quiet? And now my sister, as well? If what Ernie was saying was true—well, no wonder she was as messed up as she was.

There was so much I wanted to ask Ernie Collier, so much I felt I needed to know. But his internal switch had flipped to "sleep," and his head slowly tipped back on his thin neck. His mouth dropped open and within seconds he was snoring, his chest rising and falling in a slow, steady rhythm.

Back in the car I found my sister's phone number in my call log and hit redial. It took a moment for the call to go through, and even longer for her to answer. Eventually she did.

"Where are you?" I asked her, no formalities or small talk.

"Where do you think?" she answered flippantly.

I had no patience for her games, but the sledgehammer approach never worked with Karen. Now I suspected I knew why. "Probably halfway to Atlanta," I guessed. "Look…there's something I need to ask you."

"You know the fountain in Hampton Park?" she asked.

"The what?"

"Remember? Mom and Dad took us there for the Spoleto Festival one summer. There used to be a zoo, but then the city redid everything. Anyways, there's a fountain right in the middle. Meet me there in a half-hour."

"So you're not in Atlanta?" I asked her.

"Silly rabbit, Trix are for kids. See you in thirty minutes."

It took me more like forty, since I didn't remember where the park was located and neither did my GPS app. By the time I'd found a place to park and had wandered past the rusty old baseball stadium I was sure I'd missed her deadline, but then I saw Karen stretched out on one of the picnic tables soaking in some lowcountry sun. She didn't seem to mind that I was late.

My shadow crossed her closed eyes and she opened them with a jolt. "I was about to give up on you," she said as she shielded her face with her hand. "What's this about?"

"I just came from Ernie Collier's place."

She said nothing at first, just lowered her head to the table and closed her eyes. Then she said, "You talked to Stumpy."

I'd had forty minutes since leaving Ernie's tidy house to try to draw some clarity from what he'd told me. The more I tried, however, the murkier things got. "You've been carrying a big burden over a lot of years," I told her.

"So, you finally took your head out of your ass," she said without opening her eyes.

It's difficult carrying on a conversation with someone who isn't looking at you, much less making an effort not to. My sister never made things easy, something I'd grown accustomed to, but today I think she kept her eyes shut so she couldn't see the ghosts of the past.

"You were there the day Jimmy Holland was killed," I said.

She dipped her head in what I guessed was the slightest of nods, then said, "Wrong place at the very worst time."

"Care to talk about it?"

"I really like Adeline," she said, deftly shifting the topic. "She's beautiful but doesn't quite know it yet, and smart, and very caring. You should be proud."

"I am. Sometimes she seems like she's fifteen going on thirty."

"She's a girl," Karen said. "Get used to it. I was a volunteer that summer."

She was a master of changing subjects on the fly, and just like that we were back on Jimmy Holland. "What were you volunteering for?" I asked, going with her flow.

I had no reason to think she would answer my question, at least not directly, but she surprised me. "I'd just finished my freshman year at Clemson, and I'd started working with a campus organization that was trying to provide scholarships to minority kids. I was doing outreach around here, and one day Mr. Collier told me about this kid who somehow was part of his extended family. He lived up on a dirt road outside Orangeburg. He really wanted to go to Clemson, but there was no way his family could afford it. Mr. Collier asked if I might drive up and talk to him about his chances for one of those scholarships."

"So that's how you came to be walking down the road with him that day."

She jerked her head from side to side, almost violently, and said, "I don't want to talk about that day."

Understandable, but I couldn't let it go. "You saw what happened."

"What I saw was how dark a human soul can turn when hatred is allowed to consume the heart," she said.

I reached out and touched her hand, but she snatched it away. "It wasn't your fault," I told her. "You have to know that."

"I tried to help him," she replied, her voice ragged and torn. "It only made things worse."

I tried not to imagine what she had seen and heard that day, how the imagery must have invaded her mind and lingered ever since. "What did you do afterwards?" I asked her.

"What I did was learn what a coward I was," she said, her words coming out as a whimper. "A fucking gutless, yellow-bellied coward."

She was anything but, yet I knew I wouldn't be able to convince her of that. "You must have been terrified out of your mind," I told her.

"That day and every day since."

I felt as if I'd only learned a fraction of the story, but I knew with my sister it was best to tread lightly and not poke her too many times. I was still numb from what she had told me, and likely had not told me. I knew Reverend King spoke eloquently about light driving out darkness and love conquering hate, but what if that darkness and hate was just the shadow of pure evil lurking behind the mask of human depravity, for which love and light were no match.

"You told Dad," I finally said.

"Not right away," she replied, softly. "Not until summer was almost over. The whole thing was in the news for days, but no one was ever caught."

I was ashamed to admit that I'd paid no attention to that sort of thing that summer, preoccupied as I was with Laurie and my adolescent attempt to commit my own sins of the flesh. "Did you get a good look at them?" I asked her.

She opened her eyes and I could see the self-loathing deeply rooted within. Then she sat up and turned away from the sun. "There were three of them," she finally said. "Two were brothers. Greasy hair, brown eyes. Body odor and breath that smelled like rancid pickles. The third one was older. Black hair, devil's eyes. I think he went to U.S.C."

"How could you tell?" I asked patiently, letting her remember at her own pace.

"Class ring," she said. "I saw it when he put his finger in me."

"When he *what?*"

"Jimmy Holland wasn't the only one who was attacked that day."

"Shit...you...he..." I tried to wrap my mind around what she was telling me, then said, "He was attacking you and you were *looking at his ring?*"

"You do strange things when someone's trying to rape you—"

Her voice trailed off, and I felt my blood begin to boil. I couldn't imagine how my sister had lived with this secret all these years. It explained so much and, all of a sudden, I wanted to wrap my arms around her and hold her close. But that was not my sister's way. Nor mine, I suddenly realized.

Still, I said, "What did Dad do when you told him?"

"What do you think? He went berserk. He was furious. Not with me, but with what had happened. And with himself. You remember how he was: everything was about jigaboos and spics and slants."

I nodded, but said nothing. There was no need to. As Ernie Collier had said, he'd been conflicted by many things, in many ways.

"He was raised to believe that whites and blacks had their places on this earth, and as long as everyone knew theirs, no harm could come of it. Like dogs and pigs, ducks and geese. Peaceful coexistence. But he did not abide violence, and when I told him what happened to Jimmy—and to me—he went pyrotechnic."

"So what did he do?" I asked her.

"He told me not to think about it again, that he'd take care of it."

Take care of it? What the hell did that mean? I wondered. "Did he ask you any details? I mean, about those three shit bags, or the truck?"

She nodded. "I told him what I just told you. He wanted to bring in sketch artists and detectives and all that, but I didn't let him. I was too afraid. I knew they'd kill me if they ever found out who I was, and I was just too scared. Too much of a coward."

"Don't blame yourself, or shame yourself," I told her.

"Way too late for that," she replied.

"Dad must have gone to the police—"

Another shrug, mostly one of indifference. "If he did, he never mentioned it to me."

"And when was this?" I pressed her, as gently as I knew how. "When you finally spoke with him?"

"At the end of August," she said. "About ten days before Mom died."

My sister didn't want to talk anymore, and she made this clear when she just slid off the picnic table and shambled off. I wanted to go after her, tell her all sorts of things I'd wished I'd known to tell her way back then. I also had more questions, but I knew she was all talked out. She said nothing as she made her way toward the path that ringed the park, just raised her hand in the air and waggled her fingers. *Good-bye.* I would have to be patient, but at least she was still in town. She hadn't gone back to Atlanta, and as long as she stuck around I might get another chance to know what she knew.

What she had implied, but had not directly said, was that Henry Stump had been assigned to guard us against unknown forces that might try to kill us. Not reporters or cameramen, or the hecklers who had been calling for the death sentence for our father. No, he was there to protect us from the bastards who had killed Jimmy Holland and assaulted her, and would come after us if even a hint of the truth got out. Stumpy had brought up Jimmy Holland's name in the first place, then implied that Ernie Collier had knowledge of the young man's death.

Karen had said she thought two brothers had been involved with Jimmy Holland's death, and my brain immediately went to Rudy and Gerald Aiken. Jenkins III had told me that Rudy could place my father at a meeting of White River the night of the murder, but what did that mean? I was convinced he'd been a party to Jimmy Holland's dragging, and reluctantly agreed to testify because of what my sister had seen. Did he also have proof that Dad had not killed our mother? Or had Jenkins III just relied on him to provide an alternate explanation that could have planted reasonable doubt in the minds of some jurors? However it played out, he'd been shot in the neck out on Dog Swamp Road A, and Gerald had been found with a hole in his head in the Congaree Swamp.

How could I have missed all this? Had I been so engrossed in my own reflection that I'd overlooked all these whispers and nuances? My sister had witnessed an inhumane act upon another person, and also had suffered a vicious attack herself that simmering July afternoon. I understood that my father and his lawyer had tried to shield me—*us*—from whatever blowback might come from Karen's involvement in those horrible events, but now I felt the weight of guilt for being so blind, so oblivious. And a growing anger that, for some reason, they had felt a need to build a wall of lies in order to protect me from the truth, however dangerous it might be.

It was mid-afternoon, and I hoped Addie was enjoying her time at the beach. I thought about calling her but decided to shoot her a short text instead, just to check in while trying not to hover like a drone.

`Hope you're having a good time. I still have one more thing to do, but should be home by 6:00. What would you like to do for dinner?`

It took her a few minutes to get back to me, and I received her reply when I was stopped at a light on Old Savannah Highway, heading south. I've heard all the warnings, and merely holding a cell phone while behind the wheel gets you a hefty fine in California. But she was my daughter, and the light was red.

`There may be a cook-out later. OK if I go? TTYL.`

I had to pull into the parking lot of a homegrown barbecue joint to text my reply, which was:

Yes, but be home by 11. Who's driving?

To which she answered,

Not sure yet. Don't worry, it's at Beverly's house on Isle of Palms.

Don't worry? I thought. *Wait until you're the parent of a teenager.* What I wrote instead was:

Sounds good. Keep me posted.

An hour later I was pulling down the long, shrouded drive that led to Jenkins III's house on the edge of the South Edisto River. The air was still and the sun was throwing deep shadows across the dirt road. It hadn't rained in several days and my tires churned up a wake of dust as I bounced down the corrugated lane that cut through the trees. I bumped along, under the same clumps of moss dripping from the oaks and sweet gums, same twisted Carolina creeper strangling the life out of the newer growth.

Eventually I came to the clearing where the log home stood, looking out over the shimmering water. The lawyer's silver Mercedes was parked where it had been a week ago, and Diesel was curled up in the shade of a river birch. I pulled my rental Chevy through the circular drive and cut the engine, then climbed out just as I heard the kitchen door open.

"Jesus, Devlin," Jenkins III barked. Clearly not overjoyed to see me. "What the hell do you want this time?"

"Answers, dammit," I shot back. "Sprinkled with a bit of the fucking truth, for once."

"What the devil are you talking about?" he said, his words guttural and coming from deep in his throat.

"Let's start with Jimmy Holland and go from there," I snapped. As I moved toward him he crossed his arms, a classic gesture of defensive body language. "That takes us to my sister, who had a front-row seat when he was killed. Then there's Rudy Aiken, who disappeared the week before he was to go on the stand. Which brings us to White River and Avery Dunham and Gerald Aiken, whose truck was burned up in the warehouse fire. And let's not forget Ed Landry, however he fits into all this. Should I keep going, or is that enough to jog your memory?"

He stared at me, then shook his head and glanced back over his shoulder at the kitchen door. "Christ almighty, son. Whatever the hell you think you're doing, it's time to undo it and let old ghosts die."

"My father gave up thirty years of his life because of those old ghosts, *sir*," I said. Even during times of impassioned debate, the southern civility thing found a way to come out. "And they won't find any peace until they come into the light."

He inhaled a long breath, then let it out slowly. It seemed that whatever secrets he'd carried with him all these years were about to squeeze out, and there wasn't a damn thing he could do about it. "Christ, get your persistent ass inside before it gets shot off," he sighed. "And I mean for you to take that literally."

Unlike the last time I was there, we sat in hard wooden chairs at the dining table. He offered me no sweet tea, no beer, no water. I couldn't even see the bird feeder from where I was sitting. The message being: this was not a social call. He sat across from me, four feet of polished maple between us. Hunched forward, hands folded on the table in front of him. Neither of us said anything for a long time, until eventually he spoke.

"Your sister saw Jimmy Holland get dragged that day," he said. "But you already know that by now. What you may not know is that she also was assaulted."

"She hit me with that just a few hours ago," I said.

"Well, there were three dickheads in that truck to start, but only two were actually in it when the black boy got killed."

"Rudy Aiken and his brother Gerald," I said, taking a stab at it.

"Damn, son. How'd you get to that?"

"Gerald's truck burned up when his uncle's warehouse went up in smoke. He'd hidden it there, 'cause everyone in the state was looking for it."

The old lawyer shook his head. "Christ—I totally missed that."

I couldn't tell if he was being honest, and it didn't much matter. Instead I said, "How did you learn about Rudy in the first place?"

"That shit-for-brains suddenly grew a conscience," Jenkins explained. "Something about hearing the voice of God, and he wanted to come clean."

"The voice of God?"

"He wouldn't be the first around these parts. No one ever accused Rudy Aiken of being a genius. He was just a kid who'd done something hideous and he was scared to death."

"And he ratted out his own brother?"

"Not directly," Jenkins III replied. "It took some hard-ball tactics just to convince him to talk."

"What about the third motherfucker?" I asked him. "The one who assaulted my sister?"

Jenkins III shook his head at that. "I never was able to figure that out, and Rudy was too terrified to say. I was going to try to get it out of him on the stand, if Judge Carter let me, but I never got the chance."

"Whoever it was, the bastard needs to pay."

"That's what your mother said, when she found out what happened to Karen," the aging lawyer said. "She never stood a chance."

"Is that why she was killed?" I demanded. "Because she knew who killed Jimmy Holland?"

He dipped his head in what either was a neck spasm or a nod; it was hard to tell which. "Nothing I could ever come close to proving to a jury," he said.

"You've known this all along and did absolutely nothing?"

Jenkins III pressed his palms against the table top and rose to his feet. "I did everything I could do. All I needed was to stir up some doubt, just enough to spare your father a guilty verdict. But the judge knocked down everything I tried. He cut me a short leash and yanked me back every time I tried to pull. The prosecutor, Blackwood, knew what I was trying to do, but he had an airtight case and had an eye on your father's senate seat. He was looking for a win rather than the truth. Politics and ambition sent your father to jail, son. Not me."

"And it never crossed your mind to take it to the cops?" I pushed him. "SLED even opened an anonymous tip line."

"Your father was convinced there was a bullseye on your back," he said. "You and your sister *both*."

I shook my head, more out of disappointment than disbelief. I stood up and stared the old man square in the eye. "So let me say it again: you did absolutely nothing."

"Rudy was in the wind by then, and I figured he was dead," Jenkins III explained. "Your father was convinced the same thing would happen to the two of you, and he ordered me to drop it."

I got the distinct feeling it was an order he was eager to follow.

"The mystery witness you never called. After Rudy Aiken vanished. It was my sister, wasn't it?"

"She was one brave young woman, son. But after what they did to your mother, and Rudy's disappearance, I couldn't put her up there. Your father was adamant, and I had to agree. She wouldn't have stood a chance, not with what they did to your mother. When Rudy disappeared, our fears were confirmed. The fact that both he and his brother were shot and dumped in the middle of nowhere… well, over time that convinced me we'd made the right choice."

"You didn't give a shit what Jimmy Holland's family was going through? That maybe they deserved some justice for what happened to the poor kid?"

"I'm not proud of the course we chose, but what's done is done."

Typical lawyer response, totally devoid of any compassion or remorse. "How did they do it?" I asked him. "Make it look like my father killed her?"

"Any answer to that would be speculation, at best," he said as he walked me to the door. "The tox tests showed that Frank had so much alcohol and narcotics in his system that he couldn't have driven himself home from the meeting. Plus, Rudy swore on both testicles that he wasn't at your house that night. That leaves his brother Gerald and this other motherfucker, as you so eloquently put it."

George Kovacs, I thought as I reflexively balled my hand into a fist. *Time to put that sack of shit in the ground.*

There are studies that show many people would rather dig their heels deeper into an exposed lie than admit they were wrong, and I was faced with that quandary now. I'd spent the last three decades convinced that the jury had to be correct, that seven men and five women could not have convicted my father unless he was guilty as sin. Reasonable doubt, and all that. I'd accepted their verdict and had moved on with my life, and even my father's refusal to see me when he was in prison played into the convenient storyline in my head. The same line that had been hammered into the minds of the jurors: State Senator is skunked on booze and benzos, gets into a fight with his wife, whom he believes is having a torrid affair with a black man from church. The closet racist grabs a knife from the block in the kitchen and comes at her in a fit of rage. Even after she's been stabbed, she defends herself and pushes him away, causing him to hit his head on the edge of the Formica counter and black out. No memory, no alibi. Nearly everyone in the courtroom bought it, except maybe Lily Elliott, my father, and his crack legal team.

Now I was faced with accepting that the jury was wrong. The prosecutor was wrong, and the judge was wrong. So was I, and that truth was a weight on my heart while I drove back down Jenkins III's long driveway. As I pulled out onto the two-lane county road I realized it wasn't just a case of me being wrong, either. It was a matter of bad faith, of being swept up in an easy conclusion that allowed me to compartmentalize my father many years ago so I could move on with my own life.

There were so many different emotions pinging through my mind that I had difficulty keeping track. Remorse, for believing my father could have done what I now realized was a false accusation. Anger, at him and his lawyer for permitting him to rot in jail while my mother's real killer went free. Yes, there had been appeals, but Jenkins easily could have played the Jimmy Holland card and blown the case wide open. Then there was guilt: guilt for how easily I had abandoned the man who, despite all his human faults, had brought me into this world and had done all he thought he could to protect me, and my sister.

I'd been blind on so many levels, and now I didn't even have the chance to look my father in the eyes and tell him just how very, very sorry I was. He had spent the last three decades in prison for a crime he knew in his heart he could not have committed, and he shut my sister and me out of his world in order to protect us from whoever had likely killed our mother. And now his death had taken from me the chance to confess the sense of regret that was hammering my chest, trying to get out, a lost opportunity I never could regain.

I was still struggling with how he possibly could have sacrificed thirty years of his life, just to make sure his son and daughter would remain out of harm's way. Who does something like that? Then my mind went to my own daughter, and I knew I would go to the same lengths to protect her, to keep her safe, to forfeit my own life for hers. As a father there is no choice, no decision. You just do.

There was no way I could know at that moment just how soon my own moment of truth would come along.

CHAPTER 26

Laurie Cobb called me on my way back from Edisto. Since no one else was in the car I switched to the Bluetooth function to keep my hands free.

"You never call, you never write…" she said in a cordial rebuke. Cordial because she said it in a lighthearted way, rebuke because I also knew there was a touch of honesty in it.

"I plead the Fifth," I responded. "I should have called before now, but parenting and scattering my dad's ashes have been a bit of a distraction. Plus, my sister showed up out of the blue."

"Karen's in town?"

"Has been since yesterday, and so far the cops have only been called once. But let's not talk about her."

"So, what would you like to talk about?"

"You called me," I reminded her. "But since you're asking, I sure could get into a replay of happy hour."

"God help you if that's all you think about," she said.

"My brain multi-tasks just fine. You just tend to set it in a certain direction."

She giggled. "It's Thursday night," she reminded me. "That means the start of a very busy weekend if you run a restaurant."

"If we don't embrace the challenges of life we will only diminish the possibilities," I told her.

"Is that something someone once said?" she asked.

"Me, just now. What's a man to do?"

She was silent for a few seconds, then said, "Well, maybe a man can park his car in a secluded space at the far end of my parking lot behind the dumpster," she suggested. "After dark, of course."

"Seriously? Dumpster diving at our age?"

"Don't get too excited," Laurie said. "We won't be alone. There's lots of cats and raccoons and other things hanging around."

"Howling creatures of the night gnawing on old shrimp skins and sour coleslaw. Sounds like the perfect date."

"We'll leave the windows up," she offered. "That way they'll fog up faster."

"Unless we turn on the AC the car will turn into a sauna—"

"C'mon, Rick…embrace the challenge and imagine the possibilities."

I realized she was serious about this, and my sense of adventure was up for any new experience. "Okay…I'll bring the champagne," I finally agreed. "Just like old times."

"You never once brought me champagne back then—"

"I was on a beer budget in those days, but the sentiment was the same. When shall we plan this sensory trip down memory lane?"

"I won't know until I see how busy it is," Laurie said. "I'll give you a call later."

"Operators will be standing by," I replied, and clicked off.

I knew where George Kovacs lived and, since I didn't need to fix dinner for Addie, I drove out to Ladson to see if he was home. I didn't have a clear plan for when I got there, and I had no intention of doing anything stupid. My GPS guided me to his address on Limehouse Lane, a plain one-story brick house with peeling white shutters and a one-vehicle carport. Thousands of these homes had been built around the lowcountry in the fifties and sixties, and they were remarkable only in their uninspired similarity. Kovacs' lawn was mostly patches of brown weeds enclosed behind a chain-link fence with driveway gates that were securely closed. A sign fastened to one of the steel fence posts warned:

`Ignore the Dog…Beware of Owner`

The black Ram 1500 he had been driving the day I'd picked up Addie at the airport was nowhere in sight, which was good news. It told me he probably wasn't home, which gave me even less reason to try something dumb. Like walk up to his front door and ring the bell.

I did it anyway, three times, but no one answered. I peered through the glass in the door, then walked into the empty carport and peered through the glass there, as well. No sign of life in the kitchen, and I wasn't about to let myself into the backyard. The background report I'd received from Kat Rattigan said Kovacs was divorced, but didn't mention whether he had a girlfriend or kids. If he did, none of them seemed to be around, so there was no point in any further snooping. Besides, there was a state police vehicle parked several doors up on the other side of the street, a Charger with a light bar gripping the roof, and I didn't feel like being asked questions to which I didn't have answers.

I'd done a lot of ruminating on my way back from Edisto, and something had been bothering me. I hadn't been able to put my finger on it but now, as I sat behind the wheel in front of Kovacs' house, I realized what it was. Rudy and Gerald Aiken in all likelihood had been in the truck that dragged Jimmy Holland, and I'd assumed Kovacs was the sonofabitch who had assaulted my sister. On one level it made sense, if only because he had slipped the note to my father and had tailed me to the airport. Plus, he was about the right age. But something Karen had said finally clicked into place, something that now caused me to push Kovacs to the margins of my suspicion. She'd told me that the man who assaulted her had been wearing a U.S.C. class ring, but I'd seen no such jewelry on either of Kovacs' hands when I'd busted him in the jaw. That itself wasn't conclusive—after all, it had been thirty years—but the background check reported no further education in his life beyond high school. There was little chance that he'd worn a ring for a university he had not attended, unless it was an heirloom from a relative or maybe a gift from a girlfriend. Even so, the odds of him being Jimmy Holland's third assailant slipped a few notches in my mind.

I picked up some moo shu chicken on the way back to the condo, and finally found a stretch of time to tackle the book for which I was being paid to write. Several glasses of wine were involved, which helped with the tedium, as did the phone call from Laurie a few minutes before nine.

"Is this the operator?" she inquired when I answered.

"That's what I've been told," I replied.

"Well, now…aren't we just a little cocky?" she giggled. "I just wanted to let you know the dinner rush is winding down, and the parking lot is emptying out."

"Give me twenty minutes," I said, already saving the Word file on my computer as we spoke. "I'll be in the unmarked Chevy parked behind your trash bin."

Laurie was right: the space at the far end of her lot was ideal for what we had in mind. For just a second I wondered if she knew this from past experience, or if she just had a snapshot memory of her restaurant's parking lot. In no way did any of that matter as much as my rental car's awkwardly placed steering wheel and gear shift. Even the back seat was cramped and claustrophobic, a tight squeeze for someone who once had tried—but had not succeeded—to acquire membership in the mile-high club in the confines of an airplane restroom.

The dumpster was set under a clump of trees that shielded my car from the bright lights of the parking lot. It was out of view of anyone who might be heading to or from their vehicles and, except for the occasional feral cat, there was not another living being in sight. Laurie seemed to be particularly stressed by work and nearly attacked me as soon we were properly concealed in the back seat. I reciprocated fully, and within seconds we were tightly entwined in a crazy embrace, fingers fumbling at buttons and zippers while our lips and tongues unleashed our pent-up passions.

The champagne helped, at least at the start. But I soon learned from the Mount Pleasant police officer who rapped on the window with the butt of his flashlight—just like in the movies—that drinking from an open container in a car was considered a DUI even if the vehicle was parked behind a dumpster at the edge of a dark parking lot.

"It's my lot," Laurie explained to the officer as she hurriedly fastened the buttons of her blouse, light blue with dark blue pagodas on it. "Private property."

"Technically it belongs to the city," replied the cop, who kept sweeping the beam around the interior of the car. Looking for probable cause that would permit him to toss the vehicle from bumper to bumper. "The businesses along the creek pay for the upkeep and maintenance."

"Look, Officer," she said. "No harm, no foul. I own Jake's On The Creek, and I have to get back to the kitchen."

"Ma'am, with all due respect, you have committed a serious misdemeanor, and the law requires that I write you up."

"You're arresting us?" I asked him. Laurie shot me a look of warning and gave me an almost invisible shake of her head. Translation: *Let me take care of this.*

"It's not for me to make that determination, sir," he said. "That would be up to the captain. Or a judge. Let me see some identification."

"Both of us?" Laurie asked.

"Which one of you was driving?"

This was something he couldn't determine from where we were positioned, and I realized it could provide us some legal room if he tried to pursue this angle.

Neither of us said a word, which caused the officer's nostrils to flare. "There's a rental sticker on the bumper," he said, changing his tactic. "Whose name is on the agreement?"

I admitted my legal culpability, and he flashed a smile of victory. We were still in the back seat and he couldn't legally reach into the glove box, so he ordered us both out of the car. I tucked in my shirt and pulled up my fly, then handed him the packet of papers from the rental company. I also handed him my license, which he noted was from California, as if it were a bad word. Then he said, "You're both going to have to come with me."

"*What?*" Laurie said. "That's...ridiculous."

"Lady Justice does not have a sense of humor," the officer said. "We'll sort this all out down at HQ."

"My daughter's going to be home by eleven, and I have to be there," I protested.

"Let's hope she has more sense than her father," he replied, not the least bit interested in my plight. Or Laurie's, for that matter.

That's how we both ended up sitting in the lobby of the Mount Pleasant Police Department. The arresting officer—J. Beckwith, according to the brass tag pinned to his shirt—had not cuffed us, and since neither of us was drunk we were not considered risks to ourselves or others. Nor were we likely to flee, since both our cars were back at the creek. We both sat there fuming for what seemed like an eternity as the wheels of justice turned at the speed of a lava flow.

By the time the night shift captain came out to speak with us the clock on the wall had ticked well past midnight. Officer Beckwith had confiscated our cell phones, and had not granted either of us our one legal call. "That's only in the movies," he'd said with a snort.

"Mrs. Mitchell," the night captain now said, genuinely surprised to see her sitting in the hallway at such a late hour. "What are you doing here?"

"I'm still trying to figure that out," Laurie replied, polite but firm. "Your very efficient officer was doing what he clearly thought was his job, but I believe he got a bit overzealous in his interpretation of the law."

"I see," the captain said. His badge said his name was Darryl Baar, and he looked to be in his late thirties. He had darkish hair cut close to his scalp, revealing a fresh scar above his right ear. He had a flat nose that looked more genetic than the product of a fight, and dull gray eyes that seemed weary and drained. "Care to fill me in?"

She did, explaining that she and I were old high school friends and had decided to share a bottle of champagne in a car parked on private property, since the dumpster and the small patch of real estate around it was property she legally rented from the town. "I have a copy of the lease back at the restaurant, but your officer refused to let me go and get it," she fumed. "He brought us here instead."

"When was this?" Captain Baar asked her.

"About three hours ago," she replied. "I haven't been able to call my kids or Tommy at the restaurant. He's the kitchen manager."

"What about your husband?" he inquired, glancing at the ring on her finger.

"He wasn't invited," Laurie said. "We're separated."

Captain Baar nodded in understanding, then drew his eyes to me. "What do you have to say about all this?" he asked.

"Everything she said," I replied.

He massaged his upper lip tiredly, then said, "I apologize for this, Mrs. Mitchell. You're right: Beckwith can be a bit zealous when it comes to the letter of the law. But I've been eating at your family's restaurant since my parents took me there as a kid, and you're a respectable member of this community. You should not have had to go through this, and you're free to go. You, too, Mr. Devlin. I watched you pitch once, against the Braves. As I recall you had a stinger of a fastball."

I wondered how Captain Baar knew about my major league history, although we'd been sitting there long enough for him to run an extensive search. He arranged to have one of his cops—not Beckwith—drive us back to where we'd parked our cars. On the way Laurie called the restaurant to let anyone who might still be on the premises know that she was on the way. Meanwhile, I phoned Addie to apologize for not being there when she got home. It rang five times and then went into voicemail, which told me she either had turned it off or had left it somewhere out of earshot. I hoped that meant she was home and in bed, but this night had already been full of surprises. I didn't want another one.

We said goodbye against the fender of my Impala. It involved a long kiss, passionate but still somewhat rushed because new priorities had set in. We lamented the missed opportunity of the night and agreed to connect in the morning to reschedule our botched rendezvous. We were laughing about it now and discussed the possibility of a quickie, right then and there. But our mutual responsibilities were calling, so we exchanged one more prolonged kiss and then went our separate ways.

I tried calling Addie again, twice, but her phone still rang through to voicemail. I realized then that I didn't have Sam's phone number, nor that of his parents. Big mistake on my part, and as I drove across the bridge back into Charleston I hoped I wouldn't come to regret the oversight. Knowing Addie, she probably was sound asleep in her bed, but the worst-case scenario side of my brain began playing out all sorts of dark and dismal options.

When I pulled into the covered parking garage under the condo building I was tired, worried, and still a bit buzzed from the events of the evening. Getting hauled down to the slammer was not part of my plans, and I felt miserable because I hadn't been able to let Addie know what had happened. I'd told her to be back by eleven, and then I was gone when she would have let herself in. I'd had her in my care for less than a week, and already I'd screwed things up.

My mind was racing as I drove toward my assigned parking space, playing out in my head what I would tell my daughter. My headlights bounced across the other cars in the garage, most residents being safely home at this hour of the night. That's when the worst of all the scenarios—one that I had not anticipated on the way home—hit me with a resounding thud.

Backed into my designated slot was a large black Ram 1500 quad cab pick-up, tinted glass and blacked-out bumpers and plastic-dipped rims. Unquestionably the same truck that had followed me to the airport Sunday morning, and its presence meant only one thing.

George Kovacs was in the house.

CHAPTER 26

An icy needle stung my spine as a hundred horrid thoughts gripped me. I braked to a halt directly in front of his truck and stared at the illegal tint job. The fluorescent glow from the overhead lighting cast enough illumination inside for me to see the cab was empty. That opened another host of possibilities I didn't want to consider, as I realized Addie was upstairs with a sicko who only had revenge on his mind.

I left my car where it was. If Kovacs made a fast break he would have to go through the rental Impala first. I hit the "lock" button on the fob, then raced across the garage to the bank of elevators. I knew they defaulted to the first floor, so I took the stairs two at a time up to the lobby. I only had to wait a second before the bell rang and a door to my right opened. I jumped in and hit "12," then waited for the interminably slow climb to my floor.

Instinctively I knew Kovacs was not just going to hang around and wait patiently for me to come home. He was a man of action, and it was clear he had come here with a purpose. By parking his truck in my space he was taunting me, announcing his presence with a bold statement when I showed up. By now I seriously doubted he was directly involved with Jimmy Holland's death or my sister's assault. Still, he'd shown a perverse interest in my father—and, by extension, me. He'd slipped the handwritten note to Benita, then had followed me Sunday morning to the airport. And, most likely, tailed me to Beaufort the day before. If he wasn't operating out of his own self-interest, then what was his game and whose team was he playing on?

None of that mattered now. What mattered was that I had left for my rendezvous with Laurie a little before nine, and now it was one in the morning. That meant Kovacs had a four-hour window to break in while I was gone. There was a good chance he had not known about Addie, and if he'd shown up before she had arrived home he would have settled in to wait for me to return. At some point she would have let herself in with her own key and found him in the condo. Even if she'd already been there when he arrived she would have been a bonus prize, and that was something I didn't want to think about.

I'd already tried her cell phone three times, and that now drove me to a point of panic. Addie never had her phone turned off, and even if she was talking to Sam she would have put him on hold to let me know she was home, even though I was not.

As the elevator slowed to a halt I hit her number one more time. A wave of dread was building in my heart, and the scenarios of what I might find on the other side of the door numbed me to the core. If George Kovacs was in there—and there was no reason to believe otherwise—he could have unleashed the fires of hell. His rap sheet read like a Stephen King novel, and the sonofabitch was as depraved and demented as anyone I'd ever known.

Again the phone rang right into voicemail. Bad sign. The elevator doors slid open and I bolted down the hallway, not knowing—nor really caring—what my next move might be. I still had my phone in my hand, and all of a sudden I felt it vibrate, a fraction of a second before it began to ring. I stopped just a few feet from my door and stared at the screen, which read "Addie."

A tsunami of relief collided with a tide of dread as I hit the "answer" button and said, "Sweetie—"

"Ah…such a beautiful fatherly sentiment," Kovacs jeered. "We've been waiting for you to show up."

"Let me talk to her," I said, trying not to give in to my worst fear.

"Come on in," he replied, his voice almost a hiss. "I know you're out there. I heard the phone ring."

"You are one sick bastard—"

"You have no idea, dickhead. Your daughter and I have arranged a most thrilling welcoming party, just for you. And I know you're too smart to call the police."

Then I heard Addie scream something like "Dad…stay out! There's a bomb!" Her words were followed by a ferocious slap, and then another scream.

"You do anything to her and you will die regretting it," I yelled into the phone.

"Talk, talk, talk," he taunted me. "Let's get this party started."

I'd already fumbled my keys out of my pocket and was set to slip them into the lock when Addie's words lodged in my brain. *Bomb! Stay out!* My hand froze just inches from the doorknob, giving my mind time to catch up and give this a second of thought.

My top priority—*my only priority*—was to get to Addie, but I knew Kovacs was not going to let that happen. I was a fool to think otherwise. If there was a bomb I'd be dead two seconds after I came through the door, and then there was no telling what the sick bastard might do to her. Even if his plan was only to break a lot of bones, I didn't want to think about what might be on the other side of that door.

What I did next was the most difficult decision I ever made in my life. The wash of adrenaline chilled my blood as I quietly ended the call and backed down the hallway to the elevator. I started to hit the button, but I knew a bell would chime as soon as it arrived. Instead, I raced to the fire door and quietly let myself into the stairwell. I guided the door closed slowly so it wouldn't slam, then took the steps two at a time up to the next floor.

As I pushed the door open I took out my phone and dialed 9-1-1. The plan that was forming in my head had a high chance of failure and, whatever happened to me, I needed to make sure Addie stood a chance.

"Nine-one-one. What's your emergency?" the dispatcher on the other end.

"This is Rick Devlin. I live at Riverfront Tower. I just heard from my daughter and she said a man broke into the condo. I think he has a gun and there may be a bomb."

"Excuse me, sir, did you say bomb?"

"That's what she said. I'm on my way there…please send someone."

She asked me the address and unit number, then said, "Officers are *en route*. Can you stay on the line?"

Not easily, not with what I had in mind. I hung up, then switched my phone to vibrate as I sprinted down the corridor to Mrs. Adams' apartment. I leaned on the bell for a good five seconds, but got no answer. I tried it twice more but still no one responded to the buzzer. *Damn.* Even if she was a sound sleeper I knew Sparky would hear me, but there was no eruption of yapping that was typical of dogs with a Napoleon complex.

Convinced that no one was home, I tipped back the heavy jade foo dog at the side of her door. The key was right where she'd said it would be. My hands were trembling and I had a little trouble getting it into the lock, but eventually I was able to turn it. The door swung inward and I slipped inside, flipping the light switch just inside and to the left. I heard no telltale beeping, and I didn't really care. If a silent alarm was ringing right now at the security headquarters—or the Charleston P.D.—they could join the cops that were already on the way. But there was no way I was going to wait for them.

I closed the door behind me and moved across the living room to the master suite. The floorplan in here seemed identical to mine, so I knew the guest room would be on the other side of the living room, next to the guest bath, one floor above Addie's room. The master bedroom would be set off to the left, so I poked my head in to see if Mrs. Adams was actually gone or just a seriously deep sleeper.

The bed was empty and made up perfectly, lots of pillows and a folded quilt at the bottom. No sign of Sparky, either. I yanked the comforter back and pulled off the top sheet, which seemed to be some kind of synthetic blend woven into a high thread count. I dragged it out into the kitchen and found a knife to slice the side hem; then I ripped it into three long strips.

I unlatched the balcony lock and slowly eased open the slider, not sure whether Kovacs could hear the low rumble of the door as I pushed it aside. I stepped out onto the balcony, where I tied all three pieces of the ripped sheet together. I slipped one end under my arms and pulled it snug with a double knot, then quietly moved to the metal railing. I hesitated a second, realized I only had once chance to get this right. I tied the other end of the sheet-rope to the base of an upright stanchion that secured the rail to the concrete terrace. At least if I slipped I had a bit of a lifeline.

I then hoisted myself over the balcony and made the conscious effort not to look down. Thirteen floors is a lot deadlier than the single story I'd navigated years ago when I'd escaped from Laurie's bedroom above the front porch of her old home. I'd made it safely back then—twice—and I told myself if I didn't look down I'd be okay this time, as well. It was still just a single story, except there were twelve more below that.

The next five seconds gave me a new appreciation for Hollywood stuntmen. I managed to lower myself from the terrace, then extended a leg in an attempt to touch my foot to the top of my own railing below. If I looked down, my eyes would be drawn all the way to the parking lot, and my gut was already twisted enough. I focused my strength inwardly and lowered myself inch by inch, knowing that eventually my shoes would touch the cold, steel surface.

Eventually they did. I lowered myself another inch or two and placed a bit more weight on my foot, then dropped the other one incrementally until both were firmly planted on the railing. I was almost there, but now came the hard part. At some point I had to let go of the concrete lip of Mrs. Adams' balcony, and that point was now. I released one hand, then grabbed the sheet-rope and slowly lowered myself until I was able to slide my feet forward and then slide onto the hard surface of my own terrace. I swung my body over the rail, and gently let myself sink into a dark shadow at the end of the balcony. I gasped for a breath that I'd dared not inhale for the last ten seconds, which seemed to have lasted ten minutes.

I didn't allow myself to think about what I had just done. I was entirely focused on what I still had to do, and I needed to do it quickly. I untied the sheet from my waist, then silently edged up to the sliding door of my bedroom and pressed my face to the glass. The room was dark and the space inside appeared to be empty. Wherever Kovacs might be holding Addie, it was not in there. Then I edged down the terrace a few yards and ventured a guarded peek into the living room, whereupon my heart turned stone-cold.

The three-way lamp beside the couch was turned on low, casting an eerie amber glow throughout the room. Addie was sitting in one of the dining chairs near the front door, dressed only in her panties and bra. She was bound by ties made from bedsheets, torn the same way I had ripped Mrs. Adams' luxury linen. Kovacs had knotted her ankles, waist, hands, and chest to the chair, and he'd wrapped another length of cloth around her mouth as a gag. The look of terror in her eyes told me all I needed to know, and it was all I could do to keep myself from blowing through the glass in a full tilt of rage.

That's when I noticed the device set on the floor to the left of the door. It looked like a small gray football, maybe a dog's toy, with some sort of tripwire connecting it to the doorknob. That's when I realized it was a grenade, rigged to explode if someone came through the door. Enough force to kill me—and Addie, whose chair was only a few feet away from it.

I didn't see Kovacs, which worried me. I was hoping he'd be stationary, sitting in a chair or maybe on the couch, but I couldn't see him at all. I knew he had to be in there, but I had no idea what he might be up to. Then I caught a flash of movement as he stepped out of the kitchen, and I realized he had a gun about the size of a small cannon in his hand.

Thirty seconds, I told myself. *Where were the cops?*

My cell phone had vibrated several times while I was lowering myself to my balcony. I knew Kovacs would be getting anxious, which meant he might flip out at any second. I edged back to the master bedroom slider and gently pulled it back, just enough for me to slip inside. I hadn't locked it since hospice moved my father in, and Kovacs hadn't done so, either. I moved across the carpet noiselessly, aided by the fact that Kovacs was blasting the rhythmic pulse of gangsta rap on the high-end stereo in the living room.

The walk-in closet was fitted with older accordion doors that squeaked when I tried to push them open. I had to move slowly, so I lost a few seconds there. I regained them, however, when my fingers found Kovacs' gun almost instantly. I'd stashed it under a blanket on the shelf, and now I hefted it in the darkness. The room was dark and I couldn't see past my hand, but I didn't need to. I'd racked the slide when I brought it home from the airport, found that the expanded magazine was fully loaded, with one in the chamber.

I slipped a finger through the guard and felt the tension of the trigger. I'd never been faced with the need to shoot someone, but I knew I could if I had to. And I'd know *that* in just a few more seconds. And since it was a Glock I knew there was no safety to switch off. Just point and shoot.

My bedroom door opened directly into the foyer inside the front door. It would save me time to go in that way, but I'd be far more exposed than I wanted to be. The element of surprise was critical, so I quietly padded back across the bedroom carpet and slipped back out onto the balcony. A gentle breeze had kicked up, and the rope of sheets dangling from the railing above was beginning to billow in the wind. A good gust might blow it just far enough across Kovacs' field of vision to catch his eye. I thought about tying it down, but that would cost me too many valuable seconds.

I crouch-walked along the terrace until I came to the frame of the living room slider. It opened left to right, which worked in my favor—as long as Kovacs didn't see me. Fortunately, the glow from the table lamp made it lighter inside than out here in the dark of night. I would be little more than a shadow to him, but I had a satisfactory view of what was going on inside. As long as the door was unlocked I had the advantage on my side.

It was. I gently eased the glass open until I'd created just enough of a gap to slip inside. I worried that the wind might rustle the curtains, so I quickly slid the door closed before I crouched behind the overstuffed sofa. I was about ten feet from where Addie was strapped to her chair, but her back was to me so she couldn't see me.

That's when Kovacs came into view. He clearly was agitated, enraged that I wasn't answering his calls. He had Addie's phone in one hand and the gun in the other. A large bandage was taped to his jaw, and he was close enough for me to see a splotch of dried blood on the white gauze. He punched the redial button again, and for a second I was afraid that he might hear my phone vibrating in my pocket. But the gangsta rap drowned it out, and again he recoiled in disgust when I didn't answer.

This gave me an idea. I thumbed my phone out of my pocket and dialed him back. The sudden shrill of Addie's ringtone was drowned out by the music, but the illuminated screen caught his attention. At the same time Addie's eyes flew open in fear. Kovacs glanced at the phone, then screamed, "You goddamned son-of-a-whore—!"

That's when I shot him. Justifiable, and totally in self-defense if anyone ever asked. I fired four rounds in his direction, one of them hitting him in the shoulder. The phone flew against the wall as he spun around and clutched his upper arm. He brought his gun up but had no idea where to aim. He'd seen the flashes and heard the gunfire, but the speed and pain that had accompanied my shots had disoriented him. I glanced over to Addie, who had stiffened from fear, then fired off two more shots at him.

"Drop it, asshole," I roared at the same time, over the thump of the music. I rose out of the shadows, aiming the gun at his head as I edged forward.

"You motherfucker," he snarled. "You and your cock sucking daughter are so going to die!"

No one said that about Addie, so I shot him again, this time in the thigh. He fell against the wall and cursed in pain as the gun skittered across the floor.

Addie made a muffled scream through her gag. I caught a flurry of motion to my left as another man slammed into me. The Glock slipped from my fingers as he drove me to the floor, and I felt my head explode against the hard tile.

CHAPTER 27

A galaxy of stars erupted inside my skull, but I did not black out. I felt as if I'd just been struck by a freight train. Almost instantly came a blow to my stomach and another to my ear as my attacker began to pummel me with his fists. He'd knocked me down and intended to keep me there, but I was not going anywhere without a fight. As he brought his fist back for yet another strike I saw his face about twelve inches from mine, and I reared up hard and cracked him in the nose with my forehead. He let out a yelp as he continued with his punch, but it went wide. My sudden movement had caught him off guard and his fist smashed into the floor with a resounding crunch.

Out of the corner of my eye I saw Kovacs edging toward his gun, which had clattered to a stop near the entrance to the kitchen. A few more seconds and he'd be armed. If I was going to come out on top of this I had to take control of the situation, and fast.

My attacker had followed his punch through to the tile, causing him to lose his balance just enough to let me push him off. My head was still throbbing, but I pressed down the pain and scrambled to my feet. He rolled into a sitting position and started to get up, but I landed a solid kick to his chin.

In the same motion I spun around, using the same foot to sweep Kovacs back just as I took a wild dive for the loose gun. Kovacs clawed at my leg but then recoiled as my foot crunched his nose, his head jerking back from the impact. Blood spurted on the walls and floor as I grabbed the Glock before he had another chance to get to it. At the same time Addie screamed; she had managed to rip away the strip of sheet that was gagging her, so her voice was loud and clear.

"Dad! Watch out!"

I didn't see him coming, but her words registered in my head before the other man's foot did. He'd aimed for my jaw but only caught my shoulder as his kick circled through. The force of his shoe stung like a sonofabitch, but he'd only been able to wing me. I whirled around as I raised the gun and squeezed the trigger several times.

At first I thought I'd only hit the sliding door. A million stars exploded behind him like an entire galaxy dropping into a black hole, all at once. His mouth gaped open and his eyes widened with surprise. He stared at me and tried to speak, but no words would come. Then I noticed that blood was oozing from a hole in his black T-shirt, just below his rib cage. He began to stagger backwards, his feet crunching on the broken jewels of glass as he backpedaled onto the balcony. His life seemed to be draining from his eyes, and it was at that point I realized I'd seen his pasty skin and red hair before. He was the state cop who'd been posted outside my father's door at the Hospice Center when I'd first pulled into town.

He stumbled up against the railing, and for a moment it appeared he might simply collapse to the hard terrace. But he was a tall man and his momentum caused him to lose his balance; the laws of gravity took over from there. The off-duty cop teetered for a moment on the edge of the rail, a wild look of horror in his eyes, and then he folded over it and disappeared into the night. Several seconds later a loud *crunch* resounded from the parking lot below.

"Dad!" Addie screamed again, and I whipped around to find Kovacs struggling to get to his feet.

"Don't. You. Move!" I yelled.

Kovacs did not seem to be the kind of man who took orders from anyone. He struggled to move toward me, no matter that I had a gun and he did not.

"The two of you killed Lily Elliott," I said, killing the music and jerking my head to where my attacker had gone over the rail.

"And you just killed a cop," he seethed.

"Didn't look like a cop to me. No uniform, no badge."

"You are in such…deep shit," Kovacs said. "You don't have a fucking clue."

"Come any closer I'll blow your head off."

He hesitated for a moment, then settled to the hard tile as a big grin creased his lips. "You are so fucked," he said. His words were coming out ragged, even though I doubted I'd hit anything vital with my shots.

"Your cop friend, there." I gave a nod in the direction of where he'd fallen into the night. "He was outside the hospice room. He's the one who told you my father had started talking about the murder."

"Blow it out your tailpipe, shithead."

"Watch your language," I replied. "There's a lady present."

I kept the gun aimed at him as I backed up toward where my daughter was sitting. I used one hand to loosen the bonds holding her wrists to the chair, and she was able to do the rest.

"You okay, Addie?" I asked her.

"Yeah, except for that...scumbag."

"Did he do anything to you?"

"All hat, no cattle," she said. "But he wired a grenade to the door."

"Up yours," Kovacs snarled. "You try to dismantle that thing and it'll blow this place right to hell."

I took a menacing step toward him, then hesitated. "Do you hear that?"

"What the fuck are you talking about?"

"Sirens." Keeping the gun aimed at Kovacs I edged out onto the balcony, looked down at a pair of vehicles with blue strobes flashing in the night. Turning full speed ahead from the street into the parking lot. The nine-one-one cops had finally arrived.

I retreated back inside and said, "Cavalry's here."

A few seconds passed and I heard the elevator ding out in the corridor, then the pounding of feet in the hallway. There was a sharp knock on the door, and then someone yelled, "Charleston Police. Open up!"

"Please, Officers. Don't touch that door," I yelled. "It's wired with a grenade!"

"What?" yelled the voice from the hallway.

"There's a grenade wired to the door."

"Who is this?"

"My name is Rick Devlin. I called nine-one-one. A couple of thugs broke in and booby-trapped the door."

I heard some muffled chatter, then the same voice called out, "Are you okay in there?"

I glanced at Kovacs, made a threatening gesture with the gun. "Under control, sir. Home invasion, but my daughter and I are fine. One of the attackers went off the balcony, and another is in here wounded."

"Got it. Okay, I want you to stay put and listen to what I tell you."

"Not going anywhere, sir," I assured him. "But you're going to need the bomb squad."

The grenade was simple military issue, with a wire looped from the pin through an eyelet that had been screwed into the wooden jamb. Still, it took twenty minutes for the cops to rappel from the balcony above and defuse it and, while they did, Kovacs continued to bleed on the tile floor. He clearly was too weak to be a threat, or even move, but until they came in through the busted slider I kept the gun trained on him anyway. By the time the door was finally secured a full squadron of officers, detectives, firefighters, and state police had arrived on the twelfth floor, and then in an instant they were swarming throughout the condo.

A large, burly cop cuffed Kovacs, who squirmed in defiance. Two med techs tried to load him onto a gurney, but he wasn't having it. The big cop roughly twisted Kovacs arm behind his back, and this time there was no protest. A separate team of officers reported they had found the body of a state trooper down below in the parking lot, next to a Mercedes sedan. In the eyes of the law I had taken the life of one of their own, but they seemed to understand that he'd broken into my home. He'd also aided and abetted the kidnapping and confinement of my daughter, and physically attacked me when I confronted Kovacs.

A stream of questions from various detectives followed, and by the time they finished, the first light of day was beginning to glow on the eastern horizon. Addie and I had been interviewed rigorously and repeatedly for hours, separately and together. She patiently explained that she'd come home a little after eleven, and the parents of one of her friends had waited downstairs in their car until she called and assured them that she was safely inside. Seconds after that Kovacs had jumped her, threatening to choke her if she kept struggling. He'd tied her to the chair and demanded to know where I was. When she told him she didn't know, he grew more furious and threatened to throw her—chair and all—over the railing.

My story was considerably more embarrassing. I'd been with Laurie Cobb since a little after nine, most of that time at the police station in Mount Pleasant. We'd both had eyewitnesses and surveillance cameras trained on us until we were released by the night captain. When Kovacs found my parking space empty he apparently backed his truck into it just to alert me that he was there to play ball. Then he and the state cop rigged the grenade and waited for me to show up. When Addie let herself in she was forced to make the "all clear" call, and then they'd tied her to a chair. When she'd yelled to me about the bomb, they'd stuffed a dirty dishrag in her mouth.

Kovacs didn't confess to any of that; he was far too wily and arrogant. In fact, from the stray fragments of conversation I'd overheard while the EMTs were treating his wounds, he seemed confident that he'd be back on the street by noon. Friends in high places, and all that bullshit. He refused to cooperate with the SLED detectives who were badgering him about the grenade, as well as the two guns they'd recovered in my condo. He denied any knowledge of them, and had no response when they asked him about the stash of weapons they'd found in the tool locker bolted to the bed of his pick-up downstairs. Both handguns and several of the rifles in the truck later would show up in FBI computers as stolen during a pawn shop burglary, but by then it was a moot point.

Throughout the grilling I insisted I had no clue why Kovacs was after my daughter and me. I'd already told Amos Brady, the SLED investigator who'd questioned me the other day, I believed Kovacs had killed Lily Elliott. Likewise, Brady had good reason to believe I'd busted his jaw with my fist. The truth was, I'd had no idea what the sick bastard or his state trooper friend were up to, only that it had something to do with my father, and probably my mother's murder. I didn't want to complicate matters now by saying anything more than I had to.

For obvious reasons, Addie and I were forced to move to a hotel, a suite on the third floor of a national chain located across the river in Mount Pleasant. We had a spectacular view of the traffic rushing by on Highway 17, and Detective Brady cautioned me not to leave town. While Kovacs had an alibi for the time frame of the novelist's death, there was ample reason to believe he had been working directly with the state cop, whom Brady eventually informed me was named Malcolm Egan. Even though the man was dead, the police still wanted to clear the case, and he seemed like the best target to hang the writer's murder on. Especially since a witness claimed she had seen a state trooper's vehicle pulling out of Ms. Elliott's driveway around the estimated time of her death.

That's when I recalled seeing a lot of cop cars, too. Or maybe just one that seemed to show up wherever I happened to be: outside the retirement community where Alice Marion lived, and then again at the Berkeley County records building. There had even been one parked across the street from Kovacs' house that afternoon. Had Malcolm Egan been following me all along?

By noon the reporters began calling. How they got our phone numbers I do not know, but they were incessant and persistent and rude. Spewing crap like, "the people have a right to know" and "in the public interest." Eventually we both turned off our ringers and were able to get some sleep.

Around four in the afternoon I woke up to the sound of Addie shrieking. I was dozing on the fold-out couch in the outer room and she had taken the California king in the bedroom. I found her standing in the middle of the mattress in utter terror, pointing a trembling finger at something on the floor.

"What is…*that?*" she screamed.

I thought she had been awakened from a nightmare, which was understandable considering the traumatic events she had just survived.

"What?" I asked her as calmly as I could.

"That!"

That turned out to be a colossal palmetto bug, close to two inches long and now lying on its back on the carpet. Apparently it had crawled across Addie's cheek while she was sleeping, and the tickling of its tiny feet had awakened her with a fright. When she swept it to the floor she went off like a firecracker.

"It's just a bug," I told her.

"I know it's a bug! *It was on my face*!"

Which brought me back to the grim reality of the weeks to come. The panic brought on by a common brown cockroach was nothing compared to the post-traumatic stress that in all likelihood would creep into her mind at some point. Being bound and gagged and tied to a chair during a home invasion was not an easy thing to forget, and Addie might need professional help to cope with the shock.

I rounded the foot of the bed and stepped on the critter, hard. She shrieked again and said, "You killed it, Dad…that's bad Karma."

"Not for him," I said, picking it up with my bare hand. "Now he can come back as a butterfly that much sooner."

She stared at me as I carried it to the bathroom and dropped it into the toilet. Then I came back into her room and sat down on the bed, where she now was folded up in a classic lotus position. Her lower lip was quivering, meaning she was on the verge of tears and just wanted permission to let go. I reached out my arms and drew her into a tight hug, and the flood began.

Eventually she pushed away and wiped an arm along her nose. I went into the bathroom again and got a wad of tissue, and handed her one. She sniffed as she dabbed her nose again, and her eyes, then said, "That was all real, wasn't it?"

"Yes, it was, Addie," I told her. "But it's all over now. No one can hurt you."

She nodded at that and sniffed again. Then she said, "You killed that man—"

"I had to," I assured her. "I had no choice."

"I know. Just like in the movies. But—"

"But what?"

"That makes you a murderer. Just like Grandpa."

I could see where her mind was going with this, someplace dark and macabre. I'd had to live for thirty years believing my father was a cold-blooded killer, and I didn't want my daughter having to endure the same thing.

"It was self-defense," I explained. "Those men were going to kill us. Both of us."

"I know." A few more tears trickled down her face, which she quickly wiped away. Then she said, "You saved my life."

"It's my fault…I should never have put you in danger like that."

"You couldn't have known, Dad. They were bad men. Crazy

motherfu…mother*fingers*."

If she made that up on the spot I had to give her credit for quick thinking. "Is that a real word?" I asked her.

She grinned. "It is now. Look…just so you know, I'm okay. Seriously. You don't need to worry about me."

"I'll always worry about you," I told her. "You're my daughter. And I need you to tell me, again, if they hurt you."

A female officer last night had taken her aside and asked her all the sensitive questions, mostly to ascertain that she hadn't been sexually assaulted. Addie insisted that the roughest George Kovacs had gotten was when he twisted her arms behind her back and bound her wrists with strips of the ripped sheet. The other man—Officer Egan—hadn't laid a finger on her. No, she didn't need to go to the hospital to get checked out, and there was no need for a rape kit. She actually winced at the thought.

"I'm fine, Dad. Really. Okay, I admit I was scared. Terrified. I didn't know what they were going to do, especially when they wired that thing to the door. I knew you were out there, talking to *that creep* on my phone. I screamed at you not to come through it, but then you went away."

"I'm sorry about that," I told her. "I needed to find another way in."

"Did you actually come down from the condo upstairs?"

"It was the only thing I could think of."

She offered up another grin, and said, "*Dad du Soleil*."

CHAPTER 28

A little after five we walked to a southwestern-style restaurant located across the road from the hotel. Addie found a Santa Fe bean and rice wrap that fit her diet, and she wolfed it down as if she hadn't eaten in days. I focused more on the wine list and nibbled on a plate of nachos while we talked.

Earlier in the day I had received word that Belinda was resting comfortably at Cedars-Sinai, but her pneumonia still put her at great risk. The sepsis she had contracted from shooting up with an unsterilized needle didn't help, and a new test had just revealed she had contracted Hepatitis C. Her doctors were cautiously optimistic that a prolonged regimen of antibiotics and antivirals would help her pull through, but her recovery would be lengthy and expensive.

The charge nurse reluctantly put her on the phone and Addie was able to say a few words to her. She was smart enough not to agitate her mother by mentioning what had happened last night, and their exchange was light and brief. I could sense the worry in my daughter's eyes when she handed the phone back to me.

"She sounds real bad," Addie said, when I ended the call. "I'm scared."

"Me, too, sweetie," I said. "But she's in the best place she can be, and she's getting the best care there is."

"It's going to be expensive."

"I'm sure Carl has insurance," I assured her. "That's not something you need to be concerned with."

Another nod, but I could see the worry weighing down her eyes.

We were seated outside on a covered patio that was cooled with overhead fans. The inside dining room was air conditioned, but neither of us wanted to be in an enclosed space right now. Traffic hummed by on the highway on the other side of the tall pines, while lizards and skinks scurried across the flagstone terrace. A television set bolted under the eaves had been showing a re-run of last weekend's NASCAR race, but someone had switched it to the local newscast.

It was almost sixteen hours after the first cops arrived at the condo, and a lot of news had broken since then. I'd managed to hold off the reporters' calls, but that didn't keep them from doing their thing. The "home invasion at the Riverfront" was the station's top story, and the local anchor team played it as if it were the headline of the century. I didn't realize it was even on the TV until about twenty seconds into the story, and then we both put down our forks and focused on the screen:

"According to police, Mr. Devlin arrived at the high-rise condominium near East Bay Street to find two armed men holed up inside his home," an anchorwoman with a solid athletic build was saying. "He made telephone contact with one of the invaders, who caused him to believe his teenage daughter was in danger."

She then handed the story off to her male co-anchor, who explained, "Rather than go through the front door—which he suspected would have brought bodily harm to himself and his daughter—Mr. Devlin called nine-one-one, and then climbed down to his condo from the balcony above. Details are still coming in, but it appears he shot one of the intruders, George Kovacs, before he himself was attacked by an off-duty state trooper who allegedly had accompanied Kovacs to the scene."

The camera switched back to the anchorwoman, who observed, "Mr. Devlin, a Charleston native and former major league pitcher, is in town with his daughter to attend the memorial service of his father, Frank Devlin. The elder Devlin, who was convicted in 1990 for fatally stabbing his wife, reportedly passed away last week."

The newscast then switched to a young reporter who looked as if he was still in high school. He was standing in front of the Charleston Police Station on Lockwood Drive near the River Dogs baseball stadium, and filled in a few unenlightened details about last night's events.

"...Kovacs is not cooperating with authorities and has refused to explain his motive for the alleged break-in. Police say he was in possession of several weapons, both of which had been reported stolen in a burglary last year," the rookie reporter said. "He also was in possession of a military-style grenade, with which he allegedly booby-trapped the front door."

The anchorwoman thanked the rookie reporter for his live story, then switched to an equally young woman who was positioned in front of Al Cannon Detention Center on Leeds Avenue, otherwise known as the Charleston County Jail. Her name was Irene Walker, and her job was to dig up the dirt on the surviving suspect. "As we just heard, Kovacs has an extensive criminal background, with numerous arrests and convictions going back to his teens," she explained. "Most of these crimes involved assault, aggravated battery, weapons violations, domestic abuse, and armed robbery. He's also suspected in the deaths of several men, but charges have never been filed due to lack of evidence. Due to his record and the seriousness of the charges filed in this home invasion, a bond judge this morning ordered Kovacs be held without bail."

So much for his highly placed connections.

I'd given a lot of thought to Kovacs' actions over the last few days, and it was clear that he must have been aware of my father's release since the very beginning. Officer Egan had been positioned outside his hospice room to keep eyes and ears on the situation, and must have heard him speaking with me about DNA and rejected evidence. He must have relayed this information to Kovacs, who then had gotten a note into the hands of Benita Juarez. Of course, this series of events still begged the question: who was Kovacs working for? Aside from Jenkins III and IV, the members of the parole board, and the warden at the prison in Ridgeville, no one was aware my father was even being released. Not even the doctors and nurses in the prison hospital knew where he was going to be transferred. Secrecy was critical to the plan, yet there obviously was a leak somewhere along the pipeline.

Then the anchorwoman said something that caused a deep shiver to shoot up my spine. "Interestingly, our sister station in Columbia reports that Officer Egan was part of a team of off-duty officers who worked for a private security firm that has ties to white supremacist groups. Egan was involved with a scuffle at a controversial rally in Charlottesville several years ago, and you can see him in this video clip recorded at that event." The news director then froze a frame on the screen and positioned a red circle around the face of the now-deceased state trooper. The image was grainy and imperfect, but the anchorwoman was correct: the man in an official looking black uniform and a shiny cap on his head clearly was Egan, looking stiff and important. But that was only half of the story, because standing behind him was George Kovacs, in similar black garb. And next to him, at the very edge of the photo, was a man who looked remarkably like Ed Landry, the racist neo-Nazi and founder of White Makes Might. I'd come across several pictures of him in my Google searches, and that pointy nose and weak chin had been etched into my brain.

When we got back to the room I phoned Laurie. I hadn't talked to her all day so I figured she hadn't heard the news, and I wanted to let her know that Addie and I were fine. My call went straight through to voicemail, which told me she was having another busy night at the restaurant. As I listened to her voicemail greeting I had time to think of what I would tell her, and at the beep I said, "Laurie…I don't know if you've watched the news today, but I just wanted to let you know we're both okay. Addie and me. I'll fill you in on the details when we talk. Call me when you get a minute."

I also placed a call to Stumpy, who informed me he was home having a dinner of what he insisted was the best tomato pie from Georgia to Virginia. He'd just watched the local news, too, and was mortified by what he'd seen on the screen. Then he said, through a mouthful of pie, "Remember what I told you?"

"You told me lots of things," I replied.

"And it looks like you ignored it all. But I distinctly remember saying that if you kept poking your nose into this, nothing good would come of it."

"Yes, you did say that," I admitted.

"Well, that advice still stands, although I have cause to believe you won't pay attention to any of it. Now, tomato pie is best when it's eaten hot, so I'll be saying good night, my friend."

I had another question I wanted to ask him about Jimmy Holland, but he'd already hung up and I wasn't about to call back. Instead I sat down at my laptop and typed "Ed Landry" into Google. I'd done a perfunctory search before, but now I learned that he had been in the Marines for nine years before being kicked out on a general discharge. I could not find a direct reason for his dismissal, but there were rumors about the hazing of a fellow soldier—behavior that may have been racially motivated. In any event, he found himself a day job as a driver for a propane delivery company and seemed to remain on the right side of the law.

Sometime over the next few years, however, he became active in the white supremacy movement, which was becoming more visible and vocal. He ascended through the ranks of the organization known as White Makes Might, and had just been anointed the group's leader when violence erupted at the alt-right demonstration in Charlottesville a few years back. During a counter-protest a young woman had been killed in a deliberate hit-and-run, and the suspect who had been driving the car was charged with first degree murder. Ed Landry announced the group's full support for him and formed a legal defense fund to pay for this lawyer.

Every drop of blood in my body wanted Landry to be the third redneck who had killed Jimmy Holland that day in 1989, but there were two problems: First, he had attended the University of West Virginia, not U.S.C. Second, he was two years younger than I was, which would have made him just fifteen when the dragging had occurred. If the man who had assaulted my sister was just a kid, she would have told me. As despicable as he was, Landry had nothing to do with the poor kid's death.

One of the stories I found during my search included a photograph that appeared to be taken from the same video I'd seen earlier on the TV newscast. Unlike that report, however, this image had an expanded field of vision and depicted four men, not just three. I didn't recognize the fourth man in the frame, but the website had provided identification for each of them. Once again, my brain caught the name before I could figure out where my eye had found it, but then I saw the photo caption and my blood turned cold:

`Controversial megachurch pastor Rev. William McCann was widely criticized for his appearance at a white supremacist event`

> in Charlottesville over the weekend. Never one to back down from criticism, McCann told reporters that, "All souls are in need of saving, and Jesus extends his love to all men, no matter their color, creed, or conviction." Pictured with Rev. McCann are White Makes Might leader Ed Landry, and two members of Landry's private security force. [AP Photo]

Holy shit. Reverend McCann was the Carolina Cross preacher whom Jenkins IV had sicced on me to oversee my father's release, and I'd relinquished my better judgment to his compassion-drenched theatrics. As most good southerners are wont to do, our mother had dutifully driven my sister and me to church every Sunday morning and had imbued us with chapter and verse from both testaments of the Bible. As a boy I had found a perverse interest in the human devastation caused by the Great Flood, and also how God had rained fire and brimstone down on Sodom and Gomorrah. I don't know how much truth my mother placed in the scripture, but she'd found personal comfort in some of the more meaningful passages. Thus, when Rev. McCann had unloaded his sermon about forgiveness and redemption on me, a voice in the back of my brain told me to listen. That voice sounded an awful lot like my mother, and her distant words of empathy and understanding had caused me to shift my perspective on the parole deal.

On a whim I ran a new search—several of them, in fact. I learned that McCann was a homegrown Carolinian, born and raised in the Spartanburg area. But that's where any sense of normalcy ended; his father had been four-term U.S. Senator Alfred James McCann, and young William had enjoyed a charmed and privileged upbringing. He'd played varsity football at a private Christian school in Spartanburg, and then enrolled at U.S.C., where he eschewed his father's fondness for politics in favor of a marketing degree. He graduated in 1989, and took two years off while trying to find himself, eventually shifting gears entirely and earning an advanced degree in theological studies at Liberty University.

It was those two years off that interested me, and I spent the next hour trying to fill that gap. I knew I could run another search through

Kat Rattigan's online service, but I was growing impatient and wanted results now, not tomorrow. I entered numerous combinations of search terms, extrapolating and changing my parameters whenever I met a dead end. Each empty attempt convinced me I was rapidly running out of options, until one random hit flushed a jolt of adrenaline through my veins.

McCann, William Raymond: Theologian in Spartanburg, SC - Televangelist - Author https://www.LukesWork.org/profile/376917 W.R. McCann: Bio * Childhood * Education * Family * ...father Senator A.J. McCann... ... University of South Carolina..."preacher to the prisoners"...second cousin once-removed Avery Dunham (federal prison)...The Carolina Cross...satellite channel 2371...

My eyes almost missed the name, but then they came back to it: *Avery Dunham.* What in the name of Jesus was that SOB's connection to Reverend McCann?

From that point forward my search became easier. When I coupled the two names together I learned that Senator Alfred McCann was related by marriage to Avery Dunham's second wife, who just happened to be the mother of Rudy and Gerald Aiken. Dunham's short-haul transportation business was based in Hanahan, where the burned-out warehouse had been located, but he also had buildings in Jacksonville, Richmond, and—*of course*—Orangeburg. He owned a small horse farm on State Road S 38-74 just a few miles outside of town, twelve acres with stalls for six animals and several small worker cabins.

I wasn't sure what the connection to William McCann might be, if there was one, so I kept hunting. Eventually I found a passage in a memoir penned by the aging Senator and published online by Google Books, and it all came clear:

"For a few years in the 1980s and early '90s, Mr. Dunham used the farm to board horses for neighbors. On occasion he employed his two stepsons to maintain the property. It was a modest concern, but Dunham took pride in the place and kept it clean and functional.

The summer after my son William graduated from college—back when he was still trying to determine what the good Lord had in mind for him—he worked there as a farmhand for six or eight weeks. It was an attempt, as he put it, "*to get my hands dirty and develop a feel for the warm earth and the good people of God's creation.*"

That was it: the link that placed William McCann in the Orangeburg area, working side-by-side with Rudy and Gerald Aiken the same summer Jimmy Holland had been killed. I sat back in my chair and felt another shot of adrenaline race through my system. *Goddamn!* The slimy, sanctimonious preacher who had convinced me to mind my father during his dying days very likely had been involved in dragging the poor black kid to his death. He'd also assaulted my sister and, in my mind, somehow was involved with my mother's murder. I wasn't sure how, but the dots were there for me to connect, if I could only find them. Easy to see why the sonofabitch now preached about sin and forgiveness to millions of followers every Sunday morning.

Guilt and redemption.

Goddamn.

I checked my phone and saw it was a little after nine. I'd turned the ringer off earlier, and had not turned it on after I'd talked to Stumpy. Since Addie was safe in the other room I wasn't on parent duty, so there was no urgency to remain connected with the rest of the world. Only a handful of people left voice messages, and one of these was from Laurie Cobb, who was almost apoplectic from what she'd seen on the news: "My God, Rick. I had no idea what happened to you after you left last night. I can't believe what you must be going through, you and Addie. Please give me a call whenever you get this. It's Friday, so it's a long night for me. Call as late as you want, but do call." She made a few kissing sounds, and then the message ended.

The only other voicemail worth listening to was from Detective Brady, who had called just twelve minutes before. His message was short and cryptic, noting that, "It seems your boy Kovacs met bail, but not in the way he expected." There was no urgency about his message, and no request that I call him back.

I didn't, so I wouldn't know until the eleven o'clock news what he meant. That's when the late-night anchor—another from a crop of freshly minted puerile reporters—led with the news that "alleged home invasion suspect George Kovacs was found unresponsive in his cell at the Charleston County Detention Center earlier this evening. Authorities say he'd been stabbed in the chest with a handmade object and was rushed to the jail infirmary, where he was pronounced dead."

That didn't take long, I said to myself. South Carolina justice was fast and sweet. I wondered who had gotten to him, and how quickly it had happened. He'd boasted about his connections that would get him out on the street by noon, so he must have spoken with someone. Ed Landry? Reverend McCann? Another interested party who had someone on the inside—a guard or even an inmate—who could have gotten in and out of his cell unnoticed? Addie would probably call it karma, although my mother used to tell my sister and me that the Bible was full of eye-for-an-eye lessons. A pacifist at heart, she was particularly fond of Matthew, who insisted that, "whosoever shall smite thee on thy right cheek, turn to him the other also." That was all well and good, but when it came to playground bullies my favorite was the eternally vicious Leviticus, who said, "He who causes an injury to a neighbor must receive the same kind of injury in return. Broken bone for broken bone, tooth for tooth."

I glanced toward Addie's bedroom door, but she had crashed not long after we got back from dinner. I suspected she would probably sleep until morning, which was just as well. The news that Kovacs had been shanked certainly could wait. She'd find out soon enough, either from Sam or someone else in her new posse.

I waited until after the Kovacs story ended to return Laurie's call. Her phone again sent me straight into voicemail, so I left her a brief message, letting her know it had been a long day and I was heading to bed. I would call her again in the morning when things returned to normal. What I didn't say—what we'd both left unsaid—was that, with my father gone and Addie's mother in critical condition in an L.A. hospital, there was no sensible reason for my daughter or me to hang around.

Addie was up before I was and I found her sitting on her bed, FaceTiming with Sam. She hardly looked up from her phone when I knocked, except to say, "Come in." Then she explained that she was coordinating plans for later, and she'd only be a few minutes longer. That was fine with me, since it meant she was functioning like a typical fifteen-year-old.

A few minutes turned into a half-hour, but I didn't mind. I had a publisher who was growing more anxious by the day, and I needed to ease her mind. I didn't hear my daughter again until she was standing almost right behind me.

"We're famous," she said. Gone was the fear and disquiet from yesterday, replaced by a newfound exhilaration. "We're all over TV."

"It's our fifteen minutes," I replied. She looked at me as if I'd grown a second head, so I added, "Andy Warhol."

The confusion in her face told me she still didn't get the reference, but we both let it go. Instead she informed me that some of her friends were planning to go up to the Boardwalk in Myrtle Beach, and could she please go. "Bethany's older sister is going to drive, and she's almost twenty," she said.

Every instinct in my body told me to say "no." My daughter already had one brush with death and I didn't want to invite another. I'd seen enough stories in the news about how cars full of teenagers veer off the road into the trees or get struck by eighteen-wheelers, killing everyone instantly. I could never forgive myself if something happened to her, especially on my watch. Then again, I'd been solely responsible for what had happened at the condo the night before last, so my record was already sullied.

"I'll want to meet her," I reluctantly told her. "This older sister of Bethany."

Addie rolled her eyes, but I could see by the slight gleam in them that I'd given her the answer she wanted.

CHAPTER 29

Ernie Collier was working a hoe in the rich loam of his rose garden when I pulled up in front of his place an hour later. He gave me an expressionless glance, then went back to work until I was out of the car and heading toward him. He slowly straightened, then leaned against the handle of the hoe as I approached.

"I figured I'd be seein' you again," he said with an air of resignation. "Just as sure as the sun rises and the cock crows."

"You got a minute?" I asked him.

"Last time took a lot longer than that," he said. "But sure, let's go sit a spell."

I followed him up onto his front porch and we sat down in the same chairs we'd occupied the last time I was there. I got the feeling he didn't appreciate me just dropping by, and he stared at me long and hard. "I saw the news on TV," he finally said. "Seems you've been swimming with the sharks."

"A couple folks got a little overzealous," I conceded. "But it's all settled down now."

"How's that daughter of yours? I believe the news said her name is Adeline."

"A little shaken up, but she'll be okay. She's a strong girl."

Ernie said nothing for a bit, just watched me intently, as if he was waiting for something to happen. Eventually he said, "You obviously got something on your mind, so come out with it, Mister Rick."

Now it was my turn to study him: dark, weary eyes that had borne witness to so many of the world's greatest triumphs…and a good number of its cruelties. I remembered back to what he had told me about the Korean War, when he had served in one of the first Army units ever to allow blacks to fight side-by-side with white soldiers. Something he had told me all those years ago had stuck with me, something I now wished to ask him about.

"I remember you once telling me that you were in one of the first integrated divisions in Korea," I said.

"You got a good memory on you," he confirmed. "503rd Field Artillery, 2nd Infantry. Although they later moved me to a different division that was organized to take advantage of certain specialized skills."

"Skills that had to do with your ability to hit a rabbit at two hundred yards."

He eyed me warily, either wondering where I was going with my line of questioning, or already knowing and not liking it. "Good practice for what was to come," he said.

"Are we still talking about Korea?" I inquired.

Ernie did not reply. I had known him since I was a young boy, and the passage of time hadn't diminished my recollection of what he had told me on those long summer afternoons while he was repairing this or that.

"Life comes at you in a blur," he finally said.

"Did you know you're mentioned in Wikipedia?" I asked him.

That was something he did not appear to know, and it got his attention. "What are you talking about, boy?"

"Well, not you by name, but I did a little checking. I don't have a photographic memory, but there's a line that says something about how one of the Army's top sharpshooters in that war was a black man from South Carolina. I'm figuring they're talking about you."

Ernie tapped his fingers nervously on the arm of his chair. The paint had been worn thin in that spot, which told me he did a lot of tapping. "Let me tell you somethin', Mister Rick," he said. "You listen real good, cuz you might learn somethin' real important. There are good men in this world, and there are bad men. Plain and simple. It's like day and night, darkness and light. Some might say black and white, but that's another can of worms. Fact is, war is one of those things where we learn about good and bad, and right and wrong. We're supposed to be fighting for freedom, but when you're in the middle of it all, that notion goes all to hell. You're taught all your life that killing another man is wrong, but then you're expected—*ordered*—to kill as many of the bad guys as you can. When you're in a war, you know who the good men are because it's all laid out for you. But the men on the other side, they know who the good guys are because *they're* told who the bad guys are. You follow what I'm sayin'?"

"I believe so, Mr. Collier," I said.

He gave a slight nod of satisfaction, then began again. "Everyone thinks they're fighting on the side of good, cuz that's what they're told by the generals who move pieces around on a board in a room far away from the battle. Thing is, war doesn't always stop with the generals, and it doesn't always stop *over there*. There's a whole spectrum of light and dark when you've seen good and bad, black and white. And sometimes we have to fight our own war, on our own terms. Wherever that war may be."

The thing about Ernie's stories—which in reality were morality tales—was that a kernel of rectitude usually was buried at the end of them. I never knew where he was going when he started, but he never let me down when we got there. I assumed the same would be true today, so I just nodded and told him, "Go on."

"I was in Korea for eight months," he continued. "Seems a drop in a bucket now, and I saw a lot of death in that time. Caused a lot of it, too. A lot of dark and light, a lot of good and bad. You get a good sense of that, growing up here in white man's country. No offense."

"None taken," I assured him.

"Now, I want you to listen real close to what I'm about to tell you," he continued. He fixed me with his eyes so hard that I didn't dare look away. "One day many years ago, in a different kind of war, I heard tell about a man who had done a serious wrong to someone. The when and where ain't important, and I can't tell you how I learned it, 'cept to say there's folks been doing battle around these parts longer than you might care to know. And on this particularly fine day I came to know about this man who was involved with the death of another man—a most hideous, painful, torturous death. You still following what I'm telling you?"

"Loud and clear," I said, wondering if this was headed where I suspected it was.

"Now, this man, he'd been hidden away by forces that believed they had righteousness and justice on their side. But me and my men, we found out where this fella was holed up, and we took him for a road trip. We put him in a car and drove him far out into the middle of perdition. He was pretty much soiling his pants, that man was so terrified of what he knew was coming. When we found him he was all defiant and bigheaded, warned us God would smite us for what we were doing. Like he was an expert on that sort of thing. Anyways, we took him out to a forest of tall pines and thick creepers where we could have a word with him. Just to run a few questions by him, no interruptions. You still with me?"

A nod indicated that I was.

"Well, pretty quick he began to realize this situation was a bit more ominous than he suspected. No one was coming to help him, no one would be punishing us. And Lord, it didn't take him more than a couple of minutes to start confessing to all sorts of things."

"Fear does that to a man," I observed.

"So does pain," he replied. "And I must say, there was a good deal of both that day. Any event, that boy knew a lot: names and locations and other details that convinced us he knew of which he was speaking. By this time he was crying his eyes out, and his trousers were soaked with last night's beer. He begged us to let him go. Eventually we got everything we'd come to get, so we pushed him out of the car and told him to start running. Gave him a five-second head start, in fact."

"The woods are pretty thick along that stretch of woods," I guessed. "Nowhere for him to go but up the road."

Ernie lowered his head in such an exaggerated nod that I thought he was rocking in his chair. Then he said, "Anyway, that boy got his ass pretty damned far up the road in those five seconds. Fifty, sixty yards, I reckon. But like you said, they'd pulled me out of the Second Infantry and put a sniper rifle in my hands cuz I could shoot a damn rabbit at a distance far greater than that. A man running a straight line down a road was no match for a good eye, a steady finger, and a purpose so strong even God drew a sigh of relief when he dropped. That fella barely knew what hit him."

"The medical examiner said he was shot in the neck," I pointed out.

"That would be a fair assessment," Ernie said with a shrug of indifference.

"And the others?" I asked him. "The running man's brother was found in the Congaree Swamp."

"Seems about right."

"And the third man. What became of him?"

Ernie shook his head in resignation as he rose to his feet and started down the wooden stairs. "Never was able to figure out who he was, where he was from. We tried and tried to get it out of the kid, but alls he said was 'Billy Ray.' You know how many Billy Rays there are in this state?"

He had a point: the south sure did love its double first names. Tommy Lee, Emma Sue. Billy Ray. I followed him down the creaky front steps and stopped at the bottom to admire his roses, big and red and aromatic, like a bottle of perfume.

"They sure don't smell like that in the flower shop," I told him.

"Chrysler Imperials. Named after the automobile."

I took another sniff, then walked to my car and opened the door. "Rudy Aiken was going to testify at Dad's trial," I said as I got inside. "When he disappeared, my father went to jail for a crime he did not commit."

"A regrettable miscalculation," Ernie replied, staring up at the brilliant blue sky. "I had no knowledge of what that lawyer of his was planning, and no one else was going to do a damned thing to those bastards for what they did to Jimmy Holland."

Poor man's justice, and I could hardly blame him. Americans of African descent had been on the losing end of the law since they began arriving in slave ships over four hundred years ago. The heels of rectitude dragged deep in a world mired in privilege and entitlement.

"So this sonofabitch named Billy Ray is still out there?" I asked.

"I reckon so," Ernie said through his teeth. "And this old integrated black soldier from the Second Infantry's still got his vision and his touch. And a whole world of patience. All he's been waiting for is a confirmed target to set this matter right, once and for all."

I grasped what he was telling me, but decided not to respond to his words directly. "Thank you for the conversation," I replied as I turned the key. "I look forward to paying you another visit sometime soon."

Two miles down the road I pulled into a parking lot and cut the engine. I had a direct view of a cell phone tower, so I knew reception had to be good. I opened the browser function on my phone and typed in a name: first, middle, and last. The nearby transmitter accelerated the results, and less than a minute later I had what I was looking for.

Next, I called my sister, who was in a mood that would best be described as borderline. That meant she was functioning at the junction of reality and disassociation, and she could flip either way with the slightest provocation. The worst-case part of my brain told me how that would go, but I really needed to see her as soon as possible

"I'm heading back to Atlanta today," she informed me. "For real. I can't deal with all this shit I'm seeing on the TV."

We'd spoken briefly yesterday by phone and I had thought she'd already gone home by now. It was clear that she was stressed by the events of the previous thirty hours, and back here in Charleston had reopened old wounds. The trauma she had endured on that country road thirty years ago had never slipped far beneath the surface, and now it had clawed its way back into the open. She was wise to get out of town and try to lock away the old memories—but not before I had one more chance to talk to her.

"I don't blame you one bit," I told her. "Addie and I checked into a hotel, and so far no one's been able to find us." Not quite true, but close enough.

"I'm meeting someone for something in thirty minutes," she replied. "Then I'm outta here."

"Well, I have something I want to show you before you go," I said.

"Can you bring Addie?"

"She's up in Myrtle Beach with friends for the day."

Karen hesitated a second, then said, "So…this thing you want to show me. What is it?"

"It's best if I not tell you up front."

"Is it absolutely necessary? I really want to get home."

"It'll only take a couple minutes, and it might provide some closure."

She let out a dramatic sigh. "All right. I'll be downtown, so maybe we can meet at White Point Garden."

"What time?"

"Let's do noon. Traffic's going to suck as it is."

That gave me a little over an hour. I headed back to the hotel, where I pulled a dozen images out of Google and loaded them onto my back-up flash drive. Then I went to the business office on the first floor and made prints of all twelve. They were all black and white, from the same era, with the same vintage look. I wanted to make this as conclusive, yet random, as possible, and I didn't wish to expose my sister to any more distress than necessary.

I found a convenient parking space two blocks from the Battery on Murray Street, along the sea wall across from a row of Charleston's priciest mansions. Here, vast replicas of Georgian architecture coexisted side-by-side with Federalist and Greek classical and neo-Victorian styles, each home with its own expansive view of the Ashley River and the mouth of the harbor in the glimmering distance. I locked the car and hustled toward the historic tree-lined garden situated at the tip of Charleston, worried that I was late again and Karen would get impatient. We hadn't said precisely where we would meet, but as I hurried into the park I saw her sitting on the steps of the old bandstand. When we were children our parents would bring us here for the afternoon, and we would climb all over the cannons and statues and monuments, sometimes reenacting the Civil War bombardment, pretending to aim the rusted guns at imaginary ships out beyond Fort Sumter, doing our best to fend off the Union troops.

"Sorry I'm late," I apologized as I sat down beside her on the wooden steps.

"I've always loved this place," she said, ignoring my words as she gazed out at the water. "So beautiful and quiet and soothing."

"We used to get ice cream from the truck that came down King Street over there," I said. "You always liked those nutty cones."

"The nuttier the better," she said. "Just like me."

"Not nutty…just traumatized from a horrendous experience that was swept under the rug," I said. "I had no idea about any of this back then."

"You were in your own world," she said. "Baseball scouts, sex on the beach, beer and bourbon. Getting kicked off the football team. You didn't think I knew all that, but I did."

"I guess I was more obvious than I thought."

"You were seventeen, is all. So what is it that's so important to show me?"

I expected her to be in a hurry; I also knew I could inadvertently flip a very dark switch with what I had in my pocket. There was no telling how Karen might react to the photos, what errant spark might flash across a dysfunctional synapse. But there was no turning back now, so I reached into my pocket and took out the black-and-white prints.

I'd folded them into quarters, and it took a moment to arrange them in a neat stack in my lap. "I have twelve pictures I'd like to run by you, see if any of them mean anything," I told her.

"Like a photo line-up on a cop show?" she asked.

"Something like that. Are you up for it?'

She flexed her shoulders and said, "Go for it."

I handed her the top photo and waited for her reaction. Any reaction, whatever it might bring. She studied the face for a second, then handed it back to me. "Who's he supposed to be?" she asked.

"Just a guy," I said. "No one in particular."

She shook her head, so I handed her the next photo, similar to the first one. I'd gotten eleven of the twelve from a high school yearbook website, enlarged them all to the same five-by-seven size. They were all pictures of graduating seniors, all boys, all with various haircuts that were popular back in the day. All were wearing suit jackets and most had ties neatly knotted at the neck.

She looked at it, handed it back. "Don't know him."

I handed her the next one, and she gave it back, shaking her head and saying "nope."

We kept going. If she sensed what was coming she was trying not to make a big deal of it. I'd shuffled all twelve photos randomly so there was no telling which picture would turn up next, but when I handed her Number Nine she froze. She stared at the face with a mix of horror and contempt; then her hand tightened on the sheet of paper and gripped it so hard that it crumpled in her fist.

"Sonofabitch," she said in a muffled voice. "That fucking bastard robbed me of my life that day." Then she wadded the picture into a ball and hurled it at the trunk of an old water oak.

"I'm so sorry," I said, putting my arm around her.

"How…did you know?" she stammered. Then she turned and buried her face in my shoulder, the tears streaming down her face as she let out a sound that could only be described as keening.

Neither of us said anything for a long time. My sister had an overwhelming need to cry herself out and finally had found closure for the events that had strangled her soul for most of her life. That could not be done in a single afternoon, or a month, or a year. Maybe never. The torment she had tucked away in a dark corner of her mind on that summer afternoon thirty years ago now had a face, and a name. And one way or another he would pay.

"Who is he?" she finally asked, wiping the back of her hand across her nose.

"William Raymond McCann," I told her. She didn't seem to recognize the name, so I added, "He's a big-name preacher and televangelist around these parts."

"What the hell…this is for real?"

"That was his yearbook photo," I explained, cocking my head to where the balled-up paper lay on the ground. "Pulled it from the web less than an hour ago."

"Holy shit. That motherfucker killed Jimmy—"

"Not to mention what he did to you."

She either didn't hear what I'd said, or ignored it completely. A coping strategy she'd used for years, and it came to her naturally. Push that tragic incident out of her mind and it would simply go away.

"I've got to go," she said suddenly. "I need to get home."

"You sure you're good to drive?"

"Never felt better, actually," she said as she stood up.

I didn't believe her; she looked as if she had just been squeezed through an old mangler washing machine. I waited for her to exhibit signs of dissociation, or maybe for an absorbing blackness to take hold and spill a torrent of rage. But none of that happened, so I said, "That's probably a good idea. Sort this all out, try to make some sense of it all."

But she shook her head rapidly. "No…that's not it. I need to find something."

I had no idea what she was thinking, so I said, "What sort of something?"

"Back then…the day that fucker attacked me. I still remember

Jimmy's screams, as they bound his wrists and then tied the rope to the bumper. There was nothing I could do because that bastard…*he was on top of me*. I managed to get away, hide in the scrub at the edge of the road."

She hesitated, and it was clear she wanted me to give her a verbal nudge. So I said, "Go on—"

"But before that, back when he was…you know…well, I scratched at his eyes and bit his face. Then I grabbed his hair, and yanked a bunch of it out. Made for a nice memento over the years."

"You saved it?"

"Pretty sick, huh?" she said with a wicked grin. "They didn't really have DNA tests back then, but I always knew a rainy day might come along."

CHAPTER 30

I walked my sister to her car and wished her a safe drive back to Atlanta. Her plan was to find the clump of hair that she'd squirreled away in a box and get it to me, via FedEx or in person. The odds of matching it to McCann's DNA were slim to none: the arrogant hypocrite would lie all the way to next Sunday before agreeing to any kind of test. Meanwhile his sycophants would do their best to cast ridicule and scorn on any hint of an allegation. Reverend McCann was a malignant narcissist who had risen to the top of his game through his vicious cunning and scheming, and I believed he would not go down without taking everyone with him.

What I was having trouble understanding was why he would have gone out of his way to recommend that my father be released to my care, after all these years. McCann was almost home free—just a week or two away from being rid of the man who knew the whole truth, and nothing but. Had he succumbed to the ravages of guilt? Could he have been inflicted with some tormenting sense of compassion or remorse? Was he attempting to repent his sins before a God that looked unkindly on charlatans and trespassers?

Or was it just the sheer arrogance of a sociopath who had come to believe his own P.R.?

Once Karen was on her way I drove to Jenkins IV's office on Broad Street. The receptionist told me he was busy, so I told her I'd wait. When she said his appointment might go long, I explained I could wait as long as necessary.

He came out fifteen minutes later, a perplexed look on his face. "Most of my clients call ahead and set up a time to come in," he said with a touch of exasperation.

"I have a question about the preacher," I said, ignoring his sarcasm.

"What preacher?" he asked, impatience in his voice.

"The one you roped in to convince me to do this." I gestured broadly with my hands to indicate I meant everything I'd been involved with over the last ten days.

"You mean Reverend McCann?"

"That's the one," I confirmed. "What was his role in my father's release?"

"Like I told you before, he's the 'prisoners' preacher.' He's helped a lot of inmates find a personal path to God."

"There's more to it than that," I said. "Why him? And why now?"

Jenkins glared at me and said, "For Chrissakes, Rick…can this wait?"

"Two minutes," I promised him. "I just want to know what part McCann played in this whole parole deal."

Jenkins IV sighed in vexation, then said, "Off the record…it was his idea. He heard about your father's cancer through the prison grapevine and initiated the petition. When it came up before the parole board he made an impassioned plea on your father's behalf."

So the great Reverend McCann had been overcome by guilt, thirty years after the fact. Or maybe it was some sort of time-lapse penitence. "He knew Dad was being taken to the Hospice Center when he was released, didn't he?"

"So now he's 'Dad' instead of your 'old man'?"

"Circumstances have changed," I replied. "Please answer the question."

"Yes, he knew about all that," Jenkins IV said with an impassive shrug. "Christ, that was his condo you were staying in, just so you know. Then you went and trashed it."

"*What the fuck?*" I snapped, thinking that all I wanted to do was punch the smug lawyer in the nose. On an entirely different level, however, it made sense, although I didn't show my cards. Not right then, at least. "That belongs to McCann?"

"It was a gesture of compassion, Rick. You might try it some time."

Compassion, my ass. I was convinced the charlatan preacher had killed my mother, and my father had spent thirty years in prison because of it. McCann was feeling the flames of purgatory on the soles of his feet, but I suspected his actions were driven by the blind arrogance of narcissism.

I didn't want to mention any of this to him, not yet. It occurred to me that I didn't have a clue what Jenkins IV's role might have been in my father's release, aside other than he was the son of the attorney who had represented him at trial. What was his personal interest in how and where my father died?

So I asked him, "What's all this to you, anyway? Why did you care so much about whether Dad got paroled or not?"

"Jesus, Rick," he sighed with exasperation. "It's all in the past. Your father is dead and there's bullet holes and glass all over the condo. Whatever you're trying to prove, end it."

"I can't end it," I told him. "The jury convicted the wrong man, and I'm going to prove it."

"My father tried that thirty years ago," Jenkins IV replied. "I know you want to believe your dad died an innocent man, but you just need to let it go."

"Rudy Aiken was going to get up on the stand and blow the doors off the case," I reminded him. "Then he disappeared and your father's plan went down in flames."

The lawyer gave an obvious glance at his watch, a thick gold Rolex that seemed heavy on his wrist. Then he said, "The only thing Aiken was there for was to give your father a potential alibi. Just enough to aim for reasonable doubt."

"And when he disappeared, *your father* gave up."

The darkness in his eyes revealed the anger that was building inside him. "We're done, Rick," he said, his voice almost a growl. "Put it to rest. Jimmy Holland, your mother, your father: they're all gone. Whoever did what to whom, it's all in the past."

"Rudy Aiken killed the Holland kid," I said. "He and his brother got their tickets punched years ago, and the third shitbag is coasting on borrowed time." Again, there was no need to mention McCann, not until I had solid proof.

Jenkins IV looked at me as if I'd lost my mind. Maybe I had, trying to convince this high-priced Broad Street lawyer of something that, on its face, sounded utterly preposterous.

"You think you solved a case that no one has been able to close in thirty years?" The sarcasm in his voice was thick and patronizing and annoying as hell.

"It pretty much solved itself," I told him. "Rudy Aiken knew what happened the night my mother was killed. Dad wasn't in any shape to drive home after that Nazi meeting, or whatever it was, on account of all the benzos they hit him with. Someone did the driving for him, and whoever it was had to have gotten a ride back. That means at least two people were in our kitchen that night, and I know who they were."

"Look…can we do all this speculating later?" Jenkins IV said, checking his Rolex again.

But I was tired of listening to him. "They killed my mother and damned near killed my father, too," I continued. "Probably thought they had, in fact."

"This is total horseshit—"

"Just one last thing," I said. "What happens to evidence after a trial is over?"

"It's usually placed in storage, in the event of an appeal or in case there's some legal issue that comes up."

"What about Dad's trial?"

"You'll have to ask my father."

"I believe he's grown a bit weary of my questions," I confessed. He gave me a look that said *I don't blame him*, which I ignored. "Who would I speak with to see if any of that stuff is in a warehouse somewhere?"

"The Solicitor's Office," Jenkins IV replied. "If the physical evidence still exists, they'll know where it is."

I thanked him for the information and his time, then said, "For what it's worth, I'd like to thank you."

"Thank me? For what?"

"Well, to be honest, at the start of this I was wondering why I agreed to do this, and to what end," I said. "Then I realized that if you hadn't pressed me into spending those last few days with my father, the truth about my mother's murder would have remained buried for all time."

"I think we've talked through this bullshit more than enough," he replied. "I actually have paying clients waiting in my office."

"Good for you," I told him. "I Googled you, you know."

"You have way too much time on your hands."

I ignored the jab and said, "The thing about the internet is, you can run all you want, but you can't hide."

He had turned to go, but now he stopped and glared at me. "What the hell are you talking about, Devlin?"

"I'm talking about a little blurb I found about you online. Something I saw on the Carolina Cross website that lists you as general counsel for McCann's megachurch."

"One of many," he said, trying to sound bored. "It's a big church. So what?"

"So, a little more digging told me you filed an *amicus curiae* brief for Ed Landry, in support of the defendant in that hit-and-run in Charlottesville a few years back. You're not only cuddled up in bed with that fucking preacher; you're a goddamned Nazi."

Jenkins IV glared at me, his gaze dark and blistering. "My business is none of yours, and I have nothing further to say to you," he snarled as he pivoted on one foot and stalked off. Then, not bothering to look back, he added, "My office will be in touch regarding your parents' trust, and another attorney will be handling the matter from this point forward."

"Works for me," I said to his back. "Now that I've come to see the content of your character, or the lack thereof."

This time Jenkins III called me, no more than twenty minutes after I left his son's office. He was too old to drive much of a distance, so he asked if we could meet at a place called Connie's Kitchen on Old Savannah Highway, a few miles south of Ravenel. He wouldn't tell me what he wanted to discuss, but since Addie wasn't due back from Myrtle Beach for a few more hours I had a little time on my hands. With George Kovacs and Malcolm Egan both dead I believed she was safe, and I wanted her to have as much time with her new friends before we headed back to L.A.

Connie's was a homespun gift shop and general store with weathered tables set in the shade of an ancient live oak. Tidy and quaint, the place looked like a converted house with Victorian finishes, white with a red tin roof that was starting to show signs of age. The store sold everything from handmade jellies and berry pies to painted shells and sand sculptures. It also served fresh ground coffee and an assortment of other non-alcoholic beverages. I ordered a glass of sweet tea and took it outside to one of the tables, where I relaxed to the gentle thrum of insects in the grass and the whir of tires on hot asphalt.

I passed the time while I waited thinking about Laurie. I missed her voice and knew I should give her a call, but I was afraid she might ask the question that was inevitable and imminent: When do you plan on going home to L.A.? I had no easy answer for that, so I left my phone where it was, on the table in front of me.

Jenkins III's Mercedes pulled into the dusty parking lot five minutes later. He made a wide circle and slipped in next to my rental under the same oak tree. The weary lawyer climbed out and lifted a hand in recognition, then shuffled over to where I was sitting and lowered his frame into the chair opposite me.

"What you got there?" he asked, nodding at my glass.

"Sweet tea," I told him. "May I get you something?"

"Nah…I don't plan on staying long enough to finish it."

I studied him a minute, wondering what would be so important that he would drive thirty miles out of his way to see me in person. Then again, I'd driven down to his home on the creek twice, so who was I to talk?

"We have to stop meeting like this," I said, trying to break the ice with a joke.

"Trust me, this is the last time." He stretched his body out in the chair so his legs extended beyond the table, then gently rubbed his right hip. His eyes followed a scarlet tanager as it hopped along a fence rail, then he flicked his attention back to me. "You shouldn't have brought your sister into this matter," he finally said, a weary duskiness in his eyes.

"She's been in it from the beginning," I reminded him.

"Karen has suffered enough pain, Rick," he said in a slow rasp. "You had no business resurrecting the traumas of the past."

"Excuse me, sir, but you had your chance thirty years ago to right an incredible wrong. Several of them, in fact. Yet you did nothing except collect your fees and send my father to jail for a crime he had no part of."

"Be careful, son," he said. His voice was hard-edged, almost sounding like a threat. "You are venturing onto very thin ice."

"You knew about Jimmy Holland, yet you did nothing," I continued. "You knew what happened to my sister, yet you did nothing. You kicked my father under the bus."

"You've been in California for too long," he replied, shaking his head.

"Meaning what, exactly?"

"It's softened you," Jenkins III said. "It's caused you to forget your roots."

"Forget them? Dammit, old man—it's caused me to realize how totally root bound this place is. All the tangled lies, the courteous smiles and gracious manners on the surface while the fires of hate simmer just beneath. It's no wonder there's more churches per person here in the good old land of Dixie than anywhere else in America. Makes it easy to go nigger-knocking on Saturday night and then bow before the Lord on Sunday morning."

"I will not allow the 'n-word' to be uttered in my presence!" he snapped at me.

"But you don't give a shit if it's used a thousand times a day if you *can't* hear it," I shot back. "You didn't give one goddamn that my sister was a witness to Jimmy Holland's death. A young black kid who had no bearing on your own life. She all but handed you Rudy Aiken, but rather than give him up to the cops for a savage murder against a black boy you played him like a pawn in your own game."

"That pawn would have spared your father a life in jail," he seethed in a wet voice that was little more than a whisper. "I was doing whatever I could to create reasonable doubt. It would've worked, too, except they got to him."

"And who might 'they' be?" I asked. "Who got to him?"

"Cousins, brothers, nephews…whatever. Silent tongues don't talk."

Jenkins III clearly had never heard Ernie Collier's parable about Korea, and I wasn't about to fill him in now. I still wasn't sure what he'd hoped to accomplish with this face-to-face meeting, but as long as he was here I intended to make the most of the opportunity.

"What were you going to ask my sister?" I said. I had been close to asking Karen the same question, but she was always so close to the edge that I was afraid I might tip her over. "Up there on the witness stand?"

"It was a long time ago," he sighed. "None of that matters now."

"Who the hell are you to decide what matters?" I snapped at him. A young couple sipping from white porcelain mugs glanced over, so I lowered my voice. "You had justice in your hands, and you let it slip away like a bird on the wind. Why?"

He said nothing, just stared at a lone grackle standing in a field across the road.

"I know who it was," I told him then. He turned his head slightly so he could see me out of the corner of his eye. "The scumbag who raped my sister, I mean."

"Like I said, you shouldn't have brought her into this."

"Tell me what she was going to say up there on the stand."

"Your father is gone, Rick. You need to let it go."

"I'll let it go when I'm good and ready," I countered. "Meantime, I hope you sleep well every night knowing you could have done something honorable with your life. Instead you let evil walk free while a good man rotted in prison. And a black kid dragged behind a truck was all but forgotten. If those are the roots you're so proud of, you can take them with you to hell."

I abruptly stood up and scuffed back to where I'd parked my car. I yanked open the door and climbed behind the wheel. I could see Jenkins III rise from his chair and turn in my direction, but I was done with him. Done with his stonewalling and superficial pride, his empty answers and his false propriety. When I was seventeen I'd convinced myself that he'd done all he could to defend my father, but now it was clear he'd allowed him to burn in purgatory for another man's crimes.

I started the engine and backed out of my parking space in the dusty lot. I shifted into drive, but then was forced to brake to a sudden halt as he stepped in front of the car and raised his hands, palms outward. His lips were moving but I couldn't hear him because my air conditioning was blasting. He edged around the front of the car and motioned for me to roll the window down. At that point I just wanted to be gone, but I hit the button on the armrest and the glass slid into the door.

"You are one impudent, cocky, insolent, vulgar sonofabitch," he said.

"Get away from the car."

"But you're also clever, smart, astute, and remarkably shrewd. Your father would be very proud."

"Are you through?"

Jenkins III placed his withered hands on my windowsill so I couldn't drive off without injuring him. "Just so you know, I never once believed your father killed your mother," he said, his voice full of sadness. "But we had an uphill battle proving it. He was found passed out at the scene and couldn't remember where he'd been. His prints were all over the knife. He had possible motive, and plenty of opportunity. All of it was circumstantial, but the jury bought it. My challenge was to place someone else there that night, someone who could convince the jury of an alternate scenario."

"Rudy Aiken." It was a statement, not a question.

Jenkins III shook his head. "No, Aiken was at that meeting, like I said. But it wasn't really enough to prove anything except that Frank was there, too. The timeframe of the murder was so broad that he still could have come home and had plenty of time to stab your mother."

"So how did Dad get home?" I asked. "If he'd been that wasted he couldn't possibly have driven himself. That means whoever drove him had to have a ride back, and that means at least two people were involved."

"Like I said, you're very clever and smart. Problem was, Aiken didn't see him leave the meeting."

"You really believe that?"

"He swore he didn't. But someone else was there that night, at the meeting. And she got a good look at them."

"My sister," I replied.

"She drove down from Clemson," Jenkins confirmed. "The thing is, your father wasn't a member of White River; he only went there to confront the bastards who killed the Holland boy. And attacked his daughter."

"How did he know where they'd be?" I asked.

Jenkins let go of my windowsill and brushed a fly from his forehead. "The day that boy was killed, your sister saw a sticker on the back of that truck. It read 'Keep White River free of black mud.' She didn't know what it meant, but it stuck with her. She told Frank, and he did a little digging. He was a State Senator, and it didn't take long to track them down. He found out about the meeting and went there, professing an interest in joining."

"And my sister met up with him there?"

"No. Your father had let it slip that he was going to confront them, but he never imagined in a million years that she'd go there, too. Karen knew he'd be furious if he saw her, so she hid in the parking lot."

"But she still saw who brought him home."

Jenkins III nodded slowly. "She didn't know their names, but she recognized them both."

"From the dragging."

"And the rape, yes."

I could only imagine what my sister had gone through, witnessing what had happened to Jimmy Holland while at the same time suffering through the humiliation that had been inflicted upon her. "And after that she was still able to drive back to Clemson?"

The retired attorney tightened his lips and managed a slight nod. "In fact, she got pulled over for speeding outside Greenville just after midnight," he said. "I felt it was my obligation to confirm her whereabouts."

It all was starting to make sense now, except for one thing. "Why didn't you put her on the stand?" I asked.

"After Aiken disappeared she totally freaked out," he said, creases of guilt etched deeply in his face. "She was terrified they would get to her and she refused to say a word. She was babbling incoherently, and there was no way I was going to let that egotistical prosecutor have a crack at her."

"There had to be another way to introduce what she saw," I said. "Sworn deposition, video testimony…something."

"I tried all that," he said. "Judge Carter wasn't agreeable in the slightest. He ruled against it all, and in the end I had no case."

"What about the media?" I asked. "You could have gone to them."

"I did. Don't you remember the rumors of armed thugs maybe breaking into the house, confronting your mother and killing her?"

Of course I did, and I told him so. "I thought it was stupid," I said. "It was obvious no one took anything, and there were no signs of forced entry. And no burglar would have stabbed Mom like that."

"It was the best we could do, but the obfuscation infuriated the judge. Blackstone claimed the jury pool had been unduly tainted, all that sort of bullshit. And when I told your father I needed to have Karen testify on his behalf, he shut me down. He wouldn't put her through that, said he'd place his faith in the grace of God. I argued with him, but he was adamant. His daughter was not going to risk her life for his."

"What led you to Aiken in the first place?" I asked him then.

"He was at the meeting that night. He felt worse than shit for what he'd done to the Holland kid, like the devil himself had trapped his soul. Later, when your father went on trial, he sent me a letter saying he knew who killed your mother. The truth was killing him, he said, and he wanted to be judged by the Lord. Roll over on his brother, too. But then—when he disappeared a week before the trial—well, we had no proof. No witness. And your sister just about lost her mind."

Truer words were never spoken, especially by a lawyer. "I appreciate your efforts," I told him, too detached from his version of the past to worry if I sounded cynical or contemptuous. "Look, sir. A dozen wrongs will never make what you did anything close to right. Not in your lifetime, or my father's. But what you said a minute ago is correct: I'm insolent and shrewd. But I'm also pretty damned calculating and slick when I need to be, and many were the days I might have adjusted a fastball when I thought someone was deserving of a quick lesson. Back in the day, of course."

"What are you saying, Rick?"

"I'm just explaining that my fastball has slowed up a bit," I replied. "But I still have a damned wicked curve."

I could tell by the way his fingers gripped my door that he still had something more to say, one last word, but I was done with Jenkins III. I hit the window button and the glass slid upward, until he was forced to let go. Then I pressed my foot to the pedal and left him standing there, his face contorted in a scowl reminiscent of when the Lord had rejected Cain.

Dammit, Ernie, I thought as I drove away. *Why couldn't you have waited one week?*

Detective Brady pretty much laughed in my face.

When I'd told Jenkins III I had to be somewhere I wasn't lying. The SLED investigator had agreed to meet me at the IHOP near the airport out in North Charleston, and after I told him my idea, he said, "You're out of your mind."

"Just hear me out," I pushed him. I took a sip of coffee, then said, "I know it sounds ludicrous, but you have a chance to crack an old case."

"Ludicrous isn't the word for it," he agreed. "You're talking about one of the most popular preachers in the South. My wife watches him every Sunday."

"I know his pedigree," I said. "But that's all beside the point. If we can prove what he did, he's going to jail."

"There's no 'we,' and nothing's going to happen," Brady said, shaking his head. "He's the voice of God all over the South. No one's going to buy it."

"They don't have to buy it," I argued. "The DNA will sell it."

"DNA from hair ripped out of the head of a man over thirty years ago," Brady said as he shoveled the forkful of thick pancakes into his mouth. "Hair that's been sitting in a box ever since. Then your sister sees an old photo of the creep she thinks assaulted her, and she's absolutely certain it's him. And now you want to match it to DNA that may or may not be on a knife that was used to kill your mother—again over thirty years ago. No judge in this state will look at it."

"Look—I know it sounds preposterous," I told him. "All I want is permission to have an independent lab pull samples of DNA from the knife so we can test it. No one needs to know whose DNA we're looking for. This sort of thing is done all the time, for crimes that were committed before DNA testing existed."

"Your father is dead," Brady reminded me needlessly. "Exoneration won't mean anything to him now."

"But it might mean everything to my sister," I pushed back. "It could bring closure for an assault that has traumatized her for decades."

"'Might.' 'May.' 'Could.' Those aren't words I can take up the chain to justify reopening that evidence box."

"C'mon, Brady…what can it hurt? There's no taxpayer dollars involved, no reputation on the line. It's just a routine inquiry from a private party. If it turns out to be nothing, no harm, no foul. But if something does come of it, this could be huge."

"I don't want huge," he sighed as he washed the pancakes down with coffee. "I want 'by the book.' I want to keep my job. I want to be on my boat out in the marsh on weekends, casting for redfish."

"It's only a DNA test," I told him. "Your signature on a single page could bring a lot of closure to a lot of people."

He didn't say anything to that, which I took as a sign of hope.

CHAPTER 31

The next day Addie and I were on a plane heading west.

She and Sam said their goodbyes at the hotel as I loaded our bags into the trunk of the rental car. I gave them a few moments of privacy while I checked out at the front desk. As Juliet had told her Romeo, parting is very sweet sorrow, although I sincerely hoped the outcome in this case would be different than Shakespeare's star-crossed romantics.

Laurie and I made up for our botched "dumpster diving" escapade. The night before, she and I managed to find a quiet place in the sand on Sullivan's Island to share a blanket and crack another bottle of bubbly. It was not far from where we had done the same thing for the first time many years ago, although I'm quite certain neither a blanket nor champagne were involved. It was a bittersweet moment for both of us, because as much as the past tries to catch up to the present, tomorrow always lies one day beyond.

"You'll be back?" she asked me.

"That's the plan," I told her. "But probably not until the holidays. School vacation, and all that."

"It's been marvelous seeing you again," she replied. "Too many years have run off the clock."

"We still have a few innings to go," I said. Different sports metaphors, but neither of us was keeping score.

We drank a toast to many things then: the innocence of youth, the raw desires of a young boy and girl fumbling in the sand, the rushed passage of time. Years that have come and gone so fast that the memories have grown ragged around the edges. There's a song with a similar melancholy refrain that comes on the radio at the end of every year; I think it's by the late Dan Fogelberg.

"There's something from way back then that I need to confess to you," she said at one point. "In the spirit of full disclosure."

"If it's about Matt Harris, I already know," I said.

"Damn," she said, suddenly looking contrite and embarrassed. "How did you find out?"

"It was a small high school back then," I reminded her.

"Just so you know, it was only once—"

"Twice," I corrected her. "Once in the gym and once in the back of his car."

"Double damn," she said, shaking her head. "What about you?"

"A gentleman never tells."

She frowned at me, then said, "Well, then, I want some of that gentleman right now."

I snapped a photo of her afterwards, before we packed up the bottle and the blanket and headed back to the car. Addie caught me looking at that photo now, from the middle seat beside me, somewhere over Kansas.

"I like her," she said.

"Me, too," I replied. And then for good measure I added, "Sam seems like a good kid."

She nodded and said, "I wish this plane had Wi-Fi."

"We'll come back soon," I assured her.

"Soon is still a long time."

I knew what she meant as I took one more look at Laurie's deep blue eyes, then closed the photo app and slipped my phone back into my pocket.

We scattered Belinda's ashes two weeks later. She had been transferred back to I.C.U. the day after we returned from Charleston. The doctors continued to watch her closely, but her condition worsened and one night she slipped into a coma. Addie and I rushed to the hospital as soon as I got the call, but by then there was nothing the doctors could do. She died in Addie's arms, something I will always be grateful to the hospital for permitting. I had not been able to do that with either of my parents, and even though the tears flowed for days afterwards, I know my daughter took great comfort in being able to hold her mother in those last moments of life.

Detective Brady came through on the DNA test. He simply retrieved the carton of trial evidence and, taking great pains to establish a legal chain of custody, forwarded the knife to a forensics lab Kat Rattigan had recommended. As I'd assured him, no taxpayer dollars were involved; an advance on my father's trust paid for everything. It was the same lab to which I'd sent the hair samples Karen delivered to me, and then weeks went by as backlogged cases dripped through the bottleneck.

The hair DNA came back first, but it meant nothing unless there was something to match it to. That made the wait for the other results even more frustrating, until one afternoon I received a call from a lab technician who wished to speak to me personally. He introduced himself as Reyansh Patel, then told me that he was looking at the results of the knife DNA test on his computer screen.

"We collected twenty-four samples of DNA from all over the weapon," he said. "Blade and handle. Now, most normal humans have a total of forty-six chromosomes—twenty-three pair—as well as some mitochondrial DNA. If you look at this mitochondrial DNA, as well as twenty-two of the twenty-three chromosome pairs, there's nothing to tell you if it came from a man or a woman. The genetic difference between them is found only in the sex chromosome pair, where women have two X chromosomes, while men have one X chromosome and one Y chromosome."

"I assume you're telling me this because you needed to rule out the female victim's DNA in the samples," I said.

"Our instructions were to look for the DNA of a male subject, so yes. That's what I'm saying. The process of identifying male and female DNA in all twenty-four samples would have been time-consuming and expensive, so what we did was determine that one sample definitely was from a woman, and then we compared it to all the other samples. If they matched we knew we wouldn't have to test for sex, because they clearly would have come from the same person. Do you follow?"

"Like *y* follows *x*," I said.

"So, of the twenty-four samples, all but two came back as being from the same female," the lab tech said.

My mother. "And?" I asked him.

"And the other two were male."

This was the tricky part. I'd already figured that if any of the samples came back as male they could have come either from my father—which then would prove that his DNA had been on the knife—or another, unidentified male. This was a critical point, and I almost didn't want to hear the results.

"In fact, the two male samples were from the same male subject," Patel said. "That made it much simpler for the next step, which was to compare it against the previously analyzed sample that came from the hair."

"And you have the results of those comparisons?"

"Yes," he replied. "Both of them are perfect matches. The DNA from the knife and the hair came from the same person."

Detective Brady was intrigued by the test results, up to a point. That point was when I demanded that he get a DNA sample from Reverend McCann.

"That takes a subpoena," he said. "No judge is going to sign one based on such flimsy evidence."

"What are you talking about?" I screamed into the phone all the way from L.A. "The tests were a match."

"The tests showed that the person who belonged to a clump of hair left DNA on the knife that killed your mother," he explained. "Nowhere does it say anything about McCann."

"But my sister identified him as her attacker—"

"A thirty-year-old memory from a woman with a history of drug use and borderline disorders," Brady said. "Picking him out of a line-up of old photos that her brother pulled off the internet."

"Still—"

"Still nothing," he said. "I warned you I couldn't take this any further than it's gone. It's out of my hands."

"There has to be someone who will look at the evidence—"

"There is no evidence," he said, his voice edged with exasperation. "Listen to what I'm saying, Rick. You have your match, but this is as far as I can take it. Unless the preacher's DNA is already on file, there's nothing more I can do."

Maybe Brady couldn't do anything more, but as soon as I hung up I called Kat Rattigan. She was busy and her assistant told me she would have to call me back, but when she did I explained what I'd found.

"I don't have access to those records," she said after I told her what I was after. "I'm sorry, Rick."

"But it does exist…a database, I mean."

"It's called CODIS," she replied. "It's an acronym for the Combined DNA Index System. It's the FBI's database and it takes high-level clearance to tap into it. Way above my pay grade. In other words, SOL."

I swore, then explained what I was trying to do. When I mentioned the name "McCann" she said, "You're talking about that money-sucking con artist on TV? My mother forked over fifty grand to him before I was able to tie up her purse strings."

"That's the one," I told her.

She let out a full line of George Carlin curse words, then said, "Wait a sec…I may have an idea."

"What kind of idea?" I asked her.

"You don't want to know," she said. "Plausible deniability."

Laurie and I spoke on the phone a lot. Not every night, but close to it, and to the point where my cell battery would be almost drained by the end of the call. She explained how her eldest daughter was adjusting well to college up in New England, and how it had suddenly gotten a little quieter around the house. Quieter except for her husband who, in her words, was becoming a real dick and was starting to make her life miserable. He'd found out about our summer interlude and was making noise about raising a moral turpitude argument in family court.

"After all the running around that slime ball did?" I asked.

"I didn't tell you the half of it," she replied.

When it was my turn I would fill her in about our life in the canyon. After Belinda's death Addie had moved into my A-frame, which meant long drives to school and forced seclusion from her friends. She had been engulfed in a tide of grief, and we both were coping as best we could. It was a frustrating and trying time that I filled by finishing the celebrity tell-all, which I sent off to my agent just two days past my contracted deadline. I still wouldn't see a check until the publisher accepted it, a process that was impeded by the immense size of the young celebrity's inflated ego. She kept wanting to add more and more to her story, tweak every phrase, touch up every line of dialogue, and embellish the already-pervasive sexual innuendoes. In other words, put lipstick on a pig.

A week after I finished my agent called to tell me she had secured another book for me to write, this one a little different from all the others. "It's sort of a *where-are-they-now* look at a dozen child TV stars," I told Laurie. "Apparently there's quite a market for that sort of stuff."

"Well, you're the best writer I know who can tackle it, and you're in a good town to do it," she replied.

"The great thing is, I don't have to be in L.A. to pull this thing together," I explained. "I can do it just about anywhere."

I let my words hang there, because I suspected I knew what we both were thinking.

Kat Rattigan called me back in early October. She got right to it, just about screaming into the phone, "I did it!"

"Did what?"

"Got the preacher's DNA. It was a little dicey and I'll probably go to hell, but I have it."

She explained that she had done a little digging and learned that McCann occasionally served as a guest pastor at a large church in Charleston, and afterwards he would meet with the congregation for coffee and pastries. Kat personally had attended his most recent sermon, then went up to introduce herself to him afterwards. They chatted a bit, and when they were finished she offered to take his empty plate and coffee cup into the church kitchen.

"You stole it?"

"Sitting in a Ziploc bag right here on my desk. Just tell me where you want it to go and I'll put it in FedEx this afternoon."

Several weeks later Reyansh Patel from the DNA lab called back. He started to take me through the scientific process one more time, but I asked to hit the fast-forward button. "Just tell me if it's a match," I told him.

He sounded a little miffed that he couldn't show off his scientific expertise again, but quickly got over it. "We analyzed five samples from the rim of the coffee cup we received from your investigator," he said. "They were all identical, meaning they were from the same individual."

"Please…just tell me."

"Okay, okay. It definitely came from a man, so we then compared it to the previous samples taken from the knife and the hair. After thorough analysis, I can tell you without a doubt that the DNA from all three samples came from the same individual."

Holy mother of God, I thought, and then the irony of my words hit me.

Detective Brady still said there was nothing he could do. Fruit of the poison tree, and all that bullshit. The hair sample was old and questionable, while the sample from the coffee cup was obtained under false pretenses. In a house of worship, no less. There was no legal chain of evidence in either case, and no judge would sign a subpoena for an official DNA sample.

"I'm terribly sorry," he said. "I just don't see where this goes any further."

"You're just going to let it go?"

"I have no choice, Devlin. And it's time for you to do the same. Put this behind you and move on."

Damn. I was tired of people telling me that. Jenkins III and IV, Stumpy, and especially this SLED detective, whose job was to protect and to serve and to enforce the law—hence the name State *Law Enforcement* Division. But I decided not to press the issue, because I had an alternate plan that did not involve Brady. Or, for that matter, the law.

I invited my sister to visit us for Thanksgiving. She declined, just as I thought she would, but my offer was sincere and I think she felt that. Instead, we spoke on the phone for a long time, mostly about peripheral memories that were safe and secure. My "Karen radar" was on full alert the entire time, but I sensed none of the anxiety or borderline hysteria that always seemed to lurk below the surface of her conscious self. Eventually we worked our way around to the events of the past summer, and I informed her that I had recently received proof of what we already knew.

"So, it was that bastard after all?" she asked me. "The preacher?"

"No doubt about it," I assured her.

"What now? Is he going to be arrested?"

"Not likely. Tainted evidence, and all that."

"That dirt bag can't just go free—"

"Don't worry," I interrupted her, holding off the tsunami of indignation that I knew was coming. "He has a different kind of due process coming to him."

"What are you going to do?" she asked warily.

"You don't want to know," I told her. Addie had prepared a vegan turkey pot pie and I could smell it baking in the oven. Not the traditional Thanksgiving dinner I remembered as a child, but the times do change, and I'm comfortable with that. I glanced into the kitchen, where my daughter was wiping up a thin layer of flour, then said, "I owe you an apology."

"An apology?" Karen said. "What do you have to apologize for? You tracked that asshole down. You *nailed* that bastard."

"I need to apologize for back then," I told her. "For being such a dick. Caught up in my own world, thinking only about myself and how fast I could throw a baseball. I had no idea what you were dealing with, or any sense of the truth."

"Maybe, but you damned sure made up for it. And anyway, that was then, and this is now. You can choose to live in one or the other, but remember: the past is never what you think it was." Katherine Anne Porter again, but this time she sounded cheerful and bright.

"I guess so," I said. "But in any event, I'm sorry I was so far behind the times. I'm going to make up for it, for your sake and mine."

"I'd like that," Karen said.

"Maybe Christmas?" I hadn't told her of my Charleston plans, but I wanted to open the door just a crack.

"We'll see," she said. "One day at a time."

CHAPTER 32

I made good on my pledge to Addie that we would return to Charleston for the holidays. When I'd made that promise I didn't know that her mother would have passed away, or that we would have scattered her ashes at Point Dume in Malibu. By December my daughter had begun to unfold the blanket of darkness in which she'd wrapped herself, and managed to smile from time to time. Her schoolwork definitely suffered during the fall semester, and her friends started to shun her for not being her usual bubbly self. Social media bullying reared its ugly face, and Addie withdrew into herself. The teachers at her magnet school were very understanding and gave her a pass, but it was still a difficult time. I knew what it was like to lose a mother at that age so I could empathize, and I reflected back on what a rude boor I'd become during those final months of high school.

I rented a small house one block back from the beach on Sullivan's Island for two weeks. It was off-season and, despite the holiday surcharge, I got what I considered a good deal on it. It was just two bedrooms and one bath, older kitchen with turquoise refrigerator, but it was an easy hike to the sand and a short walk to the tiny downtown area. The water was chillier than last summer but not much colder than the L.A. beaches my daughter had grown up with. A southeasterly breeze kept the days unseasonably warm, while evenings were perfect for a blaze in the wood-burning fireplace.

Laurie and I wasted no time making up for all those lonely nights on the phone. That first evening Addie and I were back in town she came by the rental cottage and whipped up a magnificent shellfish pasta and goat cheese salad. Dessert was left up to our combined imaginations, cooked up on the spur of the moment and having nothing to do with the kitchen. The small dining room table did play a major role, but details are not necessary.

Our intimate dinner was made possible by the fact that Sam had gotten his driver's license, and he'd invited Addie to a movie. I didn't know how I felt about that, but she had a good head on her shoulders and I trusted her instincts. I didn't necessarily trust Sam or his intentions, but lessons of the last few months taught me that I should not live my daughter's life through my own rearview mirror. A difficult thing for a father to do.

The night before Christmas, Addie and I had dinner at a restaurant on the island that's locally famous for its fresh ground cheeseburgers. She was having none of that, opting instead for a veggie burger while I tried the fish tacos. I'd insisted that she keep her phone in her purse until we were back outside, which caused her to eat a little more quickly than usual. Her Charleston friends had surprised her that afternoon by checking out all three of her mother's old horror movies from the public library, and they planned on binge-watching them as soon as I dropped her off at Sam's house. It was an *ad hoc* tribute, quite a contrast to the petty ostracism she had been subjected to by her superficial west coast clique. Addie told me it was no big deal, but the tear in the corner of her eye suggested otherwise.

The television behind the bar was showing a basketball game that I had no interest in watching. Addie and I were discussing various plans for the coming days, so it took me a moment to realize the TV station had switched to a special news report. I hadn't noticed the change until I caught murmurs of "oh, my God" and "in cold blood" rumbling throughout the dining room. I turned in my chair to see what was going on, and found a local newscaster saying, "… was shot just moments ago while walking in a field near his country home outside the town of Pickens. We don't have many details yet, but sources tell us that the popular TV pastor was struck in the head by a single bullet that appeared to have been fired from the trees at the edge of a clearing. There are reports that he has died at the scene, but authorities refuse to comment at this time."

I don't know how long I stared at the TV before Addie said, "Earth to Dad—"

"Sorry, sweetie," I said. "It looks like someone important has just been shot."

"Holy shit…I mean *crap*," she replied. "You mean, like, dead?"

"They don't know yet," I told her. "Or at least they're not saying."

I felt the cold chill of winter race up my spine, or maybe it was a twinge of guilt. Guilt because the first full day after Addie and I had checked into our rented island house I'd paid a visit to Ernie Collier, who had been cutting back the stalks of his now-barren Chrysler Imperials.

"I been wondering if I'd see you again," he'd called to me, not bothering to come over to my car.

I climbed out and walked to where he was hunched over with a pair of garden shears. "I just wanted a quick word with an old black soldier from the Second Infantry," I told him.

That got his attention, and he straightened his spine as far as it would go. "What sort of business you got with him?" he wanted to know.

"Last time I was here he said that all he needed for justice to be done was a name," I told him. "Just wanted to know if that's still the case."

"Could be," he said. "Doctor says the cancer's spreading."

I told him what I could, which wasn't everything, but enough. I fully understood what I was doing and what the ramifications might be, but the path to righteousness is not always straight and true; nor does it always pass through the doors of a courtroom. When I finished my story, he just stared at me and said, "The Lord surely does work in mysterious ways."

I turned to go, then stopped. "Do you mind if I ask you a question?"

"If there's something you think you need to know, now's the time," he replied.

"Gerald Aiken was found in the Congaree Swamp, with a hole in his head."

"I think we've done worn that subject out, Mister Rick."

I raised my hand politely, a signal for him to hear me out. "I know he was at our house that night my mother was killed, and I suspect he might have told you how that all went down."

Ernie Collier took a deep breath and stared at the ground for a long, long time. Then he looked at me and said, "The Aiken boy was under some duress that day in the swamp, being that it was the last one of his life. But you are correct. He confessed to many things, and your mother's murder was one of them."

He hesitated a second, then launched forth on what Gerald Aiken had revealed to him that day in the swamp, just before he caught a bullet in his brain. He explained how my father had made a lot of noise at the White River meeting that night in Cottageville, going on about Jimmy Holland and the attack on his daughter. Demanding that the perps step forward and admit their crimes. It was a small group of loyal racists, and everyone there knew what had gone down earlier that summer. Dad had poured himself a stiff bourbon when he'd arrived, and when he started raising his ruckus Gerald Aiken secretly spiked it with the benzos.

A couple minutes later Dad got sick and passed out on the floor. That's when Aiken and his partner in crime—whom I'd since identified as the young Reverend McCann—hatched a plan to kill him. His address was on his driver's license so they drove him home, and at some point discussed driving him off the road and making his death look like an accident. Then they realized his wife also knew about Jimmy Holland's murder, and they knew they had to silence both of them. It would look too suspicious if our parents died in separate incidents the same night, so they decided to kill them together and let the cops sort it all out.

"When they got to your place Aiken and this other guy carried him into the house," Ernie explained. "They surprised your mother and took a knife to her, then went after your father. He hit his head and they thought he was dead, too. By that time they were hopped up on drugs and adrenaline, and got the devil out of there."

"How did they get home?" I asked. "If they drove my father's car, I mean."

"Aiken drove your father home in his car, and the other guy followed him. They were both pretty shaken up later when they found out your dad hadn't died, but then he was charged with the murder and the jury sent him to prison."

"And Gerald. He never coughed up the name of the third dirt

bag?" I asked.

"Billy Ray is all I ever had," Ernie said. "Until now."

That was four days ago. Now I studied the TV, wondering where old Ernie might be at that very moment. Was he in the warmth of his living room, wailing away on a sad Sonny Rollins tune on the sax my father had bought for him many years before? Or was he dragging his crooked and tired body through a forest of pines and sweet gums in the Carolina upstate, hunting rifle with long-range scope slung over his back? Maybe he'd enlisted the help of someone else, someone with a little less mileage on him but just as good of an eye. I hoped I'd never know, and I knew it wouldn't bother me one bit one way or the other.

Just then the wail of a horn rocked the wood frame building. It was the same siren that had blown me back to my childhood last summer when I'd met Laurie for a drink at Swampie's. Addie was sipping from her glass of Cheerwine, just as I had done many times when I was her age, and she splashed some of it on her new U.S.C. sweatshirt. The one from South Carolina, not Southern California.

"What the *heck* was that?" she said, rattled by the abrupt blast.

"Seven-thirty Thursday," I explained to her, glancing at my watch. "They test the fire horn here once a week just to make sure it's working."

"You mean they do it *every* Thursday?"

"Ever since I was a kid. You can set your watch by it."

"Holy *crapola*," she said, rolling her eyes. "That is way annoying."

Better get used to it, I thought but did not yet say. I hadn't told Addie this, but I'd already contacted a realtor and we were meeting with her the day after Christmas.

"After a while you don't even notice," I told her instead.

That wasn't quite true. I had been guided by that harsh noise through the first seventeen years of my life, until the night before my mother had died. In an odd deliverance of irony, Judge Carter had finished reading his instructions to the jury just a few minutes before five on the Thursday of my father's trial, and those twelve men and women returned just two hours and fourteen minutes later. The foreman had read the guilty verdict just as I watched the clock in the courtroom click forward to half past seven. A similar synchronicity occurred the night I started my very first major league game, on a warm Thursday evening in Kansas City that had been delayed a few minutes by a short drizzle. I'd thrown my first big league strike at seven-thirty, on the dot.

"How can you not notice?" Addie said with a shudder. I heard her cell phone vibrate and her eyes momentarily shifted to her purse. The suspense was killing her.

"As a kid it made me feel safe," I explained to her. "It told me that everything was good, and confirmed for me that the world was still here. It's all a part of my past."

"You have to release your past in order to live in the now," she replied. She'd been reading a lot of Eckart Tolle lately as a way to move beyond her mother's death.

"So I've heard," I told her with a smile.

What I wanted to tell her then, and someday will, is that while our past is etched in stone and never can change, it remains the outline of who and what we are today. It imbues in us our sense of certainty and purpose, and sometimes it even lies to us, for no reason but to challenge our values and our principles. With luck and a little wisdom, we can learn from what has come before—the truths and falsehoods that color the stories of our existence. We cannot alter what already is, but by gaining a sense of clarity and understanding of what has shaped our individual selves, we can forge a future that provides confidence and meaning to who we are. And who we will become.

That is what I wish to tell my daughter, someday. For now, however, I will tell her that it is seven-thirty on a Thursday evening, the night before Christmas in South Carolina, and all is right in her small corner of the world. Also, if she really wants to, she now can take her phone out of her purse and read the text that I know Sam just sent her.

—End—

AUTHOR'S NOTE

Sullivan's Island, South Carolina has a magnificent fire and rescue department, but there has never been—at least to my knowledge—a regular testing of the horn exactly at seven-thirty on Thursday evenings. But the concept is not a figment of my imagination: the fire department in the small town in which I grew up far from the Carolina coast did, in fact, test its emergency si-ren precisely at that moment, once a week, without fail. It was a distant wail I would hear as I was getting ready for bed (as a young child) and later, when my bedtime advanced, a signal to let me know that the latest episode of *Batman* was about to air. Despite its sudden blast into the night, the horn always seemed a reassuring constant during my childhood, its predictability and comfort serving to soften the edges of growing dysfunction that all children sense but may not yet understand.

As usual, there are a few folks to whom I would like to extend my sincerest gratitude for their guidance during the writing of this book:

My agent extraordinaire, Kimberley Cameron, for always taking the finest care of my novels and finding a good home for the characters therein. So many thanks!

Shannon and John Raab, and all the other professionals at Suspense Publishing, for be-lieving in this book and—I hope—more to come.

Anne Olvey Vocino, licensed P.I. and go-to person for all there is to know about the seedy side of background checks.

Pete Rock, Sarah Rock, and Freddie Jenkins, for being my eyes and ears on the ground in Mount Pleasant thirty years ago.

My daughter, Jennifer Nantell, for her unique spirit and invaluable input along the way.

And, of course, my amazing and remarkably patient wife Diana, whose reassurance and encouragement were inestimable in the conception and delivery of this book. As always, thank you for sharing this bold and dashing adventure with me.

ABOUT THE AUTHOR

Reed Bunzel is the author of a half dozen mystery novels, as well as several nonfiction books.

A former media industry executive, Bunzel served as President/CEO of a streaming music company (TheRadio.com), as well as COO/Executive VP of Al Bell Presents LLC. Previously, he was editor-in-chief for United News and Media's San Francisco publishing operations; earlier in his career he was editor-in-chief of Streamline Publishing's *Radio Ink* and *Streaming* magazines, as well as an editor at *Radio & Records* and *Broadcasting* magazine. Additionally, he served in an executive capacity at both the National Association of Broadcasters and the Radio Advertising Bureau.

A graduate of Bowdoin College in Brunswick, Maine, Bunzel holds a Bachelor of Science degree in Anthropology, *cum laude*. A native of the San Francisco Bay Area, he currently resides with his wife Diana in Charleston, South Carolina.

CPSIA information can be obtained
at www.ICGtesting.com
Printed in the USA
LVHW041709141019
634150LV00011B/747/P